DEMONHEART
2023 Edition

I0615002

Abbas Daya

DEMONHEART
2023 Edition

DOUBLE DRAGON

Glossary of Rittershafen terms

Das Viertel der verlorenenSeelen: The district of lost souls. The nickname given to the South Bank District of Rittershafen where the poor live and where the strongholds of most of the city's criminals and gangs are to be found. The name is often shortened to the 'Viertel' by the city's inhabitants.

Hochmeister: Grand Master.

Meister: Master.

Schwertbrüderorden; The Sword Brothers Order also known as the Sword Brethren or Sword Brothers, *Schwertbrüder*. Little is known about them except rumours of fighting monks and nuns who combine martial arts with mystic magic.

Aufmerksamkeit: Lingering mind, awareness, or sixth sense.

Komtur: Commander.

Sonderbarer Stahl: Special Steel. A form of enchanted steel that when in contact with human flesh absorbs magic from beings thus preventing the casting of sorcery.

Heiligesstahl: Divine steel, also called Empyrean steel. Steel from heaven which when enchanted with divine magic has sentience. The hardest known metal, it is indestructible.

Vis: (Latin. Pronounced "Wees".) The magic energy that surrounds the world and is found in all living things. Sorcerers use their internal *Vis* to manipulate the *Vis* of the world.

Drachenholtz: Dragonwood. A magical wood with strange properties.

Nachahmen: Mimic demons that can assume the form of people or animals.

Rittershafen Map

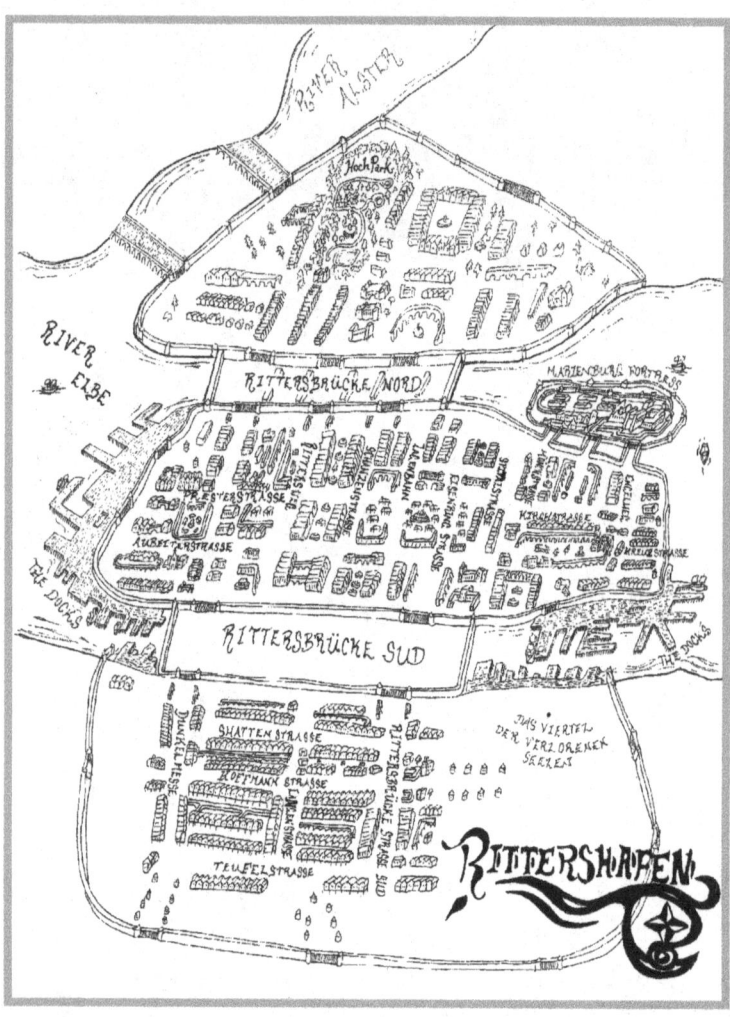

Drawn by Daniel Kettle
danielkettle@icloud.com

Prologue

'I am ready now, *Meister*,' the sorcerer said to the figure behind him.

The master stared at his student with blue eyes set in a face of indeterminable age as white as bleached bone. 'I have my doubts,' he replied. 'Serious doubts. This is not like summoning your steward or a lesser demon. These are very rare and this particular breed is going to be far more powerful. Even the Exiles hesitated to summon this.'

'I understand. But I *am* strong enough to control it and when I do, my power will grow.'

'Very well.' The master took a last look around the room as he listened to it breathe, deep and slow, like air pumping through the lungs of a giant bellows.

He doubted he was ever going to return.

The chamber was devoid of windows and furnishings, apart from a small ornate wooden cabinet in the far corner.

The walls, ceiling and floor were the colour and texture of flint – black with a creamy fudge-coloured vein swirling through it and seamlessly joined as though it were shaped from a single piece of stone. A perfection which was beautiful, alien and frightening, *and so very like my student,* the master thought.

'Then I bid you farewell. This stage is for you and you alone. And know that I wish you every success.' He dipped his head.

The sorcerer bowed his thanks.

The master vanished.

The sorcerer looked down at the circle where he stood which was etched in silver as was the flowing sorcerous script within and without.

Satisfied that his protective circle was without error, the sorcerer scooped up his spellbook, a large black leather-bound tome with a metal clasp fashioned in the likeness of a snarling, horned demon. He brushed his fingers lightly over the metal clasp and it sprang open, the pages of the book flicking of their own accord to the page the sorcerer desired.

He placed his book on the floor in front of him and began to chant. A slower but considerably safer method of casting, as the book itself aided the sorcerer in his struggle to master the arcane words which writhed and twisted, resisting all attempts to bend to his will.

The sorcerer flicked his gaze to the other occupant in the room and smiled.

Lying in another circle was a young man with fair hair and innocent blue eyes now wide with terror. He moaned, bucking and jerking as he struggled to break free of his bonds. His efforts to escape were so desperate that blood had started pouring from his wrists and ankles where the hemp rope had sanded away his skin and flesh.

The sorcerer stopped his chanting, interrupted by the sudden stench– the foul odour of a fetid sewer on a sweltering day. He looked up from his book to find himself staring at a handsome man of average height, possibly middle age, with a face devoid of lines. Even the corners of his eyes lacked crow's feet. His dark hair, which was short and slicked back, only accentuated his pale skin and small neatly trimmed goatee and moustache. But it wasn't his appearance that mesmerised the sorcerer, it was his eyes, large and black, like a shark's.

The newcomer smiled, revealing teeth which were sharp and pointed and stained with a thick tallow-coloured filth.

'Good evening,' the figure said with a cheerful smile.

'Greetings, honoured messenger of Lord Beraak.' The sorcerer dropped to his knees and bowed his head.

'Call me Francis.'

Though he carried himself with the air of a nobleman, charming and debonair, Francis' raiment spoke otherwise. His boots were worn and cracked, his once-fine silk shirt, cloak and linen trousers were stained with the muck of ages, frayed and pocked with ragged holes. Flies, thick and black, orbited his head, buzzing noisily. He leaned on an elegant cane, expertly polished and lacquered. It was topped with a silver knob in the likeness of a fly's head, complete with curling horns.

'Lord Francis...' the sorcerer began, looking up at the figure, wide-eyed.

'Just Francis.' He gestured to the sorcerer to rise.

The sorcerer obeyed.

'Now, why am I here?' Francis' hideous smile was still fixed in place.

'But…I…didn't finish the incantation. Lord…Francis.'

'No matter!' Francis waved dismissively. 'It's not the words, my good man, it's the intent that Lord Beraak hears and the sacrifice of that small bit of you,' he held up his thumb and forefinger an inch apart, 'that really counts!'

'Yes, Francis.' The sorcerer bowed low, suddenly noticing the unnaturally long grimy nails sprouting from the visitor's fingers.

'Why don't you stop all the fawning and get down to business? What do you want – and tell me honestly – what do you *really* want?'

'Greater knowledge of sorcery, Francis.'

'And power, yes?'

'Yes. And power.'

'And what are you willing to sacrifice for this power?'

'Anything.'

'Anything?'

'Anything!' the sorcerer confirmed.

'You're certain? The price will be steep.'

'Yes. Anything you command.'

'And my payment?' Francis asked casually, admiring his grubby nails.

'Whatever you ask for. Whatever Lord Beraak demands.'

'Very well. I'll grant you the name of a powerful demon *and* the identity of a powerful sorcerer whose magic you can seize. In return, you must feed Lord Beraak the souls of the innocent and the pious, the ones fat with *Vis*, but especially the devout. Do you agree to this?'

'I do, Francis.'

'Excellent!' Francis clapped his hands. 'Then we have an agreement.'

The sorcerer dipped his head. 'We do.'

'Now, if there's nothing else…'

'Our business is concluded.'

Francis gave an exaggerated bow and, with his yellowed smile still playing on his face, vanished, leaving behind the faint smell of faeces and the buzz of a single fat fly.

The sorcerer bent his head to his spellbook where the long, graceful script of sorcery had appeared sinuously slithering its way across the pages. He chanted again and blue flames erupted from the boy's circle, swaying and roaring as they grew in intensity.

The young man was no fool. He had been schooled in this kind of lore and knew what the flames heralded.

The knowledge only fuelled his fear, and he started mewling and sobbing in terror.

And then he froze.

Through the dancing flames, he had spied a figure.

It looked like a person, but the creature, the size of a newborn babe, had no skin to speak of. It moved by dragging itself, using its arms like a seal, as it shuffled forward, staring at the young man with milky orbs. It stopped an arm's length away from him and opened its mouth, stretching its jaws impossibly wide to reveal rows of pointed white

13

teeth with long sticky strands of saliva stretched between them like webbing.

The young man was still, eyes wide, caught in the depths of its soulless mesmerising gaze. The creature reared, swaying for a moment before it shot forward with blinding speed.

It punched straight into the young man's abdomen, folding him in half and throwing him backwards. He clutched at his gut and screamed, curling into a foetal position, thrashing as tears poured from his eyes while his lifeblood leaked through his fingers.

Tearing into the stomach was just the beginning of the creature's journey. It set off, munching its way through the young man's innards and then up, using the spine like a set of bone stairs spiralling upwards towards the real prize.

The young man's body arched in pure agony as his screams and pleas echoed around the chamber.

The creature's hunger caused it to kill slowly but after an eternity of pain, the young man's prayers were answered as, with a final shudder, his body slumped and his soul floated free of his flesh.

The creature was indifferent. It continued with its feast-journey, chewing its way through meat and crunching bone until it reached the brain.

The sorcerer could hear it slavering and smiled in satisfaction when he saw the young man's skull writhe and pulsate as the creature scrambled inside.

The body jerked and thrashed violently again and then, as swiftly as the fits had started, they ceased.

The body sat up and looked around with eyes that belonged to a serpent – yellow lamps with black slits which he fixed on the sorcerer as he fluidly rose to his feet, smiling. He blinked and his eyes reverted to the innocent blue of the novice whose innards he had just dined on.

'Why have you summoned me?' He looked around at his prison, the blue-flaming circle.

'To do my bidding, demon.'

'I need to feed, master.'

'What do you require, my servant?

'The energy of the gifted.'

The sorcerer fell silent as he and the demon locked gazes, neither moving nor wavering. The battle of wills lasted for a few heartbeats before the demon brought it to an end by bowing low. 'What is your will, master?'

The sorcerer flicked his hand in a dismissive gesture and the circle's blues flames vanished. The creature was a prisoner no longer.

The sorcerer beckoned the young man forward.

The demon within the body resisted, refusing to obey.

The sorcerer smiled and exerted his will, and the demon found its feet moving of their own accord as he walked obediently to the sorcerer who spoke softly to it. When he finished, the creature bowed low again before departing.

***

It was dark when the novice entered the cloisters of the seminary. He nodded to the guards on patrol who bowed, never thinking to stop and challenge a familiar person.

Once past the unsuspecting guardsmen, he glided quickly and silently through the shadows of the cloister and up the stairs to the first-floor gallery where he moved along the rows of sturdy arched wooden doors. He stopped at one, halfway along the corridor, and pressed his ear to it.

He knocked.

The scratching quill stopped, followed by a soft curse and the scraping of a chair being moved and then the slapping of sandaled feet on stone as someone approached the door.

It was opened by an old man whose eyes widened slightly in surprise at the figure, but the frown vanished in the light of recognition, and he smiled.

'Ah dear boy…wait a minute, you're not–' The old priest's words were cut short when the initiate's hand shot out, grasping him by the throat. He struggled to break the grip but was held fast.

The novice pushed him effortlessly back into the room, still maintaining a hold on the old man, and with his other hand closed the door behind him. He brought his face near to the priest's and opened his mouth, stretching it unnaturally wide to reveal row upon row of pointed teeth.

The old priest's eyes widened in horror.

'Kiss me, Father,' he whispered, grinning as he gripped the priest's face with his other hand. 'I hunger for it.'

The initiate pressed his mouth over the old priest's while the cleric squirmed in his grasp, swatting ineffectually at the boy, trying to break free of his grip and pull away from the sucking lips.

Eventually his protestations grew weaker until they completely subsided and his body sagged.

The boy pulled back and sighed with pleasure, looking at the old cleric with swollen eyes that now resembled a snake's. 'Delicious!' He smiled, licking his lips.

'My *Vis*...' the old priest croaked.

'Exquisite!' the boy replied. He brushed his lips delicately against the cleric's ear. 'Thank you for your power, old one. Go into the void knowing that I will feed on *all* your brethren.'

The old man tried to scream but could only choke and gasp as the novice, with the effort of a child squashing a moth, crushed his neck with a soft crunch. He lowered the body to the floor and left as silently as he had arrived.

He glided back down the stairs and along the gallery, gesturing to the guards again as he passed them and left the seminary behind him.

Chapter 1

The sign above the door depicted a naked elf maid making a suggestive face while below it, two large bald heavies searched punters at the door and fed them the standard line, 'No weapons in the Lewd Elf.'

They didn't search the lean figure swathed in a black cloak with a black wide-brimmed hat. Him, they gave a nod and let pass unmolested. In turn, he threw them a wink and slipped a couple of silver coins in their pockets; it always paid to keep the muscle sweet.

Once past the door guards, the lean figure was met by a tall beauty with the kind of curves men duelled over, large blue eyes and chestnut-coloured hair which spilled down to her slim waist.

This evening she wore a flowing red dress which exposed plenty of her ample bosom on which glinted a snowflake-shaped pendent made of platinum and diamonds.

She drifted up to him with a sway that drew every gaze in the room.

'Vogel,' she said in a husky voice, offering a silk-gloved hand.

'Marianne.' Vogel raised her hand to his lips while he gazed into her cool blue eyes.

'The usual?'

'Please.'

She smiled, slipped her arm through his and led him through the common room where men lounged on couches with scantily clad women hanging on them, towards a set of stairs leading to the upper floors. As they drifted through the crowd, Vogel took his time to eye up the clientele and note their appearance, class and profession. He wasn't concerned about being surreptitious, not when Marianne was on his arm. He could have been dressed as a capering court jester with a jingling cap and bells on and no one would have paid him any mind. Every eye in the room was locked onto her as she sauntered through, smiling and nodding to the crowd, her every movement utterly graceful and mesmerising.

A far cry from the woman he had first met those many years ago.

Vogel is fourteen when he first meets Marianne Breitmeyer.

He's working in the Sunken Galleon in the docks district, tending tables and picking pockets in the evening when she shuffles through from the kitchen one morning, head low, her long dark unwashed hair covering her face.

Vogel greets her with a smile and a, 'Hello.'

She responds by looking up and shooting him a nervous glance before hurrying on. Her face is pale, her cheeks sunken and her almost skeletal arms and legs make it apparent that she could do with a few more hearty meals. But that's not what makes Vogel stare after her with his brows furrowed in anger – it's the large angry bruises covering the left side of her face.

19

It's several days later before Vogel has the pleasure of meeting her husband, Herr Eric Breitmeyer, a large man rolling in fat and muscle with a bald head and small eyes, who elbows the staff aside as he barges into the kitchen.

The screams draw Vogel, the staff and Father Pohl Heinz, a priest.

The Innkeeper ignores the screams, preferring to keep out of a domestic row.

The group rush into the kitchen to find Marianne on the floor, trying to shield her face from Herr Breitmeyer, who is gripping her long hair in one fist and hammering at her face with the other. He pulls back for another punch, but Father Pohl steps in and catches his arm.

Eric responds by shoving the cleric back and closing on him with the threat of violence clearly written on his face. A mistake. Father Pohl is a witch hunter and has faced far worse than abusive husbands. In a heartbeat, his form is wreathed in the golden flames of divine magic which whip and tear at his cassock. He invites Eric to take the first swing.

Nobody has ever seen a priest or templar fling divine fire at an ordinary person, but everyone knows that the clergy use their powers to combat demons, sorcerers and the undead, so it's a safe bet that they could easily melt the flesh off the bones of most tossers. When it comes to giving women and the weak a good beating, Eric is a hero, but against clergy wielding divine magic he all but shits himself and withdraws, pushing past Father Pohl but not without giving the old priest a defiant glare.

Marianne is helped to a bench, her wounds are washed and a cup of wine pressed into her hand. An hour later she's back at work washing and cooking, and in the evening she'll return to the man who uses her face as a punchbag.

Father Pohl offers to talk to her husband on her behalf, even threatening to have him arrested for his behaviour, but Marianne begs him not to interfere.

Vogel has seen this behaviour countless times from the mothers of the children in the gangs he's run with; boys and girls who have left home because of the Marianne and Eric Breitmeyers of the world, where mum is unable or unwilling to stand up to dad's constant brutality, or mum is the brute herself.

Vogel tries to stay out of the matter, but he just can't. The only way he can sleep soundly is if he deals with Eric Breitmeyer personally.

It's a month before the opportunity presents itself.

Marianne is accompanying her husband home after an evening in the Angel on the South Bank. She has one of Eric's arms draped over her shoulders, supporting him, as they totter along the streets.

Vogel leaps out of the darkness, a throwing knife in his raised hand, poised to end Eric's life.

Eric's in no shape to challenge Vogel. He can barely stand.

Marianne is shrieking and begging Vogel to stop, not kill them. She tosses the pouch of meagre coins they have to the floor, swearing that they have nothing more.

It's clear from the rags Marianne wears that she's poor, and if Vogel was an ordinary footpad after loot, he might have grabbed the pouch and left, but not tonight.

Tonight he has other business.

He ignores Marianne's pleas and lets his knife fly.

Marianne's fear reaches hysterical proportions and something within her snaps. Suddenly she and her husband are wrapped in golden flames which cause Vogel's knife to ricochet off the divine magic shield she has managed to create.

Vogel quickly shrugs off his shock and flees.

Events pass in a blur after that.

Word spreads, thanks to Vogel, of Marianne's divine magic gift and the Church swiftly descends upon her. Within days she has disappeared into its ranks while Eric Breitmeyer is given a fortune by the Church and told to fuck off and forget his wife.

He happily does so.

Vogel sees Eric weeks later strutting along with a skinny girl of seventeen summers trailing behind him; probably the daughter of a destitute family who sold her to him.

She looks at Vogel and he notes the large bruises on one side of her face before she quickly turns away.

Vogel sighs, shakes his head and walks on.

Marianne led him upstairs to a private room with an ornate table and plush rugs on the floor. Once she had closed the door, she pulled off her silk gloves and kicked off her shoes and sat at the table, rubbing her feet and sighing.

Vogel smiled and tossed his hat on the table and his cloak over the seat opposite her before he sat.

Marianne smiled at him. 'Do you want to go first?'

Vogel shook his head. 'Ladies first.'

Marianne snorted. 'I'm hardly that.'

'You've always been a lady.'

Marianne dipped her head in gratitude. 'Ever the charmer.'

Vogel shrugged. 'So, what's the news?'

'Nothing concrete, I'm afraid. Just the usual gossip and hysteria about sorcerers, demons and monsters, all blamed on the foreigners and Jews. I've checked a few of them out. They're nothing.'

'And the rest?'

'I'm still investigating.'

'Anything else?'

'Just more rumours. Something about a sorcerer in the *Viertel*, but that's not your concern. That said, I have got something up your street.'

Vogel raised an eyebrow.

'I think I've discovered the money behind the Crescent Moon – a Sicilian, by the looks of him. I don't have a name yet but I have seen him with Mathilda. They've also got foreign guards on the doors –inside and out.'

'I've seen 'em, big scary fellas with scalp locks and long thin moustaches. Are they from the Dragon Empire?'

Marianne shrugged. 'That's on the outside.' She smiled slyly. 'On the inside, she's got women from the same land as the men. They're dressed like exotic houris but they're not working girls. I've seen them use their swords, and I can tell you, they're experts!'

'You managed to get into the Crescent Moon – how did you wangle that?'

Marianne winked. 'You're not the only one with charm and training, Vogel. Besides, as one madam to another, Mathilda and I get along.'

Vogel drew a breath. *Fair enough.*

'I'm trying to seduce the sword houris into working for me,' Marianne said, 'but no joy so far.'

'Didn't Mathilda say her husband was the money behind the place?'

'Turns out *Herr* Rositzke is skint.'

'So what's Mathilda hiding?'

Marianne shook her head. 'Perhaps nothing. Maybe she's just embarrassed that they've fallen on hard times and rather the world didn't know. Who knows?'

Vogel understood. *Pride – the deadliest sin.* 'There again, it could be that she *is* hiding something – a front for a gang?'

'It's the "or something" that concerns me. I'll investigate and give you a shout if there's anything juicy.'

'Appreciate it.'

'Now, what do you have for me?'

Vogel pulled out a piece of parchment and slid it over to her.

She unrolled it and Vogel watched as her eyes took in the scroll's contents while she played with her diamond pendant. Only the closest of examinations would have revealed a small symbol of a three-pointed throwing star with a cross at its centre etched into the heart of the gem.

'Three?' Marianne said.

'Yes.'

'And you're sure they're bad?'

'Foul. I've seen the bruises on their wives and kids.'

Marianne rolled the parchment up and stuffed it down her bosom. 'A pleasure doing business with you, Vogel.'

She rose and crossed to a small dresser in a corner of the room on which was a tray with a jug and two cups. She brought it back to Vogel and poured wine for them both which they drank as they leaned back in their chairs and gossiped and relaxed.

Vogel rose an hour later, snatching up his cloak and hat before he kissed Marianne's hand. For all her grace and beauty, her hands and knuckles were heavily calloused from years spent pounding sand, wood and stone.

Vogel gently stroked them. 'Same time, next week?'

She smiled. 'Until then.'

Once outside, the spy paused to take a deep breath of the fresh night air while he gazed at the Lewd Elf. He turned slightly at the sound of a figure approaching.

'Evening, Vogel.'

'Evening, Kris.' Vogel smiled at the newcomer, a boy of about fifteen summers with mud-coloured hair and blue eyes.

'Anything new?' Kristian asked.

Vogel shook his head before motioning that they should move, and the pair strolled to the end of the street where they stopped in front of a small house.

Vogel and Kristian looked around to ensure that there were no eyes on them before Kristian unlocked the door and they slipped inside.

They stood in a small entrance hall with a kitchen before them and a room to their left. To their right a set of stairs led to the house's top floors.

The old man sitting in the kitchen raised a hand in greeting to Vogel.

'Evening, Wulfram, everything all right?' Vogel smiled.

The old man nodded. He was a soul of few words and though nearly eighty summers old still had bright eyes and the body of an athlete – all lean and hard muscles.

Vogel tossed him two pouches, one of which clinked slightly.

The old man ignored the pouch of coins and fumbled at the other pouch from which he took a large pinch of tobacco which he stuffed into his pipe. He lit it and leaned back in his chair, puffing contentedly.

Kristian shook his head as he followed Vogel up the stairs.

'A pipe, a full belly, a warm roof over his head and some coin in his hand, and old Wulfy is as happy as a pig in shit,' the boy said.

'Amen!' Vogel replied.

The attic room was swept every day – at Wulfram's insistence – and covered with a thick rug and lit with lamps hanging from beams criss-crossing the room. It had a single window and five cots, two for the girls and three for the boys, all aged between ten to twelve who sat on the floor in the centre of the room passing around a leather bag. From it, they fished cheap trinkets.

'Vogel!' They cheered when he and Kristian entered the room.

'Evening all!' Vogel greeted his urchins with a smile as he swept off his hat and unfastened his cloak. It was warm in the attic thanks to the fire from the kitchen below.

'Evening, Vogel, evening, Kris!' they replied as they shifted to make room for the newcomers.

'What's this?' Vogel pointed at the leather bag.

'Yeah, this should be good.' Kristian grinned as he leaned against a beam with his arms folded.

The sound of the front door opening and closing caused Vogel to turn to Kristian.

The lad waved dismissively. 'That's just Wulfy off to the Elf for a beer and a cuddle.'

Vogel turned back to the urchins. 'Well?'

'We're celebrating!' one of the youngsters said.

Vogel looked at Kristian who shook his head.

'Celebrating what, Julian?'

Julian's eyes darted between his gang. 'Er, my twelfth birthday.'

27

'You're twelve now?' Vogel said.

'Yes.'

'And when was your birthday?'

'Yesterday?'

'And how did you celebrate?'

'You said that we could thieve when it was someone's birthday. Soooo...' He looked at the leather bag.

'Julian also got another ink,' a girl called Bettina said.

Julian pulled up his shirt to reveal two robins tattooed on his back.

'So you celebrated Julian's birthday by getting him inked and nicking junk?' Vogel said to Julian and the children.

'Er, yeah,' Julian said with a doubtful look at the others who giggled and stared at the floor.

'So, if you're nicked by the watch and they look at your back, they'll have no idea what gang you belong to, will they?'

'But we all have the ink!' Julian said. 'It's our gang ink...'

The kids burst into laughter.

'You fuckers!' he roared at them 'You told me we *all* have the same ink!'

Vogel turned to Kristian who was still chuckling and shaking his hung head. The spy grinned at the kids. 'I was your age once.'

'A long time ago,' Kristian added.

'Piss off,' Vogel said. 'Anyway, I remember the thrill of stealing, but you kids are getting older.' He indicated Julian. 'Time to consider settling down and a proper career.'

'What, like being an agent for the Teutonic Order? Like you?' Julian pulled a thoughtful face.

'Why not?' Vogel shrugged and looked at Kristian who nodded his support. 'You really want to spend all your lives thievin'? And when you're too old to thieve, what then – back to the streets?'

The children exchanged looks before turning back to Vogel and shaking their heads.

'Sod that,' Bettina said. 'I'm never goin' back to livin' on the streets.'

And the begging and the beatings, Vogel thought, and that's if you were lucky.

Far worse happened to children on the streets. Most never lived beyond their twelfth birthdays.

'Yeah, why not?' Julian said looking at the others. 'I could be like you, couldn't I, Vogel? I could spy for the Order and still thieve every now and then.'

'Oi!' Vogel protested. 'I don't thieve.'

They all gave him unconvinced looks.

'Well, not too often,' Vogel mumbled. 'Anyway, just consider what I've said. Right, well, seeing as it's Julian's birthday,' he said to the children, 'let's have some presents.'

The children grinned broadly as Vogel waved to Kristian who tossed over another pack which the spy rummaged in for a few seconds before his hand emerged clutching a number of pouches. He tossed one to each child who caught them with ease.

The children emptied the contents of their pouches into their palms and when they saw the silver coins shining up at them, gave Vogel five large grins.

29

'Right,' Vogel said to them. 'Anyone have any news for me?'

Julian stood. 'Anna from the Elf.'

The spy turned to Kristian who raised a curious eyebrow.

'What about her?' Vogel said.

'She's been seeing this fella, Bernd, says he's a ship's captain. Anyway, she's more than a bit keen for him and he feeds her shit about taking her away from the brothel.'

'And what's so special about this Bernd?' Vogel said.

'He's a smuggler, or so he says.' Julian shrugged. 'Trades in *sorcery*, smuggles in books an' magical stuff.'

'Right, boys and girls!' He held up five more pouches. 'Which of you clever little devils know where I can find him at this time of night?'

Five hands went up.

Vogel grinned and tossed the pouches to the children.

'You got anything else for us, Vogel?' Julian asked.

Vogel spread his arms wide. 'Of course I have. You know I wouldn't come here without treats.' He turned to Kristian and smiled.

Kristian tossed him another sack and from it Vogel produced ale skins and bundles wrapped in cloth. He laid the items on the bed and when he unwrapped them, the children gasped at the sight of the roasted hams and beef, soft bread and wheels of ripe yellow cheese.

'Dig in, gang!'

Vogel and Kristian staggered from the house a couple of hours later, having eaten a little and drunk a lot with the children.

'Do you think they'll do as I suggested,' Vogel asked Kristian, 'and seriously consider jacking in the thieving?'

'They respect you, Vogel. You're the nearest thing they have to a proper parent.' Kristian shrugged. 'You look after them. Protect them.'

'I'm no dad. Wulfy'd make a better parent that I would,' Vogel said.

Kristian shook his head. 'Nah! He's the embarrassing grandad that farts loudly and pisses himself.'

Vogel chuckled. Wulfram Brenner was anything but that as he recalled the evening they met.

Vogel was staggering down *Arbeiterstrasse* behind an old man who was suddenly set upon by four n'er do wells intent from parting him from his purse. In heartbeats, he left them lying on the ground, bloody and battered.

Yeah, he could see old Wulfy kicking the bells out of thieves, but never a doddering old has been.

Kristian put his hand on Vogel's shoulder. 'If you tell 'em to do something, Vogel, they'll do it. For you.'

Vogel rumbled thoughtfully.

'Anyway, what the fuck is Bernd up to now?' Kristian said as they walked along *Zimmermannstrasse* towards the Artisans Quarter.

Vogel shrugged. 'I hope the shit he fed Anna about dealing in sorcery really was that – shit. One of these days that arse is going to get himself killed. Er, why are we going this way? Aren't we going to the Drowning Duck?'

Kristian shook his head. 'The littluns are right about Bernd drinking in the Drowning Duck, but I know for a fact that tonight he'll be in the Sunken Galleon in the south docks.'

Vogel slapped him on the shoulder. 'Good lad.'

'And what about Anna? What's going to happen to her?'

'Don't worry about her,' Vogel said softly. 'I'll deal with it.'

Which meant he'd have a word with Marianne.

Anna would be bribed and scared into forgetting her beau and keeping her mouth shut – Marianne was an expert at that. If not, Anna would wind up floating in the Elbe – Marianne Breitmeyer was *really* good at that too.

***

Bernd Engel was no angel. But then Vogel had known that for some time.

'He's smuggling what?'

'Sorcery,' the old man seated next to him said.

They sat in a cosy corner of the Sunken Galleon, eyeing up a card game with eight players all of which had that "sea dog" air about them with long moustaches, white shirts and tall leather boots.

Bernd lounged in a chair with his leather coat and rapier slung over the back of it, his eyes already drooping from boozing and gambling all evening.

'How long's this been going on?'

'Nearly a year. I'd have told you sooner, lad, but I've had no proper shore leave.'

Vogel waved away the apology. 'Who's the buyer?'

'Noble. Von Dassel.'

Vogel snorted. Herbert von Dassel was a notorious philanderer and hedonist into all kinds of sick and twisted pleasures.

The old man sighed and shook his head. 'I should have left when Hendryk died.'

'Is it really that bad, Kurt?'

The old man cursed. 'I've said it once, and I'll say it again, Vogel. Bernd's always been bad fruit. When he was Hendryk's first mate, he was always pushing to up the smuggling.'

He had, once Hendryk had died and he inherited the *Dolphin*.

According to the intelligence Kurt had been feeding Vogel, for several years now, Bernd had taken the crew from petty smuggling to shifting large numbers of slaves and underworld criminals in and out of Rittershafen. The smuggling of slaves had never really sat right with the *Dolphin's* crew but now Bernd was gambling with everyone's life by dealing in sorcery.

'He's got to know the risk he's taking,' Vogel said.

'That's why I want out. You know what'll happen to us if the Church or Order catches us with sorcerous gear.'

'Oh yeah,' said Vogel. *Red-hot pokers up the arse followed by being burnt at the stake in public.*

'Don't worry about the Church or the Teutonic Order, Kurt. I'll vouch for you and your mates.'

'Appreciate that, Vogel.'

'Feeling's mutual,' Vogel replied. 'You've helped me out. Your info's always been solid.'

The agent handed the old man a pouch of coins under the table. It vanished inside Kurt's jacket.

'So, this sorcery…' Vogel began.

Kurt shook his head and stared into space, blowing out a cloud of smoke. 'Nothing good, and that's a fact. It's in a long box securely locked in a hatch in the hold. Whatever it is, we were all given orders not to go anywhere near it. Bernd only told us that it was potent sorcery and that, unless we wanted to lose our lives and immortal souls, we weren't to go anywhere near it. Not that some of the crew hadn't tried.'

'They tried to steal it?'

Kurt shook his head. 'Nah! Not these lads. They were just curious and wanted a look.'

'And?'

'We found 'em dead. They'd murdered one another.'

Vogel clicked his tongue. 'Greed.'

Kurt shook his head. 'They hadn't got past the locks. They didn't even get a look at it. Besides, they were a close bunch.'

'Thick as thieves.' Vogel winked at Kurt.

The old man chuckled. 'Whatever is in that box, the accursed thing drove them to kill each other.' He pulled out a cross pendant from under his shirt and kissed it before stuffing it back.

Vogel raised an eyebrow. 'How did Bernd handle it?'

'Had men bring it aboard; guys swathed in black robes. Moors, I think?' Kurt spat and grimaced. 'They must have told him how to handle the cargo.'

'And he never checked on it during your journey?'

'Only when he heard some of the lads went down to see it for themselves. And after he had their bodies tossed over the side. He only checked on it when we docked day before yesterday. As first mate, I went with him.'

'No dead bodies?'

'None human.'

Vogel frowned. 'Huh?'

'Vogel – there were a few dead rats around the thing when Bernd opened the hatch where it's stashed. There were no rats on the ship by the time we docked. None anywhere.'

'You know what happened to them?'

Kurt dipped his head. 'I asked the lads when we was alone. One of them said he saw 'em all, the rats, one night not long after we left Marrok. They were diving over the side of the ship into the sea. They'd rather drown then stay on the ship with that thing.'

Vogel swore softly.

'Too right. I want it as far away from me as possible.'

'Understood.'

'I've had enough of this business, Vogel. I'm done. I'll stay on for another year. After that, I've more than enough coin to retire.'

'Fair enough. And do you think Bernd's just going to let his first mate walk away with a handshake and an, *"Auf Wiedersehen"*?'

Kurt laughed and snorted. 'I'll leave him a letter. You can arrange for me to leave the city?'

'No problem. Just tell me when.'

Kurt raised his mug. Vogel did the same and they knocked their steins together before Kurt drained his cup.

The old man rose and threw on his coat. 'Watch Bernd, Vogel. He's a snake, and a demon with the rapier.'

'Will do.' Vogel winked.

Kurt threw him a wink in return before he slapped on his hat and rolled out of the inn.

Vogel waited a few minutes before he too slipped out of the pub and quickly made his way to the quays where Kristian was waiting for him.

The boy indicated to Vogel he had located the *Dolphin*.

They found the two-masted cog gently bobbing on the swell moored to a pier in the north-west docks of Central Isle. A skeleton crew of a half a dozen surly scoundrels had been left to guard the ship, not that they were doing a good job as the main deck was deserted.

Vogel looked around to ensure that there were no eyes on him and Kristian before they moved closer to the ship and crouched behind some wooden crates stacked on the dock.

'Any movement?'

Kristian shook his head. 'A few comings and goings but no cargo shifted.'

'Good,' Vogel said. He motioned with his head and they walked back to the harbour front and the Sunken Galleon where the agent pressed some coins into his young assistant's hand.

'You know the drill. Keep a watch on Bernd.'

'I know, I know. You're going for reinforcements.'

Vogel smiled and slapped him on the shoulder before hurrying away.

***

Stefan von Stern floated in darkness with his eyes closed in the deep trance of rapturous prayer.

His devotions were interrupted by the rattle of metal armour and thump of hobnail boots echoing on stone indicating someone rapidly approaching down the aisle.

He finished his prayers, crossed himself and rose. He turned to find himself staring at a woman with close-cropped blonde hair, dressed in chain armour over which was draped a white tabard with the black cross emblem of the Teutonic Order. An arming sword was strapped to her left hip and a dagger and shortsword on the right. Slung on her back was a large shield.

'Sorry for the intrusion, Stefan, but there's an agent for the Teutonic Order demanding to see a templar.'

'How's the leg, Stef?'

'It's alright. This hurts more.' Stefanie pointed to her face and the bandage wrapped around it and part of her head.

Stefan clamped a hand on her shoulder. 'I saw the other bloke and he's doing far worse. Don't worry, the Benedictines and Franciscans will be here soon and we'll have you driving the blokes wild again in no time.'

Stefanie grinned and snorted. 'But not for a while.'

Stefan shrugged before gesturing to Stefanie to lead on. 'Come on then, let's go and see what this agent wants.'

The agent was wrapped in a black cloak and wore a broad-brimmed hat pulled low to cover most of his face. He was leaning against a lamp post with his head constantly turning to scan his surroundings.

Not dodgy at all, Stefan thought when he emerged from the church. The templar could clearly see, by the agent's constant shifting, that he was anxious.

'Sorry to bother you, Brother.' Vogel held up his seal of office which identified him as an agent of the Teutonic Order. 'I'm Vogel Schlosser. I need help apprehending a dangerous individual involved with the supernatural.'

'Really?' Stefan stared down at the agent with his fists on his hips and a frown at the short, slight figure swathed in black with his goatee and earring.

'Yes,' Vogel said. 'What?' he asked the templar when he saw the grimace on the big man's face. *What the fuck is beefcake's problem? Aside from the impossibly square jaw and tan.*

'Nothing,' Stefan growled, shaking his head. 'So what's all this about, then?'

Of course he'd have a deep voice, too. 'He's a smuggler by the name of Bernd Engel. I have credible information that says he's trafficking in sorcery. I left him in the Sunken Galleon on the harbour front. His ship, the *Dolphin*, is berthed in the north docks.'

'You left him alone?' Stefan asked.

Vogel shook his head. 'One of my men is keeping an eye on him.'

'And the ship?'

'I've no eyes on that.'

Stefan gave a sigh.

Vogel noticed that the Teutonic Knight's robes and surcoat were covered in grime and mud. There were rents in his garments and his chain armour was missing a few links.

The Order soldiers with the templar looked equally worn and battered and some of them sported bandages – evidently the group had recently seen action although the templar didn't have a scratch on him.

'Sorry, Brother. I can see you and your soldiers are weary, but I wouldn't ask if the matter wasn't pressing,' Vogel said.

'Very well, agent.' Stefan turned to one of his men and was about to say something when Vogel chimed in.

'You'll need to send men to secure Bernd's ship.'

'Thank you, *agent,* for telling me how to do my job,' Stefan growled.

The way he spat the word "agent" sounded to Vogel like something that had been squeezed out of a dog's arse.

Vogel held his hands up by way of apology. *Arsehole.*

Stefan barked orders to one of his soldiers about fetching the watch before turning to Vogel. 'Lead on then, agent, and you can tell me all about it as we go.'

'My name's...' Vogel began but the templar had already marched away.

The spy rolled his eyes and shook his head as he followed the big man.

***

The Sunken Galleon was heaving with bodies and obscured by a thick cloud of pipe smoke when Stefan and Vogel entered.

Bernd's card game had swollen into an epic spectacle involving several extra players and large amounts of coin which had subsequently drawn a large and loud crowd.

'Bernd! Bernd Engel!' Stefan's roar instantly silenced the crowd.

Men and women edged away from the table.

The smuggler's eyes widened at the sight of the huge templar, well over six foot tall, bulging with muscle, draped in the distinctive Teutonic Order's white surcoat with its black cross emblem and hefting a war pick in each hand.

Bernd's eyes flicked around the tap room as he sought an escape but, to his horror, Order soldiers blocked them all. He started to rise, but Vogel was faster, crossing the distance to stand beside him and place a hand on his shoulder.

'Don't even try, mate,' the agent said, leaning close to the smuggler. 'There's no escape. Best come peacefully.'

Bernd stared at Vogel with wide eyes and opened his mouth to say something, but all he could do was gape before he sighed and slumped.

'Bollocks!' he said, before Vogel led him out.

***

The *Dolphin* was crawling with Stefan's soldiers and the watch when Vogel, Stefan and Bernd arrived.

Stefan left Bernd in the care of four of the watch while he talked with the commander of his soldiers who had secured the ship and herded the crew together on the main deck.

To his dismay, Vogel noticed Kurt Wechsler among them.

Kurt shot him a glance filled with fear.

Vogel shook his head, indicating that he should keep calm and silent.

'This your ship?' Stefan said to Bernd.

The smuggler shook his head emphatically. 'Never seen it before.'

'You lot!' Vogel yelled to the crew, as he tossed several gold coins at their feet. 'Where's your captain?'

The crew pointed to Bernd before scrabbling for the coins.

41

Bernd groaned and hung his head.

Stefan grabbed the smuggler by the throat and pulled him close.

Vogel drew close too.

'What's in the hold?' asked the templar. 'Tell me now and there'll be no torture and no death.'

Bernd hesitated.

'Tell me!' Stefan roared, shaking the smuggler. 'Or by God I'll walk into the hold with you held before me. Let's see what it does to you then!'

'It's a sword,' Bernd said.

'Where did you get it from? How did you get it on board?'

'I got it from Marrakec,' Bernd said. 'From traders in the bazaar. They handled it, and loaded it, and showed me how to store it.'

'You expect me to believe you just picked up a sorcerous item from the bazaar?' Stefan sneered.

'It wasn't outside. Its owners traded it from a house in the city. I didn't find them - they found me through one of my Marrok contacts.'

'Which of your contacts?' Vogel asked.

Bernd shrugged. 'They didn't say. I didn't ask.'

Stefan shook his head and pursed his lips. 'And how many of your crew have died since you brought the thing on board?'

Bernd shook his head. 'None, I swear.'

'Don't lie to me! I know your men have died. Tell me the truth.'

Bernd hesitated for a moment before shaking his head.

'You bloody fool!' Stefan growled.

For a moment, Vogel thought the templar was going to strike Bernd, such was the fury blazing in his blue eyes.

'Let me have a word with him,' Vogel said to Stefan. 'I know him.'

Stefan glared at Vogel for a moment before turning back to Bernd. He tossed the smuggler to the watch.

'Clap him in irons,' he ordered, 'and hold him for the Trinitarians and witch hunters.'

Bernd's eyes widened in terror. 'Wait! Wait! All right. Four of my men died. I told them not to go near the thing - I warned them. It wasn't my fault.'

'Of course it was your fault!' Stefan roared. 'You knew this was dangerous sorcery. You broke the law and now you'll answer for it, and the deaths of those men.'

Bernd looked at Vogel, but all the agent could do was shake his head sadly.

'Brother Stefan, please can I have a word?'

Stefan glared at the agent in reply.

'This man,' Vogel nodded at Bernd, 'is one of my best informers. I understand he broke the law and trafficked in sorcery, and I absolutely understand he must be punished.'

Bernd's eyes widened.

'But if he's killed over this, we lose a valuable source of information that may prove vital in apprehending threats to the Order and the Church in the future. Threats greater than this.' Vogel indicated the *Dolphin* and its sorcerous cargo. 'It could save lives. Please, spare his.'

Stefan opened his mouth but whatever he was going to say was interrupted by a shout from one of his soldiers.

Vogel saw figures approaching, some wearing the long black cassocks of the Dominican Witch Hunters Order and others in short grey robes with an emblem on their right breasts of a triangular throwing star with a cross at its heart.

'Why are the Trinitarians here?' Bernd asked Vogel, indicating the figures in the short grey robes. He was sweating buckets and his eyes were wide.

Vogel knew how he felt. The Trinitarians, with their cat-like grace and flea-like speed, scared the shit out of him too, as they did everyone.

'They're not here for you,' Stefan said to the smuggler. 'They're here for security and to ensure that there isn't anything else dangerous in your hold. There isn't, is there?'

Bernd shook his head vigorously. 'Only the blade – I swear!'

Stefan moved to greet and speak to the clergy and stopped to talk with a witch hunter and Trinitarian Vogel knew by name only – Father Hubertus Schweinebraten and Brother Martin.

Vogel left them to their conversation and slipped aboard the ship while the Order soldiers were rounding up the crew and searching the vessel. His seal of office allowed him past any guards that challenged him, and he quickly made his way to the hold where he found two Order soldiers guarding the entrance. They barred his way, refusing to budge even when he flashed his seal of office.

When the begging and threats failed, Vogel had to reluctantly resort to bribery and parted with a hefty chunk of silver before they let him in.

The hatch was untouched with the padlocks still in place.

Vogel didn't hesitate; he dug in his pack for a cloth bundle which held his precious lockpicks. He unrolled it, selected two picks and within heartbeats had the padlocks open and tossed aside.

He took a breath before opening the hatch and drew back slightly, as though he were opening an oven door and expected to be blasted with a wave of heat. To his relief there was no sorcerous attack, no wards and protections, and he was able to safely get a good look at the item.

It was in a box, well over six feet long, made of black lacquered wood with images of mythic beasts formed from a collage of bits of coloured shell around which sorcerous script flowed, traced in silver.

Vogel paused a moment before shrugging and opening the box.

He sat back and gasped softly.

It was a sword with a long, slim double-edged blade and hilt made of a black glassy substance which glittered like polished jet. Even as Vogel watched, silvery sorcerous script suddenly appeared, flowing across the blade before vanishing again. It reappeared and disappeared like a sea creature breaking the water's surface for a moment before sliding back beneath the waves. Delicate blue flames flickered along the length of the sword.

Vogel reached for the blade, but before he could grasp the hilt, hands suddenly grabbed him, and he was hoisted back and to his feet.

He turned to find himself staring into the hard eyes of three Trinitarians.

Vogel blinked in surprise. He hadn't heard them approach. He was about to explain his presence when they dragged him out of the hold, off the ship and shoved him before Stefan, Father Hubertus and Brother Martin.

'He was in the hold with the item,' one of the Trinitarians told the clergy.

Stefan stared at Vogel for a moment before grabbing the spy by the front of his tunic.

'Are you insane?' the templar roared. 'Do you have *any* idea how dangerous that thing in the hold is?'

'As it goes, I do…' Vogel began.

'And you still chose to ignore the warning. People have *died* because of that thing. If you're not trained to deal with it, it'll kill you or drive you insane.'

'It had no effect on me!' the spy yelled back, freeing himself from Stefan's grip.

Stefan turned and exchanged a look with Father Hubertus who raised an eyebrow.

'Probably because you were not in there for very long,' the witch hunter said. 'You were lucky, my son. Very lucky.'

He turned away when Brother Martin placed a hand on his shoulder and suggested, in a whisper, to detain and question the crew and move the sword to the citadel of Marienburg.

Father Hubertus bobbed his head in agreement and Stefan wordlessly complied when Brother Martin asked him to clear the area. He barked orders to the soldiers and watched as they quickly shepherded any onlookers from the quays back to the harbour front.

Bernd was taken into custody by a pair of Trinitarians while his crew were escorted by Order soldiers, and the whole group was quickly spirited away.

Stefan turned to the Trinitarians who had apprehended Vogel. 'Get him out of here!' He glared at the agent.

'Wait, wait!' Vogel turned to Stefan as the Trinitarians seized his arms. 'I have informants among the crew.'

Stefan turned and walked away. 'Make enquiries at the Dominican abbey in the morning,' he shouted back over his shoulder.

Vogel heard him tell Father Hubertus that they were off to the von Dassel estate in the Nobles Quarter on the North Bank.

Fucking arsehole! Vogel cursed as the Trinitarians escorted him from the pier to the harbour front where they gave him a gentle shove. They folded their arms in front of their chests and watched him walk away.

He glared at them as Kristian came up to him and leaned on his shoulder.

'Who's that, then?' the boy asked with a nod to Stefan.

Vogel shook his head. 'A knob jockey. Come on.' He wrapped an arm around Kristian's shoulders. 'Let's go drown my sorrows.'

Chapter 2

'Come,' replied the voice to the knock at the door.

A young, tonsured novice entered and bowed. *'Hochmeister* Heinrich von Wilnowe II to see you, my lord.'

'Thank you, Wolfgang. Show the Grand Master in,' the bishop said without turning around.

'Yes, my lord.' The novice bowed again and hastily left.

The bishop stood at the largest window in the room, an arched lattice affair, his hands clasped behind his back as he stared out over the city.

On the South Bank, fires burned.

From his high vantage point atop the tallest tower of Rittershafen Cathedral, they looked like the tiny camp fires of an army and not the houses of the poor being burned and pulled down as riot and disorder swept through the *Viertel*.

The bishop couldn't help wondering if the fire was sent by the divine to cleanse the "district of lost souls" of its vice and crime.

Another knock at the door interrupted his reverie. Before he could utter a word, a figure walked in.

Hochmeister Heinrich von Wilnowe II was not a tall man, but years in the militant Teutonic Knights Order had forged him into a mass of muscle as hard as the tempered steel longsword he wore. Not bad for a man of nearly sixty winters. Age may have robbed him of his hair, and age-lines cracked his face, yet his fierce grey eyes were as bright as a youth's.

He smiled when he saw the bishop, which only highlighted the web-work of scars on his clean-shaven face.

The man he had come to see, on the other hand, was the moon to his sun.

Bishop Vassiliev Ignovovitch was a tall, bony, hard-faced individual whose musculature had all but melted off his frame, leaving it sparse. His lack of facial hair only accentuated his gauntness, and his purple robes of office hung on his frame like sackcloth on a scarecrow.

'Ah, Heinrich!' Vassiliev smiled as they embraced. 'How are you, my friend?'

'Well, Vassily,' Heinrich rasped. 'And you?'

'Well, thank the Almighty. Any news?'

The Grand Master of the Teutonic Order shook his head and pursed his lips. 'None yet. I'm expecting Martin to join us shortly and give us a report of the Trinitarians' findings.'

Heinrich clanked down into a sturdy chair at the bishop's large desk and slung his sword and belt over the back of it. He was clad in his full-length mail and wearing the Order's distinctive white tabard with a black cross.

'Let us hope that he brings good news,' the bishop said, as he crossed to a cabinet and returned with a wine carafe and three goblets. He poured wine into two of the cups and handed one to the Grand Master.

Heinrich took it and muttered his thanks as Vassiliev sank into the chair at his desk and sighed.

The two men sat in silent contemplation for a moment, staring into their wine cups, before another knock shattered the moment.

Bishop Vassiliev's young novice poked his head into the room again. 'My lord, *Hochmeister*, Brother Martin is here.'

'Send him in, Wolfgang, and please ensure that we are not disturbed,' Vassiliev said.

'Yes, my lord.' The young man bowed and departed.

The monk who entered the room had short, cropped hair, once raven coloured though now shot through with more grey than black. His fierce blue eyes sparkled with energy and his wiry frame moved with the grace of a cat.

Unlike the other holy and militant orders, the monk wore a grey tunic, short trousers tied at the knee and soft leather shoes. On his short habit, which also fell to the knees, was an insignia on the right breast of a three-pointed throwing star with a cross at its heart.

'My lord bishop, Grand Master.' Brother Martin embraced Vassiliev and Heinrich.

'Martin,' Heinrich said.

'Martin, I hope you are well. What news from the Trinitarians?'

'Some, my lord,' Brother Martin replied. 'Unfortunately, none of it good.'

Heinrich grunted and sat while the bishop returned to his seat and gestured to Brother Martin to sit.

51

He shook his head and held up his hands indicating he'd rather stand. 'We've had no luck at finding Konrad.'

'And?' Heinrich growled. He could feel there was more bad news to come.

'There have been two more murders, both novices in the Dominican Order.' Martin spoke without expression.

Bishop Vassiliev crossed himself, a grim look on his face.

'Bollocks!' Heinrich cursed.

'And what of your other investigations?' the bishop asked.

Brother Martin shook his head. 'Nothing, my lord.'

Vassiliev steepled his fingers in front of his face and stared through them, lost in thought.

Heinrich looked between the bishop and the monk before turning to Vassiliev. 'You think it's sorcery, don't you, Vassily?'

The bishop looked at him. 'How else do you explain it, Heinrich? A disturbed novice vanishes and is seen moments before and after our fathers are killed–'

'The seminary guards only thought it was Konrad,' Heinrich interrupted.

'With their necks crushed. What novice could do that?' Vassiliev concluded. 'This whole affair stinks of sorcery.'

'What do you think, Martin?' Heinrich asked.

'I'm not one for guessing, *Hochmeister*,' Martin said. 'We know Konrad was definitely off his head when he disappeared.'

The bishop nodded in agreement.

'So it could be the work of a deranged individual driven mad by his experience of the supernatural, or it could very well be sorcery. We'll know more when we have the boy.'

Heinrich snorted.

Vassiliev had returned to his contemplation.

Heinrich looked at the men before staring out of the window.

'How is he eluding us?' The Grand Master turned back to the bishop and monk. 'How is one novice proving so difficult to find when we have Trinitarians and agents out hunting him?'

'Not all the Order's and Church's agents are looking for him,' Martin said. 'Only those who deal with the supernatural, and that's not many. We also have a lot of territory to cover, not just the city but Rittershafen's lands.'

'And Konrad might be hiding among the underworld,' Vassiliev observed.

'We've people looking for him there,' Martin said.

'Maybe not enough people,' Heinrich grumbled.

Vassiliev and Martin exchanged a look before the bishop raised an eyebrow.

'You're thinking we put more agents on the hunt?' Vassiliev asked Heinrich.

'I think we'll have to,' Heinrich said. 'It's been a fortnight since Fathers Pohl and Dieter died, and Konrad vanished, and now we have two more clergy deaths with these novices.'

'You're right, Heinrich,' Vassiliev said. 'But maybe it's not more people we need, but the *right* people.'

Now it was Heinrich's turn to raise an eyebrow.

'What we really need here is a bloodhound,' Vassiliev explained. 'Someone who understands the underworld inside and out – a thieftaker of exceptional ability.'

Heinrich stood up abruptly. 'Our thieftaker's going to need help if he's never gone up against the supernatural.'

'You have someone in mind?' Vassiliev asked.

The Grand Master shook his head. 'No. But we know a man who might.'

Brother Martin crossed his arms and frowned at the bishop and the Grand Master. 'Who?'

Heinrich grinned. 'I'll arrange a meet later today.'

'Well, then.' Vassiliev refilled his and Heinrich's goblet and poured a cup for Brother Martin. 'I think we have something to drink to,'

Heinrich raised his goblet and the bishop and Brother Martin followed. 'Here's to our thieftaker.'

'Amen,' Bishop Vassiliev replied as they knocked their cups together.

***

An hour later a slightly drunk Heinrich rose, with the bishop escorting him.

'I've posted templars to guard you and the fathers, men I hand-picked myself.'

'Thank you, Heinrich.' The bishop hugged his friend goodbye.

'Keep safe. Keep vigilant, Vassily.'

'I was a witch hunter once, my friend,' Vassiliev said. 'I may have lost some of my edge but there's still a little left.'

The *Hochmeister* of the Teutonic Order smiled before he turned, jingling noisily as he walked down the steps and out of the cathedral.

Heinrich did not glance back as he left Rittershafen Cathedral. Waiting outside for him was his six-and-a-half foot bodyguard, nearly as old as the Grand Master himself, with snow-coloured locks that fell to his shoulders, and a long silver handlebar moustache.

'Well?' he said, staring at Heinrich.

'Well what?' Heinrich replied, staring into his bright blue eyes.

'What news of the fathers and Konrad?'

'Martin needs more agents to help him find Konrad, and Vassiliev thinks sorcery's behind this deviltry.'

'So nothing to worry about, then,'

Heinrich smirked. 'We'll just have to keep a careful watch on him – on all our fathers. Speaking of which, where's Gunther?'

'Probably out and about doing what any good spymaster does – minding everyone's business.'

'Good. Bring him to me, and your protégé. It's time to do what we discussed and put him to the test.'

'About bloody time,' Heinrich's bodyguard declared. 'He's climbing the walls babysitting new recruits.'

Heinrich's evil grin was impossible to ignore.

'What?'

'He's going to be doing more babysitting, unfortunately,' Heinrich said.

His bodyguard groaned as they wheeled their horses round and clopped across the *Mönchsplatz*, the cathedral square in the Church Quarter of Rittershafen.

Chapter 3

Vogel was still suffering from the previous night's excesses at the Drowning Duck when he was rudely roused by a pounding on his door.

He cursed as he rolled out of bed, shuffled to the door and poked out a dishevelled bleary-eyed head. He found himself staring at the bulky upper torso of a tall figure wearing chainmail armour and draped in the distinctive white tabard of the Teutonic Knights. Panning up to the face, Vogel saw that the templar was an old boy with long white hair and a handlebar moustache. The sturdy old geezer looked like he meant business and was more than capable of handling a good deal of trouble.

'Wot?' Vogel croaked. His throat burned and he was in no mood to be courteous. 'It's too early, mate.'

The man stood with his feet wide apart and his fists on his hips. He let his sneering gaze travel slowly up and down the figure standing before him and fought back the urge to pound the little shit for his insolence. He cleared his throat.

'It's lunchtime,' the figure replied coolly. 'I am Brother Arnold Guerk - you know whom I serve. I'm looking for Herr Gunther Hahne. Do you know where I may find him?'

'Maybe,' Vogel replied, one eye narrowing suspiciously. 'Why?'

Arnold levelled a murderous glare at him before clearing his throat again. 'Grand Master

Heinrich von Wilnowe II, of the Teutonic Order, would like a word with him. His services are needed.'

'Bad luck, mate. He's not in.'

'When will he be back?'

'Dunno.' Vogel shrugged.

'Do you know where he is?' Arnold said through gritted teeth.

Vogel shook his head. 'Nah.'

'And who are you to Herr Hahne?'

'Order agent.'

'Do you have a name, agent?'

'Yeah.'

Arnold clenched his fists and closed his eyes for a moment.

'Well, what is it?'

Vogel stared at him for a few heartbeats. 'Vogel.'

'Well then,' Arnold declared loudly. 'That's fortunate – just the man I'm looking for. I was told to fetch you and your *Meister*, but you'll do. Grab your things - you're coming with me!'

'Wot, now?'

'No. Christmas.'

'Really?'

'Of course not, you insolent little shit!' Arnold roared. 'Now move!'

Vogel paused only long enough to wipe off Arnold's spittle, splash some water on his face and collect his cloak and hat before Arnold marched him out of the inn.

***

There were two horses waiting for them outside, but the press of people and wagons in the narrow cobbled streets meant that they had to walk their horses through them, not that Vogel minded.

A kaleidoscope of colours, sounds and smells assaulted their senses as they wound their way through the stalls and shops of the Artisans Quarter and the markets of the *Rathaus Markt* where Rittershafen's town hall loomed. They passed bawling hawkers selling everything from melons and lemons to strange creatures from far-off lands.

Cages held a menagerie of chittering, screaming beasts as variable as the people who thronged the market, dressed in every conceivable colour and design, from plain flowing robes to ornate silk gowns, from tight leathers to metal-clad mercenaries drifting menacingly through the streets.

In the Merchants Quarter, people from all corners of the known world rubbed shoulders with each other, while food as exotic as the cultures they came from sizzled on spits or bubbled in pots.

Vogel drank it all in with a smile on his face while Brother Arnold grumbled under his breath. He glared with disapproval at the shantytowns that had sprung up in the squares and parks of the Artisans and Merchants Quarters; refugees who had fled the fire in the *Viertel*.

Arnold turned to Vogel and glared at the smile on the agent's face. He rewarded Vogel's friendly nod with a scathing grunt before motioning to him to mount up. They were out of the hive of humanity that was the Artisans and Merchants Quarters and would now ride to the Teutonic Order's stronghold.

***

It was a grey and thoroughly miserable late summer afternoon when Vogel first entered Marienburg– the fortress monastery and seat of power of the Teutonic Knights, sited on an island between the Central Isle and the Nobles Quarter on the north bank. It loomed over the city of Rittershafen which huddled to its south while the estates and mansions of the rich and gentry sprawled to the north.

It was connected to the Central Isle by three long walled and narrow bridges interrupted at intervals with gatehouses.

As they passed through Marienburg's western gatehouse, Vogel couldn't help marvel at the sheer size and intimidation of the fortress.

The entire complex was surrounded by three rings of red brick walls, each well over forty feet high, with battlements roofed in red tiles. The walls were punctuated at intervals by soaring towers with tall, pointed roofs which looked like witches hats and were likewise covered in red tiles.

They clopped over the drawbridge of the first moat and passed unchallenged through the second wall's barbican. At the third, or inner, wall's main gatehouse, Arnold halted and indicated to the spy to dismount. Servants came rushing up to the Knight and spy and took the reins of their horses. It was on foot from here onwards.

Passing through the gatehouse's long tunnel, with its unsettling murder holes on either side tracking their progress, Vogel and Arnold found themselves in the Lower Castle. This was a large and bustling bailey, a mini-city within the fortress complex, complete with workshops and warehouses, armouries, breweries and kitchens.

Vogel and Arnold exchanged curt greetings with the servants, soldiers and knights they passed and strolled beneath the portcullis of yet another barbican flanked by a pair of squat conical towers into the first of the fortresses-monastery castles, the Middle Castle.

On entering the courtyard, Vogel paused, smiling as the din of the Lower Castle receded and the serenity of the Middle Castle washed over him, although he would never have called it a "castle".

It was comprised of four long cloistered wings creating a square, two-story high, building built of red brick with tall arched windows and red tiled roofs with a large grass courtyard at its heart.

Each side of the monastery catered to an aspect of the martial monks and nuns dwelling there, providing them with dormitories and cells, living quarters, armouries and training halls for practice indoors when the weather was foul. The other buildings of the Middle Castle were given over to providing the living needs of the brothers and sisters and included kitchens, studies and chambers for meditation, prayer and chapter meetings.

When Vogel asked Brother Arnold about the Middle Castle, the surly Teutonic Knight informed him that below it were storage cellars, saunas and bathrooms. These were cunningly engineered to allow steam from the bathhouses to filter up through special vents and grates to heat the entire Middle Castle, a blessing when cold winters fell upon the city.

Arnold allowed Vogel a few moments of awestruck silence to drink in the splendour of the monastery before ushering him on.

'This isn't it?' he asked the large templar.

'No,' Arnold replied. 'This is the Middle Castle, the abbey of the *Schwertbrüderorden*.'

Everyone in Rittershafen had heard of the *Schwertbrüderorden or Sword Brethren* – once feared warrior monks who were now reduced to a handful of individuals. No one knew why, Vogel included. Whenever he asked Gunther about it, the old rogue would grunt and dismiss it with a wave.

'Our destination is there.' Arnold pointed to a large gatehouse, the entrance to a huge Gothic monastery keep towering above the fortress complex. 'The High Castle, the seat of the Teutonic Order.'

As they strode through the courtyard of the Middle Castle, Vogel noticed that even the sanctums of the warrior monks were a hive of activity. Servants scurried in and out of doors laden with bags or trays of food, while others rolled barrels towards underground cellars.

The barbican that led to the High Castle had its drawbridge down and was guarded by a pair of Order soldiers who bowed to Brother Arnold as he and Vogel passed through.

They emerged at the other end only to find themselves crossing a moat which separated the Middle and High Castles before proceeding to another gatehouse, the High Castle barbican, which was only slightly smaller than the one they had just walked through. It too had a long passage that could be sealed by a portcullis with holes and slits in the walls where defenders could pour arrow fire and all manner of horrific murder on invaders.

The thought made Vogel slightly edgy as he walked along the cool dark passage, but it evaporated as he passed into the courtyard at the heart of the High Castle.

The High Castle was even more impressive than the Middle Castle and stood overlooking the entire Marienburg complex, partly because it was the tallest building and partly because it was built on a hill.

It too was a square-shaped monastic building built entirely of red brick with three stories of cloistered galleries and an open courtyard at its centre dominated by a large roofed well.

Arnold didn't pause to give Vogel any more time to admire the High Castle, rushing him quickly up three flights of stairs to the Teutonic *Hochmeister's* study.

'Wait there,' he said, motioning to a bench. 'A brother squire will fetch you when the Grand Master is ready.' With that, Arnold turned on his heel and strode off.

Vogel shrugged and sat down. He contented himself with gazing at the beautiful, cloistered gallery with its elaborate pointed arch windows, vaulted ceiling and red brick walls adorned with artwork depicting the knights in battle with mundane and supernatural foes.

The spy shook his head at this alien world of monasteries and warrior monks. *Still*, he thought as he leaned back and let the peaceful atmosphere of the building flow over him. *If only I had a jug of ale and my pipe*.

***

Fetching Vogel had left Arnold in a foul mood and so, after he had seen the Order's agent to the Grand Master's private chambers, he went into one of the High Castle's baileys. Long before he reached it, he could hear the sweet ring of steel on steel and entered it to find his protégé fencing with Reinhard Schiller, the Order's master-at-arms.

Reinhard was perspiring hard but, much to Arnold's delight and pride, Stefan von Stern was not.

He was twenty-eight summers old and hugely muscled. He wielded the *zweihander*, two-handed sword, like a light bamboo cane and it wasn't just his strength which was awesome but his skill. His mother, Katharine, had died giving birth to Stefan, something his father, Eric, of the noble von Sterns, had never forgiven him for. So his childhood was marked by torment and torture, not just from his parent but also his siblings who were raised to believe Stefan was a curse on the family. They brutalized him as maliciously as their father and had howled with laughter when he had knocked the ten-year-old Stefan unconscious one night in a fit of drunken rage.

Stefan had finally been saved by the kind-hearted and gentle priest, Father Pohl Heinz, who could no longer bear silent witness to the boy's torment. Fearing for the boy's life, he had carried the unconscious Stefan from his father's banqueting hall, bundled him onto a wagon and battled through a stormy night to deliver the boy to his closest friend, Arnold Guerk, then a junior knight in the Teutonic Order.

And so Stefan grew up in the Order where every knight was his brother and Arnold doubled as a surrogate father. Here he stood years later, six and a half foot of solid muscle – a fearless killing machine forged by the Order, tempered and polished by Arnold.

Even as Arnold watched, Stefan drove the master-at-arms back before knocking his blade aside and delivering a punishing blow to the side of the head. Schiller stumbled to one knee. *A prudent moment to interrupt,* thought Arnold.

'Stefan!' he barked, calling the combat to an end.

Reinhard and Stefan separated, saluted each other and wordlessly turned away.

'*Meister* Arnold.' Stefan turned to his mentor and peeled off his helmet, stroking back his long sweat-streaked hair. 'I missed you in this morning's training session.'

'I was with the Grand Master and attending to duties.'

They sat on a bench where Arnold helped Stefan to unbuckle his padded fencing armour.

'What's the order of business today?'

'Grand Master Heinrich demands our presence. So when you're done stowing this,' he indicated Stefan's fencing gear, 'collect your armour and blade and meet me in his chambers.'

'Back in the field?' Stefan's blue eyes were wide and he had a broad smile on his square jaw.

'Your talents are wasted training the Order's knights and soldiers, not that they're not appreciated. But we need you back where you belong, in the heart of battle, doing what you do best – slaughtering the enemy.' Arnold patted him on the shoulder. 'Get going, boy!'

'Yes, *Meister*!' Stefan leapt to his feet and sprinted away.

***

'Come!'

Vogel entered the Grand Master's study to find Heinrich with company.

Surly Arnold Guerk was present, and he recognised the scrawny sharp-faced old cleric dressed in purple robes, Bishop Vassiliev, but not the younger cleric with the close-cropped hair and beard who stood behind the bishop. He was dressed in the cassock of a witch hunter.

Vogel groaned inwardly when he saw the figure standing next to Brother Arnold–Stefan von Stern. Now that Vogel had the chance to get a good look at the templar in the sober light of day, he realised that

66

he had never seen so much muscle on a human being.

'My lord, Grand Master.' Vogel bowed to Heinrich and the bishop. 'Father, Brothers,' he greeted the others.

The gathering bobbed their heads and mumbled greetings.

'Ah, Vogel, good,' Heinrich said, acknowledging the agent before turning to the gathering. 'Gentlemen, allow me to make the introductions. Everybody, that's Vogel. Vogel, allow me to present his lordship, Bishop Vassiliev Ignovovitch. You know my *Komtur,* Arnold Guerk, my second-in-command, and his protégé Stefan von Stern. Behind his lordship is Father Jozef Richter.'

Thanks for introducing me like a piece of turd. Vogel bowed again to the group.

'Gentlemen, I've asked Vogel here as he's one of our most promising agents,' Heinrich continued.

Vogel puffed out his chest at that introduction. *That was more like it.*

'Vogel,' von Wilnowe continued. 'I am assigning you a new job. I've discussed this with your *Meister*, Gunther, and cleared it with him. You and Brother Stefan will be working together on this case.'

Stefan and Vogel exchanged a glance and Vogel raised a questioning eyebrow.

Heinrich turned to Arnold. 'Have you told him?' He gestured toward Stefan.

Arnold shook his head.

Heinrich turned back to the agent and templar. 'I'll keep it short, boys. A fortnight ago two priests were killed, Father Pohl Heinz and Father Dieter Schenk – may God rest their souls.'

The men in the room bowed their heads, muttered prayers and crossed themselves.

Heinrich could see the shock in Stefan's face at the mention of Father Pohl. The jolly, tubby old cleric had not just been Stefan's teacher, friend and mentor. He was family.

He rose, went to stand in front of Stefan and placed his hands on the templar's broad shoulders.

'I'm sorry lad. I know you and Father Pohl were close, but we decided to hold off the funeral, and making the deaths of our fathers known, until we had caught the culprit and learned the reason for the murders.'

'I understand, Grand Master,' Stefan said softly.

'Your relationship with Father Pohl was why I chose you for this job. I know your devotion to him will mean you'll do whatever it takes to catch whoever's responsible. I know we trained you for the battlefield, but now we want you to enter a different arena and learn different skills. We want you to work with agents of the order to sniff out supernatural foes and use your templar gifts against them.'

'You think the supernatural is involved, Grand Master?' Stefan asked.

Heinrich looked serious. 'We think so, but we also know that sometimes that's not the case.' He looked pointedly at Vogel who knew exactly what the Grand Master was alluding to. It was not unknown for criminals to dress up crimes, like murder, to make it look as though the supernatural was responsible. Some even went as far as donning masks and applying makeup to appear like demons, even using theatrics like fire breathing to add believability.

'But,' Heinrich barked, 'if the supernatural is involved, Vogel will need some divinely aided muscle on this job, and that's you, boy – are you up to it?'

'Absolutely, Grand Master!' Stefan replied as tears tracked down his cheek. 'For Father Pohl! For our Fathers! For God and the Order!'

Supernatural, Vogel thought. *Fucking great.*

'Good lad,' said Heinrich. 'You could both learn from each other, and that's what we want.'

He turned to address the gathering. 'Bishop Vassiliev has something vital to add. My lord bishop.'

Bishop Vassiliev cleared his throat. 'Vogel, Stefan, I want you to attend to Father Jozef - he's one of the finest witch hunters in our order. You won't find a more knowledgeable man on the subject of the supernatural, and his speciality is sorcery.'

'Thank you, my lord,' Richter said with a smile and wink at the templar and spy.

'It's true, Jozef,' the bishop replied. 'Vogel, Stefan, you will report to Father Richter who will oversee your actions on this case. He will be your teacher–'

'And ensure you play well together,' Heinrich growled.

'Quite,' Vassiliev said, with a nod to the *Hochmeister*. 'Now gentlemen, about the murders of our poor fathers, there's something vital you should know.' Bishop Vassiliev took a deep breath before continuing. 'I believe I brought the murderer to Rittershafen, and for that, I beg your forgiveness.' Vassiliev smiled wryly and shook his head. 'And to think, I came here to battle dark forces - instead I come bringing the serpent with me.'

Like the templars and Father Richter, Vogel remained patiently unmoved by the melodrama.

The bishop continued. 'I believe the murderer *may* be one of my own novices, a young man named Konrad Stich.'

The men in the room exchanged looks.

'A year ago,' Vassiliev said, 'Konrad accompanied myself and some of the brothers as we hunted a witch called Sabine Halmer. We tracked her to the *Geistwald* forest but when we were a day from her lair, her demons attacked us. Many knights fell in that battle. Konrad was attacked by her demons and, being of a fragile mind, was unhinged by the encounter. He began having nightmares and started behaving aggressively to everyone around him. Eventually, he even started eating raw meat.'

Vogel looked at Stefan, who stared at the bishop, unmoved.

'I felt responsible for the boy and had him working in the hospital, which suited his once-gentle nature. But to no avail,' the bishop said. 'It did nothing to quell his aggression. And then, a little over a fortnight ago, the boy vanished and the

70

murders occurred. And it's not just senior clergy that have been killed. Since Konrad went missing, two novices have also been found dead.'

'We have good reason to believe it is the boy,' Heinrich said to Stefan and Vogel. 'Bring him in – unharmed. Understood?'

'Yes, Grand Master,' they chorused.

'Questions?' Heinrich barked.

'Begging your pardon, Grand Master,' Vogel said. 'Did anyone see anything the night Father Pohl and Father Dieter were killed?'

Bishop Vassiliev grimaced. 'The guards at the seminary where they lived said they saw a novice enter and leave the good fathers' rooms moments before and after they were killed, but they couldn't confirm who it was. To them, one novice looks much like the next, especially when it's dark.'

'And did Konrad have a grudge against the fathers?'

Vassiliev shook his head.

'So Konrad may not actually be the killer or connected in any way to the murders?'

'We don't know, Vogel,' Heinrich said. 'That's why we've called you in. Find out if he is responsible for their deaths, and if he's not, then find the killer or killers.'

'Understood, Grand Master,' Vogel said, clearing his throat.

'Any more questions?' The Grand Master glared at the spy.

Stefan and Vogel shook their heads.

Heinrich grunted in approval. 'Good luck, boys. Dismissed.'

71

Vogel and Stefan bowed to the group and left with Father Richter behind them. Once outside, the priest put an arm over their shoulders and pulled them close.

'Vogel, Stefan, before you begin your search for Konrad, I have a small job for you. There is a party tonight at the von Gruenbaum mansion. I want you both to attend and see what information you can glean about the von Gruenbaums and their guests. Report your findings back to me tomorrow at the Witch Hunters convent. All right?'

Vogel and Stefan exchanged looks.

'This is a test, isn't it, Father?' Vogel said.

Father Richter stood before the duo with his hands folded behind his back. 'Absolutely. This will tell us all what you're both capable of and if you can play nicely together.'

Vogel sighed.

Stefan remained silent.

'Anything else, my boys?'

The spy and templar shook their heads.

'Cheer up, lads,' Richter said. 'You two will get on famously.' He slapped the spy on the arm. 'God be with you.'

'And with you, Father,' they chorused.

Father Richter gave them a big grin before he strode back into Heinrich's study and closed the door behind him.

Vogel and Stefan stood staring at the door for a few moments before Stefan turned to Vogel.

'Where to now?'

'The Honey Bee,' Vogel replied. 'Just off the *Rathaus Markt Platz*.'

'Ah!' Stefan smiled. 'You plan to start the investigation there?'

'No,' Vogel said. 'I eat there.'

'What...' Stefan began, but Vogel had already started walking down the stairs and out of the High Castle.

Chapter 4

The von Gruenbaum mansion was a beautiful three-story manor with fluted columns, tall windows and gleaming tiles, occupying nearly an acre of impeccably tended ground in the Nobles Quarter on the north bank.

Vogel and Stefan clopped up a gravel drive, lined with lit lanterns, as manicured lawns fell away on either side of them, scattered with fragrant-smelling fruit trees and wildly colourful displays of summer flowers while crickets chirped in the warm evening air.

Vogel stared in dreamy awe at the wealth and splendour of his surroundings and at the looming house a hundred yards away which blazed with light. He looked up at the stone gargoyles perched on the roof leering down at him. They kept watch over the grounds around the house as well as the straight gravelled drive which stretched from the main gates to the front of the mansion where it ended at a stone fountain of a unicorn spewing water from its mouth.

He turned to Stefan, who was fidgeting and looking surly.

'This place is gorgeous, isn't it?'

The templar grunted.

'What's wrong with you?' Vogel raised an eyebrow.

'We should be hunting Konrad and the killer of our fathers, not attending a soiree.' Stefan had a face like a thundercloud.

'We might pick up clues to the murder here. Somebody might've seen something, or know the murderer and let the information slip. Stranger things have happened.'

'I feel like a bloody fool.' Stefan pulled at his shirt.

'You look fine,' Vogel lied.

Vogel was dressed as a young noble should with a fine shirt and doublet, boots and hat, and a neatly trimmed goatee and moustache.

Stefan wore trousers, boots and tunic and had a longsword and dagger strapped to his hip as befitted a noble's bodyguard.

'So how did I get us in here then?' Vogel gave the templar a sidelong glance, trying to take Stefan's mind off just how ridiculous he looked.

Stefan snorted. 'You didn't. Father Richter arranged for our invite.'

Vogel rolled his eyes. *Arsehole.*

'Actually *I* did get us in. If it was known that the Church or Order had arranged our invites, everybody here would know we're agents and how many people do you think would talk to us then?' He held up his finger and thumb in the form of a zero.

'So how did you get us in?' Stefan asked.

'How do you think?'

'Thievery? Blackmail?'

'Not quite. I bribed *and* blackmailed our way in.' Vogel puffed out his chest, looking pleased with himself.

'So I was right,' the templar said.

'Agents don't always use bribery and extortion. Sometimes we use sex – it's one of the most potent weapons in our arsenal.'

Stefan turned away in disgust, muttering something about agents having no shame and even fewer morals.

Vogel smirked, feeling better at having nettled the pious templar.

A queue of carriages had started to form as guests took their time to disembark or wait for a servant to lead their horses to the stables. This gave Vogel a chance to get his first good look at their hosts.

Lady Silke von Gruenbaum was a spectacle to behold with her slender waist, full bosom and pale skin. Her long golden hair was wrapped up in a beehive and encased in a delicate silver net kept in place with silver and pearl pins.

Pearls also adorned the long dress she wore which was as red as the rouge on her lips.

Vogel gawped at her, especially her jewellery which was worth a small fortune. He also noted Stefan staring enthralled at the lady. He cleared his throat loudly when he noticed the agent staring at him and turned as red as the lady's lips.

Vogel grinned and nudged the templar in the ribs. He was starting to enjoy himself.

'Alex von Hessen,' Vogel said with a low flourishing bow when their turn had come to greet the hosts. 'And may I present my man, Gunther.' He gestured to Stefan.

Silke stared at him with the coolest and bluest eyes Vogel had ever lost himself in before her gaze drifted to the templar.

Stefan bowed to them. 'My lady, my lord.'

Silke smiled and dipped her head, as did Olaf, who was dressed similarly to Vogel, before they turned away, which was the templar and agent's cue to leave.

They entered the house to find themselves in a circular foyer large enough to house a small army, tiled with elaborate and costly mosaics. A sweeping staircase to their right wound up to the upper floors of the mansion, guarded by a pair of rhino-sized guards sporting maces who had been squeezed into thick leather armour. Halls branched off from the foyer, leading to other wings of the house.

Vogel tapped Stefan on the shoulder and pointed to a pair of double doors on their left from which the sound of music washed through. It could only be the ballroom.

Stefan led the way, ploughing through the crowd of richly dressed men and women as the music guided them past the ornate doors into a brightly lit world of whirling gowns and stirring melodies as nobles, young and old, danced in groups and pairs.

Vogel squinted as he entered the ballroom, almost blinded by the rainbow of light cast by three huge crystalline chandeliers hanging from the cavernous ceiling.

Stefan was sweating and frowning. His was a world of piety and battle and now he was plunged into a maelstrom of powdered and simpering sharks in a sea of courtly etiquette, where the weapons of choice were gossip and whispers in shadows.

Stefan focused on the familiar and made a beeline for the tables lining one side of the room, laden with piles of meats, cheeses, fruit and other fancies from Rittershafen as well as far flung lands.

He moved behind the tables with his back to the wall and stood staring at the throng with wide eyes that darted furiously around.

'Are you ill?' the spy whispered to him.

'I can't dance!' Stefan hissed back.

Vogel nearly laughed out loud but swallowed it on seeing the templar's face drenched in sweat.

'Relax; no one's going to ask you to dance. You're a bodyguard.'

'Really?'

'Yes.'

The templar breathed a sigh of relief and Vogel thought he caught a whispered prayer of thanks.

'I'm off to see what I can learn,' Vogel said. 'Why don't you just lurk here and keep your eyes peeled and ears open?'

'Shouldn't I come with you? Listen to how you interact with people and be on hand in case things get nasty?'

Vogel shook his head. 'Nah, no need. I can handle myself and, to be honest, you'd learn far more by just listening to people.'

Stefan frowned in doubt.

'As a bodyguard, nobles won't pay you any mind – you're invisible to 'em and when you're invisible, the things you overhear people say…'

'All right! Fair enough.' Stefan looked happier. 'Sounds like a good idea.'

'Brilliant,' Vogel said, slapping him on the arm. 'I'll come and find you in a few hours and remember – no food!'

'I know.' Stefan sighed. 'Guests only, not servants.'

Vogel grinned. 'Remember why we're here.'

'We're fishing.'

'And what are we hoping to catch?'

'Anything juicy.' Stefan gave the thumbs up.

'Good man. Remember,' he pointed to his ears, eyes and nose, 'keep 'em peeled!'

Stefan gave him a wink.

Vogel winked back and disappeared.

Stefan stood vigil for over an hour before he relaxed enough to think about his current situation and Vogel's hasty exit. It occurred to him that the spy had placed him in his current position to keep him out of his hair.

Stefan shrugged. He didn't care - he was happy to watch the dancers and try to pick up some conversation, but after a further hour of hearing nothing important, not that he could hear over the sound of the musicians, he decided he needed a change of scene and to stretch his legs.

He walked out of the ballroom, pushed past the hordes still swilling around the foyer, and into the fresh air outside. He took a moment to stare at the giggling and flirting crowds before he shook his head and started ambling along the drive which led to the main gate.

There were halfa dozen guards at the gate standing around a brazier, chatting softly, but they fell instantly silent when Stefan appeared.

The templar smiled in understanding. Fighting men and women were close-knit families who were suspicious of outsiders, but after a few minutes talking with the templar, they warmed up and were happy to let him share their fire and swap banter on soldiering and combat.

He lingered with them for a while before he made his excuses and returned to the mansion, where he noted that the crowds had swollen. As he was unwilling to return to the throng, Stefan decided to extend his stroll and have a wander around the grounds.

It was a fine summer's evening and Stefan found he had plenty of company as groups of guests drank and gossiped in gazebos or lovers drifted, looking to steal intimate moments alone. Stefan gave them a wide berth and soon found himself behind the mansion, facing a pair of guards who, unlike the others at the front gate, were not welcoming at all. They greeted him with stony stares and politely but firmly insisted that he piss off and return to the party. With a deep sigh and a shrug, the templar slouched back to the main entrance, steeling himself to plunge back into the chaos of the ball.

***

80

Vogel walked away from Stefan grinning to himself. He almost felt sorry for the templar – almost. *He'll be alright*, the spy reasoned, *as long as he stays put and keeps out of everyone's way.*

His adrenaline pumped as he went to work.

There was a set behaviour that Gunther had seared into him from the outset so it became instinctive when he was on the prowl – work on the drunkards first, they'll have the loosest tongues. Make friends where you can, snoop when you can't and treat all gossip as gospel. *Always* seduce the servants.

Vogel spent the next couple of hours flitting from guest to guest, chatting and flirting, howling with pretentious laughter at every shit joke that he heard and feigning genuine interest in every eye-drooping story related to him. When he wasn't listening to tall tales, or regaling guests with his own, he lurked and listened and, though he spied groups of nobles who acted furtive, further investigation revealed their secrets were nothing more than the sordid infidelity of the rich and bored. Even the servants he wooed yielded nothing scandalous and certainly nothing for the Order or Church to concern itself about.

Vogel sighed as he drifted on through this sea of feckless and privileged humanity.

On the other side of the vast expanse of the foyer were two large rooms, not as large as the ballroom but with enough space to accommodate the horde of guests that thronged the von Gruenbaum's party. Both rooms were also far enough away from the raucous music and revelry to permit the guests to have normal conversations and not shout.

Vogel was thankful for that. He was also grateful at being able to hide in the haze of smoke that hung in the air of the study he currently stood in. It was littered with large sofas and armchairs where the older guests lounged, grouped into tribes of gossiping men and women, nibbling on cheeses and quaffing glasses of brandy and wine. Two blazing hearths provided additional light and heat, though the latter was unnecessary as it was a fine evening.

Vogel spotted Gunther seated at a table with four elderly noblemen heatedly engaged in some debate, waving his hand dramatically and pointing emphatically with his pipe as he argued some irrelevant point.

Of course he would be here, Vogel said to himself. This was a prominent party, it was only right that he be present to find out if there were any threats to the Church and Order brewing from within the city's nobility.

Mentor and mentee rightly refused to acknowledge each other and Vogel drifted on, leaving Gunther to his work although he couldn't resist a little smirk. The old rogue seemed perfectly at home with the rich and privileged as he laughed and joked with them, but then he would – they were all thieves and cutthroats.

The next room Vogel visited was also mostly full of old boys and girls who offered nothing scandalous except for one old dear with more money than sense who was keen to purchase Vogel's companionship as a bedfellow.

The agent fled.

The evening was drawing on and Vogel had discovered no information of value among the toffs, so he decided it was time to do some serious snooping and explore the rest of the house.

Aside from the main staircase in the foyer, there was another set of stairs at the back of the ballroom which Vogel had noted earlier led to the upper floors.

The spy made his way back to the dancers, swaying slightly in feigned drunkenness as he staggered to the door at the back of the ballroom, noticing that Stefan had disappeared. He slipped through the door to find himself in a tiny foyer with a set of circular stairs to his right, which he climbed silently.

There were two squat and powerfully built dogs with large drooling jaws lounging at the top of the stairs. They rose and started growling softly the moment Vogel appeared.

Bollocks! He froze. 'Good doggies,' he whispered as he slowly backed down the stairs with a nervous smile and his hands held up.

He weaved his way back through the ballroom and foyer and staggered outside where he stood, eyeing up the house and weighing his options before he shrugged.

Time for some breaking and entering. He smiled broadly at the thought of that.

***

Stefan resumed his position behind the buffet tables with the enthusiasm of a wretch being dragged to the gallows. He watched the dancers for a while before hunger tugged him to the platters. After a quick look around to ensure that there were no eyes on him, he grabbed a chunk of bread and a couple of smoked sausages which he stuffed under his jerkin.

'Wine, *Mein Herr*?'

Stefan jumped before turning to find himself staring into a pair of the greenest eyes he had ever seen. The serving girl beamed at him in amusement.

'No!'

The maid raised a surprised eyebrow and leaned back slightly.

Stefan cursed himself and blushed. 'No, thank you, *Fraulein*.'

'Beer, sir?' She was smiling again and moving closer to the templar.

'I'm on duty,' Stefan said as he backed up and pressed himself into the wall. Somehow, he found himself sweating and unable to meet the maid's lovely eyes.

'Oh?' She looked him up and down, drinking in the templar's fine physique, and her smile broadened at his awkwardness. 'What duty would that be?'

'Bodyguard.'

The maid looked at the guests swirling around the ballroom. 'Who are you guarding? Is it a lord?'

Stefan shook his head. 'He's not here,' he mumbled.

'Well, how are you going to guard him when you're not with him?'

Stefan stared at her, his mouth gaping, caught completely off guard at how to respond.

The maid laughed softly. 'What's your name?'

'St…Gunther,' Stefan stammered.

'Well, Stagunther, I'm Marie.'

'Er…' Stefan said as he struggled to think of a reply. 'Good name. After the Virgin.' He turned away from Marie, still red faced, to stare at the dancers, shooting the occasional sidelong glance at her as she smiled at him.

'Do you like dancing, Stagunther?'

'Only with swords,' Stefan blurted. He closed his eyes in frustration, immediately regretting what he had said. 'And you, Marie? Do you like dancing?'

'Yes!' She moved to stand in front of him. 'Whenever I have time. What do you do in your free time?'

'Prayer.'

'Every day?' Marie raised an eyebrow.

'Of course. All good Christians should devote time to prayer!' Stefan said, beaming. 'I love it –it lightens my soul.'

Marie was about to burst into laughter but on seeing the zeal in his eyes, it died on her lips.

'Well, speaking of duty, I have to return to mine. Have a good evening, *Mein Herr*.' She shot Stefan a wan smile before beating a hasty exit.

Stefan sighed and shrugged. Stick to swords and leave the bullshitting and seduction to Vogel – he's the expert at it.

He turned, feeling a presence by his side, and found himself staring at a young serving man.

'Good evening, *Mein Herr*,' he said to the templar with a broad smile and a wink. 'I'm Holger.'

Stefan groaned and shook his head before he strode out.

***

'Beg your pardon, sir,' the stable boy said, leaping to his feet. 'I didn't see you enter.'

'Think nothing of it, dear boy,' the young nobleman slurred as he shuffled unsteadily towards the boy.

'Can I help you, sir?'

'As a matter of fact, you can.' Vogel fumbled in his pockets and fished out a silver coin which he tossed to the boy who deftly caught it, stared at it wide-eyed and then quickly pocketed it.

'There's another of those if you can help me find my money pouch.' Vogel beckoned him closer and when the boy edged forward, the spy wrapped a friendly arm around his broad shoulders. 'Now then, keep this between you and me, but I was in the bushes at the back of the mansion, er, showing a very nice young lady my brand new pocket watch. It's solid gold, you know?' The stench of spirits that washed from the nobleman made the stable boy gag and lean back.

'Why did you have to take her into the bushes to show it to her? Wouldn't it have been easier to see it in the house with the lights?' The stable boy stared into the swaying nobleman's drooping eyes.

'Don't be impertinent!' Vogel sputtered. 'Anyway, when we finished, I noticed my pouch had gone. I must have dropped it in the bushes back there. Now, if you'd be a dear and find it for me, I'll give you another of those shiny silver coins for your trouble. What say you, eh?'

The boy stared at Vogel for a moment before dashing off.

The spy knew that if there really *was* a money pouch, he would never see it again, unless the boy was a proper moron. Or pious.

Vogel dropped the pissed nobleman act and quickly located the carriage Gunther had arrived in. He reached inside, took out a blanket from under the seat and laid it on the floor so as not to dirty his fine cape and clothes. He lay on it and reached under the carriage to a secret compartment where he and Gunther kept their gear. He groped around before producing a length of rope, padded grapnel, small shuttered lantern and a set of climbing claws. He closed the compartment, crawled back out from under the carriage and replaced the blanket before he pulled up his shirt, coiled the rope about his body and concealed the grapnel and lantern under his cloak. He muttered a silent prayer of thanks that Gunther had attended the party as he crossed to the stall where the servants had tied his horse. His saddle was on a bench beside it and he quickly located a secret compartment on it where he stashed his beloved lockpicks, which he stuffed under his shirt. With a last quick look around, he left the stables.

Many of the guests had drifted outside to take a break from the noise and have a breath of fresh air. Luckily for Vogel, who had stumbled out of the stables and wobbled his way to the rear of the mansion, there were no guests loitering there. Instead, he found a couple of beefcakes who the von Gruenbaums had squeezed into servant attire and who were standing around a brazier, passing a wineskin back and forth.

Vogel looked towards the heavens and gave silent thanks to the Lord that they didn't have any dogs with them. He took a moment to calm himself as he focused.

Vogel breathed deeply, focusing on his fear but instead of trying to bring it under control, he surrendered to it, vividly picturing what the guards would do to him if they caught him – the pain, the shame, the embarrassment.

The anxiety was having the desired effect. As he moved towards the guards, still keeping in shadow, he could feel the hot flush suffuse his body and knew his ability had triggered.

His jogged out of the darkness, his arm blurring twice. He was rewarded with the sounds of two meaty thwacks and grunts as the hilts of his heavy throwing knives struck the guards in the head, knocking them out cold. Without pausing, he stooped to snatch up his knives before making his way to the house where he pressed his back to the base of the mansion's rear wall. He looked up and saw a number of open windows on the upper floors.

Vogel decided to forgo the rope and strapped on his climbing claws – his favoured method of scaling. He lit his small lantern, shuttered it and, with a last look around, started effortlessly up the wall of the house, lizard fashion, towards an open window on the top floor.

The room he entered was neat and clean with a small rug on the floor and a single bed with sheets and blankets neatly folded on top. The wardrobe and chest of drawers were empty, and a quick search of the walls and floors yielded no secret compartments.

Just a guest room, he said to himself as he glided to the door and pressed his ear against it. He could clearly hear the music from the ballroom below but nothing else.

He opened the door and cringed when it creaked, a noise that sounded as loud as a cannon's discharge. He dismissed his fears with a shake of his head – the party would drown out the sound. Besides, if any servants or the good lord and lady had found grease on the hinges of the door, they might suspect that an intruder had been in the room, and that was the last thing Vogel wanted. He had been taught to leave no trace of his presence when sneaking. Grease would have been fine if he was burgling the place or wanted it to look like a burglar had been present, but tonight he needed to remain invisible.

He drifted out onto the landing and peeped over the balcony at the party and oblivious guests below before moving on with his reconnoitre.

The hallway, dimly lit by a couple of lanterns on the walls, had three other doors. An investigation of the next room, also a guest room, showed that that it too was unoccupied.

The next door along was locked and, when he pressed his ear to it, he could hear nothing.

Vogel fished out his lockpicks and set to work on it and after a few moments of delicate fiddling with the slender metal rods in the lock, was rewarded by the click of tumblers falling.

Grinning with excitement, he packed away his picks and slipped into the room.

Judging by the number of bags and feminine clothes and the absence of any male attire or accessories, the occupant was a woman staying on her own.

It didn't take long for Vogel to locate her poorly concealed valuables which she had secreted under a loose floorboard.

Silly cow. Vogel stuffed them, along with a fairly weighty pouch of coins, into his shirt. Finding nothing else of value, or interest, in the room, he moved onto the last door on the landing which was also locked but proved no match for Vogel's lock-picking skills.

He opened it in a heartbeat and nipped inside.

It could only be Silke and Olaf's room.

The huge chamber had an en-suite closet as expensive and fine as the furniture in the bedroom – large wooden drawers, all lacquered and ornately carved, as were the matching wardrobe and tables. There were a pair of expensive crystal chandeliers hanging from the ceiling and the monstrous four-poster bed, dominating the centre of the room, had silk and satin sheets.

Vogel didn't have to worry about stealth as he crossed the room. The floors were carpeted in thick luxurious rugs from far-off Persia, providing padding enough to muffle the sound of a hunting party riding through.

The spy stood for some moments, staring in wonder at the room before surrendering to his desire. He kicked off his boots and stripped naked before he dropped to the floor, writhing and rolling around in the thick carpet just to feel the texture of the rugs softly kissing his face and body. Since it was likely to be the only opportunity he would ever get, he decided to frolic on the bed as well and was soon giggling like a child as he tossed and turned amid the swirl of the fine sheets. He lost himself in the sheer pleasure of savouring another person's wealth before rolling off the bed, straightening his hair and dressing.

Right, back to business.

After rearranging the rug and making the bed, he searched the room from top to bottom and aside from some fine clothes, parchment and writing materials, could locate nothing of interest.

Bollocks. Nobles always jealously guarded their wealth. *Now, where would the von Gruenbaums store their loot?* Vogel rubbed his chin as his gaze slowly panned around the room.

It would be somewhere heavily guarded, and Vogel hadn't found anywhere like that in the house. Then it would be well hidden. Likely, it would be somewhere the lord and lady were expected to go alone. A place where the servants could enter occasionally but were otherwise not granted access to.

One place sprang to Vogel's mind.

***

Stefan was unsure for how long he had walked. After his encounter with the von Gruenbaum maid, Marie, he decided that he had had enough for one evening and walked out of the party, lost in his own thoughts about Father Pohl's and Father Dieter's deaths and his inadequacy to blend in at the ball. When he eventually looked up, he found that he had managed to wander across the *Rittersbrücken Nord*, the north Knightsbridge, and found himself standing in the middle of the Church Quarter. He relaxed considerably, at home once more in the world of the ecclesiastic.

He walked along the *Kirchenstrasse*, the main street of the Church district, and passed groups of men and women clad in white robes with a symbol of a silver cross within a circle on their right breasts. These were members of the Scholars Order who practiced magic at the College of Sorcerous Studies at Rittershafen University under the watchful eye of the Church. They had either finished, or were close to completing, their evening chore of using their sorcery to light streetlamps. All the main streets of Rittershafen's districts were lit as well as the residential streets of the Church, Nobles and Artisans Quarters. This was a duty and ritual provided by the novices of the Scholars and, aside from providing an essential service for the city, it also stood as a potent reminder to all that the Church wielded sorcery along with their divine might.

Only the *Viertel* was left in darkness, not because the scholars refused to light the lamps there but because whenever they did, the ne'er do wells would break the lamps and try to steal the light. After a while the authorities admitted defeat and left the poorest quarter of the city to wallow in the darkness they so craved.

Stefan walked on until the calm and serenity of the Church Quarter gave way to the chaos and bustle of the Artisans and Merchants Quarters.

Standing with his hands on his hips, Stefan weighed his options – go back to the party or return to Marienburg? He couldn't face returning to the ball but he had a duty to protect Vogel. Or did he?

The spy was clearly in his own element and didn't need protection, and what if Stefan seriously blundered and compromised him? Wouldn't that be worse? He decided that Vogel was better off without him at the party. His best option would be to find an inn, spend time there and possibly track Vogel down later, although how in God's name he was going to do that remained a mystery. With a nod, he turned and made his way towards the Honey Bee, an inn he knew was one of Vogel's regular haunts. Maybe somebody there might know where to find him?

'No, mate,' the innkeeper replied, hawking and spitting a mouthful of phlegm into a mug which he wiped clean with a grimy rag. 'I 'aven't seen Vogel all day. I can give 'im a message if you want?'

'No, it's fine,' Stefan said.

'As you will, friend.' The innkeeper shrugged. He held up the stein he had cleaned. 'Could I interest you in a pint? Finest ale in the Artisans Quarter.'

'I'll have wine, thanks, innkeeper,' Stefan said.

The innkeeper reached for a cup, but Stefan held up a hand. 'Make that a flagon.' He shot the cup a horrified glance.

'Right you are, mate!' The innkeeper smiled. 'Take a seat and I'll bring it to you.'

Stefan muttered his thanks and slid into a quiet corner. He slung his sword over his chair and leaned back in it, sighing as the evening's stress drained out of his body. He let his gaze pan over the patrons, a mix of local craftsmen and shopkeepers of the district along with some artists, playwrights and actor types.

'Evening, mate.'

The boy had made no attempt to hide his approach but had walked boldly up to the templar and presented himself, smiling broadly at the brooding Stefan.

Stefan raised an eyebrow.

'I'm not in the mood, boy. Best you be off,' Stefan growled.

The boy leaned forward and spoke softly. 'Well, mate, I thought that maybe *I* could help you.'

'Really? And how could you do that?'

'You looking for someone?'

'Yes. He drinks in here a lot. Average height, dodgy and dishonest type. A ne'er do well called Vogel.'

'What do you want 'im for?'

'To talk. I'm not going to hurt him.'

'I know 'im.' The boy had a feral grin. 'I know where you can find 'im too.'

'And you'll tell me, just like that?'

The boy smiled and shook his head. 'I'm a businessman, mate. I'm afraid I'll have to charge you a small finder's fee and I won't be telling you where he is – I'll be showing you.'

'I see.' Stefan grinned at the boy's nerve and felt his mood lighten. 'How much? And, mind you, I'm only a humble sellsword, not a rich man.'

'Yeah, right,' the lad replied. 'Anyway, who said anything about coin? Favours can be as good as coin – sometimes even better.'

'Oh ho, it's like that, is it? You should know I won't agree to anything which breaks the law.'

The boy raised an eyebrow. 'A moral and honest mercenary – that's a first.'

Stefan shrugged.

'Fair enough. Understood, and I wouldn't ask you to do anything untoward.'

'Very well. What's the favour?'

The boy shrugged. 'Dunno yet. You can owe it to me and I'll collect on it when you're available. How's that?'

'Agreed.' Stefan stuck out his hand.

The boy grasped it and they shook.

'Well now, since we're business associates, it would be rude if we didn't formally introduce ourselves. I'm Stefan.'

'Kristian,' the boy replied.

'Now that,' the templar said with an approving look and smile, 'is a good name.'

***

The von Gruenbaum family chapel was a small building nestled in a quiet corner of the grounds, surrounded by a small copse of trees. To the untrained eye it was designed to look like a place of serene contemplation and worship.

Vogel knew that the greenery wasn't designed for ascetic purposes but for subterfuge. The chapel was designed to be concealed. He was about to move towards it when he froze.

The doors were open with the padlock that normally sealed them lying on the ground.

He drew a throwing knife and moved closer, reaching the walls of the little church without incident. He looked around and up in case the competition was hiding behind any greenery or on the roof of the building, but couldn't see anything. All seemed clear, but Vogel knew there could always be somebody hiding in the shadows. So he closed his eyes and concentrated.

He calmed his breathing and flicked on his hearing, sending it through the doors and into the chapel.

And then he heard it – the faint crunch of footsteps swiftly approaching, far too quiet for ordinary ears, but not Vogel's.

With no time to hide in the bushes or behind a tree, Vogel pressed his back into a corner of the chapel, melting into the shadows.

A short, slim figure emerged from the building. It quickly replaced the padlock on the doors and, after a cursory look around, silently disappeared into the darkness of the surrounding foliage. If it saw anyone, it gave no indication.

Vogel ghosted after it.

As he trailed his quarry, Vogel noted the figure's diminutive stature. *A child?* Regardless, he was certain of one thing – this was no ordinary thief. His stealth, if it was a he, was far too good. Only someone with formal training could move with such speed and skill, not to mention bypassing the padlock on the chapel with ease.

Vogel was sure that this was no cat-burglar looking for riches. *Another agent maybe, but whose?*

The figure reached the east wall of the grounds and, without breaking stride, sprang up and over it.

Slick fucker, he grudgingly acknowledged as he too nimbly bounded over the wall after the little phantom.

***

'I thought you said you were going to take me to him, Kristian.'

'I have, Stefan. This is where he lives.'

They were standing in front of an arch and stairs which led up to a landing and series of rooms behind the Drowning Duck where Kristian insisted Vogel lived.

'Those are his rooms, I swear.'

Stefan sighed. He had considered waiting for Vogel but the rogue was likely up to his eyeballs in vice. The templar was about to give up and return to the Honey Bee in the morning when Kristian started climbing up the wall.

'What are you doing?' Stefan hissed.

'Having a gander. There's nothing like being on the roof of a tall building to see what's around, is there?'

'Apparently not.'

He watched the boy clamber nimbly up the wall, using window ledges and crumbling masonry for hand and foot holds. Within moments he had reached the roof and straightened up. He looked one way and then the other before craning forward, as if something had caught his interest. He took a moment to watch the drama in the distance before quickly shinnying down.

'What?'

'Two figures, over there,' the boy pointed off into the darkness. 'Both dressed for stealth, both moving fast, one following the other.'

Stefan didn't pause for thought. 'Let's go and have a look, shall we?'

He gave Kristian a big grin and together they dashed off in pursuit of the fleeing shadows.

***

98

By God! Vogel thought, the fucker was sublime, no doubt about it. Nearly all thieves thought they were excellent at stealth, but the reality was that very few were good and even fewer gifted. But this one was exceptional – falling snow made more sound than the little man.

Vogel looked up and gave the Almighty another nod of thanks. If he hadn't had his special hearing, he would never have been able to track the figure.

Another set of rapidly approaching footsteps tickled Vogel's awareness, but he was too focused on using his hearing to track his little shadow. It wasn't until the footsteps were close enough to suggest someone approaching him that he gave them some attention – and by then it was too late.

Something crashed into his side and the world became a spinning blur as he rolled on the cobbled streets, locked in an embrace with an unknown assailant.

Where's my beefcake when I really need him! Vogel cursed.

He tried to right himself, to lash out with fist and foot, or a knife, but all he could manage was a string of loud curses. The curses turned to yells of pain as the figure easily managed to get on top of him and lock his arm before hoisting him to his feet.

'Who are you?' a deep voice asked in his ear.

'Stefan?'

'Vogel?'

The lock on the spy's arm disappeared and he stood and flexed his limb, massaging the circulation back.

'For fuck's sake, Stefan, I was chasing someone!'

'How was I supposed to know it was you?' Stefan roared back. 'All I saw was a dodgy cloaked figure chasing a smaller cloaked figure. I thought it was a child.'

'Fuck!'

Stefan was about to say something when he suddenly turned and drew his sword in a fluid motion.

Aufmerksamkeit.

Vogel had heard about it but until that moment had never seen it in action.

The word meant lingering mind or awareness – a skill developed by the Sword Brethren through rigorous contemplation and shared with their Teutonic Knights brethren.

Stefan's *Aufmerksamkeit* screamed at him, and he obeyed. He didn't need to see or hear the attack to know that it was coming; his awareness took care of that. It pulled him aside, forced him to dive and roll, just as a knife rang off the cobbles and skittered into the darkness.

Vogel cursed softly as he eased back into the shadows.

Stefan assumed *Vom Tag*, a high guard, as his attackers materialised from the darkness of an alley.

Fanned out in front of him were three men, their clothing dirty and rank. Their faces, equally unclean, were screwed into masks of hatred. He sensed three more to his rear.

The three before him carried longswords - their feet widely spaced indicated a modicum of training, but their stances were horribly unbalanced.

They edged forward.

Vogel pressed himself against the wall on Stefan's left flank.

The templar grinned fiercely. Sod parties – this was more like it!

The bandits felt the first slivers of fear. The men they outnumbered three to one showed no signs of fear. Far from it. They reacted to the threat with cool, competent speed, and as for the mercenary in front of them, he seemed positively ecstatic.

The tension was broken by the bandit at the centre.

'Your sword and purse, big lad, throw them to the ground and we'll let you walk aw–'

He never finished.

Stefan's blade was a blur as he swung. The bandit at the centre struggled to block, but a life dedicated to the way of the brandy bottle had dulled his reflexes and Stefan's technique tore open his throat. He collapsed, thrashing and gurgling, clutching at his throat and the crimson tide gushing from it.

The attack was so quick it stunned the bandits on either side of their former leader, and they froze for a split second.

It was all the time Stefan needed.

His sword flashed again, severing the neck of the bandit on his right flank and, before the body could drop, Stefan spun. He pirouetted clockwise and let the momentum of his turn, and longsword, behead the bandit on his left flank.

Their corpses sagged to the floor, blood spraying from their headless bodies.

The cries behind him caused Stefan to whirl around and face the threat to his rear.

Vogel had not been idle and, as soon as Stefan had moved, so had the spy. He unleashed a pair of throwing knives at the attackers to their rear. They dropped with his blades growing from their eyeballs.

Stefan turned to the remaining thug, who screamed, venting his terror as he launched an all-out attack on the templar.

Stefan assumed the *Ochs* guard as he danced aside from his opponent's overhead cut, letting it pass harmlessly by his side, before delivering his own overhead slash in return. The timing and technique were impeccable and the man screamed as his hand went spinning away. He gawped at his wrist stump which continued pumping blood like a burst pipe before Stefan's longsword thrust through his heart. Blood burst from his mouth as he sagged to the cobbles.

Stefan wiped the blood from his sword and sheathed it before he turned to Vogel.

The spy raised an eyebrow. He was no stranger to swordplay and had once witnessed a duel between two knights, who, by all accounts, were quite skilled. But the fight rapidly degenerated into a messy affair with both men clumsily hewing at each other until they collapsed, grunting and panting like bellows. In the end, one knight won by stabbing the other in the groin with a dagger and then hysterically plunged his blade into his already dying opponent's neck, groin and anywhere that was not armoured until the loser expired in a lake of blood.

Stefan's fight, on the other hand, looked like a dance with the big man gracefully pirouetting away from his opponents' swings as he casually sliced off limbs and heads, or ducked and weaved before he sheared off other bits.

'That was seriously impressive,' Vogel said with a nod.

Stefan shrugged. 'They had no training or experience to speak of. I didn't think they were going to be a problem.'

Vogel pulled a thoughtful face. Anybody waving any kind of weapon at him was considered dangerous. But then, he wasn't a templar gifted with divine magic.

'Speaking of impressive,' Stefan said as he nodded at the thugs Vogel had taken down with his throwing knives. 'I've only ever seen that kind of accuracy from the Trinitarians – and they use magic.'

Vogel shrugged. 'Yeah, well, my magic's constant practice,' he said, patting his sheathed blades. 'What now?'

Stefan searched the corpses and held up their purses. 'Now we go back to the Church Quarter with a short detour to deposit this coin in a small chapel.'

'It's a considerable sum.' Vogel eyed the plunder. 'I think these men were placed here to delay me.'

'From the man you were chasing?' Stefan asked.

'How did you know I was following someone?'

'I had help,' Stefan replied.

'Oh?'

Both men turned at the sound of running footsteps approaching. A panting Kristian rounded a corner and stopped. He leaned against a wall, clutching at his scrawny belly, heaving hard at the effort of having tried to keep up with Stefan. 'What did I miss?' He grinned.

'From him.' Stefan jerked a thumb at the boy.

'I see,' Vogel replied.

Stefan turned and motioned to the bodies of the men he had just cut down. 'But how did they know to ambush you here?'

Vogel shrugged. 'The figure I was chasing must have been following a pre-planned route with prepared delays.'

Stefan didn't reply. Instead, he continued to stare at the bloody bodies, frowning and shaking his head. *What a waste.*

Chapter 5

'What's the problem, driver?'

'Beg your pardon, Father, but there's a mercenary blocking the path.'

Father Jozef Richter climbed out of his carriage and pushed through his guards to the fore.

'What is the meaning of this? Brother Stefan, is that you?'

'God be with you, Father,' Stefan greeted the priest.

'Evening, Father,' Vogel added.

'I noticed Church soldiers accompanying a carriage with the holy seal and wondered if we could be of any assistance,' Stefan said.

The templar and spy had quickly left the scene of the ambush and had just walked out of a small chapel on *Spittalstrasse*, where they had stopped to donate their attackers' coin when they saw a carriage with the emblem of the Witch Hunters Order accompanied by a group of Church soldiers.

Father Richter smiled broadly. Not just a Teutonic Knight and agent to help out tonight but *his* agent and Teutonic Knight.

'Absolutely, Brother Stefan, Vogel,' Father Richter said. 'I'm on my way to arrest a woman for the illegal practice of sorcery.'

'Is she connected to the deaths of our fathers and brethren?' Stefan asked.

'Possibly. We'll know more once we have her in custody and question her.'

'A fortuitous meeting then.'

'As you say, Stefan. How is it that you are out in the streets at this time of night? Has the party finished? Did you discover something there?'

'Er…' Stefan began.

'We were following up a rumour we overheard at the party, Father,' Vogel interjected. 'It led us here.'

'And what was this rumour?'

'It turned out to be nothing.' Vogel shrugged. 'Just drunken lies.'

'And who is the urchin?' The priest looked at Kristian.

'We lost our bearings in the warrens of these streets. The boy was acting as our guide,' Vogel explained. 'We don't need him now, so I'll send him on his way.'

The spy went to Kristian and pressed a coin into the boy's hand. 'Where did you take Stefan?'

'Behind the Drowning Duck.' Kristian grinned.

'Good lad!' Vogel gave him another coin along with a wink and a nudge.

'Thanks! Later, Vogel.'

'Later, Kris. Go carefully now.'

The boy disappeared into the shadows.

Vogel turned back to the priest and templar, who had watched the exchange between Vogel and urchin and were wearing curious expressions.

'Well then, if there are no more delays, gentlemen, shall we proceed?' Father Richter gestured to his carriage.

They climbed into the priest's carriage after him.

'Driver,' Father Richter barked, 'make haste, the night is dwindling.'

Beneath his hood, Vogel frowned. The night hadn't gone well. They had discovered nothing of value at the von Gruenbaum's except the small shady figure Vogel had chased and they'd let him slip through their fingers.

The spy looked at Father Richter and then Stefan and back to the witch hunter. They were both adrift in their own thoughts, but there was something about the chance meeting with Father Richter that made Vogel uneasy.

He dismissed the thought and eased back into his seat as the carriage shook and rattled its way along the Central Isle and the *Rittersbrücke Nord*.

We're going north? 'Father Richter, is your suspect in the Nobles Quarter?'

'She is, Vogel.'

She? This was no mere coincidence – there had to be a connection between the von Gruenbaum party and Father Richter's presence.

Beneath his cloak, Vogel rested his hand on the hilt of a throwing knife and fingered it for reassurance. Whatever was coming tonight, he was going to be ready for it.

Chapter 6

The procession pulled up to the gates of the von Gruenbaum mansion an hour after Lauds and, judging by the sound of the music, which easily carried that far, the party was still in full swing.

The guards at the main gate who were gathered around their brazier rose, hands on the hilts of their swords, as the Church contingent rumbled into view.

Vogel poked his head out of the carriage window for a good look before shaking it as he hopped out.

Stefan climbed out of the carriage after Father Richter and stood for a moment, facing the mansion with his hands on his hips and a frown.

'Yes,' Father Richter said, placing a hand on Stefan's shoulder. 'Do not be enchanted by the beauty of the place, or your hosts, my son. It's all an illusion designed to mask the evil beneath. You there – guards!'

Vogel stared at the priest thoughtfully. He must have had an agent at the party, and it could only have been the diminutive man he had chased.

The guards at the gate exchanged concerned looks before one of them stepped forward.

'Evening, Father,' he said evenly.

Vogel had to nod in grudging respect at the guard's cool. Though he was faced with a witch hunter and a score of footmen in thick chain armour, he didn't allow himself to be intimidated.

'I am Father Jozef Richter, a priest in the Order of the Witch Hunters. I demand you open the gates and grant me entrance in the name of the Church and the Teutonic Order.'

'As you command, Father,' he said with a curt nod before he unlocked the gates and pushed them wide open to allow the carriage entrance.

Though he hid it well, Vogel could see the tension in the guard's face.

The procession clopped on, jingling and rattling as it passed through the portals but to the spy's surprise, stopped just inside the gates. At Father Richter's insistence, the gate guards were stripped of their arms and a few Church soldiers left to supervise them. The priest then left the carriage at the gates and motioned for the rest of his guards, along with Stefan and Vogel, to follow him and set off unerringly in the direction of the chapel.

Yep, Vogel said to himself as he trailed after the priest, the little man was definitely one of Richter's people.

Vogel flicked a glance at Stefan, who was following after Father Richter like a bloodhound on the scent.

***

To the untrained eye, the chapel's interior would have betrayed nothing, but to a person trained to observe, the signs were present. Yes, the floor showed scuffing, but not much, and the benches and pews showed no signs of wear whatsoever.

And then there were the bibles.

Vogel flicked through them, holding them close to his nose to breathe in the scent of ink on paper. They were in pristine condition. Not a blemish or crease on any of the pages. They had never been touched, never been opened and read.

The evidence clearly pointed to an unquestionable fact – no one worshipped in this chapel.

If Father Richter knew this, he gave no indication of it. Instead, on entering the chapel, he strode straight to the vestry.

On entering the room, one of the witch hunter's soldiers pulled aside a rug to reveal a stone floor.

Vogel started as Father Richter's hands became wreathed in golden flames as he weaved them and sang for blessings of Sight before they died, leaving the priest's eyes shining with golden light. He took a moment to scan the floor before smiling and sang again, this time calling for blessings of Smite. A blast of divine fire shot from his outstretched hand and slammed into the floor.

Vogel heard a small shriek followed by a flare of blue light as black smoke drifted up and disappeared to reveal a trap door sealed with a sturdy padlock.

'She had a guardian demon bound into the floor,' Father Richter said to the group.

At a nod from the priest, Stefan smashed the lock and cast it aside before he grasped the ring of the trapdoor and heaved it open to reveal a set of stairs descending into the dark.

Seeing Vogel reach for his lantern, the group started lighting torches and lanterns collected from the cupboards and drawers in the room. Once light had been found, Father Richter and Stefan led the way down the stairs with the witch hunter's soldiers and Vogel behind them.

The stairs wound down for about thirty feet into a short passage at the end of which was a thick wooden door reinforced with riveted bands of steel. An iron doorknob, in the shape of a demon head, leered at the group.

'There's no lock?' Vogel said to Father Richter and Stefan as he pushed his way to the front and tried to open the locked door. 'How do you enter?' He leaned closer to the door before leaping back.

The rivets had morphed into little demonic faces, along with the doorknob, which had leered at him.

'What?' Stefan said.

Vogel shook his head. 'Nothing.'

Father Richter pulled Vogel behind him, his eyes still glowing with magic sight. 'This is no ordinary door. It's another guardian and opens only at the bidding of its mistress.'

The priest held his hand out again, palm turned towards the door, and sang for another blessing of Smite. His hand became wreathed in a storm of golden flames before a bolt of golden brilliance shot from it. When it struck the door, it bathed the entire passage in light which forced the spy to shield his eyes from the glare. The door itself flared for a moment before turning to ash.

Vogel heard it wail before it was destroyed.

111

'Fuck me!' the spy blurted. 'Sorry.' He looked sheepishly at the group, who glared at him disapprovingly, except Father Richter, who leaned against one of the walls of the passage panting hard.

Stefan stepped forward and Vogel heard the templar softly ask the priest if he needed assistance.

Father Richter shook his head and patted the templar's shoulder in gratitude. When he looked up at the group, his face was bathed in sweat and Vogel thought he was going to collapse. He didn't. Instead, he signalled for Vogel and Stefan to lead on, which Vogel did but not before looking back and catching the frown of confusion plastered on the templar's face.

'What?'

Stefan shook his head dismissively.

Vogel shrugged and turned back to the passage where he could see a room just beyond where the door had stood.

Burning with curiosity, and before anyone could stop him, Vogel quickly shuffled forward into the room.

And was instantly rooted to the spot.

The floors, walls and columns in the room were carved from what looked like a seamless piece of marble with blue veins running through it. Yet when Vogel brushed his fingers along one of the columns, the stone felt warm and soft to the touch, like cork. In one corner of the room stood a small, very ornate and richly wrought cupboard made of lacquered wood and chased in elaborate silverwork.

Standing in the room and gazing around at the splendour of its construction left no doubt in the spy's mind what this alien chamber was.

The floor was covered in several large and small circles decorated with the flowing script of sorcery all etched in silver.

A single arched window was the only other portal in the room and, as Vogel approached it, he found himself gazing out over a lush forest that stretched away on all sides, as far as the eye could see. Snaking its way through the verdant greenery was a broad river with scattered lights winking on the surface where the sunlight reflected off it.

Gazing up, the spy found himself squinting at a sun blazing in an azure sky as clear as any the spy had ever seen.

Vogel inhaled deeply and felt as though he were breathing in a warm and fragrant summer's morning which lifted his spirits and left him feeling invigorated.

Vogel smiled. *So* this *is a ritual chamber.* A room used by sorcerers to practice and hone their arts and to tear beasts and beings from their native pits and planes and summon them to this world. All the whispers had suggested that ritual chambers were dark places, tainted by the foul practices of their sorcerers. But not this one. Where this ritual chamber was concerned, Vogel felt that he could have stayed in the room forever.

***

By three in the morning, the majority of the older nobles had long since left. One or two had arranged to stay over and so had retired to comfortable beds while the remaining few lay scattered across the ballroom and ground floor rooms, snoring loudly in alcohol-induced sleep.

Silke and Olaf took a stroll in the cool early morning air, watching a younger noble totter drunkenly around the gardens before finally collapsing.

'A fitting end to a fine evening,' Olaf said to his wife as he kissed her cheek.

She beamed and flushed and slipped her arm through his before suddenly frowning.

'What's wrong?' Olaf said.

'The connection to my Guardian is gone,' Silke replied. 'Someone has breached my sanctuary!'

'The study!' Olaf hissed.

Silke turned and walked quickly back into the mansion and had just entered the foyer when a series of screams exploded through the house at the sudden arrival of soldiers in armour with tabards bearing the Church's emblem.

The clergy's gate-crashing had a profound impact on the gathering, instantly silencing all conversation and merriment. People recoiled in fear - some gasped in shock.

'What is the meaning of this rude intrusion?' Olaf demanded angrily, stepping forward.

A priest stepped forward to meet him. 'Lord Olaf, Lady Silke, I am Father Jozef Richter of the Witch Hunters Order. Pardon the intrusion, but this was a matter that could not wait. Madam,' Father

Richter turned to Silke, 'I have evidence that you are a practitioner of sorcery. Is this true?'

There was another round of gasps from the guests at this revelation.

'It is,' Silke declared, raising her chin.

'And are you a member of the Order of the Magi?'

She paused before replying. 'I am not.'

Yet more gasps and whispers.

'The meaning, Lord Gruenbaum,' Father Richter said, 'is that your wife has been illegally practising sorcery and we have discovered her ritual chamber beneath your chapel.'

'What!' Olaf exploded.

'Lady Silke,' Father Richter continued, 'I charge you with the illegal practice of sorcery and arrest you for said crime and hereby exercise my authority as a witch hunter to take you into custody for questioning.'

More people gasped. A few screamed. One or two fainted.

'Take her!' Father Richter ordered his men.

As the Church soldiers moved forward, Olaf and a few young noblemen stepped between them and Silke, the light of confrontation in their eyes. Steel rasped on leather as both sides drew blades.

'Enough!' Silke cried. 'I will have no blood spilled here. Father Richter,' she said to the witch hunter, 'I will go with you – peacefully.' She turned to the young noblemen standing before her and addressed them too. 'Peacefully.'

They slowly lowered their blades and she stepped from behind them as Father Richter's soldiers took charge of her. She shot a desperate last look at her husband before being led outside.

The silence after Silke's departure lasted for a few heartbeats before the torrent of the guests' excited babbling washed noisily out.

***

Stefan and Vogel accompanied Father Richter, Silke and the Church soldiers to the main gates and the witch hunter's carriage.

Olaf and a few young nobles, friends of the couple and still bristling with anger over Silke's arrest, followed. When they reached the gates, Olaf bid Silke farewell, planting a tender kiss on her forehead and whispered a vow to set her free. She smiled and climbed into the carriage.

Father Richter turned to Stefan and Vogel and beckoned them aside.

'Well, my boys, here's a test for you and a chance to learn something,' the priest said with a pointed look at Stefan. 'Stefan, Vogel, I want you to question Lord Olaf, see what you can find out about Lady Silke's practice of sorcery.'

'You want us to find out if he knew that his wife was a sorceress?'

Father Richter smiled. 'I've no doubt that he knew his wife was a sorceress, Stefan, but see if you can get him to admit it, and see what else he knows. Ask him where his wife keeps her sorcery but do not approach or touch it.'

'But you found her sorcery in the ritual chamber, Father,' Vogel said.

Before arresting Silke, Father Richter had ordered Stefan and Vogel to tear apart Silke's ritual chamber for any sorcerous items and books. The soldiers with the witch hunter could only watch from outside the room as powerful sorcery prevented them from entering, but not Vogel and Stefan.

Father Richter guessed it was because the priest and Stefan were magic users and Vogel's seal of office, which was a minor enchantment, allowed him entrance. So it fell to the three of them to conduct a search of the room, starting with the small wardrobe in the corner which contained books but nothing of interest to the witch hunter.

'Only some of it, my boy, and they were just minor magical trinkets. Her spell books and journals were not there and neither were her most powerful items.'

'If we should find it, we'll bring it to you,' Vogel said.

Father Richter shook his head. 'No. It might have wards and protections. Set a guard over it and inform me. And whatever you do, Stefan, do not threaten Lord Olaf and under no circumstances harm him. Be tactful.'

Stefan gave Father Richter a woeful look.

'Don't worry.' The priest gave the templar a slap on the arm. 'Vogel's on hand to help you; isn't that right?'

'Absolutely. When I first started questioning scumbags, Gunther was always on hand to ensure I asked the right questions, made the right bribes or threats, to teach me to read people and to make sure I didn't cock up.'

'See – you're in good hands.' Father Richter smiled.

Stefan glanced at the spy unhappily before turning back to the priest and nodding.

'And you, Vogel, have you learned anything today?'

'Lots, Father. I've seen blessings performed and I've been in a ritual chamber.'

'And what did you learn from the latter?' The priest smiled slyly at the spy.

'It felt unnatural,' Vogel said. 'It was made of a seamless stone-like substance and magic transported us across a great distance to get there. I've learned that there are spells that can do that.'

'Good lad.' Richter smiled approvingly.

Stefan cleared his throat loudly. 'Father, if Lord Olaf admits his complicity in his wife's crime, shall I arrest him?'

Father Richter shook his head. 'No, I don't think there's a need for that, unless he's actually a sorcerer himself. What loving husband wouldn't keep his wife's secrets, even if she was a sorceress? We'll post some soldiers behind to keep an eye on Olaf.'

Stefan and Vogel exchanged looks. It seemed reasonable.

'When you've finished here, report your findings to me at the Witch Hunters convent,' Father Richter said. 'Any questions, boys?'

The templar and spy shook their heads.

'God be with you,' they chorused.

'You too, my lads.' The witch hunter blessed them, along with the Church soldiers left on guard, before climbing into his carriage which rumbled quickly out of the gates.

Stefan turned to Olaf. 'Lord Olaf, may we please talk inside?'

'And him?' Olaf looked at Vogel.

'He's with me.'

Olaf flicked glances to the assembled nobles with him before reluctantly agreeing and leading the way back into the mansion with Stefan and Vogel in tow.

**

The guests left, still quietly babbling in excited tones. Getting rid of them, politely, proved to be a painfully slow process as some wanted to stay and comfort Olaf while more than a few of the younger ones wanted to have a meeting to decide the best way to free Silke.

Olaf thanked all parties for their help and concern and, after promises to keep everyone updated on Silke's plight, eventually managed to usher out the last of the guests. He gratefully slammed shut the front doors after them.

Only his best friends – Dirk, Mathias and Carsten, remained behind to comfort him and with the last of the guests finally gone he withdrew with them, and Stefan and Vogel, into one of the ground floor studies.

'Lord Olaf, I am Brother Stefan von Stern of the Teutonic Order.'

119

'We have met, Brother Stefan, though that was not the name you gave me when we did.'

Stefan's face reddened. 'That is true, my lord. Since I am going to ask you to be honest with me, I'll be honest with you. We,' he gestured at Vogel, 'were asked to attend your party incognito and ascertain if there were any threats to the Church and Teutonic Order from the nobility.'

'And who is this?' Carsten asked, pointing to Vogel.

'As I said, he's with me. His name's not important,' Stefan replied.

Vogel raised a hand in greeting.

'I recognise him too,' Olaf said. 'So you both came here to see if there were any threats to the Church and Order's rule in Rittershafen,' Olaf turned back to Stefan, 'and instead the Church and Teutonic Order now threaten my wife.'

Stefan ignored the barb. 'Did you know she was a sorceress, Lord Olaf?'

'Of course I did. And before you ask it, I would never turn my wife over to the Church for being one.'

We'd never have guessed, Vogel thought.

'So it's true, Olaf, Silke's a sorceress,' Dirk said.

'I'm sorry, but I couldn't tell any of you because Silke wanted it kept a secret. You can see why, and I'm sorry that you had to witness this humiliating debacle, all of you. I beg your forgiveness.'

'There's nothing to forgive,' Mathias said gently.

Olaf's friends mumbled their agreement.

'Well, what do we do now?' Carsten addressed only the nobles.

They looked at Olaf and then everybody looked at Stefan.

'Yes, Brother Stefan, what happens now? Am I to be arrested?' Olaf asked.

Stefan shook his head. 'No, my lord. But you may not leave the city and wherever you go, Order or Church soldiers will accompany you.'

Olaf agreed but it was clear from his clenched fists and jaw that he was less than thrilled at the news. 'Very well, but I insist on seeing my wife tonight.'

'I don't see any problem with that,' Stefan replied. He looked at Vogel to see if the spy had any further questions and when Vogel shook his head, Stefan turned back to Olaf. 'I'm going to see Father Richter when I finish here. You may accompany me if you wish.'

'I'll saddle my horse,' Olaf said. He turned to his friends to bid them good night when Stefan cleared his throat yet again.

'Lord Olaf, do you know where your wife's spell books and sorcerous items are?' the templar said. 'I'm not talking about the trinkets we found in the ritual chamber.'

Olaf shook his head. 'I don't. If they're not there, then I don't know where they are.'

Stefan turned to Vogel, who indicated with his head he wanted a quiet word with the templar.

'We'll meet you at the stables,' Stefan said before he and Vogel left the room. As they walked to the stables, Vogel leaned close to him.

'He's lying about his wife's spell books and sorcery.'

'Are you certain?'

'Oh yeah, I'm certain.'

Stefan sighed. 'It's a good thing we're taking him to the witch hunters, then. I can think of no better place to question him.'

Vogel felt a shiver down his spine at the thought of the Dominican's dungeons and the red-hot pokers that awaited Lord Olaf and his unfortunate wife.

Chapter 7

Silke von Gruenbaum half expected to be flung into a dark filthy cell and threatened with all manner of hideous tortures. Instead, Father Richter's carriage pulled up to the Witch Hunters convent, where a group of five nuns were present to greet her. They bowed, before a nun with the palest grey eyes Silke had ever seen stepped forward.

'My lady, I'm Sister Adelheid. If you'll please follow me, I'll escort you to your room.'

'You mean my dungeon, Sister?'

'No, my lady,' Sister Adelheid replied coolly, staring into Silke's eyes. 'I mean your room.'

Sister Adelheid led the way to the first floor and stopped halfway along the gallery outside an arched door. She fumbled with a set of keys for a moment before throwing open the door and gestured to Silke to enter.

Silke's room was neat and sparse, but it was no dungeon.

The wooden floors were carpeted with a simple rug, and the bed, though small, was comfortable with fresh linen and bedding neatly folded atop it. A small table with two chairs stood under the solitary arched window, and a metal basin, discreetly squatting in a corner, had been provided for Silke's toilet.

The room's most noteworthy features were the large circles and divine sigils etched into the ceiling, floors and door which glowed with a faint golden hue.

Silke knew what they were – the Sorcerer's Bane blessing.

No using sorcery to get out of here. She sighed, as the blessing prevented demons from using their abilities, and only the strongest of sorcerers could fight through them to cast spells.

Sister Adelheid crossed to the small table and placed a jug of water, a basin, some cloths and a book upon it before she turned to Silke with a bracelet in her hand. It was made from some strange black metal with silver veins streaked through it.

'I'm sorry, my lady,' she said as she moved to clamp the bracelet around Silke's wrist.

The noblewoman wanted to scream. The bracelet was made from *Sonderbarer Stahl*, a metal which prevented the casting of any sorcery.

Silke kept her composure cool as the nun locked the bracelet around her wrist.

'I don't need to tell you the penalty for trying to remove the bracelet, do I, my lady?' Sister Adelheid said.

Silke shook her head.

Sister Adelheid gave a curt nod. 'If there's anything you need, just call out.'

'Thank you.'

The nun gave her another curt nod before she left, locking the door behind her.

Silke crossed to the table and picked up the book the nun had left her. It was a bible, of course. She swore.

As expected, her next visitor came almost immediately after the nun had left.

The man who entered the room was far calmer than the wide-eyed zealot who had confronted her in her own home.

Father Jozef Richter was a tall slender man with a long chiselled face, tanned skin and eyes the colour of chestnuts. He had short hair and a close-cropped beard and moustache that fitted seamlessly together. When he moved, it was in slow and measured steps with his hands behind his back and his head held high.

Father Richter crossed the room to the table and sat opposite Silke.

'My lady.'

'Father,'

'I'll speak plainly, if I may.'

'Please do, though I suspect there are no secrets between us at this juncture.' Silke seemed surprised at the priest's gentleness.

'Lady Silke, your ritual chamber, I believe it is a room at the top of a tower somewhere, is it not?'

'In the New World,' Silke confirmed.

'And the threshold is a Gate spell, transporting whoever enters the room there. Is that correct, my lady?'

'It is, Father.'

'And you have admitted that you are not a member of the Order of the Magi. I'm sure you're aware, to practice sorcery without belonging to the Order of the Magi, or the Scholars Order, is a very serious transgression; a crime punishable by being burned at the stake.'

125

'Father Richter–'

The priest held up a hand, cutting her short. 'Please, my lady, let me finish. Though the evidence against you for your heresy is overwhelming, I am not here to threaten you with torture and death. I've seen enough blood to last a lifetime and I want no more of that.' He sighed.

Silke raised a surprised eyebrow.

'My lady, I'm going to make you an offer and I urge you to give it serious consideration.'

'I'm listening, Father.'

'I propose that we wipe the slate clean. We forgive and forget about your crimes, but first, you must go before the Church and confess and renounce your sins. If you still wish to practise sorcery, then join the Scholars Order and swear by Almighty God to follow their rules regarding practice of the art. That, or swear to renounce the practice of sorcery forever.'

Silke was stunned. That's all? All she had to do was swear an oath to obey the scholars or swear never to practice sorcery and she'd be set free? It couldn't be that easy.

Still keeping her composure cool, she slowly inclined her head. 'Would I be required to do anything else?'

'You must tell me the names of your teacher and fellow sorcerers, if any, and turn over your spell books and enchanted objects. You must also destroy your summoned entities before a group of witch hunters to act as witnesses to your oath of repentance and rejection of dark sorcery. Finally, subject yourself and your property to regular inspections by the Church. We will start with your spell books and artefacts. I will send my agent to collect these as soon as you agree to my terms.'

'And once I have done as you have asked, Father?' Silke said.

'We will drop all charges. You may go free, my lady,' Father Richter said.

'And what if I choose to leave Rittershafen after I'm freed. Will the Church let me go?'

'Why wouldn't we? Wherever you choose to live, the Church can still keep an eye on you. I needn't tell you what will happen to you if you're caught practising sorcery illegally again? Or you join the Order of the Magi?'

Silke knew the Church would never allow a sorceress of her power to join the Magi, the opposition, and there would be no second chances where the practising of sorcery was concerned.

'My lady, I believe my offer to be fair. Please rest and think on it and I will return later today.'

'I will, Father. Thank you.'

Father Richter dipped his head and rose.

Silke watched him go with an expressionless face. When he closed the door behind him, she hung her head and swore. Of course there'd be a catch - there always was. The Church wanted to exploit her magic for the scholars. She wasn't overly bitter about that and wished she could just hand it over to the priest, but to do so would mean certain death.

Bollocks! She rested her chin on her hand and stared out of her cell's window.

***

127

Father Richter was scratching in his journal when a knock on his door interrupted him. He sighed in annoyance before barking to the visitor to enter.

Two figures shuffled into the room. The first was hugely muscled, standing well over six feet tall, with long blond hair, a tanned cleanly-shaved face, and wearing the Teutonic Order's distinctive robe and white surcoat.

The second figure was smaller, of average height, with a wiry build and dark hair and eyes. He sported a goatee and small moustache and favoured dark clothes, a black cloak and broad-brimmed hat.

Stefan and Vogel bowed to the priest and then stared at the little man lounging in a corner of the priest's study – the man Vogel had followed from the von Gruenbaum mansion.

The spy glanced at Stefan, whose brows were furrowed in anger. Evidently the big templar recognised the little man and hadn't forgotten the ambush he had laid for them.

'Ah, Brother Stefan, *Vogel*, this is my agent, Franz Luber,' Father Richter said by way of introduction.

Franz sat with his arms folded and looked at the duo, his lip twisted into a sneer.

Vogel and Stefan glanced at the little man before exchanging a look. Both were disturbed by Franz's appearance with his adult face and child-like body.

Franz rose. 'Father,' he said, bowing to the priest.

Father Richter smiled in response and the little agent walked out without a backwards glance.

'Anything to report, boys?' Father Richter said when Luber had gone.

'Lord Olaf admitted to knowing his wife was a sorceress. He accompanied us here, insisting on seeing her. I didn't object,' Stefan said.

'That's fine, Stefan. Kindness and compassion are good Christian virtues.'

'And what of Lady Silke? Are we going to question her?'

The witch hunter shook his head. 'There is no need. Her guilt is without question and she knows it. She also knows that, as a noble, we cannot simply try and execute her, but neither can we let her walk free.'

'What do we do, then, Father?' Stefan said.

'I made her an offer. She could join the Scholars Order or swear oaths never to practice sorcery again, but first she must turn over *all* her sorcery to the Church.'

'And has she agreed yet?' Stefan asked.

'I thought I'd give her some time to think it over. Anything else to report of your talk with Lord Olaf?'

'Lord Olaf denied all knowledge of where his wife's sorcery is, but we think he's lying.'

Father Richter leaned back in his chair, steepled his fingers and smiled. 'And why do you think he did that, boys?'

'Maybe there's something in her spell books or journals that's seriously incriminating?' the templar replied. 'Or he's just keeping a promise never to reveal it?'

Father Richter smiled. 'Good.'

'Do you think Lady Silke will accept your offer?' the spy asked.

Father Richter pulled a thoughtful face. 'She'd be a fool to refuse, and she's anything but.'

'Well then,' Vogel said, 'a satisfactory conclusion to the night's events.'

'Quite so,' Father Richter said. '*When* Lady Silke accepts my offer, we can release her and move on. No need for any incarceration or interrogation. Yes, I think we can all agree that this is a satisfactory outcome to the situation.'

The templar and spy nodded.

'And you boys have done well tonight,' Father Richter said.

Stefan and Vogel exchanged a pleased look.

'Now, it's been a long night, boys. Stefan, why don't you rest and attend to your devotions here?'

'Thank you, Father,'

'Herr Schlosser.' Father Richter turned to Vogel. 'I bid you good night. You can both search for Konrad Stich as soon as you're refreshed.'

'Thank you, Father,' Vogel said. 'Good night.'

Father Richter was smiling happily when they left and, once outside, Stefan bid the spy a curt goodnight before stomping off to a cell.

Vogel watched him go and shook his head. It had been an interesting night.

He looked up at Lady Silke's room. Maybe in another life he'd have got to know her better, but from here on in, their paths would divide. She'd go her way, and he his.

Fare you well, my lady, he thought. Shame we'll never meet again.

Chapter 8

'I'm cold and hungry, Brother,' the urchin said, accosting the novice and his companion as they were leaving the pub.

'I've no money to spare, child,' the novice replied.

'I haven't eaten in three days and I'm cold – please help me. Please!'

The child learnt a long time ago that asking for coin never parted people from their money, but ask a person for help and they nearly always obliged. Human behaviour was a strange thing.

Aelfwine sighed. He turned to his partner, who was fishing in her robes for her pouch and placed a hand on her arm, stopping her.

'No, Aesa, let me.'

Aesa smiled at him.

Aelfwine smiled back and hoped his charity would sway his companion to be more responsive to his overtures later on.

The child knew it too and gave them his best pathetic look. It usually worked, with his curly blond locks and large blue eyes.

Aelfwine produced his pouch and took out a coin which he tossed to the boy who snatched it out of the air like a toad's tongue snaring a fly. The coin disappeared into the urchin's rags.

'God bless you,' the boy said sweetly.

'Now be off with you, child,' Aelfwine said.

'He's a little angel, isn't he?' Aesa looked back at the boy and shot him a smile.

'Yes, yes.' Aelfwine took her arm and ushered her away.

The boy watched them go, admiring the gentle sway of Aesa's hips, clearly visible beneath her white Scholar's robe and still picturing her lovely smile, framed as it was by her sandy-coloured hair and tanned face. He sighed and then whistled, which brought forth the rest of his gang.

'Well, Jürgen?' said a member of the gang.

'Yeah, he has a fat pouch, Julian. She does, too.' Jürgen nodded to Aesa.

'You know,' Julian said to the gang, leaning on Jürgen, 'he'll only waste his money on drink trying to seduce her, while she's the type to hoard her cash.'

Jürgen tutted, shaking his head. 'A pair of proper sinners. Him a lustful glutton and her a miser.'

The gang nodded their agreement.

'I think it would only be right if we took their wealth and shared some of it with the good people of the city,' Julian said.

'Charity,' Jürgen agreed.

Julian looked at the gang exchanging grins. With a nod from Julian, the gang set off after Aelfwine and Aesa, completely oblivious to the figure squatting on the rooftop of the Reaper. Concealed in the shadows, it watched the scene with the children and Aelfwine and Aesa play out, and licked its lips hungrily. The gang set off in pursuit of the young novice and his companion whilst the

133

figure on the roof smiled in anticipation as it trailed after them.

***

'Relax, we're safe here,' Aesa said as they strolled through a park in the Church Quarter.

Aelfwine agreed but Aesa could see he was tense. There were no guards in the park at this time of night, but since the murders of Fathers Pohl Heinz and Dieter Schenk and the Church's novices, the Teutonic Order and Church had increased the number of soldiers on patrol both day and night.

'Let's find a bench and sit down,' Aesa suggested.

'We could, or we could slip into a chapel for some privacy, one I happen to have a key for.' He held up a large iron key.

You mean safety – chicken!' Aesa teased.

'I'm not chicken, but if we're caught.' He drew a hand across his throat.

Aesa rolled her eyes and let Aelfwine lead her to the small chapel, deserted at such a late hour. Aelfwine unlocked the door and ushered Aesa inside and, with a quick look around to ensure they weren't seen, slipped inside after her and locked the door.

The children took their time to scout the building for a suitable entry point, knowing that Aelfwine and Aesa would be in no hurry. Eventually, they found a small open window and all five quickly and silently took turns to squeeze through.

134

The children had arrived in a toilet and there followed a few moments of wrinkled noses and whispered complaints of the smell before Julian pulled rank and hushed them into silence before he opened the toilet door and ghosted into the chapel.

There was light coming from a corner near the altar as well as the sound of soft laughter.

The children giggled and smirked.

Julian led the way and the gang padded after him. They crept to within a few yards of the novice and Scholar who were naked and intertwined and far too preoccupied with each other to notice the stealthy urchins. With a nod from Julian, one of the younger boys, Axl, scuttled forwards and dragged the lover's clothes into the darkness. After a brief rifle through them, he triumphantly held up Aelfwine's and Aesa's money pouches. The gang crowded around to get a good look at the coin, chuckling silently, eyes shining with excitement.

Julian grinned at them. It wasn't much coin, but then they didn't thieve for the money – the buzz was priceless.

'So it seems I have an audience!' Aesa said, suddenly appearing before the gang, hands on her naked hips.

The children looked up and stared openmouthed at her.

'Now, you imps,' she hissed, stooping to collect her robe and cover her nakedness, 'I'm going to teach you a lesson you won't soon forget!'

The children scurried back into the shadows but Aesa was quicker. She swung her arms and weaved her hands in strange patterns. A fat silver ring on her middle finger glowed with a fierce blue light. Her chanting lasted a heartbeat before she thrust out her hand and tendrils of blue energy sprang from it to wrap themselves around the children and pin them to the chapel floor. They cried out in fear as they writhed helplessly in their sorcerous bonds.

She drew to within two arms' lengths of the children and muttered again, swinging her arms again and weaving her hands in complex patterns.

Julian, like the rest of the gang, was crying out in fear when a small form barrelled into the sorceress, throwing her backwards, dropping her to the floor with a thump and dispelling her magical hold on the gang.

The children fled, all except Julian. Something caused him to pause. He watched while Jürgen, seemingly unaffected by Aesa's sorcery, pounded on the Scholar with a stone-filled sock, his face twisted into a vicious mask.

Aelfwine could only stare in horror as the angelic urchin he had given a coin to earlier smashed his girlfriend's face into a pulp with a cosh. He wanted to shout, to move, but shock paralysed his body and voice. When he was finally able to act, he was beaten to it by Julian who leapt on Jürgen, trying to pull him off Aesa.

'Stop, Jürgen!' Julian roared. 'You'll kill her!'

Julian cursed himself again for not getting rid of the boy years ago. Jürgen had always had a vicious temper and cruel with it too. The only reason he hadn't was that Jürgen was one of the gang, and you never desert family.

136

Jürgen shrugged him off and continued the attack on Aesa, oblivious to Julian's pleas to stop or efforts to drag him off the girl. Even the chapel's large rose window shattering failed to pierce the fury of bloodlust that had utterly consumed Jürgen. The blow to the side of his head which sent him crashing into a set of pews finally stopped his assault.

Jürgen tried to rise but fell back down as the room spun. He gained his feet, swaying for a moment, before finally folding to the floor and sinking into unconsciousness.

Julian turned from Jürgen to confront Aesa's saviour only to find himself staring at yet another novice, judging by his robes, but even as he looked into the newcomer's eyes, he knew, with a sinking feeling in his stomach, that he too should have fled.

The newcomer walked past Julian as if the child were not there and headed straight for Aelfwine, who held his hand out in a halting gesture.

The novice ignored it. He swatted aside Aelfwine's hand and grasped the novice by the throat with his left hand.

Aelfwine struggled to break the newcomer's grip, but he was held fast. He choked and wriggled for a few moments before the newcomer drew back his other hand and plunged his fingers, now unnaturally long and clawed, into Aelfwine's abdomen. He tore open the novice's belly with a spray of blood, letting Aelfwine's entrails hang down like a string of bloody sausages and, reaching deep inside the cavity, pulled out a ball of glowing energy which he sucked noisily.

Julian fled.

The novice let Aelfwine's body slump to the floor while blood continued to pump from the gut and pool over the flagstones. He turned to Aesa who was struggling to stand and grabbed her hair, hoisting her to her feet.

Aesa screamed. She turned and raked her nails across the novice's face.

The boy smiled and pressed his lips to Aesa's while he gripped her face with his other hand, preventing her from breaking their garish kiss.

She fought, trying to break their embrace as he sucked and slurped like a lover overwhelmed with lust. As he did so, Aesa's veins bulged like blue snakes slithering beneath the skin of her face and neck and her protestations grew gradually weaker.

Finally she stopped struggling and the novice broke off their kiss.

He smiled and gazed at her with bulging yellow eyes, black-slitted like a snake's, before he casually crushed her throat as easily as a child squashes a butterfly.

The novice released his hold and let her collapse, sighing contentedly. He turned to the child he had struck earlier to find him staring in wide-eyed terror.

Jürgen could only kneel frozen in horror as the new novice, who had smashed through the large rose window and murdered Aelfwine and Aesa, walked slowly up to him and crouched a handspan away from him to stare him in the eyes.

Jürgen held up a hand, as if shielding himself from attack, sobbing in terror, a vicious thug no more but a terrified child.

The novice leaned closer to the boy and inhaled deeply.

'You have the gift, boy,' he hissed.

'Please! Please!' Jürgen begged.

'Where are the others – the children? Where did they go?' the novice crooned.

'Please don't kill me! Please don't kill me! I'll do anything!'

'Where are the others? Tell me and you live.'

Jürgen couldn't resist the voice – its melody was so compelling that he told the novice everything he wanted to know. He told him where to find the gang and even about their guardian, the old ex-Trinitarian.

The novice smiled, basking in the child's terror, but the night was waning and it had to move swiftly. It also wanted to leave a message for those that would discover the bodies in the chapel. He grabbed the boy by the throat and, as with Aelfwine, tore out Jürgen's abdomen and sucked at the glowing blob he found there.

As he walked calmly out of the chapel, leaving Jürgen to bleed out on the floor, a single thought occupied the novice's mind – leave no witnesses alive.

Chapter 9

Vogel came downstairs to find Stefan von Stern in the Honey Bee's common room tucking into a hearty breakfast. The templar acknowledged him with a curt nod before returning to his food.

The spy sighed. *Another day with my favourite templar*, he thought as he slid into a chair opposite him.

Stefan continued with his breakfast without uttering a word or even acknowledging the spy.

Vogel listened to the slurping and chewing for a few moments before he pulled out his pipe. After taking a long pull from his stein, the spy leant back in his chair and gazed around the cosy common room which bustled with the regular morning crowd of artists, craftsmen and merchants.

'What do you think of the place?' he asked Stefan.

The templar grunted in reply, too busy trying to cram an enormous sandwich of cheese and smoked ham into his maw. After wrestling noisily with his breakfast for half an hour, he leant back and belched loudly.

'All right.' Stefan patted his stomach contentedly. 'Where do we start with our hunt for Konrad?'

Vogel puffed on his pipe. 'Well, as far as we know, he has no relatives or friends in Rittershafen, and little money. Shouldn't be too hard to find him.'

'Then why haven't the Trinitarians and other agents?'

Vogel shrugged. 'He's too well hidden and they don't have the right contacts.'

'They have contacts inside and outside the city, including the underworld.'

'But are their contacts in the city the *right* ones?'

'Huh?' Stefan frowned.

'Take Luber. He's probably got underworld contacts, but how well do they know him, and how far do they trust him?'

Stefan snorted. 'Trust? Among scumbags? Don't tell me there's honour among thieves.'

Vogel tilted his head to one side. 'Not honour but professionalism and mutual need.'

Stefan raised an eyebrow.

'The underworld needs people to trust. Thieves and smugglers need people they can rely on and vice versa. They need clients and fences who'll keep their word and not betray them. That kind of loyalty takes years of careful nurturing to build up and, with some, all the threats and coin in the world can't break it.'

'So you're saying that agents like Franz have underworld contacts that don't trust them?' Stefan said.

'Or contacts that just aren't in the know, or won't spill.'

'That could apply to your contacts.'

'True,' Vogel said. 'But none of my contacts have *ever* let me down, or I them until now.'

'I was wondering when we'd get to that.' Stefan sighed.

'If you'd let me take him away, Kurt wouldn't have died.'

'The Dominicans didn't touch him,' Stefan said. 'He had a weak heart.'

'Yeah, right.'

'If you've got something to say, let's hear it.'

'All right.' Vogel turned back to the templar. 'I don't care whether the witch hunters are lying or not, I care about Kurt Wechsler – and I lost him because of you.'

'We had to detain him–'

'I've known him for years. He was a good man who had a family and was about to retire.'

'He was a smuggler. He trafficked in innocents and then dealt with the supernatural. A "good" man doesn't do that.'

'He hated the smuggling and he wanted out. The only reason he didn't was because I persuaded him to stay a bit longer,' Vogel said.

'Then his death is on you,' Stefan responded. 'All you agents are the same – steeped in vice and deception.'

'So what does that make you? You're right here in the shit with me.'

Stefan opened his mouth to say something but instead muttered under his breath and shook his head before he turned away.

Vogel returned his gaze to the inn's patrons, but his thoughts were on a morning two weeks earlier when he had visited the Witch Hunters abbey to release his informant, Kurt Wechsler, first mate of the *Dolphin* and Bernd Engel's right hand man.

The Dominican monks had met him at the gates and kept him waiting over an hour before one of the senior brothers had taken him to a quiet study and informed him that Kurt Wechsler had died of a heart attack.

No one would tell him a thing about Bernd Engel.

Vogel had insisted on seeing Kurt's body and, when the monks agreed, the spy had been surprised to find there wasn't a mark on Kurt's flesh. At least the monks were telling the truth about a heart attack, not that Vogel thought they were lying. But he knew the heart attack had been brought on by his arrest and incarceration, especially when the Dominicans had thrown him into a cell where he could hear screams of those being interrogated and could see the braziers and hot irons.

'The sooner we find Konrad, the sooner we can each get back to our lives,' Stefan said, breaking the tension.

Vogel lit his pipe. 'Agreed.'

'Where do we start?'

Vogel puffed on his pipe. 'Four Fingered Rolf.'

'Colourful,' Stefan scoffed.

Vogel ignored him. 'Rolf runs a bunch of thieves that operate near the docks of Central Isle and South Bank, as well as a load of beggars,' he explained. 'He has eyes and ears all over the city. It's a place to start.'

'So where do we find this Rolf fellow?'

'He's shifty. Moves around a lot, makes him hard to find,' Vogel said. 'But I know a feller who could help us.'

'Let me guess, he's hard to find too?'

Vogel shrugged.

'The fun just doesn't stop, does it?'

Vogel lapsed into silence again. He was about to ask Stefan about the sword in the *Dolphin's* hold when a boy of fifteen summers with dark hair entered the Honey Bee. When he spotted Vogel, he waved and joined the spy.

'Kris,' Vogel said.

'Lord,' the boy said, fists on his hips at the scowls on the templar's and spy's faces. 'You two are cheery this morning.'

Vogel was about to tell him to fuck off when Kristian jerked his thumb over his shoulder. 'By the way, Weasel's on his way here.'

'Well, well.' Vogel was grinning as he tossed the boy a coin. 'Looks like the Lord's with us today.'

Stefan frowned for a moment before he grinned in understanding. 'He's your contact, isn't he?'

Vogel winked in reply.

Stefan turned to the spy. 'Is this a regular part of your work? Sitting around waiting for contacts?'

Vogel nodded, puffing on his pipe.

The templar shook his head. 'I'd go insane if I had to sit around in pubs all day waiting to swap gossip and drinking myself stupid. How do you do it?'

'Takes discipline and years of training,' Vogel replied. 'Look, um, why don't you take a break? I'll keep watch.'

Stefan frowned. 'What do you mean "take a break"? I haven't done anything. I've just sat here.'

'Yeah, that's the problem,' Vogel said, with a pained look. 'Anyone walking in would take one look at you and flee in terror – even if they weren't dodgy.'

Stefan looked like he was going to say something but bit his tongue and let his gaze pan around the room and the people shooting him nervous looks, those that mustered the courage to look at him.

He sighed. 'I'll be in the kitchen.'

Minutes after the Teutonic Knight had left, a scrawny man entered the Bee dressed in a shabby beige coat and black britches of a student, which only emphasised his rodent-like face. He sat at a small table by the hearth and raised his mug of honey beer to Vogel in greeting.

The spy raised his mug in return and tilted his head to the inn's rear as he placed a pouch of coins on his table.

Weasel necked his beer before he rose and left the inn.

Vogel dallied for a few minutes before he drank his and went to the bar where he whispered to Herr Wulf to ask Stefan to meet him behind the inn. When the innkeeper winked, Vogel slapped some coins down on the bar and walked out after his informant.

***

'Is this it?' Weasel said, holding up the pouch of coins Vogel had given him.

'How much more do you want?' the spy growled.

'For what I'm about to tell you – a lot more! Do you know what Rolf and his lot would do to me if they found out I had grassed?'

'Do you know what the Order will do to you if you don't tell us what we want to know?' Stefan said. 'I promise you, it'll be a lot worse than anything Rolf and his gang can do.'

'They're the experts at making people talk,' Vogel pointed out to Weasel. 'Look, here's a bit more incentive,' the spy pressed another pouch of silver coins into the thief's hand before adding, 'and the promise to look after you if anyone gets wind that you talked to us. We all good?'

Weasel pulled an unhappy face but nodded.

'Okay,' Vogel said to his contact. 'Let's have it.'

'Rolf has a slag, Beergit, at the Scabby Lobster near the docks.'

'Good man.' Vogel patted him on the cheek. 'Let's go,' he said to Stefan.

The templar waited until they were some distance away from the Honey Bee before he turned to Vogel.

'I need to attend the None office.' His face was red and his hands were balled into tight fists by his side. 'I need to bathe.'

Dealing with thieves like Weasel was a necessary evil, and the templar knew it. Everyone did it. The Church was no exception.

Vogel was about to ask Stefan if he truly believed his soul was soiled by simply talking to a thief, and that the Trinitarians dealt with the underworld regularly and had no issues with it, but Stefan had turned on his heel and strode away.

Vogel watched him go and shook his head before, he too, walked away.

**

Gunther was stripped to the waist and bent over a wooden tub, washing his face and neck when Vogel entered their rooms.

'Afternoon,' Vogel greeted his mentor.

'God, is it?' Gunther said.

'Yes. Where did you get off to?'

'The von Albrechts. Hooked and reeled me in with whispers of scandal. Turns out the old fucker just had a few insignificant family issues. Typical. Keeps one of the best wine cellars in the city though.' The spymaster winked. 'Speaking of treasures, did you find anything interesting at the von Gruenbaum's?'

'Nah! No loot or sedition.'

'And you did behave yourself, didn't you?'

'Absolutely.'

'Hmmm.' Gunther gave him a sidelong glance.

The spy kicked off his boots and collapsed back on his master's bed. 'Were you there when Father Richter nicked Lady Silke for sorcery?'

Gunther shook his head. 'Von Albrecht had hauled me off by then. Is it true - is she a sorceress?'

'Yep.'

'And did you see her ritual chamber?'

Vogel sat up. 'Oh yeah!'

His awe made Gunther chuckle.

'Must've been quite a sight.'

'It was, but not nearly as impressive as seeing that priest do his...' Vogel gestured with his hand like a street magician performing a trick.

'Divine magic,' Gunther finished.

'It was quite a sight.'

'I'm sure it was.'

'Actually,' Vogel began innocently, 'speaking of priests and the clergy, was there something you were supposed to tell me yesterday?'

Gunther closed his eyes in that *oh shit, I forgot* way. 'Oops! I'm sorry, son. I meant to have a word with you about your new assignment.'

'New assignment? When did this happen?'

'I had a little chat, not too long ago, with *Hochmeister* Heinrich and Bishop Vassiliev– we were talking about rooting out subversives of the supernatural kind and your name came up.'

'Me?'

'Yep. I told them you were extremely talented at finding slippery villains and we all came to the conclusion that your gifts are wasted chasing down scumbags.'

'And the spying?'

148

'With your knack for it? We still need you for that, but we also decided you'd be better utilised in helping the Order ferret out supernatural villains.'

Vogel groaned and slumped back on the bed. 'Thanks.'

'No problem.'

'I was being sarcastic.'

'I know.' Gunther sat beside Vogel and gently placed a hand on the spy's shoulder. 'Listen, do you really want to spend the rest of your days chasing down scum? Or would you prefer to do something far more rewarding and better paid?'

'Not to mention far more dangerous. I nearly got killed by a sorcerous sword a little while ago. Apparently.' The spy sat up. 'Besides, I know fuck all about the supernatural.'

'That's why you have Stefan. He's got the abilities to deal with whatever the supernatural can throw at you. Rumour has it he's one of the best around.'

Vogel looked doubtful.

'Vogel,' Gunther said in that gentle and yet serious voice that always compelled the spy to look him in the face. 'Your talents are being wasted chasing down ordinary villains. You must know that.'

'But I enjoy it.'

'Remember when we first met? I said to you the most important thing between us is to be completely honest to each other.'

'That's true.'

'Well, look in my eyes, so that you know what I'm about to say to you is from the heart. Yes, I

149

know you like what you're doing at the moment, but someday soon, maybe in a week or a month or a year or even ten, you'll wake up and find you hate the job. You'll hate it because it won't challenge you anymore and if you continue doing it you'll become bitter, and when you're old and grey, you'll be *full* of regret. Trust me, boy, I've seen it.'

Vogel continued to stare at Gunther.

'Yes, the supernatural is dangerous but working with the Teutonic Order and the Church will open up a world of possibilities for you. You'll develop new skills and enter a world you've never seen before. You'll have adventures few ever get the opportunity to experience. Think about that, don't just throw away the chance of a lifetime carelessly.'

Vogel sighed. The old rogue could sell sand to an Arab. *Bastard.*

'All right,' Vogel moaned, 'I'll work with Stefan, but if it gets too much…'

Gunther nodded. 'Fine. I'll pull you out and you can go back to hunting scumbags.'

Vogel snickered.

'Incidentally, where is Stefan?'

Vogel looked up. 'Where else? Praying.'

Gunther shrugged. 'Big surprise.'

Vogel stood up. 'Anything else you want to tell me before I leave – anymore good news, perhaps?'

Gunther smiled, cupping Vogel's head in his hands. 'Actually, speaking of underworld scum, I do have another job for you…'

Vogel groaned and fell back on the bed again.

Chapter 10

The sky rumbled ominously with the threat of thunder when Stefan and Vogel reached the Scabby Lobster an hour before Vespers. They had just entered the smoky, dimly lit interior when, with a boom of thunder, the heavens opened and rain began to sheet down in heavy torrents, helped along by fierce gusts.

'Evening, Knut.' Vogel leaned on the bar and tipped back his hat with his forefinger. 'Two pints of your finest ale, if you will.'

Knut stared back with dead eyes. He had a round flabby face with a nose that had been pulped from countless back-alley brawls and a scar that ran from his right eye to his chin. He growled softly at Vogel and Stefan before he produced a couple of mugs which he filled with a dark beer then slammed down in front of the pair.

Vogel raised his stein in thanks to the innkeeper, who glared at him before he resumed wiping cups with a dirty cloth.

Vogel remembered when Old Knut, the landlord of the Lobster, was a renowned prize-fighter in the South Bank, legendary for his vicious head butting and ear biting. His body, once lean and muscular, was now bent with age and laden with rolls of fat but Knut's eyes were still bright and his huge arms were covered in scars from countless knife fights.

A huge mace hung on the wall behind him, and Vogel knew he was also pretty handy with the heavy cocked crossbow under the bar.

Vogel and Stefan stared at the crowd in the tap room which consisted mainly of men dressed like Vogel, dark colours with wide-brimmed hats pulled low to hide their faces.

The templar and spy exchanged a look before Vogel gave his companion a nod to proceed.

Stefan took off his cloak and tossed it on the bar before striding to the middle of the room.

'A bag of gold,' Stefan boomed, 'to anyone who can tell me where Four Fingered Rolf is.'

'Never heard of him,' Knut growled. His eyes flicked nervously to a group of four men seated in a corner, sucking long-stemmed pipes beneath cowled hoods.

Stefan and Vogel had caught the innkeeper's look and the templar turned to Vogel. 'I'll deal with this,' he said eagerly.

'Be my guest,' the spy replied, leaning back against the bar and taking another pull on his pint.

Stefan strode up to the men, mail and sword rattling. He stood in front of them, feet widely spread.

'You there,' he declared in his deep voice. 'I know you know where Rolf is. Tell me now, or I beat it out of you.'

Well, at least he's direct. Inelegant, but to the point, Vogel thought.

The men exchanged glances and then, with loud scrapes, pushed back their chairs as they stood.

And charged.

Rolf's men had hoped to bring the templar to the floor by sheer weight of numbers, instead Stefan staggered back a few steps absorbing their charge. As he centred himself, he smashed his head into the face of a man holding his left arm who fell back, clutching the bloody ruin that had once been his nose.

Knut grinned in approval.

His left arm free, Stefan swung a roundhouse elbow into the thug in front of him and was rewarded with a sickening crack as it connected with the thug's jaw. He dropped to the wooden boards, out cold.

While Stefan brawled with the thugs in the corner, Vogel had been scanning the inn. A door on the upper landing opened and a man's face poked out to investigate the commotion. From the description Weasel had given him, it could only be Rolf.

Vogel raced up the stairs to the landing, but Rolf had seen him and quickly ducked back into the room, slamming the door behind him.

Vogel barged the door, smashing it open. As he stumbled into the room, he dropped low and heard the tell-tale fizz and bang, followed by a meaty *thuck* as the gun's ball lodged into the wooden door frame. Smoke obscured his vision for a second, but the spy didn't hesitate and lashed out at the nearest target – Rolf's genitals.

Vogel slammed two meaty punches into the racketeer's groin which doubled him up before he fell to his knees and rolled on the floor, mewling in agony.

Vogel stood and kicked him in the guts for good measure.

***

Stefan absorbed the thugs' punches without bothering to defend and unleashed a barrage of his own. His mailed fists won the day as he smashed them skilfully into both his opponents' faces until they collapsed to the floor, moaning and writhing, blood pumping from shattered noses and mouths. He turned this way and that, expecting more foes, but none appeared.

'Vogel!'

'Up here!' came the reply.

Stefan walked into the room to find Rolf sitting in a chair and Vogel binding his hands behind his back. He whistled in surprise at the sight of Rolf's rare and expensive guns in the spy's belt.

Vogel grabbed Rolf's greasy hair and jerked his head back to look him in the eyes. 'All right, mate,' he whispered. 'We're looking for someone, young feller, a novice. Ring any bells?'

Rolf replied by spitting at Vogel.

The spy stood back and wiped the spittle off his face. 'You know, I was going to offer you a fair bit of coin, but now I think we'll do it the hard way, unless there's anything else you care to add?'

Rolf remained tight-lipped.

Vogel shrugged and turned to Stefan. 'He's all yours.'

Stefan crouched before Rolf.

'Where's the novice? Tell us what you know and we walk away.'

Rolf turned away from him.

Stefan grabbed his chin and forced the racketeer to look him in the eyes. 'The boy's life may be in danger. For God's sake, just tell us where he is, or someone who can point us in the right direction.'

Rolf spat at Stefan and chuckled.

The templar turned to Vogel.

The spy shrugged. 'Like I said – there are those in the underworld with loyalty that can't be bought or threatened.' He turned back to the racketeer. 'You're an arse,' he whispered before walking out of the room to the meaty whacking sound of mailed fist against flesh and bone and Rolf's cries of pain.

Vogel had only gone a few steps out of the room and was lighting his pipe when Stefan let out a cry. The spy rushed back to find Rolf had grown a crossbow bolt through his neck and Stefan was standing at the window. The templar sang for blessings of speed and strength before he took a few steps back and, with a roar, crashed through the window. He dropped to the ground where he rolled smoothly to his feet and raced after the fleeing assassin.

Vogel drew a throwing knife as the flush of his special ability with the weapon triggered. He drew his arm back before hurling the weapon, which sailed through the air before slamming into the leg of Rolf's killer.

He shrieked as he dropped.

Vogel was still shivering from the adrenaline of his ability when Stefan returned to the inn, dragging a semi-conscious body.

The Teutonic Knight looked at his captive. 'One of the inn's patrons. He was sitting in the corner watching the show when we entered.'

Vogel cursed. 'He must have been placed here to keep an eye on Rolf.'

Stefan frowned. 'What?'

'Whoever is backing Rolf doesn't trust him to keep his gob shut, so he placed an assassin here to silence him, if needed,' Vogel explained.

Stefan dragged the man across the tap room and into the kitchen behind the bar with Vogel in tow.

'We're not to be disturbed, and not a word of this to anyone!' the spy said, pointing at the barman before he closed the door after them.

Stefan sat the assassin in a chair and bound his arms before slapping him awake.

He looked at the templar and Vogel, disorientated for a moment, before he realised where he was and, after a spasm of terror passed across his face, he sneered at them.

He then turned his gaze on Vogel, and they remained locked, staring at each other until Stefan's shout broke the trance.

'Vogel!' Stefan motioned with his head to the assassin.

Vogel turned to the man and held up a fat pouch. 'This'll buy you passage to anywhere you want and help you with a new start. Just tell us who your boss is.'

The assassin smirked and snorted before spitting on the floor. 'Fuck off.'

'What does he have on you? Is he threatening your family? Someone else? We'll help you all get away. Just give us a name,' Vogel pressed.

The assassin stared at the spy, sneering.

Vogel looked at Stefan, shook his head and motioned for the templar to follow him as they walked out of earshot of the assassin.

'Don't bother.' Vogel glanced at the templar's fists.

'Don't tell me,' Stefan said, glancing at the smirking assassin, 'we have another loyal soul here.'

'Beyond fear and coin.'

'He'd suffer a beating for a gang leader who doesn't give a shit about him – why?' He stared at the man and shook his head.

Vogel shrugged. 'I don't think he's afraid of his master. Some have a twisted sense of honour and loyalty, and he would die for his boss. Maybe the man saved his life or the life of his loved ones.'

'So what? We hand him to the Dominicans.'

'Let me have one last go,' the spy said.

'What will it take for you to give us what we need?' Vogel said to the assassin.

He stared at the spy thoughtfully.

'Anything you want, name it.'

'You really expect me to believe that?' the assassin said.

'We'll swear oaths on the bible, if that's what you want,' Vogel said, looking him in the eyes.

The assassin held the spy's gaze.

'I believe you,' he said. 'I believe the templar would keep his word too. But the Church doesn't forgive and forget. They'll send the Trinitarians to get me – maybe not today or tomorrow, but one day. I'll look round and they'll be there.'

Stefan scoffed. 'Don't flatter yourself. You're not important enough to warrant the retribution or effort it would take to track you down.'

'Release me and I'll send you a letter detailing everything I know about Rolf and your novice,' the assassin said. 'You have *my* word.'

Vogel and Stefan exchanged a look.

'Not a chance,' the spy replied.

The assassin shrugged. 'Then I can't help you.'

Vogel sighed and looked at Stefan, shaking his head.

'Now what?' Stefan asked. 'The Dominicans?'

Vogel shrugged. 'I'm not sure that the Dominicans can get what we need. I know how good they are at it, but I don't think he'll crack.' The spy gazed at the assassin. 'Besides, how long will it take and what do we do in the meantime?'

Stefan shook his head also at a loss as to what to do. He threw up his hands in frustration before nodding to Vogel, who fished out a set of manacles from his pack and moved behind the prisoner, who shared glares with Stefan.

'Ready?' Vogel said to the templar when he had finished cuffing the assassin.

'Yes.'

Vogel drew his dagger to slice the rope around the assassin's wrist.

'Wait!' Stefan said.

'What?'

The templar motioned with his head that they should step aside and speak privately again.

The assassin snorted and shook his head.

Vogel frowned. 'What's wrong?'

'I think I may have a way to get what we need from him.' Stefan gestured at the assassin. 'But it doesn't always work as some people may resist the blessing.'

Vogel raised an eyebrow before motioning to the templar to proceed.

Stefan laid a hand on the assassin's head and sang for blessings of love and courage which bathed his hand in golden light.

The assassin grimaced, gritting his teeth as though he was resisting painful torture, before he gasped and his body bucked and he relaxed. He looked at Stefan with his eyes and mouth wide open for a few moments before he sighed. All traces of anger had vanished from his face.

Stefan took his hand away from the assassin's forehead and the light of divine magic died.

'What was that?' the assassin asked the templar softly. 'What did you do to me?'

Stefan crouched in front of him again. 'A blessing to take away the hatred and bitterness.'

The assassin turned and stared into space.

Stefan placed a hand on his shoulder, which made the man stare the templar in the eyes. 'I know what you're thinking about, and you're right to question what you've done in the past. But now, you can do right and show contrition for all you've done by telling us who your master is and if you know anything about any missing Church novices. Help us, please.'

The assassin stared at Stefan for several heartbeats before his shoulders slumped. 'What do you want to know?'

'Everything,' Vogel replied. 'Who are you and who do you serve? Tell us everything you know about a missing Church novice called Konrad Stich. Do you know anything about the clergy murders?'

The information gushed out.

The assassin's name was Rutger. He had been hired to keep an eye on Rolf and, if needed, silence him. As for Konrad Stich, he knew of the novice and that the boy had been kidnapped by his employer, who was holding him at a warehouse.

Rutger gave directions.

Neither his employer nor Rolf knew anything about the murders of any priests and novices.

Vogel and Stefan listened carefully, exchanging looks occasionally.

'So, who's your employer?' Vogel asked. 'Who's holding Konrad?'

Rutger told them and, when he did, Vogel swore.

Chapter 11

According to Rutger, Konrad was being kept in one of the many warehouses along the docks on the South Bank. A permanent pall of smoke hung over the district as members of the city guard, masked and pushing carts laden with corpses, travelled between hovels, hauling out the bodies of those who had succumbed to the smoke of the fire which had raged through the area days ago.

'What did you do to him?' Vogel asked the templar as they walked through the smog, his eyes constantly shifting to the shadows, alert for any attack. Many in the *Viertel* were desperate and feral but, since the fire, they had become even more fierce and ruthless.

'Heart of Courage,' Stefan said. 'It's a divine blessing.'

'All right,' Vogel said, utterly baffled. 'But, I mean, what did you *do* to him?'

Stefan looked at the spy. 'I made him realise how much he loved people and that gave him the desire to do the right thing.'

'You made him regret his actions.'

Stefan nodded.

They walked on for a few minutes, each lost in their own thoughts before Vogel broke the silence.

'That was a clever move,' the spy said, without looking at Stefan. 'What you did with Rutger.'

Stefan sighed. 'What good has it done? Regardless of whether he repents or not, he'll answer for his crimes in the morning.'

'Rutger made his own bed. I know he had a hard life and that it was not wholly his fault he turned out the way he did, but the choices he made as an adult were his own.'

'Agreed. Is this it?' The templar stopped at a warehouse.

Undeterred by the large red cross painted on its doors, Vogel and Stefan ventured in.

The scene that greeted them made Vogel gag, and even Stefan, a veteran of bloody battlefields, grimaced.

There were once twelve men, but it was hard to determine exact numbers as bodies lay strewn around the building. Their limbs had been torn off and tossed aside as if an angry giant child had rampaged through the warehouse and ripped them apart, flinging their remains carelessly around so that they now lay like broken dolls. Their scattered heads and limbs wallowed in pools of dried blood.

Maggots swarmed over the putrid flesh as clouds of flies covered the corpses, creating a buzzing orchestra as they crawled in and out of noses and mouths frozen in screams of pure terror.

The spy and templar tied cloths over their faces to muffle the stench before Stefan bowed his head and mumbled a prayer, after which he crossed himself and turned to Vogel.

'So who is this Max Dietz?'

'Maximillian Dietz is the largest racketeer in the city,' the spy replied as he picked carefully through the debris and rotting flesh with his dagger. 'He owns and controls the docks of both the South Bank and the Central Isle through his lieutenants who are chosen from the hardest fuckers around, like the crime lord himself. You saw Rutger.'

'And these were his men?' Stefan asked.

Vogel picked through the carnage and mess but there was nothing of interest in the warehouse but bits of people and broken furniture.

The templar stood for a long time in the middle of the building, wordlessly scanning from side to side and up and down. He stopped when he saw the spy kneel by the shards of a chair.

Using his dagger, Vogel lifted up pieces of bloodstained rope. He held them up for Stefan to see. 'Looks like Rutger was right. Konrad was here. Taken by Dietz's men for ransom.' *Poor cunts*, the spy thought, shaking his head at the fate of the racketeer's henchmen. He looked at the floor and the dried bloody footprints, tracking them to the warehouse's entrance.

'And no one came near this place before and after the kidnapping, for fear of Dietz,' Stefan said.

'Only one set of footprints left this building.'

Stefan raised an eyebrow. 'How can you tell after all this time? There are so many bloody footprints in here.'

'This is what I do,' Vogel said. 'Dietz's men obviously tried to flee and slipped in their mates' blood as they did. But only one person made it out of here alive, days ago.'

'So what happened here?' Stefan said, frowning.

Vogel shook his head. 'We know Dietz's men kidnapped Konrad and then either he, or something else, slaughtered them. Do you think Konrad's possessed or do you think something took him?'

Stefan placed his fists on his hips and shrugged. 'Could be both, couldn't it?'

'We need to find Max Dietz - he may be able to shed more light on this.'

The spy flicked the rope down and he and Stefan walked out of the building.

Once outside they took off their masks and Vogel breathed deeply, which made him cough as he inhaled smoky air.

'We should inform Father Richter,' Stefan said.

'And we will,' the spy promised, 'but first the Honey Bee– I could murder a pint.'

Stefan shook his head disapprovingly at the pun. 'Not funny. Not funny at all.'

Chapter 12

As they passed into the Merchants Quarter, Vogel was about to suggest a change of haunt from the Honey Bee to the Grim Reaper when they spotted a familiar figure walking towards them.

Vogel flicked a look at Stefan, whose face darkened. The templar's shit day was about to get shittier.

'Good evening, Franz,' Vogel said with a big smile. 'Fancy bumping into you here.'

'Father Richter asked me to find you and give you a message,' Franz Luber said to the spy and templar.

'What, no "Good evening, Vogel, good evening, Brother Stefan and how are you this fine eve?"' Vogel said.

Luber raised an eyebrow and opened his mouth to say something. Instead he slapped his forehead. 'You're right, Herr Schlosser, how rude of me!' He smiled. 'Where are my manners?'

The little man stepped back and gave the spy and templar an exaggerated low bow before straightening with his mask of contempt securely back in place. 'The murderer struck again – last night.'

Vogel's smile disappeared as he cursed silently while Stefan muttered a prayer and crossed himself.

'Who?' Stefan asked.

'Where?' Vogel added.

'The chapel on *Mönchstrasse* near the *Kirchpark*,' Luber said. 'You can't miss it - the rose window was shattered during the attack. The murderer killed three – a novice, Scholar and a child. Father Richter said he didn't know if these deaths were connected with Konrad Stich but since they might be, this one's yours to investigate.'

'Anything else?' Vogel said.

'Yeah, don't fuck up like you have so far.'

That was too much for Stefan. He lunged forward like a viper, but Luber danced back and avoided his grab with such speed that Vogel raised an eyebrow and Stefan paused, surprised.

'All right! All right!' Luber held his arms up in surrender with all looks of contempt gone.

'You push me again, little man, and I don't care if you are weakling and a Church agent,' the templar roared. 'I'm going to beat the *shit* out of you! Now, what else did the Father say?'

'Report back to him when you're done and if you need any help – ask,' Luber said.

Vogel had to admit, for a little fellow, Franz Luber had balls the size of cannon shot.

Stefan continued to glare at the little man for several moments before storming past him.

Vogel gave the little man a wink before walking after the large templar with a big grin on his face.

***

Stefan and Vogel arrived at the chapel to find Church soldiers guarding gangs of builders and craftsmen who were repairing its large rose wheel window. The former kept their hands on their sword hilts as their heads constantly scanned the surroundings while the latter worked quickly with little or no banter.

The templar and spy could taste everyone's fear.

On entering the building, Stefan and Vogel were greeted with the coppery stench of dried blood, bile and guts which washed over them like a wave. The scene inside the chapel was as grisly as the smell.

In a corner of the chancel under a white shroud lay a naked novice with his intestines hanging out like a string of bloody sausages. Not too far from him, at the front of the nave, was the covered body of a young woman, about the same age as the novice, clad in a white robe with the symbol of a silver cross within a circle on the right breast.

Vogel and Stefan moved closer to her, and the spy noted that his companion wasn't bothered by the woman's naked body, which was on full display as her robe was open. The spy looked her body up and down before lifting her hands and examining her fingernails. 'No marks of violence there.'

They gently turned her over where Vogel discreetly examined her back which was also devoid of any signs of a struggle. The only marks on her were a blue frostbite-like tinge to her lips, and her slender neck and face were covered in bruises. Her head lolled at an unnatural angle.

'Her face was gripped with considerable force,' Stefan pointed to the bruises around her jaws and cheek, 'and her neck broken.'

The templar frowned.

'What?'

'Why did the killer grab her face and break her neck?'

'He wanted to say something to her. To look her in the eyes and savour her terror as well as to stop her from struggling.'

They covered her body with the sheet and Stefan murmured a prayer over her before they rose and moved to the last corpse in the chapel, a child of about eleven summers. He lay curled in a foetal position in a patch of dried blood so that, on entering the chapel, Vogel and Stefan had been unable to see his face.

The spy gently turned him over.

Vogel's eyes widened slightly and he shook his head at the sight of the child's face and torn stomach. When he looked at Stefan, it was with a face that had drained of colour.

Stefan frowned – surely the spy had seen dead children before?

'What was a child doing here?' the templar said.

Vogel shook his head. 'His name's Jürgen. I knew him. He was an orphan, a thief and a beggar.'

The spy suddenly stopped, staring into space as if a thought just occurred to him. Ignoring the nauseating stench in the chapel, he frantically searched Jürgen's pockets.

'What are you looking for?' Stefan asked.

'Purses.'

Stefan's frowned deepened.

Vogel crossed to Aelfwine's clothes and rummaged through them before going through Aesa's robes. His search yielded nothing.

'Vogel – what?' Stefan said.

The spy looked at the templar. 'They came here at night.' He waved towards the young couple. 'The lantern tells us that and their naked bodies tell us why.'

Stefan gave a small smile.

'But they also had purses on them,' Vogel continued. 'That wineskin,' he pointed to the flagon beside Aelfwine's clothes and lantern, 'that was purchased. I recognise the skin and the pub that sells it.'

'So where's their coin?'

Vogel gestured to Jürgen. 'He doesn't work alone. He works with a gang.'

'They were here,' Stefan said. 'They may have seen the murderer.'

The spy fled.

'Vogel!' Stefan roared, before racing after him.

* * *

From the outside, Herr Brenner's house looked perfectly normal with not a single thing out of place.

Vogel skidded to a halt outside the door and drew his dagger.

Stefan drew his too. The spy gave the templar a look before turning the handle and plunging inside.

They found the children and Herr Brenner in the attic, or what remained of them.

The children had been torn apart – their arms and legs scattered around the room mixed in with bits of shattered furniture. Everything was painted red with their blood, as were the walls.

It was a mirror-scene of Max Dietz's warehouse, albeit on a smaller scale.

Vogel crossed and knelt beside Herr Brenner, who lay on the floor looking serene with no signs of violence on his body or face whatsoever.

The spy rose and looked around the room at the flies buzzing over the children's corpses and congregating in the pools of congealing and dried blood. The summer heat combined with the smell of blood and flesh in the room, and the stench of death from the chapel and warehouse, proved too much for the spy. He turned away and staggered downstairs into the kitchen where he stood, gasping and sweating.

Stefan was no stranger to blood and death, but the sight of the children and so much carnage brought tears to the templar's eyes.

He knelt and prayed and after brushing away his tears, joined the spy in the kitchen.

Vogel was shivering and swearing under his breath with his hands balled into fists.

He looked at Stefan. 'I get it now,' he said softly. 'I understand why you want the fucker so badly. Now I do too.'

Stefan placed a hand on Vogel's shoulder. 'Come away. There's nothing more we can do here.'

Vogel was about to move when, without quite knowing why, he triggered his hearing.

And stopped.

There it was.

The weak yet unmistakable sound of a heartbeat.

Vogel dashed upstairs and, gently moving aside Herr Brenner's body, found the source of the heartbeat buried beneath two of the children's bodies.

Julian bore huge gashes on the chest and arms and his tunic was soaked in blood, but that didn't stop the spy pressing his ear to the Robin's chest.

'He's alive!' he yelled to a surprised Stefan.

'How did you–'

'No time for that - do something!'

Stefan moved forward. He knelt and placed his hand on the child's chest and sang for a blessing of preserving the spirit. As he did so, golden energy flowed from his palm to cocoon the child. The templar stopped singing and scooped up Julian's body, which was still wreathed in divine magic.

'What are you doing?' Vogel yelled.

'Getting help!' Stefan yelled back as he dashed out of Herr Brenner's house with Vogel hot on his heels.

***

They sat on a bench in a garden at the heart of the Franciscan abbey with Stefan's sword belt hanging on one side of it and Vogel's hat and cloak on the other. After the charnel reek of the

171

warehouse, chapel and Herr Brenner's house, Stefan and Vogel needed to be outside and breathe wholesome air.

The templar had crashed through the doors of the monastery, yelling for aid, kicking the abbey into a hive of frantic activity, and the brothers, to their credit, had acted with a practiced swiftness and coolness that Vogel found admirable.

They swiftly ushered the child into the infirmary where brothers hovered over him with poultices and salves as others used their divine magic to repair the boy's torn body.

Vogel and Stefan had been shooed out with the promise that they would be informed as soon as the monks had a better idea of the child's condition and, no, Vogel could not smoke.

'Thank you, for what you did back at Herr Brenner's house,' the spy said to the templar, puffing on his pipe as he stared dreamily at the garden's lush flowers and inhaled the sweet scent of honeysuckle.

'I can use my divine magic to heal others, to a certain extent, but Julian's wounds were beyond my ability. They required the art of the Benedictines or the Franciscans.'

Vogel knew that there were no better healers in the west than the monks of the holy orders, and he was grateful to them for their kindness. He smiled at them as they passed through the garden, and they returned the gesture.

'How did you know Julian was alive?' Stefan said.

172

Vogel shook his head. 'I didn't. I had a feeling that I just had to go back and check, and when I did, I could've sworn I saw his chest move.'

Stefan stared at him thoughtfully. 'And these feelings, do you get them often?'

Vogel shrugged. 'Sometimes. Does it mean I have the gift for divine magic?'

'I don't think so. Sorry.'

'Speaking of divine magic, how did Wulfram die? There wasn't a mark on him.'

'It's called the Templar's Retribution. It's a powerful divine blessing. A dying templar can use divine magic to smite a supernatural creature before they pass on. It burns and often kills the target.'

'So we *are* dealing with something supernatural.'

'It has to be. No normal person could've wreaked the carnage we saw in the warehouse and at Wulfram's.'

'And old Wulfy knew it when he confronted the killer.'

'I didn't know the guardian of your children was a retired templar,' Stefan said.

'He was a Trinitarian,' Vogel clarified.

'That was good work, by the way, in the chapel.'

Vogel frowned. 'What was?'

'You knew immediately that the murderer had gone after your – Robins, is it?'

Vogel nodded.

'...from Jürgen's body being there and something as insignificant as a wine flask. I'd never have spotted that.'

'I'm sure you would've eventually,' Vogel said. 'You strike me as being sharp.'

Stefan shrugged. 'Maybe. But you got it straight away. You connected it all immediately – Jürgen's body and the wine flask meant that the novice and his companion had money pouches and the fact that they were missing meant that the Robins had taken it.'

'Most likely,' Vogel said. 'The murderer could've always taken the money but that doesn't seem to be the way he operates. He's about killing, not theft.'

Stefan agreed. 'And if your Robins were in the chapel at the same time as the murderer, he'd be after them.'

'Are you saying I think like a murderer?' Vogel shot Stefan a sidelong glance.

Stefan smiled. 'You're experienced with the underworld and how criminals think. And you're quick here.' He tapped the side of his head.

'You know that makes me a criminal mastermind, don't you?' Vogel said.

Stefan chuckled. 'We're going to need one to catch this murderer, I think.'

'And muscle,' Vogel added. 'I don't want to tangle with a supernatural murderer.'

'I do,' Stefan said.

'That's why I'm glad to have you on board.'

Stefan turned and stared at Vogel.

'What?'

'So how did a criminal mastermind end up being a spy for the Teutonic Order?'

Vogel shrugged. 'I met Gunther, my *Meister*, when he was investigating an extortion gang operating in the Artisans Quarter. I told him I'd find the gang if there was a reward. There was, and so I tracked them down and informed on them to Gunther.'

'And he paid up?'

'Yep,' the spy replied.

'When was this?'

'When I was in my early teens,' the spy said softly as he blew a cloud of smoke.

'Chasing down a band of extortionists – that must've taken balls, and brains.' Stefan nodded approvingly.

Vogel shrugged. 'Yeah, maybe. But I've always been lucky. And I suppose when I was a teenager, I was a bit of a tearaway.'

'I'd never have guessed.'

'Piss off,' the spy replied. 'Anyway, that's how I met Gunther.'

'And you never considered doing anything else? Maybe following your father's trade?'

'Nah. My dad was a locksmith, hours spent tinkering and poring over little bits of metal. To hell with that - I preferred to follow Gunther.'

'That's the criminal mastermind in you craving vice,' Stefan said.

'Anyway, Gunther took me in not too long after that and started training me. Not that I really thought of his training as actually training.'

'Why's that?'

'Well, all he used to do was take me with him on certain jobs,' the spy replied, 'tracking people down. He'd let me tag along and told me to keep my eyes and ears open and to ask questions if I didn't understand anything.'

'Best and only way to learn.'

'Yeah, I certainly did,' Vogel replied, 'and when I wasn't with him on jobs he'd always be throwing questions at me to test me, sharpen me, like asking me how I'd go about finding someone. But he always made it fun, like a game.'

'And the future?'

'What about it?'

'You don't think about doing something else? Maybe retiring from a life of shadows and intrigue?'

'Nah, I enjoy what I do way too much,' Vogel replied. 'And what about you?'

'What about me?'

'Why did you become a divinely-aided arse kicker?' The spy used the term the Teutonic Order hated.

'I'm the youngest son of a nobleman and, besides it being an honourable career for a young knight, I felt the Calling.'

'The what?'

'God called to me,' Stefan said.

'What, you heard God? God spoke to you?'

'Sort of.'

'What do you mean *sort of*?'

'I saw an angel,' Stefan said.

Vogel was about to burst into laughter but swiftly checked himself when he saw the look of absolute seriousness in the templar's eyes. 'And?' he said, clearing his throat.

176

'She said God wanted my sword arm. That's when I officially became a templar for the Order,' Stefan replied.

'You couldn't say "No" then?'

'It's not like that,' the templar replied. 'When I was called, I was happy to serve.'

'I dunno. Sounds to me like you didn't really have much of a choice.'

'You always have a choice,' Stefan replied. 'It's always up to you which path you choose to take.'

'Like Rutger.'

'Absolutely,' Stefan said. 'So he was born into poverty and abuse - many are, and the majority *don't* choose to be hired killers.'

Vogel shrugged. 'Fair to say. What's it like then, being a knight in the Order?'

'Well,' Stefan said, leaning back and stretching out his legs. 'It's a long story.'

'We aren't going anywhere.'

'Fair point,' the templar said.

Stefan spent the next hour telling Vogel about the life of a knight in the Teutonic Order and then a further hour chatting about both their professions after which they lapsed into silence, staring at the garden lost in their thoughts while Vogel puffed on his pipe.

'The Templar's Retribution,' Vogel mused aloud.

'You've never heard of it?' Stefan said.

The spy shook his head. 'God! I thought I knew all about divine magic, but the truth is, I know bugger all.'

'Then it's about time we remedied that, *Herr* Schlosser,' Stefan said. 'I'll give you the concise version – feel free to interrupt and ask questions whenever you like.'

Vogel sat up straight. 'I'm all ears.'

'All right then. Divine magic has been around as long as people have, but was really limited to seers and prophets and seriously pious individuals who always kept it well hidden.'

'Why?'

Stefan shrugged. 'Most scholars suggest it was to avoid persecution or being exploited by the powerful.'

'I see. And what exactly can it do?'

'I'm coming to that.'

'Sorry.'

Stefan waved away the apology. 'Before the Lord appeared, divine magic was always used to heal, which it still is today–'

'What about angels?'

'Not commonly summoned by the pious prior to our Lord - more the province of the odd seer and holy man. Anyway, when the Lord appeared, he added further blessings. You know why?'

'His parents were killed by the Order of the Magi.'

'That's right. Anyway, they killed the Lord's parents when he was a teenager, after which he disappeared into the deserts of the near east, returning decades later with twelve disciples and new divine blessings.'

'The first templars and witch hunters of the Church.'

'Absolutely. The Lord gave them new divine magic – blessings to nullify sorcery, mainly boons of strength, speed and health, blessings to make weapons far more lethal to the supernatural and, as you saw with Father Richter, the Smite blessing that directly harms the supernatural. That's probably the most powerful blessing a divine magic user has alongside the Sorcerer's Bane and the summoning of angels.'

'Right.' Vogel was thinking back to his schooling and the lessons on divine magic and sorcery, which he loved. *If only the Church lets us learn a little more about magic.* He sighed. *Chance would be a fine thing.*

The Church was far too scared of people being seduced by sorcery.

'And the Smite blessing can take the form of a bolt or ring of golden fire that burns and destroys the undead and demons.'

'Not just demons and the undead, but spirits and certain supernatural creatures and elementals,' Stefan added.

'And the Sorcerer's Bane – that prohibits demons from using their magic, right? So demons can't disappear and travel somewhere.'

'It also affects the magical abilities of sorcerers, elementals and certain supernatural creatures–'

'Dragons?'

Stefan shook his head. 'Nope. Not dragons. One of them breathes on you, you're done for.'

'Supposedly.'

Stefan mused. 'Right. We haven't seen a dragon in over a thousand years, but the Church has records that chronicled encounters with dragons – and before you ask, on the few occasions where we stood against them, we nearly always lost.'

'Too powerful?'

'Far too powerful.'

Vogel blew clouds of smoke as he stared into space.

'And what about women in the Church?'

'What about them?' Stefan replied.

'How is it women can use all divine magic except for the Smite blessing and summon angels?'

Stefan shrugged. 'The Lord decreed it in the scriptures – and before you ask, I don't know why he did that!'

'And the Templar's Retribution?'

'That was from the Lord too.'

'And do all clergy have the same blessings?'

'In theory, the clergy can use any of the Church's blessings, but most are taught the blessings of their Order. So, witch hunters focus on smiting the undead and demons while the Franciscans and Benedictines specialise in healing. Templars are the exception. When we're ordained, we're given certain gifts–'

'What gifts?'

'Our bodies heal faster. We're able to take far more punishment than even the hardiest of souls and we're quite resistant to magic. We can utilise divine magic to harm the supernatural with any weapon we use, even these.' He held up his clenched fists.

Vogel raised an eyebrow and whistled. 'That's quite a gift.'

'Comes at a price.' Stefan shrugged.

'Dedicating your lives to the Church.'

'That's not to say there aren't those who fall in love and leave the Church. But once you do, divine magic starts to ebb, although it never really leaves you entirely.'

'How come?'

Stefan shrugged. 'Church scholars have all sorts of theories. Personally, I think the Lord doesn't take back a gift once it's given.'

Vogel puffed on his pipe and stared at the sky for a while before turning back to the templar. 'So, why is healing so difficult?'

'It takes phenomenal concentration and *Vis* to apply divine magic to healing even light wounds, and it's very risky!'

'Risky?'

'I'll come to that. But even with minor ailments and injuries, like cuts, it's as if the wound is a living thing which resists attempts to heal it,' Stefan said. 'That's why monks prefer to use natural remedies, like poultices, herbs and ointments, alongside divine magic to hasten the body's healing.'

'That's why I've seen a number of monks and nuns working together to heal a patient – they're pooling their powers.'

'Exactly.'

'And the more senior a cleric, the better he or she is at healing?'

'A reward from the Lord for their piety.'

'What about severed limbs – can the clergy really heal them?'

'Remember I said healing was risky?'

181

'Yes.'

'It's risky because sometimes the healing backfires.' Stefan held up a hand, stopping Vogel as he saw the spy was about to ask something. 'We don't know why it happens. It could be a lapse in concentration, or the healer isn't pious enough or hasn't enough *Vis*. Regardless, when healing backfires, the healer takes on the wound.'

'So, if a monk trying to heal a severed limb cocks up badly, *his* arm or leg becomes severed?'

'And if it's a group healing effort – they all suffer.'

Vogel swore under his breath.

'Yeah. Now you know why the clergy are choosy with healing magic.'

'And that applies to poisons and diseases too, doesn't it?'

'Certainly. They cock up, they *all* get ill, or hurt, or die.'

Vogel heard the slap of sandaled feet approaching and stuffed his pipe away. 'Speaking of healing.' He nudged the templar in the side and they rose as a Franciscan brother shuffled up to them.

'The child's wounds were serious, but we manage to heal him as best we can. We think he'll recover in time. He sleeps now,' the monk said.

'That you, Brother,' Vogel said.

'He needs plenty of rest. Come back in a couple of days and we'll see if he's well enough to receive visitors.'

Vogel and Stefan thanked the monk again and when he had disappeared, the templar turned to the spy.

'Back to the chapel?'

Vogel nodded. 'I want another look round. There may have been something we missed.'

'All right then.' Stefan buckled his sword belt around his waist. 'Let's see what we can glean from the chapel.'

Vogel grabbed his hat and cloak and led the way. As the pair strode from the gardens, the spy glanced at Stefan, who was lost in thought. A small part of him hated lying to the templar about his gifts, but what could he do? If he were to tell the Teutonic Knight about them, and misjudged Stefan, he'd find himself tied to a stake ready to be cooked. *Nope*, he reflected, best to keep his secrets confined to Mum and Sonja.

Vogel sighed and let his thoughts drift back to his childhood.

Chapter 13

Vogel is twelve when his gift first manifests.

He's alone in bed. He can't sleep. He's got the covers pulled up so that only his wide eyes are showing. He's staring at the largest spider he's ever seen. It's plastered against the wall like a gigantic eight-legged splayed mural. He's frozen in bed, unable to move because the beast's malevolence has him in its thrall. He's staring at the spider and concentrating so hard that when it moves, he almost shrieks with fear.

Almost.

But he doesn't and when the arachnid moves, it's as though the creature is wearing thick hobnailed boots. Every step it takes is a cacophony of thundering clomps and Vogel is forced to clamp his hands over his ears – it's as if he's right beside a squad of soldiers quick marching down the cobbled streets.

Vogel's terror gradually subsides and over time he soon realises, curse or not, that it's something he can control – he can block out certain sounds to focus on others and he can hear all sorts of things with his supernatural hearing, like grass growing. He also realises It's a VERY valuable gift and it's not long before he puts it to good use.

It's just before his thirteenth birthday that the men enter his dad's shop. There's four of them; large, frightening men.

Vogel's dad tells him to go to his room. He does and once there concentrates so that he can hear them clearly, so clearly that they sound like they're shouting, but they're not, they're talking to his dad in very quiet tones, but there's no mistaking the menace and very real threat in their voices. They tell his father that he now has to pay for their protection and that if he doesn't, they'll start chopping bits off his children and make him watch while they have fun with his wife. They'll do worse to his daughter. They tell him not to waste his time with informing the guard. They've paid those fuckers to look the other way at the gang's business activities and, besides, grassing will mean they'll do a lot worse than their previous threats.

Vogel's father is a good man but he's not a fighter and he knows when he's beaten. He has no doubts that the gang will carry out their threats. They're a vicious bunch, that's clear. He has no choice but to concede to their demands.

Vogel's young body shakes with fury. He can feel his father's shame and fear, but Vogel is determined to stop this gang from preying on his family and the other families in the area. He vows to put an end to them, no matter the cost, and sets about plotting their downfall.

A fortnight later he overhears an agent of the Teutonic Order talking to the guards and some of the craftsmen and shopkeepers in his street, Shanzenstrasse, about a particularly nasty gang of extortionists and it's almost as if the Lord has heard his prayers.

It takes him a couple of months before he finally gets the opportunity he's been waiting so long for to act.

He's standing outside Otto Schmidt's forge along with a crowd of locals, the district guards and a stranger with a big bushy beard who dresses and looks like he belongs in the wilds, like a hunter. Yet he's here, in the Artisans Quarter, asking questions about the smith and how he died.

Most people are too scared to say anything, so they shake their hung heads fearfully and refuse to meet the scout's gaze.

Eventually he stops asking questions and moves off.

Vogel follows him. He makes his way to the Church Quarter and eventually disappears inside a large abbey decorated with the banners of the Witch Hunters Order.

Vogel sneaks up to the building and, after a quick look round to ensure that there are no eyes on him, uses his supernatural hearing to eavesdrop on the man.

The man is in a room. Vogel can hear him kicking off his boots and shrugging off his shirt and trousers. He can hear a creak from the man's cot as he lets the pressure of his considerable bulk sink on the bed. He hears the man sigh contentedly and then groan in annoyance as a novice knocks on the door.

'Herr Gunther Hahne?'

The man groans in reply.

'The Grand Master requests your presence.'

'Tell him I'll be there shortly,' Gunther
grumbles.

*Now Vogel has a name and location. He knows
who to ask for when he completes his task.*

*He is so nervous that he welcomes the physical
chores that his father and brother set him, to help
him work off the tension. When evening falls he
hasn't much of an appetite and both his parents are
sullen and quiet, scared and desperate at the
racketeers' tax.*

*Vogel is aware that they can't take much more
and his resolve to end the gang's reign of terror is
bolstered.*

*He has never been trained in stealth but years
of running with street gangs has taught him how to
sneak, climb and hide like a professional. He retires
at the appropriate time, bidding his mother and
father goodnight, yawning and stumbling heavy-
eyed to his room. Once there he changes into an
ash-coloured tunic, a pair of tanned leather
trousers and to complete his ensemble, a large
black cloak which he pilfered from his older
brother, Ludwig. Finally, he draws out a small
leather pack from under his bed in which he keeps
his most prized possessions –his lockpicks and three
exquisitely crafted throwing knives –a gift, from
Otto Schmidt, given to him on his twelfth birthday.
Knives he secretly practises with whenever he can.
He draws one of the beautiful blades and smiles at
it affectionately before sheathing it and strapping
them to his back and waist.* I'll get them for what
they did to you, Otto, I swear!

187

Vogel slips out of his room window on the top floor of the building and scampers onto the roof with ease, like the spiders he's so afraid of. He moves into a position overlooking the entrance to his father's shop and conceals himself in the shadows and waits patiently.

He doesn't have to wait long.

The gang appear, chatting as they stroll down the dimly lit street, a bunch of friends on their way to the pub after a hard day's work. As they pass his dad's shop they pause, like customers debating over a purchase, and then after a quick look around to ensure that there are no spectators, they duck into the shop.

Vogel chooses not to use his special hearing to eavesdrop on their extortion of his father. He can't bear to hear the fear in his dad's voice.

The gang waste no time in their collection rounds. They stop only long enough to collect their due and then leave. As long as there are no delays, no excuses as to why the vendor doesn't have this week's tribute, they leave quickly without any violence.

Vogel watches them exit the shop and, as soon as they're out, they throw up the hoods of their cloaks and walk hurriedly on to their next collection.

Wrapped in the shadows of the rooftops, Vogel has no difficulty whatsoever keeping up with them as he nimbly dances along the precarious pathways of the roofs.

The gang seem unaware of their stalker as they make their rounds. They visit six more vendors in the Artisans Quarter before making for the Black Cat in the Viertel, *a seedy dive popular amongst the city's scumbags, cut-throats and poets.*

Vogel peeps through one of the pub's windows and spies the gang sitting near the door in the tap room. They spend the evening laughing, drinking and gambling away other people's hard-earned money before retiring.

He uses his hearing to track them to their room. He decides to see if this is a ruse and so settles down and waits. He's a patient lad. After a few hours, he hears them snoring like a symphony and decides that it's time to call it a night but he's not sure if this is where they regularly hang their hats so, just to be sure, he spends the next two weeks trailing them and finds out that they have two lairs. The first is the Black Cat and the other is the Blue Mermaid on the corner of Dunkelmesse and Hoffmannstrasse on the South Bank.

Now that he knows where they live, Vogel decides it's time to end the game and have a chat with the Teutonic Order's agent, the man Gunther.

He's about to move off when hooded figures suddenly appear, rising from the shadows like spectres out of nightmare. He never saw them, heard them or sensed them.

These could only be the legendary Watchers – the eyes and ears of the Thieves Guild, and their security, renowned for their ability to ghost in and out of virtually anywhere.

Every nerve in Vogel's body tells him to flee – but he's trapped. They have him surrounded.

His heart is hammering in his chest– he's so scared he can't move.

The pounding of his heart intensifies and, just as he thinks it will burst, his whole being is suddenly flushed with heat.

His second gift chooses this moment to make its debut.

He can move again, clear and calm, though the world has slowed to the pace of a snail's crawl.

He doesn't think. He just acts. He reaches for one of three throwing knives he keeps strapped to his back and lets fly at one of the Watchers. It sails lazily through the air. Vogel reaches for another knife and another. He watches them drift towards their targets like feathers on hot air and, just before they strike home, time resumes its regular rhythm.

Three muffled cries ring out as Vogel's throwing knives bury themselves into the eyeball of each of his attackers.

It's all over in less than a heartbeat. His foes are lying dead on the street below.

Vogel is still flushed with the heat of his gift and his body is trembling from the adrenaline.

He looks up and thanks the Almighty before he scrambles off the roof, dropping the last few feet to the cobbled streets. He pauses only long enough to tear his knives from the faces of the fallen before glancing around to ensure that there are no eyes on him. Satisfied there aren't any, he swiftly melts into the shadows and is gone.

He catches up with Gunther Hahne the following evening.

190

The monastery is crawling with guards and monks, but Vogel easily manages to slip past them. They're not the problem.

The main doors are guarded by a pair of rhino-sized templars. No entrance that way. So the thief decides to use his favourite route –the roof.

He crawls effortlessly up the side of the monastery and onto the rooftop and ghosts his way to a large window on the top floor of the building. He peeks through the shutters and glass and can see the room, a study, is empty. With a grin, he slips into Gunther Hahne's chambers.

Gunther is surprised at seeing Vogel, when he answers the knock at his door. He barges past the thief into the study, through which Vogel entered, opens the main door, pokes his head out into the gallery and looks around.

'How the fuck did you manage to get in here?'

Vogel grins before replying, 'Magic!'

Gunther's brows furrow and his eyes narrow. 'I didn't even hear you.'

'Like I said,' Vogel replies. 'It's magic.'

Gunther shuts the door and invites his young guest to seat himself at a table in the study.

'Well, young man, why have you gone through all this trouble to see me?'

'It's about the murder of Otto Schmidt, in the Artisans Quarter. I saw you there a few weeks ago asking questions. I know who did it and where they are.'

'Really?' Gunther sounds genuinely intrigued. 'Well, do tell.'

So Vogel does. He tells the Order agent everything he knows about the extortionists and their racket in the Artisans Quarter and Otto Schmidt's murder. He leaves out the bit about his gifts, not wanting to be burnt at the stake for being a demon or sorcerer.

Gunther listens carefully, rubbing his chin thoughtfully as Vogel's story unfolds. When the young thief finishes, Gunther remains silent for what seems like an eternity before finally speaking.

'I could arrest them and they'll probably be executed, but what then?'

'What do you mean? It's over, isn't it?'

Gunther shakes his head. 'Only until another gang steps in and there's always other wolves waiting to swoop in on a kill left undefended.'

'You're talking about us, aren't you? The craftsmen and shopkeepers in the Artisans Quarter?'

Gunther nods.

'So how can I ensure that we're always protected?'

Gunther grins broadly. 'All right,' he replies. 'I'll tell you what to do but it's going to be very dangerous and if you succeed, you have to do two things for me.'

Vogel eyes him suspiciously. 'Go on.'

'First, if you manage to pull it off, you come and work for me–'

'Doing what?'

'I'll tell you later, and second, you tell me right now how you managed to slip by all the guards unseen.'

192

So he tells Gunther about his life, about his father being a locksmith and how he helps his family out by slitting purse strings and pockets. He's also pretty good at sneaking and hiding and he can pick locks –an art partly self-taught, partly taught to him by his elder brother. They are the sons of a locksmith, after all.

Gunther listens intently, nodding every now and again. When Vogel finishes, the Order agent is beaming.

The next evening he takes Vogel to the Singing Angel, a very posh inn in the Church Quarter of the city. Upon entering, a couple of very squat, bald heavies escort the Order's agent and the young thief upstairs to a private room.

As they are ushered into the chamber, they are instantly hit by waves of heat coming from the enormous hearth at the far end of the room and, even though the weather is mild, the room's ornate and expensive glass windows are shut.

Dominating the room is a man, dressed in a plain short-sleeved shirt and trousers, as large as the wooden throne his muscular arse is perched upon.

'Gunther.' His voice is gravelly and very deep.

'Ingvald.' Gunther returns the greeting, bowing his head slightly. 'This is Vogel.' Gunther nudges the thief forward, snapping him out of his stupor.

Vogel bows.

Ingvald is a monster and no mistake.

Vogel has never seen a more muscled human being in his life. Or a more bald one, as Ingvald is devoid of any facial hair. When Ingvald beckons him forward, he finds he can't move.

Eventually Gunther steps in and shoves him again, and he stumbles before Ingvald.

'This the boy?' Ingvald growls to Gunther.

Gunther nods.

Ingvald leans forward and turns a pair of fierce green eyes, cold as ice, on Vogel, who feels his guts turn to jelly and is suddenly dying for a piss. 'Do you know why you're here, boy?'

Vogel nods. 'I'm going to break out your brother.'

This provokes a burst of guffaws from the muscled monsters surrounding Ingvald. He turns and glares at them and they instantly fall silent.

'This is not going to be easy, boy!' Ingvald is not a happy bunny. 'The man you're going to rescue is very *dangerous and has the highest security.'*

'I understand,' Vogel says.

'And what's your payment if you succeed?'

'Free protection for all the vendors in the Schanzenstrasse for as long as you and your successors control the district. And punishment for the gang that's been threatening us and that killed Otto Schmidt. Hard punishment!'

'That's a lot to ask.'

Vogel remains silent, waiting for the man-mountain's verdict.

'Agreed. Protection for you and yours for life and I make an example of the Schanzenstrasse extortionists.'

Vogel breathes again and nods.

'But understand this, Vogel. If you fail, if you return without my brother, I'll make you watch while I break the necks of your father and brothers and I'll do the same to your mum and sister, but only after I've repeatedly raped them. Clear?'

'Crystal.' Vogel knows that failure is not an option on this job.

***

'Psst! Psst!'

The prisoner sits up. He wasn't dreaming, someone called to him. He raises his head and looks around. Maybe it was a spirit? The restless ghost of an executed prisoner perhaps? He looks up. There's a small face pressed against the bars of his cell window.

'Over here, mate!'

The prisoner groans. It's a boy. Probably just here to mock him. He stretches out on his bunk again.

'Oi! I've been sent by Ingvald.'

That gets his attention. He's on his feet in an instant and climbs onto his bunk where he stands on tiptoe so he can see his young visitor.

'Ingvald sent you? What for?'

'I'm going to break you out.'

'Of course you are.'

'No, I am! I really am.'

'You're a master thief, are you?'

'You better believe it, mate.'

The man sighs. 'What's your name, boy?'

'Er, V..Gherkin.'

195

'Gherkin, huh? Why aren't I surprised. All right, Gherkin, do your stuff.'

Vogel gives the man a smile and thumbs up before he disappears.

Ingvald's brother shakes his head as he sits on his bunk.

The man is being held in a cell on the top floor of a barracks in the Church Quarter. To get to the cell involves a choice – on the one hand you could fight your way through all the skilled Church guards on the floors below. On the other hand, you could enter stealthily through one of the windows on the top floors.

But there's a problem. A very small problem that's actually a very big problem.

The windows.

Way too small for a man to squeeze through, but a boy, especially one experienced in contortions, might just be able to make it.

And then if you can somehow get in there's only the matter of the two bear-sized guards standing vigil over the prisoner's cell.

This fucker must be dangerous indeed to merit this level of security!

It's impossible to approach the cell unobserved, but what choice does Vogel have? If he doesn't make the attempt, one way or another, his family are dead.

Fuck it! He drops into the room through one of the small windows and, as his feet touch the floor, his heart is pounding so wildly, he can feel it's about to explode in his chest.

But it doesn't.

196

Instead heat flushes his body and the world narrows down to two faces – the titanic guards standing vigil outside the prisoner's cell. The young thief's hands are a blur as he sends two throwing knives at the men between him and the man he's been sent to break out.

Each one slams hilt first into the balls of a guard with the force of a battering ram and both men crumple to the wooden floor, mewling in agony and clutching at their nuts.

Vogel sprints up to them and rifles them until he finds the prize –a fat bunch of keys.

Their money pouches are his rescue fee.

The prisoner rises as he hears the sound of a key tickling the lock before his cell door is flung open.

'Ta-da!' Vogel beams from the cell's threshold.

'You'll understand if I don't applaud,' the prisoner says, holding up his manacled hands.

Vogel tosses him the keys.

As the prisoner shrugs off his shackles, Vogel takes a good look at the man he is rescuing.

The prisoner notices his young rescuer staring at him with his hands on hips and his head tilted to one side.

'What?' the prisoner asks.

'You're Ingvald's brother?'

'Siegfried,' he replies, sticking out a bony hand. 'What?'

'Well, it's just, Ingvald is huge and you're, well, so scrawny. No offence,' Vogel replies as he shakes Siegfried's hand.

Siegfried sighs again. 'None taken. Come on, Gherkin, time we fucked off!'

Vogel nods and stoops to pick up the discarded handcuffs. Unless he's mistaken, that's silver inlaid into them.

Worth a pretty penny.

'Don't!' The prisoner's tone has more than a hint of dire warning. It's fear.

There's no time to ask why and have a debate, so Vogel lets the matter drop, vowing to raise it again at a later, more convenient, time.

'Stand back,' Siegfried says to the thief. 'I'm going to make us a hole. When that happens, this place is going to be a hive of angry Church bees, so get ready!'

'What?' Vogel replies, wondering how a skinny fucker like Siegfried is going to perform the deed.

Ingvald's brother grins and chants as his eyes fill with blue flames which Vogel doesn't see before he places his palms against one of the cell walls and barks a word.

The walls disintegrate, exploding out in a shower of wood and brick splinters, with a sound like thunder.

Vogel raises a very impressed eyebrow.

Freedom beckons! Vogel doesn't pause for a moment but leaps.

So does Ingvald's brother.

They both land in the haywain that Ingvald's monsters positioned below the cell's window.

Siegfried turns to Vogel and they both give each other a wink and grin before they're up and *legging it, leaving the sounds of whistles and cries of alarm in their wake.*

The next couple of days are a whirlwind. First, and true to his word, Ingvald bribes the guards of the Artisans Quarter to stay away while he gathers a sizeable crowd of the area's residents into the district's main market square.

His men are on hand to make sure that all the area's thugs and scumbags are present to witness Ingvald's announcement. The big man proclaims the district under his protection and that anyone laying a finger on the people there will suffer the following fate. He gives his men a nod and the racketeers responsible for Otto Schmidt's death are then marched forwards.

There are six in total.

Ingvald strips down to his trousers, much to the delight of all the ladies present, and takes his time to oil up his hugely muscled torso and arms.

He really is a monster.

When he finishes, he calmly turns to the extortionists. He tells them the first of them to kill him will mean that the rest can walk away unharmed.

They're obviously shitting themselves, but they have a go anyway.

Brave men, *Vogel grudgingly acknowledges.*

The first one dies in a heartbeat as Ingvald wraps a giant arm around his neck and snaps it like a dry twig.

Ingvald breaks the back of the next and pounds the head of the one after him into mush by grabbing

199

his hair and bashing his face repeatedly into the cobbles.

Ingvald is drooling with pleasure.

His remaining foes are sobbing, and not because they've soiled themselves in public.

Number four falls to his knees before his executioner and begs for his life.

Ingvald's reply is to grab his face with both hands and crush his skull like an egg –it folds in with a muffled crunch and the squirting of blood and brains.

Number five turns to flee but is pushed back into the circle by the crowd, and Ingvald's henchmen, but not before he's managed to filch a dagger from one of them and charges Ingvald with a scream.

Ingvald lazily swats aside his thrust as he grabs and hoists him high in the air before bringing him sharply down to have his back shattered across Ingvald's knee. Finally, number six is lifted off the ground, with one hand, and his neck crushed by Ingvald's inhumanly strong grip.

The display is met with horrified silence by all watching.

Lesson learnt. Example made.

The vendors, shopkeepers and craftsmen of the Shanzenstrasse can live in peace for a long while now.

While Vogel's sacrifice is lost on his father and the other people on the Shanzenstrasse, for Ingvald and Siegfried, the young thief is a hero, and a big celebration is thrown in his honour, and to mark Siegfried's escape.

It's the early hours when Gunther walks Vogel home. The revels are still in full swing, but the young thief is tired. It's been a busy few weeks.

'That's lesson number one, incidentally,' Gunther says.

'What is?'

'Make powerful friends and earn favours from them. It's probably the most valuable lesson you'll ever learn.'

'Yes, captain,' Vogel says, saluting and yawning.

Gunther chuckles. 'How did you manage to swipe the keys off the guards?'

Vogel turns to the older man. 'I knocked them out.'

'Just like that?'

Vogel nods.

Gunther puts a hand on his shoulder, stopping him and looks him in the eyes. 'Vogel, you should know that in this relationship, there can be no secrets between us. Whatever you tell me will remain between us. No matter how deep and dark you think it is. You're my man now, and under my protection. You could be a demon and it wouldn't make a difference to me.'

'Really?'

'I swear upon the Almighty.'

'If I was a demon, you wouldn't turn me over to the Church?'

'Nope.'

'Why? Don't you serve the Order and God?'

Gunther nods. 'I'm all those things but, as I said, you're my man now. I owe you my loyalty and trust. Besides, I like to think I'm a good judge of character. I have come to trust you and, because I do, I'll protect you. And if you work for me, you're working for God anyway.'

'So I can trust you with my life?'

'Absolutely.'

'And my deepest, darkest secrets – you'll not tell a soul about them or turn me over to the Church?'

'Guaranteed.'

Vogel looks deep into Gunther's eyes. Maybe he sees something in the spymaster's eyes which engenders trust. Maybe it's because he's young and exhausted and needs a confidant, someone he can talk to about his gifts and ask for advice. Who knows?

So he tells Gunther about his special talents – his hearing and ability with knives.

When he finishes, Gunther stares at him and then shakes his head before grinning as he slaps the young thief warmly on the back. 'And it only happens when your blood gets pumping?'

'Yeah, I just feel the flush and, boom, I'm... gone!'

Gunther chuckles. 'Well, we'll have to teach you to be able to do that without so much... stress, in future.'

'Sure. Whatever,' the young man says, yawning and stretching again.

Chapter 14

'Stefan!' The priest who greeted the spy and templar wore a cassock with the Witch Hunters emblem and regarded the pair with piercing blue eyes. He reminded Vogel of Saint Nicholas with his silver hair and beard.

'God be with you, Father.' Stefan embraced him. 'May I present Herr Vogel Schlosser, an agent for the Teutonic Order. Vogel, this is Father Thomas Backstedt.'

Father Thomas smiled at the spy as he dipped his head in greeting.

Vogel returned the gesture, noting that, unlike the majority of Dominicans he had encountered, Father Thomas' eyes and lined face were given to warmth and laughter.

'So, I take it you both have been tasked with investigating this horrendous crime?' Father Thomas said.

Stefan nodded. 'Vogel and I are working together to catch the murderer of our Fathers and novices.'

The guards had disappeared to be replaced by two Teutonic Knights when Stefan and Vogel reached the chapel, and the spy's fears were confirmed when they entered the building to find that it had been cleaned and the bodies removed.

'Father Thomas, may we examine the bodies that were here, please?' Vogel asked.

'Of course.' Father Thomas beckoned for the spy and templar to follow him.

The chapel may have been small but Vogel thought the crypt below it was cavernous. There were tombs belonging to clerics and knights of the Teutonic Order and in the centre of the chamber were stone tables on which three bodies had been placed and covered with a linen cloth.

Father Thomas and Stefan paused to say a prayer and Vogel followed along by bowing his head. When they finished, Father Thomas drew back the shrouds and Vogel saw that the bodies had been washed.

'The girl is Aesa, a novice in the Scholars Order. The boy is Aelfwine, a Franciscan novice, and the child, we don't know,' Father Thomas said with a shrug.

'His name was Jürgen,' Vogel said as he examined Aesa's corpse.

Father Thomas raised an eyebrow and was going to ask the spy how he knew the child but after a glance at Stefan, who shook his head, decided to drop the matter.

The spy bent close to Aesa's lips which were discoloured a deep blue. He opened her mouth and examined her tongue before he smelled it. He reached for the wineskin, which had been placed along with Aelfwine's lantern at the foot of the plinths and unstoppered it. He took a deep sniff.

'Well, it's not poison,' he said to Stefan and Father Thomas, with a nod to Aesa and her blue lips.

The templar exchanged glances with the priest.

'Why would you be checking for poison, Vogel?' Father Thomas frowned. 'Aren't their deaths obvious?'

'Just being thorough, Father. Sometimes the underworld likes to cover up the obvious to throw suspicion elsewhere – whoever killed the girl and boys may have wanted to make it look like it was the clergy killer,' Vogel replied.

'Why?' Father Thomas looked at Stefan and Vogel.

The spy shrugged. 'Aesa and Aelfwine may have become involved with the wrong individuals – gambling debts, money owed, who knows?'

Father Thomas and Stefan exchanged a look. They knew such things were more common than the Church and authorities admitted.

Vogel could see that there was something else on the templar's and priest's minds. 'What?' he said, looking to each of them.

'These attacks bear the hallmarks of a type of demon, a very rare and powerful one, called a demonheart,' Stefan replied.

'Are you saying Konrad *is* possessed by a demon?' Vogel said.

'No,' Father Thomas said. 'I think Stefan is saying that Konrad *is* the demon. It killed the boy and is wearing his form.'

'Go on,' Vogel encouraged.

Stefan shrugged. 'I *think* Konrad is a demonheart, but I'm not sure.'

'That would explain why Herr Brenner used the Templar's Retribution,' Vogel said.

'Well, there's one way to be certain,' Stefan said.

'I'm all ears,' Vogel replied.

Chapter 15

Vogel and Stefan waited for Father Richter outside his study.

The spy sat on a bench in the gallery, blowing plumes of smoke at the vaulted fan ceiling, while the templar leaned against of one of the gallery's ornate arched windows.

Vogel watched monks at work in the garden at the heart of the abbey, silently thanking the Lord that he didn't have to toil outside, as it was a little after two o'clock in the afternoon and the day was sweltering.

The sound of rapidly approaching footsteps caused Vogel and Stefan to turn as Father Richter rushed up to them.

'Father–' Stefan began but the priest raised a hand, cutting the templar off.

'I'm sorry, my boys, but whatever the two of you have to say can wait. I need you both to accompany me. Now!' Richter was more excited than angry. 'You can tell me your news as we travel.'

The priest motioned for the templar and spy to follow and, after exchanging a brief look, they fell in step behind their mentor as he barked for his carriage to be brought to the front, and Church soldiers to accompany it.

'We're going to the von Gruenbaum mansion to collect the rest of Lady Silke's sorcerous items and spell books. I only hope Lord Olaf isn't going to give us any trouble,' Father Richter said as the carriage rumbled towards the North Bank.

He explained that he had met with Lady Silke earlier and she had accepted the offer he had made her the previous night. She would turn over her spell books and destroy her summoned entities in return for freedom and to continue her sorcerous pursuits with the Scholars Order. She then disclosed the whereabouts of the rest of her sorcery.

They were with her husband, of course.

Father Richter's smile could have lit Marienburg fortress. Out of respect and courtesy to the lady and her husband, he would personally see Lord Olaf and convince him to hand over Silke's spell books. He would reassure Lord Olaf that if he complied, Silke would be home in time for supper and everybody could put this sorry business behind them.

Silke had smiled and dipped her head in gratitude.

Father Richter had been too excited to reply. But as he had dashed out of the abbey and hurried to his carriage, doubt began to gnaw at him.

What if Olaf had destroyed the books for fear that there was something in them so incriminating that clemency to the noblewoman would be impossible?

'Are you expecting trouble, Father?' Vogel asked.

Richter shook his head, shaking off his reverie. 'No. Forgive my brooding, boys, but since this affair with Lady Silke is nearly over, my thoughts turn to our brethren and the murders, especially with these horrific killings in the chapel near the *Kirchpark* last night.'

Stefan gave him a sympathetic smile.

Father Richter smiled back. 'So tell me, what news of your investigations?'

'The bodies discovered in the chapel belong to a Franciscan novice, Aelfwine, and a Scholar, Aesa,' Stefan said. 'There was also a child.'

Father Richter frowned. 'What was a child doing in the chapel with them?'

'He was a thief,' Vogel said, 'in the wrong place at the wrong time. The murderer must've killed him along with the Scholar and novice.'

'And they were all killed in a fashion similar to that of Father Pohl and Father Dieter – the novice and child had their intestines ripped out and the Scholar had blue lips and a broken neck,' Stefan added.

Father Richter shook his head and muttered a prayer before crossing himself.

'The murders suggest a demonheart, Father,' Stefan said.

The witch hunter turned his head slowly. 'Do you understand what Stefan is referring to, Vogel?'

'Stefan explained it to me. It's a type of demon that tears out the intestines, as that is where a magic user's magic essence is stored, and consumes it. Sometimes, the demon sucks the essence through the target's mouth. This doesn't kill the victim but the demon often slays its target after feeding in this fashion.'

'Good,' Father Richter said with a wry smile. 'You are learning.' He turned back to the templar.

'You're right, Stefan, this suggests a demonheart, but you need to make sure. Have you any other evidence?' He looked at them.

'We learned that Konrad was held by one of the biggest racketeers in the city, Maximillian Dietz, and that Dietz held him at one of his warehouses. We investigated the warehouse and found Konrad gone and the men Dietz left to guard him dead.'

'All of them?' Richter said, horrified. 'How many?'

'All twelve, and Vogel noted only a single set of footprints leaving the warehouse.'

'I see.' Father Richter's face was grim. 'No novice could have done that, so it does look like this is indeed the work of something supernatural linked to Konrad. What's your next step, boys?'

'We're trying to find Dietz in the hope he may lead us to Konrad,' Stefan said. 'Vogel will question his contacts in the city this evening in the hope that they will have information that leads us to Konrad and Dietz.'

Vogel noted that Stefan left out the deaths of the Robins and Herr Brenner. Probably, as nothing would be gained by informing Father Richter that the murderer had also killed children and an old Trinitarian.

'You boys are doing good work. Keep it up. Keep me informed of your progress and don't forget, if you need any help, ask.'

The conversation was interrupted by the carriage abruptly stopping, which prompted Father Richter to stick his head out of the window and bark at the driver.

'Why have we stopped?'

'Sorry, Father,' the driver said. 'Traffic.'

Father Richter sat back, fuming at the delay.

They had come to a stop in the middle of one of the *Rittersbrücken Nord*, or north Knightsbridge, that connected the Central Isle to the North Bank.

The *Rittersbrücken* weren't just bridges but districts in their own right, large enough to house shops and residents. They were also a warren of tiny alleys and narrow roads, and a hive of activity with people and carts coming and going. The summer heat didn't help and when traffic built up on the narrow roads, and accidents happened, tempers flared leading to brawls and even more delay.

'Maybe we should walk?' Stefan suggested, swatting flies which seemed to swarm everywhere.

Vogel nodded his support.

Father Richter sighed. 'Very well,' he grumbled, flinging open the carriage door and leaping out. 'Meet us at the mansion,' he commanded the driver before motioning for the half dozen Church soldiers to follow.

Stefan and the Church soldiers took the lead, pushing people out of the way, opening a path for the group. After an eternity of jostling and cursing, they left the *Rittersbrücken Nord* and entered the North Bank.

Vogel let his breath out slowly, relaxing at the tranquillity of the district.

The deafening roar of the *Rittersbrücken Nord's* crowds gave way to broad quiet avenues lined with tall trees and well-tended parks with gushing fountains.

211

Vogel stared in awe at the houses they passed – opulent mansions with high walls and guards at the gate. *What I wouldn't give to live like these fuckers!*

As the group approached the von Gruenbaum mansion, Vogel could see the nobles' guards were back at their posts, having replaced the Church guards Father Richter had placed on the gate two nights ago.

On seeing the group, the gate commander approached Father Richter.

'Father,' he acknowledged respectfully.

'Stand aside, commander. I have business with Lord Olaf.'

The gate commander stepped reluctantly aside, letting the priest and his entourage march through.

Olaf was waiting for them in the ballroom, now transformed into a training hall with a fencing dummy and rack of metal rapiers at one end.

'Good afternoon gentlemen,' he said with a curt bow to the group.

Vogel raised a hand in greeting. Stefan and the soldiers remained silent.

'Good afternoon, my lord.' Father Richter stepped forward.

'How can I help you, Father?' Olaf mopped his brow with a towel.

Sweat soaked his sand-coloured hair as well as his white linen shirt. He wore black leather trousers and boots, and the rapiers he held, which Vogel's experienced eye recognised as fine workmanship, were worth a pretty *pfennig*.

'I apologise for disturbing your exercise, my lord, but we are here on urgent business,' Father

212

Richter said. 'Lady Silke informs us that you have her spell books and the remainder of her sorcerous items. You will kindly turn them over to us.'

'I'm afraid you'll have to wait until I've finished my exercises, Father. Then I must take a bath – cleanliness is next to Godliness, is it not?' Olaf smirked and turned back to lunge at his practice dummy.

Vogel shook his head. Yep, Lord Olaf was the quintessential nobleman – ballsy, arrogant and thick as shit.

'Take him,' Father Richter said to his soldiers in a bored tone.

Stefan moved first and Olaf whirled, swords raised to meet him.

'Mine!' the templar barked, causing the Church soldiers to pause before falling back.

They flicked each other looks and knowing smiles. They were going to enjoy this.

'I need him alive, Stefan,' Father Richter said.

In a single fluid motion, Olaf slid into a guard. He was looking forward to this too.

Stefan drew his longsword as he and Olaf warily circled each other.

The nobleman struck first, lashing out in a lightning thrust.

The templar responded by dancing away and smacking aside his opponent's blade.

Olaf seized the initiative and launched a barrage of thrusts with both rapiers. The room echoed to the chime of steel on steel as Stefan retreated, flicking his longsword out, parrying the noble's attacks or relying on his speed and skill to avoid them.

Olaf's cuts and thrusts were a blur and, although the templar was holding his own, the nobleman's speed and skill gave him no chance to counterattack.

Stefan was also aware that he couldn't fall back forever, as he was rapidly running out of room to back up.

Olaf knew it too.

Sensing Stefan's desperation, Olaf renewed his efforts and watched as the templar struggled to defend, his last parry swatting aside one of Olaf's thrusts a mere hair's breadth from his face.

The noble barked in triumphant laughter when he finally scored a gash along the templar's upper left arm, piercing Stefan's mail. He paused for a moment to savour his victory.

Stefan lashed out with a lightning-fast combination of cuts which Olaf easily parried with a derisive snort.

He wasn't quite quick enough, however, to parry the kick the templar slammed into the back of his knee. It dropped him to one leg, disrupting his combative flow just long enough to give the templar the opening he needed.

Stefan lashed out with phenomenal speed, burying his longsword deep in Olaf's shoulder. He yanked it out and traced a slash across the nobleman's throat, not deep enough to do any serious damage but enough to cause Olaf to howl in agony.

The nobleman responded with a desperate kick which caught the templar in the midriff, sending him staggering back to crash against the wall.

Olaf was on his feet in an instant and running. He dived through one of the large ornate windows, exploding out of the room in a shower of glass and wood and sprinted across the lawn.

Stefan moved to give chase, but Olaf's kick had winded him. The guards moved as well but, clad in their mail armour, they were lumbering behemoths compared to the nobleman's cat-like speed. By the time the Church soldiers and Stefan had leapt through the remains of the window, Olaf was long gone.

'Christ!' Vogel said. 'How can he *move* that fast?'

Stefan shot him a vexed look for the blasphemy before replying, 'Sorcery. I suspect his wife has given him a few magical gifts.'

The group watched in frustration as Olaf shrank into the distance.

Stefan, breathing hard, saluted the fleeing figure and laughed wryly. 'Run then. There'll be no fleeing when we have round two.'

Vogel turned from Stefan to Father Richter to find the witch hunter staring mesmerised at Lord Olaf's dwindling figure. He wasn't sure whether the priest was shocked or furious.

Father Richter blinked, which brought him out of his trance before he turned to Stefan. 'Are you all right, my boy?'

'I'm fine, Father.' He placed his hand over the cut on his left arm and sang for blessings of healing.

His hand glowed with honey-coloured light for a heartbeat before disappearing to leave a scab.

'It was a brave and honourable thing you did, Stefan, but next time I want him detained by the group – no individual duels, all right?'

'Understood.'

Father Richter patted him on the shoulder. 'Bloody good fight, Stefan. My money's always on you.'

Vogel shook his head in disbelief. 'Why didn't he just say he destroyed the spell books and Lady Silke's stuff?'

Stefan and Father Richter exchanged a look and a smile.

'They always say that,' Stefan replied. 'We'd have known he was lying.'

'And his highborn status wouldn't have prevented us from questioning him,' Father Richter added.

And that would've ended with Olaf writhing and screaming in the Dominican's dungeons until he confessed to the whereabouts of his wife's sorcery. But to deny the witch hunter Silke's spell books and items could only mean one thing – that there *was* something so damning among Lady Silke's sorcery that, were it known, she'd burn for it.

The fact that Lord Olaf hadn't destroyed his wife's spell books and sorcerous items also told the spy that they must be invaluable to the couple.

He rubbed his chin. He'd *love* to see what was in those books, and the items Lord Olaf and Lady Silke were willing to die for.

Father Richter sighed. 'I should've detained him when we arrested Lady Silke. Oh well, no matter, he won't be able to leave the city, not that I think he will while we have his wife. He's far too devoted to her.'

'What now, Father?' Vogel said.

'Round up the servants and gate guards,' Father Richter ordered the commander of the Church soldiers. 'I'm seizing this house in the name of the Church and Teutonic Order until Lord Olaf is found. Take a horse from the stables and send word to the city's gates and the docks to keep an eye out for him. Then get soldiers and escort all the von Gruenbaum servants and guards to the Dominican abbey. I want them questioned.'

The commander motioned for his squad to follow as he barked orders at them.

Father Richter turned to Vogel and Stefan and placed a hand on their shoulders. 'I know you boys have your hands full tracking down Konrad, and finding the clergy murderer, but I've another task for you.'

The templar and spy exchanged a look.

'I want you both to find Lord Olaf,' Father Richter said. 'Will you make it a priority, my boys, please? He shouldn't be too hard to find and, once you've got him, you can focus entirely on finding Konrad and the murderer of our brethren.'

Vogel groaned inwardly as he and Stefan agreed.

'Of course we will, Father,' Stefan said.

Vogel could tell from the templar's clenched fists that the murderer of the clergy was his priority, but how could he refuse the good priest's request?

He nodded his support.

'Excellent,' Father Richter said, beaming. 'I'll ask the Trinitarians to help you as well.'

'With their help, we should have him in no time,' Vogel said.

'Thank you, boys. Now, I'm going to search this house from top to bottom, as well as Lady Silke's ritual chamber, and then *I'm* going to question the servants and guards. Good luck.'

Father Richter gave them each a slap on the shoulder before striding out.

'It won't take long to find Olaf, will it?' Stefan asked.

Vogel looked at him. 'Shouldn't do.'

The templar sighed in relief.

'Unless, that is,' Vogel added, 'Lady Silke gave him sorcery that'll help him remain hidden.'

Stefan closed his eyes in frustration before walking away. 'Come on,' he called, 'let's get to it.'

Chapter 16

'Which one is he?' Vogel asked, flicking a card down on the table. He raised his cards like a fan and half covered his face.

Lutz motioned slightly with his head towards a table at the far end of the common room, by a large fire. 'Big bald bastard.'

Vogel looked. 'I see him. What's his name?'

'Steinaugen,' Mikael replied.

The three men seated in front of him also raised their cards so that only their shifty eyes showed.

'Wot?' Lutz asked Vogel when he noticed the spy staring at him.

'Been a long time since I was last here,' Vogel replied, looking around the dim and smoky tap room of the Fallen Angel tavern and the cloaked and cowled punters drinking and whispering to each other. Occasionally the odd unshaved character would glance at Vogel before turning away. One or two raised their steins to the agent who smiled back.

The old men seemed pleased.

'Yes, it has been too long, you naughty boy,' Feelix chided in his high voice, wagging a disapproving finger at Vogel.

'And look how our lad's grown!' Lutz said with an evil grin. 'Seems like only yesterday when we was schooling the little snotling, eh, lads?'

'You were always the best,' Mikael said, with a proud nod. 'Moved like a ghost and could lift anything.'

'Could steal the thoughts from a person's dreams!' Feelix added.

Vogel smiled. 'Also been a long time since I last saw you lot.' Not that he missed the old fuckers.

'Yeah, but we haven't changed, have we?' Mikael said to Lutz and Feelix as he ran his hand through his long and greasy silver hair.

That was true. They were just as hideously ugly now as they were when Vogel had first met them when he was twelve.

Feelix was a still a grossly fat, vicious and sadistic pervert with a penchant for hurting the boys he molested.

Mikael was a bald, scarecrow-thin, seemingly kind figure but had a violent and vicious streak a mile long, as had Lutz, except that Lutz's pride and joy was his hair, which he wore long and loose and didn't bother to wash for fear of it falling out. Combined with his thin face and furtive disposition, it made him look like a rodent, which was lost on Lutz who regarded himself as the consummate "ladies' man."

'Nah,' the spy replied with an insincere wink. 'You all still look beautiful.' *Even if you are a bunch of old cunts.*

The old men grinned, flashing their jagged yellow and black teeth.

'Thanks for coming, son,' Mikael said.

'Always happy to catch up with old friends. Anyway, what about this Steinaugen then?'

The old men leaned forward and brought Vogel up to date on underworld events on the South Bank.

Toby Steinaugen ran a protection racket that covered nearly half the *Viertel*. No one knew where he had come from except that one day he suddenly appeared and, like the recent fire and riots that had swept through the South Bank, had decimated a number of the larger gangs and crime lords overnight.

The sight of his rivals' heads decorating areas of the district soon brought the lesser gangs under his control with most of the area's inhabitants paying him tribute.

'I didn't know you boys fell under his protection?' Vogel asked the old men.

'Neither did we until a few months ago when his enforcers came by and told us as much. Big surprise, wasn't it?' Lutz said.

The old men nodded.

'It was such a shock,' Feelix whined.

'We can't afford to pay the bills, Vogel,' Mikael growled. 'Our boys and girls don't earn enough.'

Vogel knew exactly what they meant. He had been one of their boys once, like Julian and the Robins were his children, one of their best in fact so it came as no surprise to Vogel that they nearly had a collective heart attack when he announced that he was leaving. Of course they weren't about to let their best burglar and golden goose just walk away, so veiled threats were made.

He had casually shrugged and passed the matter to Gunther, who stepped in and made some quite overt threats of his own to the old timers. Even without the might of the Teutonic Order at his back,

221

Gunther was scary and the old master thieves' bravado had melted like ice in a hot oven when Gunther told them what *he'd* do to them if Vogel or his family were harmed. After that, they were happy to let him go. They even wished him well, and so Vogel and his old mentors had parted in relatively good faith.

'We don't want to pay him anymore,' Lutz said.

'All right,' Vogel said. 'I understand, but I need to hear you lot say it. What do you want from me?'

Lutz, Mikael and Feelix exchanged glances before Mikael cleared his throat.

'Disappear the cunt!' he hissed.

Lutz and Feelix nodded in agreement.

Vogel looked across at where Steinaugen was drinking with his colleagues, roaring and laughing and molesting the barmaids.

He was large, much bigger than his henchmen, and Vogel didn't miss the fact that the man's fat hid a large amount of muscle, the kind of muscle a professional fighter has.

'How do you want it done?' Vogel asked the old men.

Lutz shrugged, 'We don't really care as long as it's as public as possible...'

'And we want *everybody* to know that we're under the protection of the Order...' Feelix added.

Vogel shook his head. 'The Order doesn't get involved in the underworld.'

Mikael snorted derisively. 'Yeah right. You don't expect us to swallow that shit, do you, boy?'

'Not directly then,' Vogel replied. 'But what I can and will do is put you under *my* protection and believe me, I've got the muscle to protect you.'

'And the terms?' Feelix said, tracing swirls on the table with his forefinger.

Vogel took his time to stare all three directly in the eyes and let them believe he was weighing up their request, letting their doubt and desperation build so that they'd be more amenable to his terms.

'No tribute,' the spy said.

Feelix, Lutz and Mikael exchanged glances with raised eyebrows and smiles.

'But,' Vogel continued, 'no more selling boys and girls. Your thieves and beggars are to be my eyes and ears in South Bank. In return, I'll make a spectacle of Steinaugen. By the time I'm done, everyone will know you belong to me.'

Vogel continued staring at them. They exchanged glances and whispers before turning back to the spy.

'Done!' Lutz said.

Vogel spat on his hand before holding it out.

Mikael, Lutz and Feelix spat on theirs and they all shook.

'To our accord!' Feelix said, raising his mug.

Vogel did likewise and together they drank to their pact.

'In the meantime, I need to collect on the debt now,' Vogel said.

That wiped the smiles from the old rogues' faces.

'What do you need, lad?' Lutz said, giving Vogel a sidelong look.

'I need three bodies found quietly and in a hurry.'

'Anything else?' Lutz asked.

Vogel shook his head. 'That's all for now, gents.'

'Our boys and girls won't be put in any unnecessary risk, will they?' Mikael asked.

Vogel knew exactly what he meant. He couldn't give a fuck for the boys and girls who stole for him but if they were slaughtered, it would hurt his purse considerably to recruit and train up a new bunch of destitute and desperate children.

'Your boys and girls won't be at risk,' the spy reassured. 'And if any are harmed and unable to work, you'll be compensated.'

The old men smiled.

'Well, then,' Lutz continued. 'Tell us who you need found.'

Vogel grinned fiendishly, settled back in his chair and took a long pull on his ale before he replied. 'Maximillian Dietz.'

Only *the* biggest racketeer on the South Bank and Central Isle.

Vogel almost laughed at the sight of the old men's faces draining of colour.

'If Dietz *ever* found out that we helped you...' Lutz began.

'Helped the Order,' Mikael interrupted. 'He'd kill us slowly and painfully. And he'd make a show of it!'

'Yes! Like that time that racketeer, Ingvald, killed his rivals in the Artisans Quarter some years ago. You remember?' Feelix said to Mikael and Lutz.

He was trembling. They all were.

'No one will ever find out,' Vogel said. 'And if by chance you were outed, I'll ensure you're safe. I'll look after you.'

They exchanged looks, yet again, before slowly agreeing.

Vogel knew that they were scared of Max Dietz, but they were unwilling to live under Steinaugen's yoke and were prepared, albeit grudgingly, to put their trust in the spy's protection.

'And who else do we have to find?' Feelix said softly.

The spy almost felt sorry for him. Almost. But the sick fuck was a master actor.

'A novice on the run from the Church - his name's Konrad. The other one's a noble, Olaf von Gruenbaum.'

'That's it?' Lutz asked, suspiciously.

'Yes.'

Feelix and Mikael breathed a sigh of relief.

'One thing about this novice,' Vogel said, almost growling. 'I don't want him approached. Just find him and lead me to him.'

They didn't need to know about the boy being a potential demon and psychotic killing machine.

The old men weren't fools and the looks they exchanged told Vogel they knew that something was wrong but decided, whatever it was, it was Vogel's business.

'Shouldn't be too hard to track this lot down, Vogel,' Lutz said.

'We'll find him, son, don't you worry!' Mikael added.

He grinned approvingly and raised his mug again.

They knocked their steins together and the spy took a long pull on his ale, satisfied that his old rogues had the job well in hand.

Chapter 17

By day, the novice moved through the city with impunity, trading his habit for the lederhosen and shirt of an apprentice mason. He smiled at the memory of that encounter, at the slack-jawed shock on the face of the lad with his limp cock in his hands spraying urine against the wall of an alley near the Sunken Galleon. He still had the gormless look on his face when the novice staved his head in with a brick.

The boy wasn't a chance mark. He was chosen, and as he lay on the ground moaning and whimpering, blood seeping into his light hair, the novice had slithered over him, inhaling his scent deeply.

Ah, there it was. The gift – rich and sweet, and he reeked of it like perfume on a cheap whore. The novice had wanted to rip the boy's belly open there and then and feast on his *Vis* but the mess would draw too much attention so he had drained the boy through his mouth, locking his lips on the boy's and sucking him dry. Afterwards he snapped the boy's neck, stripped him of his clothes and valuables and stuffed the body under a pile of refuse.

The novice spent the evenings on the prowl for clergy and on this particularly fine night he was concealed in the upper boughs of a tall oak watching and waiting patiently for the good father to emerge.

He had marked the priest during one of his vigils as he watched the comings and goings of the clergy from their various abbeys. He had spotted the cleric, dressed in the cassock of a witch hunter, crossing the street accompanied by a lone monk wearing the short distinctive habit of the Trinitarians over a simple loose tunic and trousers. They had disappeared into a library.

This had made the priest stand out as he only had a lone bodyguard, whereas the other members of his order had been assigned three or four templars, or Trinitarians, since the clergy murders started.

The novice knew a trap when he saw one. The clergy were tempting him out with only a single guard and, as he couldn't sense any concealed bodies in the area, he assumed the Church were gambling that the witch hunter and his companion were strong enough to deal with the murderer.

The novice chuckled. The fools.

As he thought about his prospective kills and the feast to come, his mind drifted back to the attack on the children and their old guardian. His dramatic entrance – exploding through a window on the top floor in a shower of splinters and glass – had had the desired effect of terrifying the children.

They had scattered like rats, shrieking in fear but were unable to escape the novice's powerful talons in the confined space of the attic.

How he had revelled in the slaughter, howling like a banshee as he ripped open chests and tore off limbs with their hot blood splashing him and spraying the walls. He had torn out nearly all the children's throats before the old man appeared, bringing his revelry to an end.

The novice could smell the power in him like the heady bouquet of a fine wine. The boy had leaped at the old man, thinking it the easiest thing in the world to rip out his bloody stringy guts and feast on his *Vis*.

Oh, how very mistaken he had been.

The old man had danced aside, avoiding the novice's lightning-fast attacks with ease as he sang for blessings of speed and protection, causing his hands to flare with golden energy. He then thrust his glowing fingers at the boy's throat and abdomen. The novice had howled in agony as the potent divine magic seared his flesh and he had responded by clawing and kicking desperately at the old Trinitarian– who else? – who in contrast to the boy's berserk attack responded with cool focus, blocking, dodging and striking with his hammer like fists and feet, but the boy's strength was inhuman and his energy relentless. It was only a matter of time before Wulfram lapsed and the boy's attack landed which all but ripped away old Wulfram's face.

The boy had paused then to crow in triumph as the old man lay choking and spitting his lifeblood on the floor.

The novice had leaned close to him to whisper in his ear and taunt him with a detailed account of what he would do to the clergy and how he would take his time with them all.

The old man's response was to smile and shake his head as he sang one last prayer.

The novice had recognised the blessing and tried to escape by diving through the shattered window. He avoided some of it, but not all, and yet again he cried out in agony as the Templar's Retribution washed over him.

He touched his hand to his side and face and winced, even now the burns were still raw and the slightest touch sent waves of pain rippling through him.

He cursed the old monk and all clergy before he smiled. Since they harmed him *they* could heal him, and they would with their blood and *Vis*.

The novice would consume oceans of it and he would be well, and not just healed but stronger, much stronger, maybe even strong enough to break the bonds that chained him to his master.

His dreams vanished as the library door opened and the priest and his bodyguard emerged, the former with a leather satchel fat with tomes.

Part of the novice, the part that was ravenous and desperate and in pain, wanted to take them as they left the building, but his rational side held sway, knowing that all they had to do was move close to or inside the building and its divine magic protections would ward him off.

The novice scowled. The whole district burned with divine protection especially the major buildings – the libraries, larger abbeys, convents, churches and, of course, the cathedral, all protected by Sanctuary blessings – permanent divine magic which was lethal to demons and the undead. Patience, he told himself as he slipped noiselessly from his perch and ghosted after them, melting into the shadows.

They strolled casually along *Kirchenstrasse*, the Church Quarter's main street, chatting to each other as they enjoyed the respite of the cool evening from the day's sweltering heat and though it was late, the road was still busy with clergy about their business.

The novice cursed the crowds. Their presence prevented him from pouncing on his prey, and he began to growl in frustration, fearing that the priest and his companion would reach their destination before he could act.

He had no choice, he had to move now or he would lose his prizes.

The novice picked up his pace, closing on his victims as saliva dribbled from the corners of his mouth.

'I'm glad this area is so well lit,' Father Hubertus said.

Brother Martin smiled as they passed beneath the pools of sorcerous lamp light, courtesy of the Scholars Order. He couldn't agree more.

Darkness provided a cloak for all manner of unnatural things, and he had no doubt that the figure trailing after them concealed in the shadows was one of those. Speaking of which…

'It would be a perfectly glorious evening, would it not, Father, were it not for the fact that our brethren scurry around like scared mice.'

'Can't blame them, Martin, can we? We're being hunted, after all.'

'Speaking of being hunted, Father, you should ready yourself – we've picked up a shadow.'

Father Hubertus sighed.

The novice slowed slightly when he saw the priest and Trinitarian stop under a pool of lamplight to continue their heated argument on the matter of whether or not the nobility should be allowed to freely practice sorcery. He gave them a mumbled 'good evening' as he passed, keeping them in his peripheral vision as his talons elongated. He dreamed of the taste of their *Vis*.

He was still thinking these happy thoughts when the attack came.

The Trinitarian moved so quickly it was the hunter who was taken by surprise. The monk had turned just as the novice's blow was about to fall and lashed out with a spinning back kick which slammed into the boy like a ram, sending him staggering back to land painfully on his arse.

The novice snarled as he silently cursed the Trinitarians and their damned *Aufmerkamskeit*.

He flipped to his feet in an instant, rage twisting his face as he glared at the monk who now stood defiantly in front of him, daggers pulsing with the golden energy of divine magic sprouting from his fists.

The boy sprang and swiped at the monk, who darted forward to meet the attack. The novice growled as his blow was met by the monk's forearm, protected by a metal and leather bracer. Before the boy could respond, the monk unleashed a swift barrage of blows – a head butt, which snapped the boy's head back and a round-house elbow to the temple which sent the boy careening to the side. This was followed by a flurry of rabbit-punches to the temple and finally a low round-house kick to the back of the knee for good measure, which took the novice to the floor.

He recovered almost instantaneously and lashed out again with another taloned swipe.

This time the monk replied by turning aside slightly, letting the attack pass within a hair's breadth of his face. As the blow brushed past his nose, he caught and trapped the initiate's arm between his two forearms and broke it with a jerk and a muffled crack. He then twisted the arm behind the boy's back.

The pain was indescribable. The novice howled as his broken bones ground together with a crunch.

'Martin, move!' Father Hubertus boomed, his voice hollow as if he stood inside a tunnel.

The Trinitarian dived aside as a lance of golden brilliance slammed into the boy, exploding into radiating lines of sizzling blue energy as it collided with an invisible shield protecting the novice. Though unharmed by the magical bolt, the force of the impact lifted the novice off his feet, sending him flying backwards, hitting the ground so hard and fast he performed a string of flawless backwards rolls.

Father Hubertus' clothes and hair swirled, caught in the storm of divine magic raging around the priest as he gathered his energies for another assault, but the novice was aware that the battle was lost. His ambush had backfired horribly and now he faced capture or death.

He rolled from the ground into a crouch and glared with murderous fury at the witch hunter and monk. The easy kills had proved tougher than expected. He stretched his mouth wide, hissing his hatred of them for robbing him of his much-needed kills before he leaped thirty feet into the darkness of the buildings at the side of the road.

Two more herculean bounds took him safely out of range of attack from Father Hubertus' divine magic before he was lost to sight, swallowed by the evening's shadows.

'Did you see that?' Father Hubertus turned to Martin, his face drained of all colour.

'Saints preserve us!' the monk replied in his soft Irish accent, as he made the sign of the cross on himself and dismissed the golden flames around his daggers. 'That thing may dress and look like a novice but it had taloned hands.'

'That's not all, Martin. Did you see what happened when I struck him with my magic?'

'Sorcery.'

'His lordship was right after all,' Father Hubertus said softly. 'There's a sorcerer behind this.'

'What now?'

'Did you get a good look at the attacker?'

Brother Martin shook his head. 'A young man, that's all I could tell you. It was all too fast to tell exactly what he looked like.'

Father Hubertus scooped up the satchel of books he had dropped to the floor during the attack. 'We must report this to Bishop Vassiliev and Grand Master Heinrich immediately.'

'Father.' The urgency in Brother Martin's voice stopped the witch hunter and made him turn.

'What is it, Martin?'

'If a sorcerer is behind our attacker and the clergy murders, you should tread carefully.'

Father Hubertus smiled and placed a hand on his friend's shoulder. 'Come on. Somehow, I don't feel easy standing here in this empty street.'

Together, witch hunter and Trinitarian continued quickly on to the fortress of Marienburg.

Chapter 18

Stefan von Stern left his monastery immediately after Matins when it was still dark and cool though the day promised to be another sweltering one.

He felt loose and relaxed as he walked along the streets; the grace of devotion always made him feel light and at peace with the world. He smiled at the guards manning the gatehouse that connected the citadel of Marienburg to the Church District on the Central Isle, and they waved and muttered slurred good mornings, smiling good-naturedly.

Stefan paused to exchange pleasantries with them before moving on. For the templar, it was no chore to stop and chat with the men and women who guarded Marienburg and Rittershafen. It was an honour.

He passed into the Church Quarter to find it devoid of souls except for groups of the watch who saluted him as they marched past. At such an early hour the clergy would either be attending to the liturgical offices, or chores, and those that did have business abroad hurried to it under guard for fear of the clergy murderer.

Father Richter smiled when he saw Stefan, who had been waiting for him until the witch hunter's meeting had finished. He filed out of the chapter house, chatting softly with Father Hubertus and Brother Martin, both of whom greeted the templar with smiles and warm hugs. Their happiness was short-lived and swiftly replaced by grim looks.

Stefan knew the murderer had struck again but this time the news wasn't so bad.

Yes, there had been another attack during the night, Father Richter informed him, on Father Hubertus and Brother Martin, only this time the attacker had been unsuccessful but, alas, he had also escaped.

Stefan was to find Vogel and meet the Father in Marienburg, immediately.

He had bowed and dashed off. Though the templar didn't know exactly where Vogel lived, he knew enough about the miscreant to know that he could generally be found in or around the vicinity of the Honey Bee inn.

As the templar expected, at such an early hour the Bee was shut and he had to pound on the front door until a figure stuck its head out of a window on the first floor, demanding to know why the templar was disturbing good folk at such an early hour.

Stefan had profusely apologised to the Bee's proprietor, Herr Helmut Wulf, but explained that he needed to see Vogel on urgent business for the Teutonic Order.

Herr Wulf had met the request with a stream of grumbling but nevertheless had let the templar in. The innkeeper felt a lot better when he in turn forced Vogel from his cot, who also responded with a string of expletives at having been roused at such an ungodly hour.

Stefan had shaken his head and rolled his eyes at the laziness of innkeepers and spies before bidding Herr Wulf a good morning and thanking him. When the innkeeper had shuffled away, the templar explained that they were wanted in Marienburg as the murderer had struck again.

Vogel didn't give a shit and said as much, stumbling back to his bed and burrowing under the covers. An hour of conflict ensued as Stefan tried to drag him out of bed while Vogel valiantly resisted all attempts to prise him from his warm cot. Eventually the Teutonic Knight's perseverance won the day, along with a pail of cold water which he dumped over the spy's head.

Vogel had cried out piteously and admitted defeat. He dragged himself out of bed and after quickly attending to his toilet, threw a cloak over his shoulders, slapped on his hat and followed the templar out of the inn, sulking and swearing profusely.

The sun was peeping over the horizon when the duo arrived at Marienburg which, as ever, was a hive of activity as monks and priests went from prayer to breakfast and servants rushed around on errands. The smell of baking bread and the shouts of craftsmen calmed Vogel and as the sun chased away the darkness, his ill temper melted away to be replaced by his usual good cheer.

'Father Hubertus and Brother Martin, huh?' he asked the templar.

Stefan nodded.

'Do you know them well?'

'Not Brother Martin. But Father Hubertus is a good soul; he has a wicked sense of humour.'

'I hope that whatever Father Hubertus has to say, it'll help us. I'm getting tired of this hunt.'

'Amen,' Stefan replied.

***

Vogel and Stefan entered Grand Master Heinrich's study in Marienburg's High Castle to find a sizable company. In attendance were Bishop Vassiliev, Brother Arnold Guerk, Brother Martin, Fathers Hubertus and Richter and Gunther Hahne.

The spy and templar stood facing the gathering with their hands behind their backs while Heinrich conferred quietly with his gang. At length he turned to them.

'Right! You two first – report!' the Grand Master barked.

Vogel cleared his throat nervously before stepping forward. He shot Gunther a look and the latter grinned and winked back at him.

'Gentlemen,' Vogel said, addressing the assembly. 'We learned yesterday there was another attack on a Church novice and a junior member of the Scholars. They were killed in the same fashion as Fathers Pohl and Dieter, although we cannot confirm that as we haven't had a chance to examine the good Fathers' bodies.'

'We'll arrange for you to examine their corpses,' Bishop Vassiliev said. 'This will, hopefully, confirm that our brethren have been murdered by the same individual.'

'And what else will you learn from examining their corpses?' Heinrich growled.

Vogel exchanged a look with Stefan before he turned back to the Grand Master and shrugged.

'Maybe we'll find something others have missed, Grand Master.'

'And maybe you won't,' Heinrich said.

Vogel looked at them.

'Pray continue, Vogel,' Bishop Vassiliev urged, shooting Heinrich a reproachful look.

Vogel bowed his head in gratitude. 'We suspect the murderer of the novice and Scholar last night is the clergy murderer, as all the victims have similar wounds.'

'The nature of the injuries points to a demonheart, *Hochmeister*,' Stefan added. 'Also, we learned that Konrad was kidnapped by a racketeer, Maximillian Dietz, and held for some days, which explains his disappearance. Somehow Konrad was freed and his guards, twelve of Dietz's men, were slaughtered.'

The men in the room exchanged grim looks.

'The supernatural was definitely involved but we can't say whether it *was* Konrad or something else,' Vogel added.

'And where is this Dietz?' Heinrich interrupted.

'We're tracking him down now, Grand Master. I'm confident we'll have him in a day or two,' said Vogel. 'He may have information that will help us to apprehend Konrad.'

'Or again,' Heinrich growled, 'he may not.'

'Yes, Grand Master.'

Gunther cleared his throat loudly and looked pointedly at Heinrich who seemed to take the hint and nodded back.

240

'It seems you two are right – to a point,' Heinrich said. 'We have evidence the murderer is supernatural. I'll let Father Hubertus explain.' Heinrich looked to the priest.

'I won't bore everyone here with the details of last night's attack on us,' the Father said, gesturing at himself and Brother Martin.

'Thank the Lord for small mercies!' Heinrich's comment earned him a reproachful glare from Father Hubertus. 'Sorry, Huby. You were saying?'

'I can confirm we were attacked last night by a young man dressed as a novice who had a taloned hand. He was also protected by sorcery which deflected Father Hubertus' Smite blessing,' Brother Martin said.

'Whatever or whoever the murderer is, one thing is certain,' Father Hubertus added, 'a sorcerer is behind this novice.'

'Is this novice the sorcerer behind our brethren's deaths, or his apprentice or minion?' Gunther asked.

'We also need to find out if our sorcerer is an independent, or a member of the Order of the Magi,' Father Richter said, looking at the bishop.

Vassiliev smiled at the priest for voicing the thought on his mind too. Looking around at the gathering, Father Richter had evidently said what was on everyone's mind.

'Is Lady Silke a member of the Order of the Magi?' the bishop asked Father Richter.

'No, my lord, she says she is not,' the priest replied and, seeing the raised eyebrows and doubt on the bishop's face continued. 'I believe she's

241

speaking the truth, my lord, as I also have no doubt she is *not* the sorcerer behind our murderer.'

Vassiliev stared at him thoughtfully. 'If it was anyone else, Jozef, I'd say that they were letting their compassion cloud their judgement, but I trust yours. Very well, keep us appraised of Lady Silke's case.'

'Begging your pardon, Father,' Vogel said turning back to Father Hubertus, 'but was your attacker burned about the face and arms?'

Father Hubertus exchanged a curious look with Brother Martin who shook his head.

'I'm sorry for the strange question,' Vogel said to the gathering, 'but the individual who slaughtered the Scholar and novice in the chapel yesterday evening also attacked some children in a house in the Artisans Quarter. These children were known to me, as was their guardian, an ex-Trinitarian called Wulfram Brenner.'

'Apologies for not telling you about this before, Father,' Stefan said to Father Richter. 'We've been so busy that we thought we might as well catch *everyone* up on the progress of our investigations so far.'

The witch hunter shook his head, dismissing the apology.

'A good man, Wulfram,' Brother Martin said. 'He's dead?'

Vogel nodded. 'I'm sorry.'

'Before he died, he unleashed the Templar's Retribution on his attacker,' Stefan said. 'But if the attacker was protected by sorcery, maybe the spell didn't harm him or was lessened.'

'Or sorcery is being used to disguise the young man's injuries?' Bishop Vassiliev mused.

The men in the room exchanged glances.

'We're not sure if the spell did burn the murderer's face, but there's an individual who could possibly tell us more – a survivor of one of the murderer's attacks,' Stefan added. 'He's in a Franciscan hospital. We'll question him as soon as he's conscious.'

'The Sanctuary blessing should protect the lad from a demon but if this is a demonheart that would make it a greater demon. I'll put templars on him immediately just to be sure,' Arnold Guerk said. He bowed to the men in the room and told them to go with God before rushing out.

'And I'll inform all Church and Order agents and the Trinitarians to be on the lookout for a young man with burns about the body and face,' Brother Martin said. 'He may be disguised by sorcery, but maybe not. We may get lucky.'

'Excellent.' Bishop Vassiliev nodded his approval to Martin.

'What's on your mind, lad?' Gunther said to Vogel, causing everyone to turn to the spy.

The spymaster could see Vogel staring away, his brows furrowed.

Vogel turned to the gathering. 'I can't help wondering if we're looking in the wrong place for our sorcerer.'

Now it was the turn of the men in the room to exchange confused looks.

'What if the sorcerer we're looking for is clergy?' Vogel explained. 'Sorcery requires

243

resources – a ritual chamber, properties, books, potions, supplies. We suspect the wealthy as they have access to all these, but so do the Church, begging your pardon.'

Vassiliev exchanged another look with the men in the room and Father Richter smiled at Vogel.

'That's a reasonable assumption, Vogel,' the witch hunter said, 'but the clergy are too carefully watched by their brethren for a sorcerer to act without drawing suspicion.'

'Besides,' Brother Martin added, 'the Trinitarians and the witch hunters always keep an eye on the clergy to ensure such things don't happen, and if they did, we'd know it.'

Would you? Vogel said to himself.

'Right, you two,' Heinrich barked at Vogel and Stefan. 'Keep on the hunt for Konrad and the murderer. Father Richter tells us you're both doing well. Keep up the good work. Any questions?'

The spy and templar exchanged wide-eyed looks before they turned to the Grand Master and shook their heads.

'Good,' Heinrich grunted. 'Dismissed!'

'Keep us informed as to your progress,' Bishop Vassiliev added.

Vogel and Stefan bowed before leaving.

Gunther followed them out and walked with them along the gallery.

'I bet you have a few questions,' he said to Vogel.

'Too fucking right I do.'

'Excuse me, gentlemen,' Stefan said, so he could leave master and protégé to talk freely. 'I'm going to meditate in the refectory.'

Gunther smiled at the templar and gave him a playful punch on the shoulder.

'He's a good one lad, that one,' the spymaster said to Vogel when the templar had left.

'Yeah, I know. Took me a while to realise it.' Vogel gazed after Stefan. 'You know, this is something you never taught me.'

'What?' Gunther said.

'How to hunt the supernatural.'

'That's why you're here, working directly with the Teutonic Order and the Church,' Gunther replied, 'to learn how. So, what do you think?'

'About what?'

'How do you catch a supernatural killer?'

Vogel smirked. 'Fight fire with fire – use the supernatural. Set a trap like you did with Father Hubertus and Brother Martin to lure the murderer out.'

'We did that and failed. So now what do we do?'

'You keep trying, use different methods.'

Gunther smiled. 'I was thinking the same thing. Since Brother Martin and Father Hubertus failed, I think it's yours and Stefan's turn now.'

'You think we'll have better luck than them – men with powerful magic?' Vogel said, giving his mentor a sideways look.

'Yes, I do. Stefan has powerful magic *and* abilities – as do you. And I'm not just talking about…' He pointed to his ears and mimicked throwing a knife.

The spy smiled before he stopped and suddenly frowned.

'What?' Gunther said. 'I can see your devious little mind turning.'

'I *may* have an idea as to how we find Konrad.'

'There you are!' Gunther said with a broad grin and a wink. 'Good lad. Now, grab that templar and go find the fucker that's been murdering our brethren.'

Vogel saluted and left.

'And don't forget to attend to that other thing I told you about,' Gunther called after him.

Vogel's response was an obscene gesture.

Chapter 19

The Reaper was anything but grim. The inn was conveniently located opposite the Dominican monastery, which made it ideal for Vogel and Stefan to duck into after they had escorted Fathers Richter and Hubertus back to the Church Quarter.

It was well after Sext when they entered and found the taproom's flagstone floors were swept and laid with fresh sawdust and there was a feisty fire dancing in the hearth. As they threaded their way through the common room, they inhaled the rich earthy smells of bunched herbs hanging from the room's beams.

Vogel and Stefan seated themselves in a corner and said nothing to each other until they had downed their first two pints and held the next round in their hands, staring at the regulars.

The Grim Reaper swelled with the late-afternoon crowd of district guards and the odd priest or monk. All were lost in their tankards, though they did nod and mumble polite greetings to the newcomers before returning to their own musings.

'What's eating you?' Stefan said to Vogel who was staring into space as he puffed on his pipe.

'I've never had to hunt down a sorcerer.'

Stefan grunted. 'That's four we have to hunt now – Lord Olaf, Konrad, Max Dietz and the sorcerer behind the clergy killings. I wonder how many more will be added to the list?'

'Might be three if Konrad *is* the sorcerer?' Vogel said with a shrug.

Stefan shook his head. 'He doesn't have sorcerous ability – it would have come out a long time ago.'

'Hmm,' Vogel mused as he blew smoke rings.

He felt lost. He needed Gunther's guidance. He imagined sitting with his mentor in front of a roaring fire, pipes in their mouths and ales in their hands while they tackled the conundrum of how to hunt down a sorcerer.

And how would you do it? Vogel could imagine the old man asking him.

He shrugged. He knew fuck all about sorcery, but then, that was why the Church had paired him with a templar.

'If I'm to be any help in finding our sorcerer, I need to know more about the art,' he said.

'What do you want to know?' Stefan asked.

Vogel leaned forward. '*Everything.*'

'Get another round in, and I'll begin.'

Eight pints and two hours later, Vogel considered himself an authority on all things sorcery.

'So, sorcerers have to chant and wave their hands and arms about when casting a spell?' he said, swaying slightly.

'It's part of the rules. Sorcery is formulaic – one wrong word or gesture and the spell fails,' Stefan said, seemingly unaffected by the beer he had drunk.

Vogel hesitated, not really understanding what "formulaic" meant. 'But the Scholars don't have to
248

wave their arms 'cos they have their staffs. How does that work?'

'The arm waving and gestures help a sorcerer to focus the spell and their *Vis*. The Scholars use their staves as a focus,' Stefan clarified.

'And sorcerers don't really have any powerful spells; most of their spells are really about detecting things or making themselves a bit stronger or faster, right?'

'A sorcerer's real power comes from the summoning and binding of entities and creatures.'

'And that's why they have ritual chambers,' Vogel said.

Stefan nodded. 'They're also used for necromancy.'

'But that's a lost art, isn't it?' Vogel was definitely becoming an expert on the whole sorcery thing.

Stefan nodded again.

Vogel opened his mouth to say something but stopped, staring up thoughtfully before turning back to Stefan. 'How do you build a ritual chamber?'

'That's an art in itself. Most apprentice sorcerers complete their training by constructing their own ritual chambers, but they often need help with crafting the circles and etching the writing. This means knowing engravers and masons willing to keep their secrets.'

'Well that's something I didn't know. I always thought sorcerers did their own engraving and masonry, since they create their own ritual chambers,' Vogel said. 'Either way, in order to be a sorcerer, you need money and contacts.'

Stefan ordered another round before turning back to Vogel, who was staring away again lost in thought. 'Pfennig for them?'

'You'd be overcharged,' Vogel replied. 'So that's why sorcerers summon and bind demons – the power.'

'And the flexibility,' Stefan added. 'If a sorcerer wants to be able to lob fire, they bind a demon that can do that and confer that power onto its sorcerer. And they can bind the beast into an item, like a ring.'

'Or they can bind it to their own flesh? To eyeballs and teeth?'

Stefan gave him an affirmative wink. 'That's why the Church always binds and gags suspected sorcerers it captures.'

'And *that's* also why inquisitors gouge out eyeballs and cut out tongues – you never know what maybe bound there.'

'Or not?' the templar said. 'But why take the risk?'

Their beers arrived and Vogel raised his mug to Stefan who knocked his own against it.

'Yeah,' Vogel agreed, taking a long pull on his stein before wiping away the foam with the back of his hand, 'you're better off joining the Scholars. They don't need demons for their magic, do they?'

Stefan shook his head. 'Admittedly, they're reliant on their staves to cast *any* spells and their spells aren't as varied as demonic abilities, but that's a small price to pay for not having to dance with demons. And they still summon elementals.'

'And dealing with demons is always risky because demons always struggle to break free of their sorcerers, and if they do, they either kill or control them?'

'Not always,' Stefan said, shaking his head. 'Sometimes demons and their sorcerers bond – they become close.'

'But that's only because the sorcerer is evil, right?'

'The Church argues so, but the Order of the Magi would disagree,' Stefan said.

'And if a sorcerer is killed, his demons disappear back to the void?'

'Not immediately. They start to fade, to weaken. Their sorcerers are anchors keeping them chained to our world, which is why, when their masters are killed, demons will seek out another sorcerer to bind them.'

'Speaking of dancing with demons,' Vogel said, 'you were about to tell me all about 'em.'

Stefan took a long pull on his beer before belching and taking a deep breath.

'All right, here's the abridged version, which I will embellish as and when required.'

'Go on, then, Brother Stefan.'

'There are really only two types of demon – greater and lesser breeds and thankfully there are very few sorcerers that can summon the latter, or even possess the knowledge of any breeds.'

'Gotcha.'

'Demons also come in three forms, those that look like horrors…'

'With horns and barbed tails and such,' Vogel interrupted.

'They have all kinds of horrible appearances – some have tentacles and eyeballs on stalks while others have scales and slime. It varies.'

'And the other types?'

'Some are like ghosts – shadows or things that are hard to see, like mist or water. And the last are the *Nachahmen*, the mimics – those demons that resemble people or animals,' Stefan said. 'Demonhearts are one of the most powerful of those. The take over the body of a host and devour the brain, which gives them access to their host's memories, skills and abilities.'

Vogel whistled in amazement. *Fuck!*

'*Nachahmen*,' Stefan continued, 'can't be bound into objects or to the sorcerer's body. The other types can and can confer certain abilities to their sorcerer.'

'What type of abilities?' Vogel pressed.

'Whatever abilities the demon has – spitting acid, bolts of fire –depends on the type of demon–'

'Don't tell me,' Vogel said, holding up a hand, 'it varies.'

'One of the things about binding demons into things is that, depending on the demon and the object you're binding it into, you can create some *very* powerful artefacts.'

'Oh?'

'If you bind a greater demon into *Blutglas*, the item becomes an artefact capable of some serious sorcery. But as I said, few sorcerers can summon greater demons, especially the breed of demon that turns *Blutglas* into a sorcerous weapon.'

'Well we know our sorcerer can summon greater demons, which makes him a serious fucker.'

Stefan frowned. 'Not one to take lightly and neither are powerful sorcerous items – are you listening to me?'

'Yes.'

'Vogel!' Stefan said sternly, drawing the spy's full attention. 'Sorcerous items, especially the powerful demonic ones, are *never* to be taken lightly. They have intelligence and malice and are capable of subverting your will. They can make you do things you may live to regret.'

'Understood. I'm sorry for what happened with Bernd and the *Dolphin*. I was foolish.'

'You've learned, and you know better now – that's the main thing,' the templar said.

'And what was that sword's need and desire?'

Stefan shrugged. 'The Scholars will research it – carefully. Probably blood and battle.'

'And all demons have different desires and needs, right?'

'Yes. And some of them are really strange – such as drinking a baby's tears or eating fish eyes under a full moon. Some need to be sung to.'

'And all demons influence sorcerers to do what they desire,' Vogel mused.

'If the sorcerer's lucky, it's nothing more than doing strange or embarrassing things.'

'But it could also be murder.' Vogel thought again of the sword in the *Dolphin's* hold.

'Exactly.'

Vogel took another long pull on his beer and stared out of the pub window.

'Is there anything else you want to know?'

'Nah, I think that's it for now. But if I do have questions...'

'Ask. Anytime.'

''preciate it.' Vogel raised his mug and Stefan knocked his against it.

They returned to their musings for a few minutes before Vogel broke the silence. 'So how many sorcerers have you hunted?'

'Just one. And I didn't really hunt the sorcerer down. I accompanied a witch hunter and Trinitarian when they confronted him. I was just muscle – you've said it yourself, templars are divinely-aided arse kickers. That's what we do – combat the supernatural.'

Vogel leaned back in his chair and blew more smoke rings. 'I'd love to hear about it.'

The big man shrugged before taking a long pull on his stein. He set it down, leaned back in his chair and started talking about his earliest days as a templar, which started in the lands surrounding Rittershafen. But his real adventures started not long after he received the Gift of the Templars and was posted to Araby.

He shook his head at the memory of the place and, as he talked about it, Vogel was whisked away to a distant kingdom where oceans of sand shifted beneath a relentless sun. Where the dunes were swept by fierce winds into storms that scoured the face and skin as the sand seeped through armour and clothes.

And when the sun yielded to the night, the spy saw the bloodcurdling sight of hordes of mindless cadavers and skeletons, animated by the sorcery of liches dwelling in ruined cities beneath the sands, descend upon villages and towns.

He watched while desert warriors, swathed in black with curved blades in their hand, stood shoulder to shoulder with Order soldiers and armoured templars blazing with divine fire. They hacked, bludgeon and threw back the undead swarms as screams of terror and the dying split the night while the stench of fire and death carried on chill winds.

And when they weren't battling against the restless dead, there were other monstrosities to contend with – serpents as large as stallions that swam beneath the dune sea and dragged unwary travellers to their deaths beneath the sand.

There were scorpions the size of hunting hounds that spat acid, demons of fire and lightning and succubae of indescribable beauty and allure, all enslaved to the wills of eastern sorcerers.

Araby, however, wasn't all blood and death. When Stefan spoke of the cities, Vogel pictured beautiful verdant oases filled with palms and buzzing bazaars surrounded by tall, graceful towers and white-domed buildings framed against a sky set ablaze by the setting sun.

Years later, Stefan traded the blistering heat and exotic beauty of Araby for the snow-capped peaks of western lands. There the templar had honed his battlefield experience by facing the fierce Northman tribes with their large axes and swords

255

and howling painted shamans, fighting on fields of frozen ice and in thick dark forests.

The Teutonic Order had defeated them in nearly every encounter, finally routing them after a bold attack on the encampment of the Northman overlord, who Arnold Guerk had slain in single combat.

Stefan claimed the head of the leader of the Northman shamans – a devil with lizard's eyes, blackened teeth and every inch of flesh tattooed in reptile scales.

Their victory over the Northmen had been brief. Almost immediately after, Stefan and his templar brethren found themselves facing fresh horrors. These wore the forms of wolves and walked on two feet, standing well over seven feet tall with talons that could tear a man's throat out in a single swipe.

Beasts that prowled the forests at night with eyes that shone in the dark like hellish lanterns and who cloaked themselves in the skin of men and women, hiding among human settlements during the day.

Stefan had trekked these demons through forests filled with tall firs punctuated with small havens of civilisation –villages and towns of neat brick and timber with red-tiled roofs where travellers were greeted with broad smiles which hid all manner of dark secrets.

Werewolves weren't the only monsters Stefan had faced. By far the worst were the alluring men and women with ivory skin, red eyes and long fangs who ranged abroad at night to steal into villages and charm folk into letting them feed off human blood and lust.

In one settlement, Stefan and his templars were set upon by the entire village, all of whom were either shapeshifters or vampires, led by the village priest, himself a skinchanger.

'There you go,' Vogel declared. 'There's one the Church missed.'

Stefan shook his head. 'The priest had been turned into a shapeshifter long after he had taken the cloth, and he was living in a small, isolated community. It was only by chance that we actually discovered the monstrous nature of the village.'

Vogel raised his eyebrows and returned to puffing on his pipe.

'You really believe the clergy is behind this, don't you?'

'Like I said, it takes resources, which the Church has. Besides...' He hesitated.

'What?' Stefan said. 'Come on, let's hear it.'

'Sometimes the best way to hide is in plain sight,' Vogel said. 'Take the Trinitarians, for instance, how many people *really* know what they are?'

Stefan shook his head. 'Not many. Most think that they're just well-travelled monks, a bit handy with their fists, who arbitrate disputes and ransoms.'

'Exactly. And that's what people know about ordinary Trinitarians, never mind the Dragon Disciples.'

Stefan sighed. 'Fair point. So we're going to add a clerical sorcerer to our most-wanted list now, are we?'

'Unless you have any objection?'

'I've lots of objections,' the templar replied, 'but I suspect that's not going to deter you from looking.'

Vogel smiled and raised his stein. 'That's the spirit.'

Stefan knocked his mug against the spy's with a shake of his head and a scowl.

'Are you going to inform *Meister* Gunther?' the templar said after he had drained his mug and ordered another round.

Vogel shook his head. 'Nah, I think he'd just try and convince me to keep the focus on Konrad and the murderer. We'll tell him when we've got something solid to report.'

Stefan looked up with a smile as the barmaid arrived and thumped four steins down on the table before vanishing to attend to the cries of the inn's thirsty patrons.

Vogel raised one of his mugs and Stefan matched him.

'What now?'

'We wait. One of my contacts will have something soon.'

'What do we do in the meantime?'

Vogel raised his stein in answer. 'We drink, and you can attend to your templar duties.'

'And what are y*ou* going to do?'

'I'm going to put my head down a little later. I've work this evening.'

'Oh?' Stefan raised an eyebrow.

'Yeah. Let's just say, I'm on the graveyard shift.'

Chapter 20

It was a glorious summer's evening and two hours past Compline the streets were still thronged with people drifting about their business. When the working day was over, the people of Rittershafen enjoyed nothing more than sitting in a pleasant tavern garden with a tankard of cold beer, gossiping about the day's events, *except for cursed souls like me,* Vogel thought bitterly as he looked out over the graveyard from his perch in an old oak.

Who cared if a few bodies went missing, as long as they didn't get up and walk out themselves?

The Order cared, especially when it was the rich whining, which is why they had vowed to bring the graverobbers to justice and put their best man on the job, Gunther Hahne, who in turn put *his* best man on the job.

Best man, my arse, Vogel snorted to himself when Gunther had told him he needed his top agent on the case. More like the bastard who drew the short stick, which was why he was sitting in a tree overlooking a graveyard.

A fox suddenly emerged, sniffing curiously at a headstone before lifting its leg and then trotting away, nose to the ground.

Vogel watched it go before a flicker of movement brought him sharply to attention.

Shadows suddenly materialised, snapping him from his reverie and causing his hand to fly to the hilt of one of his throwing knives, but when all three waved, Vogel relaxed and smiled.

He slithered from his perch and dropped noiselessly to the ground.

'Evening, Vogel.'

'Evening, Kris,' Vogel said to the lad. 'Evening, gents.' He winked at the two children with the boy, a few years younger than him but no less feral looking.

'Evening, Vogel,' they said.

'The South Bank cemetery?'

Kristian shook his head. 'Not a peep. It was as quiet as a graveyard.'

He laughed and looked at the two urchins with him his arms out wide to see if they would find it funny but they stared back at him with a look that said, *twat.*

He rolled his eyes before turning back to Vogel. 'Nothing to report. It was dead.' He snorted a laugh again.

The urchins shook their heads and groaned at the pun.

'Can't you find someone else to watch us?' one of them asked Vogel. 'He thinks he's *so* funny.'

Kristian smacked the child across the back of the head lightly. 'Oi!' he scolded. 'I take great care of you little shits and what do I get in return? Mutiny.'

'It's betrayal,' one of the other urchins said, in a bored tone of voice. 'Mutiny is for ships at sea – dumbo.'

'Shut it, you little scrote!' Kristian loomed over the child.

The boys responded with scoffs and jeers.

Kristian pulled a menacing face and rested his hands on the hilts of the shortsword and long dagger strapped to his hips.

Vogel smiled wryly. Since the attack on the Robins, he had insisted Kristian arm himself.

'So the South Bank cemetery?' Vogel said to the group, bringing them back in order.

Kristian shook his head. 'Nothing so far. I left three more Sparrows,' he looked at the urchins, 'to keep an eye on the place. They'll report back in the morning.'

'Nice one. Thanks Kris, thanks lads,' Vogel said to the gang. He reached into his tunic and pulled out coins which he pressed into their hands.

'You been here long?' Kristian asked Vogel.

'Nah, arrived not too long before you. The girly I relieved was so happy to see me I thought my luck was in.'

'Nice,' Kris said.

Vogel shook his head. 'I wished. She just gave her report, which amounted to, "fuck all on my watch", and scarpered to the pub.'

Kristian shrugged. 'Some you win…'

'Yeah. I'll meet you tomorrow at the Bee.'

Kristian threw a mock salute. 'Tomorrow, Vogel.' He winked, grabbed the two younger boys and walked away.

Vogel watched them go, smiling, before he climbed back up the tree and nestled into his perch, folding his arms. He leaned back and sighed. Ordinarily, he would have spent his vigil slipping in and out of a gentle doze or occupied his thoughts with a book, as Gunther insisted he improve his reading. But this evening he had too much on his mind to feel tired.

Only days ago he was either attending soirees to eavesdrop on seditious gossip or up to his neck tracking down underworld scum. The world he knew had started to drift away from him. He felt lost as he journeyed with Stefan into the unfamiliar world of the supernatural. The problem was that he couldn't rely on his knowledge and instincts and had to defer to priests and templars. He felt like a twig caught in a wild river's rushing current, propelled without the means to stop and steer.

He looked up at the blue-black canvas of the heavens sprinkled with glittering stars and prayed that Gunther was right about learning new things, because so far he was floundering in this world of magic and demons.

Vogel turned his attention back to the graveyard. As he gazed at the rows of headstones and occasional mausoleum, he found himself thinking of his family and of how he hadn't visited his mother and elder siblings in a long while.

Vogel is fourteen when he leaves home to start his apprenticeship with Gunther Hahne. He learns many skills from Gunther – how to survive in the wild, which plants you can eat and which will kill.

Vogel asks his master where he learned his skills.

Gunther replies that he wasn't always a spy. In fact he was a scout and huntsman for most of his young life before joining the Order. But Gunther

Hahne had long since given up his forester ways and now uses his survival skills and instincts to hunt a different kind of game – on behalf of the Teutonic Order, as one of their chief spies.

And so Vogel is taken under Gunther's wing and told he has gifts too precious to waste on a life spent hunched over a desk tinkering with locks. If Vogel craves excitement and a life spent in the shadows, Gunther will give it to him. If Vogel wants to learn the skills of a master thief and put those skills to good use in the service of God and the Order, Gunther will help him to do that.

Vogel likes the sound of that.

So Gunther teaches Vogel all he knows, polishes and hones the boy's natural stealth and subterfuge skills and adds deception to the repertoire so that the young thief starts to mature into a promising spy with a sharp mind who hungrily devours all that Gunther can impart.

Time seems to pass so swiftly Vogel doesn't notice until one day Gunther suggests Vogel take a break from training and pay his family a visit.

The young man is shocked at the length of time he has been away from home and is grateful for the chance to spend some time with his family and show them what he has become.

Vogel is sixteen when he returns home. He envisages the door to the family home opening and greeting everyone with smiles and excited questions about both his and their lives during his absence.

But fate, it seems, is rarely so kind.

When Vogel walks through the door, he is greeted by tearful faces —his mother, brother, Ludwig, and twin sister, Sonja. But where is father?

His mother is too overcome with grief to reply. All she can do is clutch a handkerchief to her face and weep. It is Sonja that steps forward and pulls him into an embrace.

She's the one who whispers in his ear about their father's murder.

Vogel's world collapses. He doesn't hear any more. The shock causes his mind and spirit to flee his body. It's gone for an eternity and when it finally returns to the prison of his mortal flesh, all he can do is clutch his sister in disbelief.

Later, much later, he hears the whole story. How Dad was drinking in a tavern two nights past. How some scumbag, or was it a drunken sailor? – the witness reports are too vague to be clear –picks a fight with his old man.

Vogel smiles with tears pouring down his face. His father was never a fighter. A brave man and a good man, but not a fighter. At least he died quickly, Vogel is told. A single thrust to the heart. He felt no pain.

It's no comfort to young Vogel.

He is told by friends and even his siblings to remember what he loved about his father.

Vogel loved everything about his father.

Growing up, he knew many children whose fathers were either indifferent or sadistic and cruel. Few had fathers like his.

Vogel's dad always had time for his children. Always talked to them and, though he couldn't

264

afford to send them to school, struggled to give them an education and a trade. He put food in their stomachs and gave them warm beds. He sat with them when they were sick and frightened at night and told them stories when they were children. He even took them on trips, putting his work aside for his family.

And now he was gone. Taken away because some scumbag, pissed out of his head, decided he wanted to pick a fight with a gentle man. A good man. A man Vogel and his siblings would never have the joy of letting their children get to know.

Vogel doesn't feel grief, just white-hot fury. After the funeral and a period of time spent with his family to help them mourn, Vogel returns to Gunther.

He wants to hunt down the man who killed his father. He promises his teacher that if the old man helps him find the killer of his father, he'll help him hunt down and punish all the scumbags Gunther and the Order wants, from now until they nail shut his coffin.

Gunther nods. He agrees to help Vogel exact his vengeance. They use every means at their disposal to hunt the murderer down - brutality and coin, torture and bribes and in a matter of days they find their man. A vicious, washed up ex-marine. A gutless piece of shit who takes one look at the torturer's glowing red pokers and confesses straight away.

Vogel finally has his man and, as promised by his mentor, he is allowed to take his time with his father's murderer.

The fucker lasts six agonising days before his heart finally gives out. Ironic, since Vogel's heart gives out at the same time.

The loss of his father finally sinks in and Vogel spends days lost in grief and tears. When he finally surfaces, Gunther is on hand and ready to step into the shoes of a surrogate father and Vogel is more than ready to embrace him as such.

Mentor and mentee forge a bond of love and trust borne from grief and death, and they never look back.

Vogel couldn't help but smile as he wiped away a stray tear. All right, he promised himself, just a few minutes of sentimentality and then it's back to work.

He continued daydreaming until it was well after two in the morning. He was dying for a shit and was about to climb down and crap in the bushes when movement suddenly caught his attention.

A cloaked figure was moving swiftly and purposefully through the graveyard, not tall but extremely broad, like a wrestler.

This looks like our man, he thought as he smoothly unfolded himself and took a few moments to massage his limbs back to life. He then slipped down from the tree and glided silently after his cloaked quarry.

The big man threw back his hood and Vogel saw that he was bald. He unfastened his cloak, letting it fall to the floor, and the spy could also see that beneath the short-sleeved tunic he wore, the man was hugely muscled with a broad brawny chest and corded arms. He wore short loose trousers tied with a hemp rope belt which showed his legs to be twisted with muscle too.

The bald man took his time, reading the names on the gravestones carefully. He was evidently looking for someone specific. At last he grunted something, put down his lantern, produced a spade and started digging.

Vogel watched while he laboured, his powerful body pumping like a machine, swiftly building a mountain of dirt. At length Vogel heard the dull thud of his spade striking something and then the crunching, tearing sound of wood being torn apart. Moments later the figure tossed a bundle out of the hole and pulled himself out after it. He then refilled the grave, picked up the wrapped corpse and slung it over his shoulder. With a last glance around to ensure that he wasn't being watched, he walked hurriedly out of the cemetery, unaware of the shadow that trailed after him.

The grave robber had parked his horse and wagon just outside the cemetery gates as there was scant chance he'd be caught by the few guards on patrol at such a late hour. Besides, Vogel thought, if he was, he'd just bribe them to turn a blind eye to his nefarious activities.

Still keeping a careful eye out for any observers, the grave robber dumped the body into the back of the rickety-looking wagon and threw a few large sacks and blankets over it. He then climbed into the driver's seat and, with a flick of the reins and a click of his tongue, started the wagon moving.

267

Vogel jogged along in the shadows some distance behind it, letting the sound of its rumbling guide him as it rattled over the cobbles. He trailed it through the narrow streets of the Artisans Quarter before it turned off into the maze of streets and alleys that formed Rittershafen's Merchants Quarter, where most of the city's traders and merchant lords conducted business with shops squeezed into every alley and street.

The wagon rumbled past the market square, dominated by a large domed emporium with graceful columns and no walls, and continued to meander through the area's back streets. Eventually it turned into a mews which opened out into a courtyard and stables.

Moving with the stealth of a cat, Vogel scampered up the front of a shop and made his way onto the roof overlooking the courtyard where the grave robber had stopped the wagon.

Once the burly man had closed and locked the mews' gates he seemed to relax and take his time. First, he unhitched the horse and led it into the stables where he rubbed it down and settled it in for what remained of the night. He then returned to the wagon and retrieved the wrapped corpse which he again heaved over his shoulder before he entered the building through a door leading from the mews into the rear of the building.

Vogel went round to the front of the buildings to see what kind of place the grave robber had entered.

The practice was small, sandwiched between an armoury and herbalist. The sign hanging above the main door read:

"*Herr Doktor* Gerhardt Earnst Horstmann. Physician and Undertaker."

Is the good Herr Doktor experimenting on the corpses himself or flogging them to his physician mates? Vogel wondered.

He reasoned it would be unwise to break into the house while the grave robber was still awake so decided to wait until the burly chap turned in.

Choosing a comfortable and concealed niche from which to watch the doctor's house, Vogel settled back once more and resumed his vigil.

It was close to Lauds but still dark when a large black carriage pulled by two horses came rumbling and clopping up the street. It stopped outside the doctor's practice and a short be-spectacled figure with a pipe in its mouth hopped out and fumbled with a set of keys at the door of the building before disappearing into the gloom.

As soon as he did, Vogel detached himself from the shadows and glided toward the building.

Since there seemed to be no stealthy way to enter the doctor's practice from the front, Vogel decided to enter from the rear. He climbed onto the roof of the building and across it before he slithered down the other side and slipped into the courtyard.

He moved towards the wagon which the grave robber had left in the open. A quick search found it only contained a few sacks stuffed with wood chips and the rotten old blankets which the grave robber had used to cover up the corpse.

The door through which the grave robber had entered was well secured with both bars and bolts so Vogel decided to gain entrance to the building by trying a door on the first floor, easily reached by a set of winding wooden stairs.

Though this particular door was also locked, it lacked the security of the ground floor door and so Vogel was able to pick it in moments. Packing away his lockpicks, and with a big, satisfied grin on his face, he oiled the hinges and opened the door a crack. He was rewarded with stygian gloom and so opened it further and poked his head in for a better look.

Empty, just a dark hall.

After a quick look around to make sure he wasn't being watched, Vogel slipped inside.

He padded silently down the hall which stretched for about ten feet before ending at a staircase which wound down. His heart was pounding wildly as he descended the stairs which ended in another left-to-right hallway.

Vogel listened carefully and this time he could hear a raised muffled voice coming from behind a door down the hall to his left. It sounded like chanting.

He moved to the door and pressed his ear against it. No mistake about the voice - it was definitely chanting.

Looking through the keyhole didn't reveal much. All Vogel could see was a table with a body on it and by the state and stench of the corpse, it could only be the body the grave robber had just dug up.

The strange chanting, which Vogel suspected was coming from the physician, suddenly rose in volume and, even as he watched, the corpse became bathed in dancing tongues of blue fire.

It was Vogel's first exposure to sorcery and all he could do was stare open mouthed.

Then a figure stepped from the fire. It was the corpse and, judging from the translucent hue of the skin, was still a corpse. It was then Vogel noticed that the figure didn't really step out of the flames, it drifted.

Every hair on Vogel's body rose.

Time to fuck off. He stepped slowly back and kept backing up until he was a few feet away from the door. His face was bathed in sweat and he was shaking uncontrollably.

He could now hear muffled voices, this time conversing normally and, as the distance between himself and the doctor grew, so did control over his fear. After what seemed like an eternity, he finally made his way to the foot of the stairs which led back up to the door from which he had originally entered. Once there Vogel gave in to his instinct.

And bolted.

He raced up the stairs and out of the door, down the courtyard stairs and out of the mews, and kept running along the streets of the Merchants Quarter and beyond.

Fear gave him speed and energy. At any moment he expected demons or spirits to come shrieking out of the darkness to snatch him up and bear him back to the sorcerer who would rend his flesh and flail his soul for trespassing.

271

Vogel didn't stop running until he slammed against the doors of Rittershafen's cathedral. They were locked at this time of the day but he didn't care. He sank to the ground in front of them, panting and shaking with fear at the sight he just witnessed.

He started to laugh. He shook his head and told himself that he was safe. He repeated it over and over interspersed with the prayers his father and mother had taught him until he lost himself in their mantras.

Vogel sat on the ground with his arms wrapped around his knees which were drawn up to his chest and didn't stop shivering and talking to himself until the first rays of the sun peeped over the horizon, setting the sky on fire and promising another day of sticky heat.

Still panting with adrenaline, he walked to a well where he drew up the pail of water and after drinking some, splashed the rest on his face. He looked up at the emerging sun and took a deep breath and, as he did, he could feel his fear and tension drain away.

He had intended to tell Gunther everything about Doctor Horstmann and happily watch him burn, but then he stopped and stood with his hands on his hips and his head tilted to one side as he paused to have a good think.

He looked up at the lightening sky, then at the cathedral, and then back in the direction of the doctor's house. He looked at the cathedral again and snorted as he smiled – yeah, like he could ever worship in there.

He threw his hands up in the air and shrugged. *It's worth the risk*, he told himself as he walked back towards the Merchants Quarter.

***

Vogel's knock on the door was answered by the grave robber who he suspected also filled the roles of the doctor's manservant and minder.

'Morning,' said Vogel. 'I'd like to see the *Herr Doktor*, please. It's urgent.'

'Come in.' He had a deep gravelly voice.

Vogel was ushered in and asked to wait in a room on the left as he entered the building. The surgery was directly opposite it, on the right.

'You're early. The *Herr Doktor* isn't ready yet. He'll be about half an hour,' the burly man said.

'No problem,' Vogel replied. 'I'll wait here, if I may?'

The big man shrugged his broad shoulders. 'Please yourself,' and walked away.

Vogel didn't have to wait long for the good doctor and within twenty minutes the lumbering minder was back.

'The *Herr Doktor* will see you now.'

Herr Doktor Horstmann was a portly little man with a few strands of hair plastered to his skull. He had a round kind face which was clean-shaved, except for a small square moustache. He was also strangely but neatly dressed.

His shirt, waistcoat and trousers were all impeccably washed and pressed and a pair of tiny round spectacles perched on the end of his nose, giving him a mole-like look.

When Vogel entered, he was puffing on a long-stemmed and slightly curved pipe. He beckoned Vogel inside and motioned to a chair. The grave robber entered after the spy and shut the surgery door.

'Now, young man,' the doctor said, lifting his chin slightly and staring Vogel in the eyes. 'What seems to be the problem?'

Vogel took a deep breath and licked his lips.

'There's nothing physically wrong with me *Herr Doktor*, er, at least I don't think so,' he said, clearing his throat. 'I came to see you on another matter. My name's Vogel. I'm an agent for the Teutonic Order.'

The doctor raised an eyebrow. 'I see.'

'I was concealed in a graveyard last night in the Church District, as I had been tasked with investigating a spate of grave robberies in the Church Quarter cemetery. That's when I saw your man,' he gestured at the bodyguard, 'rob from a grave and I followed him back from the cemetery to your home.'

The man looked at the doctor with a surprised expression that said, *I didn't see or hear anything.*

Vogel turned to the minder. 'Don't feel bad. I'm sure you're usually quite perceptive.' He turned to the doctor before shooting Horstmann's minder a sidelong glance. 'I'm just better.'

The big man growled softly.

'After gaining entry to this building, I witnessed a…supernatural occurrence.'

Vogel could feel the grave robber move closer to him and swallowed as his throat was suddenly dry.

'I can tell you it scared the shit out of me and, initially, I had thought to report this to the Order, but I changed my mind.'

'Go on,' said Horstmann calmly. 'I'm listening.'

'Look, *Herr Doktor*, I'll lay my cards out on the table,' Vogel said, 'and if I'm wrong then I probably won't walk out of this room alive. But I don't think I am. I think a man like you could use a man like me – an information gatherer who knows this city well and has the support of the Teutonic Order.'

'And what do you propose?' Horstmann asked.

'A partnership. An exchange of services. If I help you, you help me, when I ask. Either way, your secret's safe with me.'

Horstmann leaned back in his chair, looking thoughtfully at Vogel while thick plumes of smoke curled up from his lips.

'Well, that's direct and you're a bold young man, I'll give you that.' The doctor nodded thoughtfully. 'Let's say I agree to this. What exactly would you ask of me?'

'Before today I never really knew what I wanted in life. I was content to chase down criminals and spy for my *Meister* and the Teutonic Order.'

'And what happened today?'

'I woke up. After seeing what you could do with the corpse, I realised that there's more to life

275

than chasing down scumbags. There's a world behind the ordinary world which I don't understand, and I may need to deal with it one day.'

'You have the Church to help you with magic.'

'True, if I'm on Church business. But I might not always be. I might need to consult someone on magic who isn't connected to the Church.'

Horstmann and his minder exchanged a look.

'So you need a sorcerer to help with magical contraband or illicit magic.' The doctor smiled.

'Exactly.'

Doctor Horstmann took a long puff on his pipe before exhaling. 'So why don't you go back to chasing down criminals and leave the supernatural to the supernatural experts? Forget it all.'

Vogel shook his head. 'What if the supernatural comes for me? Besides, I can't. I want to see where this leads.'

'And you're certain this is what you really want? You know how perilous this is?' Horstmann's eyes bored into Vogel's.

'This is what I want.'

The doctor continued to puff on his pipe and stare at the spy. 'And what's in it for me?'

'Anything I can provide.' He saw the doctor's eyebrow rise in surprise.

'I believe you, Vogel. May I call you Vogel?'

'Of course. What do you say, *Herr Doktor* – my information services for your sorcery?'

Horstmann remained silent for several moments as he blew clouds of smoke. 'I'd say that your conviction needs to be tested.'

'A test, eh?' Vogel nodded. 'Fair enough.'

He leaned forward and locked gazes with Vogel. 'Look into my eyes and tell me the truth. Can I trust you?'

Vogel stared at him. 'If I give you my word, I'll keep it.'

Horstmann nodded. 'Good. And what would you do to achieve your goals?'

'Anything.'

'Would you kill?'

Vogel shrugged. 'I have done. Depends.'

'Very well. Here then is my offer. Kill a priest for me. Not just any priest but a witch hunter and bring me his severed hand with his rings–'

'His rings?' Vogel was confused.

'A priest's rings are a mark of his office and status within the Church. Do this for me and we'll be partners. Oh, and I'll also provide my services as a physician at a twenty per cent discount.' Horstmann smiled.

'A priest?' Vogel said, raising an eyebrow. 'That's a big ask, *Herr Doktor*.'

'Yes it is. For the sake of your conscience, I'll make it easier. Find a bad one – they do exist, you know.'

Vogel stared at the doctor.

'You're wondering if I'm the individual responsible for the clergy killings in the city,' Horstmann said.

Vogel shook his head. 'I don't think you are. If you were, we wouldn't be speaking. I'd be floating in the Elbe.' He glanced at the doctor's minder before turning back to Horstmann.

'Well said. And if you really want to know, I'm not your murderer. And neither is he.' Horstmann pointed at his manservant.

Vogel took a breath. 'Okay, *Herr Doktor*,' he said, extending his hand. 'I'll do it.'

Herr Doktor Gerhardt Earnst Horstmann's grin broadened as he shook it, sealing their pact.

Chapter 21

Herr Helmut Wulf, proprietor of the Honey Bee tavern, descended the stairs an hour past Lauds to find the imposing form of Stefan von Stern seated at a table in the common room. Laid before him were platters of bread, cheese and sausages and a large tankard of weak beer sat at his elbow.

He waved in greeting and beckoned the innkeeper over.

Helmut smiled as he crossed to Stefan's table.

'Morning, Brother Stefan, how are we this morning?'

'Always good when I've had some of this,' Stefan replied, looking at his mug. 'I don't think I've ever tasted anything finer than your honey beer. I hope you've apprentices learning the art.'

Herr Wulf planted his fists on his hips. 'You fear I'll take the secret of my honey beer with me to my grave?'

Stefan shrugged. 'We can't have that, can we, Herr Wulf?'

'Fear not, Brother Stefan, I'm sure the Lord will send me a suitable apprentice to pass my art on to when the time comes. Have faith.'

'Amen.' Stefan raised his tankard.

'Well, well,' said Herr Wulf as the door opened and a figure entered the inn. 'Maybe here's a candidate for the position. Morning, Kristian.'

'Good morning, Herr Wulf, Brother Stefan,' the lad replied politely. 'How are we, this fine morning?'

'Very well, young'un, thank you.'

'How would you like to be an apprentice?' Stefan asked.

'To you?' Kristian said, wide-eyed and ever in awe of the titanic Teutonic Knight.

Stefan shook his head and nodded at Herr Wulf. 'To him.'

'Will it be exciting?' Kristian asked.

Herr Wulf and Stefan exchanged a look before the innkeeper nodded.

'I think it's exciting.'

'What is?' Kristian said.

'Keeping bees, extracting their honey and learning the art of brewing my secret honey beer.'

Kristian flicked a look between the templar and innkeeper before he turned back to Herr Wulf and, placing his hand over his heart, bowed low.

'I'm honoured that you'd consider me for your apprentice, Herr Wulf, but sadly I must decline. I'm already apprenticed to Vogel.'

'By God he's good,' Stefan said to Herr Wulf. 'He even sounded sincere and disappointed.'

The innkeeper grunted and shook his head. 'We're too late, Brother Stefan. This one's already been corrupted by Vogel.'

'I agree. It's hopeless,' he said with a wink at the boy and gestured to the food.

'Thank you kindly, Brother.' Kristian sat down and tucked in.

Herr Wulf vanished into the kitchens while the templar and urchin sat for well over an hour breaking their fast together with the only sounds being the gentle clatter of their cutlery, the chewing of food and the slurping of beer.

Kristian was the first to finish. He pushed back his plate, leaned back contentedly in his chair with his hands on his tiny belly, burped and sighed.

Stefan finally emerged from his breakfast bowl, wiped his mouth with a napkin and turned to Kristian. 'I take it you're here for Vogel?'

Kristian was too full to reply.

As if on cue, the door opened and the spy rolled in.

'Morning, lads,' he said, smiling at the templar and Kristian and giving the boy an added wink.

Kristian smiled and raised a hand.

'Take a seat and help yourself.' Stefan gestured at the food.

Vogel muttered his thanks. 'Well?' he asked the boy as he took a seat.

Kristian shook his head. 'Nothing in the *Viertel*. The lads kept watch all night until it opened this morning. They didn't see a soul.'

Stefan raised a curious eyebrow. 'Is this the job for Gunther?'

Yeah. A small job which turned out to be nothing.'

Vogel had returned to the lodgings he shared with Gunther, to find the old rogue scratching feverishly away on a piece of parchment.

'Ah, there you are,' he said looking up at Vogel. Though his long unkempt brown hair and

281

beard were shot through with grey streaks, and he always looked like he'd spent several days living rough in the woods, Gunther Hahne's eyes still burned with alertness.

'And?'

Vogel shook his head. 'One or two dodgy-looking blokes but no robbers. Do you want me to keep watching the place?'

'Yeah,' Gunther replied. 'How are you going to deal with it?'

Typical Gunther, always testing.

'I'll set my kids to keeping round-the-clock watches on the cemeteries in the Church Quarter and the *Viertel*,' Vogel replied.

The old wolf grinned. 'Sounds like you have the matter well in hand.'

'Whoever's responsible for the thefts, we'll get them.'

'I've no doubt,' Gunther declared. 'How's the hunt for Konrad going?'

'I've got eyes and ears out looking for him everywhere. We'll get him. It won't be long now.'

Gunther placed an understanding hand on his protégé's shoulder and looked him in the eyes. 'I've no doubt of that too. And I'll tell that to Grand Master Heinrich and Bishop Vassiliev.'

'You're off to Marienburg?'

'If you need anything, send word there.'

'Understood.'

'And be careful. Remember,' Gunther said pointing to his eyes, ears and nose. 'Keep 'em peeled.'

'Will do,' Vogel replied. 'You too.'

Gunther smiled and winked before sticking his quill in an inkwell and folding and stuffing the parchment he had been writing on into his shirt. He grabbed his pack and slammed the door behind him.

Vogel sighed. He considered kicking off his boots and putting his head down for an hour but knew that if he lay down now, he wouldn't wake up for hours. Best to return to his templar and get on with the business of finding Konrad and the clergy murderer.

'So,' he said to an intrigued Stefan. 'In order to find Konrad and the murderer of our brethren–'

And Lord Olaf,' Stefan interrupted.

'Quite,' Vogel said, 'we need to do my contacts in the underworld a favour. The getting-off-your-arses-and-cracking-heads type of favour.'

He reached for bread and sausages.

'You're hunting a lord?' Kristian said, wide-eyed and smiling.

'And a sorcerer,' Vogel added.

'Might even be one of the Order of the Magi,' Stefan said.

'Order of the Magi?' Kristian frowned.

'Don't tell me you've never heard of them?' Stefan sat with his fists on his hips in mock outrage. 'How could you not have heard of the Order of the Magi? What kind of schooling have you had?'

'The best!' Kristian replied, winking at Vogel.

'Bloody right. He can crack a lock and cut a purse in a heartbeat and without disturbing a hair.'

'Know my way around the ladies too,' the boy said, puffing his chest out.

'All right. All right.' The templar held his hands up in surrender. 'We get it – you're a *Meister* of vice, but you probably know more about the Order of the Magi than you realise.'

Kristian looked up and cocked his head to one side. 'Well, I know about the Church, of course, the Church Sorcerer wars where there were sorcerers fighting against the Church, but I don't understand why–'

'I see,' Stefan said. 'Do you want the long or the short version?'

'The short,' Kristian and Vogel chorused.

'A few thousand years ago, most of our world was ruled by the serpent people, the isstaloth,' Stefan began. 'They ruled the west and the desert lands of the east up to the borders of the Dragon Empire.'

'The Dragon Empire's real? I thought it was a myth,' Kristian said.

Stefan shook his head. 'No, it's real.'

'And it's ruled by dragons?' Kristian said.

Stefan shrugged. 'The legends say so.'

'And they stopped at the Dragon Empire's borders because they were scared of the Dragon Emperors?'

'According to the Scholars, yes,' Stefan replied.

'Fair enough,' Kristian said. 'So the isstaloth stopped at the western borders of the Dragon Empire. And?'

'Well, they and the other races of this world, the gronoin, d'hazi, nirnihain and saurials–'

'What?' Kristian shot Stefan and Vogel a baffled look.

'You've never heard of the nirnihain, gronoin, d'hazi and saurials?'

The boy shook his head.

'The gronoin were huge, about three metres tall, and said to be made of living rock,' Stefan began.

'Living rock? You're having a laugh,' the boy said.

Vogel and Stefan shook their heads.

'They were real,' Vogel declared.

'How do you defeat something like that in battle?' Kristian mused.

'With great difficulty,' Stefan replied. 'And as for the others, well, the nirnihain were lightning fast, beautiful, and found human flesh a delicacy.'

'Jesus!' Kristian blurted. 'Sorry, Brother,' he said when he saw Stefan glare.

The Teutonic Knight continued. 'As for the others, the d'hazi and saurials, well, they were all powerful in their own way.'

'And they enslaved us,' Vogel said to Kristian.

'Exactly.' Stefan nodded. 'They were superior to us in every way – in arms, war, magic and learning. They could build things that we still can't today and they used us for everything – labour, food, sport, you name it. Their most prized slaves were human sorcerers who called themselves the Order of the Magi.'

'Why?' Kristian frowned.

'They created the name to give themselves an identity,' Stefan explained.

'Go on,' Vogel urged Stefan.

'We had one thing that the other races didn't have – divine magic. We were able to fight them with it, but we were still overmatched. Over time, some of the Order of the Magi, powerful sorcerers, joined the Church in the fight to free us from the isstaloth. The fight became the Church Sorcerer wars. They came to an end a thousand years ago.'

'With the Divine Tempest,' Kristian said.

'Right.' Stefan nodded.

'But what *exactly* is the Divine Tempest?'

Stefan took a pull on his pint before replying. 'Near the end of the war, the Church was losing badly and close to defeat. The isstaloth and their allies were still awesomely powerful, especially with their magic, and the Church was desperate. In their hour of need, the Holy Father, Gregorious the Seventh, had a revelation and gathered all the clergy in the west, and near east, in the Holy City. There, he led them in prayer and they summoned the Divine Tempest – a hurricane, formed of angels, which swept through the west and deserts of the east collecting up the isstaloth and their allies and took them through a magic Gate in the Holy City to another world. They became known as the Exiles and their banishment signalled the end of the Church Sorcerer wars. The Church had won.'

'But there were still members of the Order of the Magi around?' Kristian said.

'Only the apprentices and junior sorcerers, and they surrendered immediately to the Church.'

'What happened to the senior sorcerers?'

'The Divine Tempest took a lot of them. We burned the ones that remained, that we found,' Stefan growled.

'Not all the isstaloth and their allies were taken by the Divine Tempest, Kris,' Vogel added. 'Some managed to remain behind, but the Church hunted them down. If any exist today, they are well and truly hidden.'

'Interesting! And what happened to the apprentice sorcerers of the Order of the Magi?' Kristian asked Stefan.

'The Church showed them clemency. It forbade them from summoning demons and let them settle in the far west, in the ruined cities of the isstaloth, but only after the Church had seized the isstaloth's powerful sorcery, devices and inventions. We didn't want the Order of the Magi using these against us.'

'Why would they?' Kristian asked. 'They surrendered, didn't they?'

'They may have surrendered,' Vogel said, 'but they never stopped hating the Church for taking away their masters, and with them, access to powerful sorcery. Since then, the Magi have been scheming and plotting against the Church and seek to return the Exiles to this world.'

'Wait a minute!' Kristian slapped his forehead as the light of understanding dawned. 'Those sorcerers that sided with the Church, the Order of the Magi, *they* became the kings and queens of the west and Araby! And the strongest of *them* became the first Emperor of the Holy Empire.'

'That's right,' Stefan said.

'And you think one of them, the Order of the Magi, could be responsible for the clergy murders? They want revenge against the Church for the Exiles?'

Vogel shrugged while Stefan looked grim.

'Maybe,' the spy said.

'Seems mad to hold a grudge for a thousand years.'

'Not all sorcerers are sane,' Stefan replied.

'Which explains why our sorcerer is hunting clergy,' Vogel said.

'And we'll know who it is soon enough. Vogel's contacts are about to bring us a step closer to catching our killer,' Stefan said.

'Hopefully.' Vogel grinned.

'So, what do you need?' Stefan asked the spy.

'I'll need some extra fighters from the Order, older grizzled types, the more injuries and scars, the better. You need to assemble them at the south bridge barbican entrance to the South Bank a bit later.'

'I can gather about a dozen. How's that?'

'Perfect,' Vogel said. 'Oh, one other thing. Try and pick *really* big lads and lasses. Like yourself.'

'There's no one as big as me!' the templar said, winking at Kristian.

'Kristian, go to the *Viertel* and find my "uncles." Tell them I'm coming to deal with their problem and I need to know *his* whereabouts. They'll know what you mean.'

'All right, Vogel.'

'When you have the info, meet me later–'

288

'I know, I know,' Kristian said. 'At the south bridge gatehouse entrance to the South Bank.'

Vogel smiled. 'Good lad. Take care.'

Kristian grabbed another chunk of bread and a sausage and fled.

'Where to now?' Stefan asked.

'To the Franciscan abbey.'

'To question the gate guards and examine the bodies of Fathers Pohl and Dieter,' Stefan said.

'And to look in on Julian. If he's able to talk, he may tell us about his attacker.'

'Right then.' Stefan pushed back his stool and stood up.

'Steady on there, big fella!' Vogel said. 'You may be ready to chase off, but I haven't had breakfast.'

Stefan sighed and slumped back onto his seat.

Vogel crammed a piece of greasy sausage into his mouth and grinned at the templar.

Chapter 22

Vogel and Stefan were met at the Franciscan abbey by an old man with the kindest face the spy had ever seen.

'Ah! Young von Stern, isn't it?'

'Yes, Brother Gerome, it is.' Stefan and the old monk embraced.

'Oh!' The old monk winced in mock pain. 'What have they been feeding you?'

Heretics – lightly sautéed, Vogel thought.

'A steady diet of *Meister* Arnold's fencing lessons,' Stefan replied with a raised chin.

'And how is he? I rarely see him these days.'

'Fine, and he sends his greetings. The Order's affairs keep him busy, I'm afraid, especially current events.'

'Yes, yes, very true.' Brother Gerome shook his head, his face sober. 'Anyway, it gladdens my heart to hear that he's well. And who is this?' He stared at Vogel, who took off his hat and bowed.

'Vogel, Brother. Agent for the Order.'

'Are you indeed. Is that what they call spies these days?' The old monk smiled and winked at Vogel. 'Well, boys, what can I do for you?'

'We're investigating the deaths of Father Pohl and Father Dieter,' Stefan said.

Brother Gerome smiled approvingly. 'Good. I always thought you should be learning how to hunt sorcerers.'

'The Order thinks so too - that's why they paired me with him.' Stefan jerked a thumb at Vogel.

Brother Jerome clapped Stefan on the shoulder in approval. 'Good. Now, what do you need?'

'We'd like to start by seeing where the Fathers were found and to talk with whoever found them,' Stefan said.

'Father Pohl was found by his novice, Pieter,' Brother Gerome replied.

'Can we speak to him and Father Dieter's novice?' Stefan said.

Brother Gerome's face grew serious. 'I'll send word to Pieter to meet you in the refectory but as for Markus, Father Dieter's novice, I'm sorry, boys, he disappeared a few days after Father Dieter's death.'

'We weren't told about this,' Stefan said before he and Vogel exchanged a look.

'I believe the Trinitarians are looking for him,' Brother Gerome said.

Vogel and Stefan exchanged another look which wasn't lost on Brother Gerome.

'Now wait a moment,' he began. 'If you're thinking that young Markus had anything to do with Father Dieter's death, you'd better think again. He was a gentle and sensitive soul - that's why Father Dieter chose him for an assistant. They were also very close, and he took Father Dieter's death very hard.'

'Which may explain his absence, Brother, but it doesn't look good – absconding after a murder,' Stefan said.

'How would having a sensitive assistant help Father Dieter with his work?' the spy asked the monks.

'Father Dieter and Father Pohl were seers and witch hunters,' Brother Gerome clarified, grateful for the change of subject. 'And having a sensitive nature helps with certain kinds of divine magic, especially with magic used to perceive dark forces.'

'Oh,' Vogel said.

'Not to mention,' Brother Gerome added, 'Markus had the gift for healing divine magic and was being trained by Father Dieter.'

'What about Pieter? Was his divine magic as strong as Markus'?' Stefan asked.

The old monk shook his head. 'Not as strong in healing as Markus but his offensive divine magic was strong indeed. One of the strongest we've ever seen. He was being groomed for the witch hunters.'

'Which is why Father Dieter chose to live among Franciscan monks,' Vogel said. 'The Franciscan and Benedictine Orders are the Church's greatest healers. Father Dieter wanted Markus to train with them and with him, at the same time. Is that right, Brother?'

'Yes, Vogel.'

'So he fled because he had a delicate disposition, Brother Gerome, is that what you're saying?'

Brother Gerome sighed and shook his head. 'I don't know, but my instincts say – yes. I can only assume he fled in fright. He must have seen something so terrifying his delicate nerve shattered and he ran.'

'Couldn't he have used his magic to defend himself?' Vogel asked the monks.

'His focus in divine magic was healing. He just couldn't produce offensive divine magic,' Brother Gerome said.

'I can see why Father Dieter chose to live among the Franciscans, but why did Father Pohl do the same? Were the Fathers close?'

'Yes, they were,' Brother Gerome replied. 'They were very close, the best of friends, and had travelled the world together fighting the supernatural and lending aid.'

Stefan looked at the spy and raised an eyebrow as if to say, *Do you have anything else to ask?*

Vogel shook his head.

'Can we have a look at their chambers now, Brother?' Stefan asked. He felt that they had bombarded old Brother Gerome with enough questions for the time being.

'Of course. Follow me,' the old monk said, leading the way.

***

Father Pohl and Father Dieter's chambers were sparsely furnished but neat and clean, reflecting the humility of both clerics.

Though the witch hunters and Trinitarians had already gone through the rooms with a fine-tooth comb, Vogel and Stefan searched them thoroughly but it yielded no clues, other than it appeared that neither clerics put up any kind of resistance as there were no broken or damaged items.

The doors, Vogel and Stefan noted with interest, were also undamaged, which indicated that their attacker was a familiar figure. With nothing else to observe, they trooped off with Brother Gerome to the refectory to meet with Pieter, the late Father Pohl's novice.

Pieter was waiting for them, sitting on a bench, staring into space, his leg trembling with nervous energy. He stood up, hands hidden in the folds of his habit, when the templar and spy walked in.

'Vogel, Stefan, this is Pieter, Father Pohl's novice.' Brother Gerome made the introductions. 'Give them your every co-operation, my boy,' Brother Gerome said to Pieter.

'Yes, Brother,' the skinny young novice replied, swallowing nervously.

'I'll be in my chambers when you've finished,' Gerome said before he departed.

'We'll see you later, Brother,' said Stefan. 'Now then, Pieter, tell me what happened.'

They seated themselves opposite the novice and tried not to be too intimidating.

Pieter sat too but his blue eyes were so wide and his face was pale. Vogel thought that the boy was going to faint.

So did Stefan. He reached for a jug of ale, poured the novice a cup and motioned for him to wet his palate before he started.

Pieter took a mouthful and nodded in thanks before beginning his account.

'Well, Brother, Herr Vogel–'

'Just Vogel.'

'On the night in question, we, Father Pohl and I, came back here after Vespers and I retired to my room to read some scriptures.'

'A bit late for reading, wasn't it, Pieter?' Stefan said gently.

'True, Brother. But I wasn't tired.'

'Go on, Pieter, please.'

'Yes, anyway, later, at around midnight, there was a knock on the door and I heard Father Pohl talking briefly to someone and then I heard the door open and close. A few minutes later I went in to ask Father Pohl something and that's when I found him lying on the floor. Dead.' Pieter crossed himself, muttering a prayer.

The templar did likewise.

'Father Pohl was up late too. Is that normal?' Vogel asked.

'Yeah, monks often stay up late reading or scribing,' Stefan interjected.

'Especially Father Pohl,' Pieter added.

'How did you know he was dead, Pieter?' Vogel asked.

'He was lying on the floor and not breathing, so I…I…assumed…'

'I meant, did you touch the body?' Vogel asked.

'No, I…I…for a few moments I couldn't move, then, when I could, I ran to fetch help.'

Stefan understood. The young initiate was not used to seeing corpses.

'Is there anything else, Pieter?' Stefan asked gently. 'Did anyone else visit him?'

Pieter shook his head. 'No, Brother.'

'What about your relationship with Father Dieter and his novice, Markus?'

'I never really got to know Father Dieter that well, Vogel. But Markus and I were good friends.'

'Did you see him after Father Dieter's death?'

'Yes. We were both lost after the deaths of our Fathers.'

'When was the last time you saw him?'

'A little over a week ago. On the night he went missing.'

'You were the last person to see him, then?'

'Yes, Vogel.'

'Pieter, did he see anyone else that day or maybe had a meeting arranged with anyone?'

Pieter shook his head. 'No.'

'The Fathers were witch hunters. Their Order would want to question the Fathers' novices. Have the witch hunters questioned you, Pieter?' Stefan asked.

'Yes,' Pieter said with a gulp. 'At great length. They sent an agent to fetch Markus and me.'

'Who was the witch hunter who questioned you?'

Vogel flicked the templar an approving look and nod. *He's starting to think like an agent.*

'Father Jozef Richter,' Pieter said, licking his lips nervously. 'Thank God.'

'Why would you say that, Pieter?'

'I could've been questioned by one of the other witch hunters, the harsher ones,' the novice said, 'but I was lucky. Father Richter is kind and popular among the novices. We all love him.'

Stefan nodded. 'He's a good man.'

Vogel stared directly into Pieter's eyes and the novice met his gaze, unflinching. The spy could detect no lies there, but he couldn't detect anything else either.

'And who interviewed Markus?' Stefan said.

Pieter shrugged again. 'Sorry, Brother, I don't know.'

'And that was the last time you saw Markus?' Vogel said.

'Yes.'

Stefan looked at Vogel as if to say, *Anything else?*

The spy shook his head.

'Thank you, Pieter,' Stefan said gently. 'You've been a great help.'

The templar indicated the questioning was at an end and the relieved-looking novice rose, bowed and quickly shuffled off.

Stefan was about to stand and follow him when Vogel placed his hand on the templar's arm, causing him to sit back down.

'What?' Stefan said, frowning.

'There's something about that novice that's very off,' the spy said, staring the templar squarely in the eyes.

'What do you mean?'

'He may act scared, but his eyes tell a different story. They seem...'

'What?'

Vogel shook his head, as if in disbelief. 'Hungry.'

Stefan raised his eyebrows. 'Maybe you need a break. Dealing with the supernatural can take its toll on the mind, especially for those not trained to deal with it.'

Vogel sighed. 'Look – I'm not paranoid and seeing demons everywhere. I'm not suggesting that Pieter is the murderer - he's got no burns from Wulfram's Templar's Retribution, but he's not the scared little rabbit that he'd have us believe he is.'

'And this abbey is wrapped in divine blessings which would reveal any sorcery if it was being used to hide his wounds, so he's not our demon.'

'I didn't say he was.'

'So what do you think he is?' Stefan said.

Vogel shrugged. 'I'm simply telling you what I'm trained to spot, just like you're trained to kick in the supernatural, and I'm telling you that, despite the act, Pieter had dead eyes – the sort that I've only ever seen in the most hardened of people – the Rutgers of this world.'

'All right,' the templar said, raising his hands in surrender. 'We raise your concerns with Brother Martin and Bishop Vassiliev. Let them keep an eye on Pieter and we carry on with our hunt. Good enough?'

Vogel nodded.

'Good. Come on,' the templar said, rising and slapping the spy on the shoulder. 'Let's go and see Brother Gerome and examine the late Fathers' corpses.'

'You never know,' Vogel said, cheering up considerably, 'we might find something that others missed.'

'Amen to that.'

The spy and templar took a little detour before returning to Brother Gerome to look in on Julian and talk to the guards who had been standing sentry on the night Fathers Pohl and Dieter were slain.

Julian was still recovering, unable to receive visitors, and the guards on duty that night could not clearly identify who it was. Yes, it could be young Heino or Markus or Konrad, but then it could also be someone else entirely.

Vogel had gritted his teeth in frustration while Stefan had talked to the guards cordially. After a friendly pat on their shoulders, to thank them for their help, the spy and templar had made their way back to Brother Gerome.

'I was wondering when you boys would ask to examine the bodies,' Brother Gerome said excitedly as he led them down the dark winding stone staircase of the morgue, under the Franciscan abbey.

'Why is that, Brother?' Stefan asked.

'Because I examined the bodies when they were first brought down here and made some interesting discoveries which I would like to share with you.'

'You have knowledge of anatomy and physic, Brother?'

'I'm a Franciscan monk, my son. It's what we do, practice medicine alongside our healing magic.'

The morgue was well lit and the pungent smell of preservative chemicals hung heavily in the cool, dry and musty air.

Vogel felt uneasy. Stefan took it in his stride.

The bodies were lying on stone slabs in the centre of the examination room, covered in plain white drapes with the emblem of the Church and the Witch Hunters Order.

Stefan and Brother Gerome bowed their heads, muttered prayers and crossed themselves before the old monk threw back the shrouds to reveal two naked corpses glowing with divine magic, which Vogel knew stopped the bodies from decaying.

'Look here.' He lifted the late Father Dieter's head. Bruising and swelling could clearly be seen on the face of the corpse.

'The blows to the face were designed to incapacitate, not kill,' Stefan declared.

'The murderer wanted the Father alive,' Vogel said, in agreement. 'To hold him and drain his *Vis*.'

'Yes,' Brother Gerome confirmed. 'And then the killer did this.' The monk lowered the shroud to Father Dieter's knees so that they could see the corpse's torso.

Father Dieter was killed by having his guts torn out – the stitching on his abdomen testified to that.

Stefan and Vogel exchanged knowing looks which weren't lost on Brother Gerome.

'You boys know, or strongly suspect, what did this?' He said, smiling slyly at the templar and spy. 'I know *you* definitely do – or should!' he said, pointing at Stefan.

Stefan looked solemn. 'All the evidence we've seen so far, from the other deaths which were similar to the good Fathers,' he gestured at the corpses, 'point to the killer being a demonheart. Those killed had the gift of magic and show signs of

300

having their *Vis* drained from them. Some through the mouth and some from the abdomen.'

Brother Gerome chuckled. 'Well, I'm glad to see you picked up on that. Looks like those lessons weren't wasted on you after all. But it's not really evidence of a demonheart, is it?'

'We thought that this could be the work of a mundane killer dressing up the murders to look supernatural, to make it seem like the Fathers were killed by a demonheart.'

'But we now know the murderer is boosted by sorcery,' Stefan said to the old monk.

'From the attack on Father Hubertus last night,' Brother Gerome said. 'Well, you're quite right in your assessment so far, my boys, but the attacker of Father Hubertus and Martin might not be the killer we're looking for. It might be a sorcerer or a minion and not a demonheart.'

'The Church has examined the good Fathers' bodies and there was no sign of *Vis* in them and faint traces of *Vis* around the mouth,' Stefan said.

'Which suggests sorcery and points to a demon,' Brother Gerome agreed. 'But that's not being as thorough as we should be, is it, Stefan?'

Stefan frowned.

Brother Gerome tutted as he rolled his eyes. 'There's something more, boy,' he said to Stefan. 'Something *everyone's* missed so far. Take a closer look at both bodies.'

The spy gingerly leaned forward. Stefan craned closer still, unaffected by the sight or smell of the bodies.

The only differences Vogel could discern was that Father Dieter had his guts ripped open whereas Father Pohl was strangled and had his neck broken, the bruising around it testified to that.

Brother Gerome waited patiently.

Stefan sang for blessings of Sight and examined the Fathers again, taking time to examine their abdomens, even Father Pohl, whose stomach was intact, as well as their lips.

'Well,' the templar murmured as he slowly scanned the priests' bodies, 'I can confirm there's traces of *Vis* on their lips, consistent with sorcery and no *Vis* in their bodies, again consistent with having it sucked out, and that points to a demonheart. If a demon didn't drain them of their *Vis*, the preservation blessing on the Fathers would have kept it in their bodies. It's exactly the same as the Scholar Aesa and the novice Aelfwine, who were killed the previous night.'

'That's what the monks examining our Fathers' bodies also declared. But corners have been cut,' Brother Gerome said. 'Remember what I taught you of magic and energy in the body, Stefan?'

The templar looked at him before looking back at the bodies.

'By God!'

'What is it, my boy?' Brother Gerome asked. 'What have you discovered?'

Vogel looked at Stefan questioningly.

'The brain!' Stefan cried. 'Their souls have been consumed too!'

'Huh?' Vogel looked at the monks.

'If this hadn't been a demonheart, the soul, which resides in the brain, would still be present,' Stefan explained. 'But it's not–'

'Which means it's been consumed – proof of a demon, of a demonheart!' Vogel said.

'Exactly! One of the trademarks of a demonheart is that it consumes its victims' souls,' Stefan explained.

'Bravo, boys!' Brother Gerome said, clapping his hands together and smiling.

'And we nearly missed it,' Stefan said, wide-eyed with horror.

'Don't feel bad, Stefan. Everyone missed it,' the old monk said with a shrug.

'Pays to be thorough, Brother,' Vogel said to the old monk with a smile and a wink.

'So, now you know that the murderer *definitely* is a demonheart,' Brother Gerome said.

Stefan hugged the old monk, who patted him on the back.

'Thank you for your help.'

The old man cupped Stefan's face. 'My pleasure, my boy.'

'Trying to hunt this creature down is proving challenging, Brother,' Vogel said. 'Any advice there?'

'Subject the entire city to a Smite blessing?' Brother Gerome replied.

Stefan barked a laugh. 'If only!'

'Thanks, Brother,' Vogel said sourly.

'I'm sorry, my lad,' the old monk chuckled. 'I've no idea how you hunt one down, but it sounds as though you boys are closing in on it. Hopefully, it will be easier, now that you know for sure what your prey is.'

'Oh, we know what it is. And it's done far worse than this.' Stefan gestured to the Fathers' corpses. 'And it doesn't discriminate between men and women, boys and girls.'

Brother Gerome agreed. 'A demonheart is a truly evil thing – I hope you boys catch it soon.'

'Yes,' Stefan said softly. 'I thought I'd seen worse...when I was younger...'

Brother Gerome squeezed the templar's shoulder in sympathy.

Vogel raised an eyebrow.

'Yes, my boy. And now you've the chance to hunt these things down, and the sorcerers that summon them, and send the foul lot screaming back to hell!'

'It's not really the demon that's important, though, is it?' Vogel said. 'We need to get the sorcerer that summoned it. I was taught that if you kill a sorcerer, you destroy all its demons as well.' He shot Stefan a smile.

'Quite right. So what now, boys?'

Stefan looked at Vogel questioningly.

'We still continue our hunt for the demonheart, for Konrad, if it even *is* Konrad,' Vogel said.

'And the sorcerer?'

'That's being dealt with,' Vogel said.

'We believe the sorcerer is a member of the clergy,' Stefan said to Brother Gerome.

Vogel shot Stefan a glance which said, *Are you sure he's trustworthy?*

'I've known Brother Gerome since I was a child,' Stefan explained to Vogel. 'I'd trust him with my life. Besides, he no longer practices sorcery.'

'You're a sorcerer, Brother?' *Jesus' hairy balls! Is there anything these fuckers don't get up to?*

'I know the lure of sorcery, but I also know its curse – and I'd never go back to that.'

'Amen,' Stefan said.

'You were a Scholar, Brother?' Vogel raised an eyebrow.

Brother Gerome shook his head. 'With the Order of the Magi, but I left a lifetime ago.'

'I'd like to hear that story.' He smiled at the old man who smiled back.

'Maybe when this is all over, Vogel. Anyway, about this sorcerer. What makes you boys think it's clergy?'

'The evidence,' Vogel replied. 'The resources needed to summon and maintain the demon, point to clergy.'

Brother Gerome pulled a thoughtful face. 'True, it could be clergy.'

'We're hoping it's not,' Vogel said.

'We're praying it's not,' Stefan added.

'Well, happy hunting, boys. If there's anything I can do to help, you need only ask.'

'Thank you, Brother,' they chorused.

'Go with God.'

He walked them to the abbey gates to see them off. He blessed them again and received a warm crushing hug from Stefan and, much to Vogel's

305

surprise and pleasure, a hug from the old monk which left him with a warm feeling. When Brother Gerome smiled, his eyes shone with humour and kindness.

Stefan was right, Vogel decided, *the old monk was a good egg.*

As he walked away from the abbey, watching Brother Gerome standing at the gates and waving at them, somehow, Vogel felt as though he were seeing his old dad again, smiling at them and wishing them well, and that made him feel lighter than he had in a long time.

Chapter 23

'Tell us again why we have to change into these?' Stefan whined, holding up a thick leather cuirass and set of greaves, the type of armour favoured by less wealthy mercenaries.

After the visit to Brother Gerome, Vogel had accompanied Stefan to Marienburg where the templar had burst into the infirmary and stirred the old veterans up with a rousing speech about fighting criminals and punishing the Godless.

Vogel noted it was hardly necessary. When the old boys and girls heard the templar's call to arms they tore off their bandages, tossed away their crutches and almost trampled over each other in their rush to the armoury. Within minutes, they were marching to the *Rittersbrücke Sud*, the south side Knightsbridge, joking and laughing like a merry Sunday picnic outing with Vogel and Stefan bringing up the rear, shaking their heads.

Once inside the *Rittersbrücke Sud* gatehouse, Vogel briefed the group on the job at hand – they were to play the muscle to his racketeer.

Though they listened attentively, Vogel knew from the hungry looks on their faces and the drool at the corners of their mouths, that they were being polite – they didn't really give a fuck who they were bashing as long as they could bash somebody.

Stefan, on the other hand, pulled a face like a kicked arse when Vogel asked him to don his disguise. Nevertheless, after a good grumble, he did as Vogel requested, after which he turned and faced the old templars, who had done the same, and elbowed his way to the front of their ranks. They all turned and faced Vogel, newly dressed and disguised in their "mercenary" leathers.

'How do we look?' Stefan said, cheerfully.

'Hmm.' Vogel cocked his head to the side and cupped his chin as he stared at them.

Something was wrong. They were too clean and neat.

'We're going to have to dirty you up,' Vogel declared.

'What?' Stefan's face fell.

A few minutes later, it was a surly and grimy bunch that left the barbican with a grinning Vogel in the lead.

Yep, that's more like it, he thought. *They looked the perfect thuggish mercenaries!*

'All this just to get information,' Stefan said to Vogel, still scowling.

'That's how the game works,' Vogel said with a shrug. 'We do this for Lutz, Mikael and Felix–'

'I know, I know. They give us the information we want.'

'It's not just about that,' Vogel said.

Stefan looked at him with a raised eyebrow.

'We do this and we have 'em!' the spy said, holding out his open hand and pointing at his palm. 'Right there! Them, their network, they all become our eyes and ears in the *Viertel. That's* how it works.'

'All right then.' Stefan cracked his knuckles and pulled a truly evil face. 'Let's go be villains.'

Toby Steinaugen had been holding court at the Fallen Angel every other *Freitag*, according to the information Vogel's "uncles" – Lutz, Felix and Mikael – had fed Kristian.

Vogel was relieved to find the information wasn't wrong.

All conversation ceased when the spy and his muscle entered the dimly lit tap room, which was shrouded in shadow. Coupled with the dense fog of pipe smoke in the air, the room provided the perfect venue to conduct the kind of transactions that required privacy and anonymity. Not that the clientele didn't take the extra precaution of doing business heavily cloaked and hooded, just to add that extra touch of shadiness to the inn's ambience.

Vogel walked to the centre of the tap room and stood in a pool of lantern light, hooded so that only a part of his goateed face showed.

The regulars knew trouble had walked in, and those not wanting to be part of it rose and beat a hasty exit, leaving behind only witnesses and those about to engage in nastiness.

'Which of you cunts is called Steinaugen!' Vogel growled.

In one corner, a table of men stood up.

Vogel counted fourteen beefy bodies.

The spy's eyes flicked to the side where he saw the bartender slowly reach under the counter for something.

Vogel's arm was a blur as he flicked something at the barman. He was rewarded with the audible *thunk* of his throwing knife burying itself a hair's breadth from the barman's hand where it stood, quivering.

'Keep moving and your wife becomes a widow,' he promised the now pale and wide-eyed bartender.

A figure, its bulk and muscle stretching tight the leather coat of a stevedore, pushed its way to the front of the men that had stood up.

'I'm Steinaugen,' the figure rasped.

Vogel swallowed. Adrenaline was roaring through his veins like a raging river.

That was how he had done it, Vogel realised. Risen to prominence. He had started off working the docks of the *Viertel* and no doubt earned a reputation for being ruthless and handy with his fists. This would have garnered him followers, like-minded tough and brutal enforcers who he made his captains. Together, they had maimed, murdered and threatened their way to their current position.

Steinaugen looked at Vogel and the veterans at his back and snorted.

'You made a big mistake, boy. I'm goin–'

He never finished his sentence.

Vogel's hand flicked twice in rapid succession.

Steinaugen collapsed back, a throwing knife growing out of each eye socket.

Stefan and the templars exchanged looks and approving nods at Vogel's prowess with the throwing blade.

Steinaugen's men turned to a tall brute for guidance. A rangy and lethal-looking enforcer with two shortswords.

'Markus?' one of them growled.

Steinaugen's   second-in-command,   Vogel reasoned.

Markus remained thoughtfully silent. He was no fool and, taking a good look at Vogel and his crew of eager old fuckers, somehow he suspected that the newcomer and his gang were special.

The sight of Stefan with a war pick in each hand and a big grin on his face was enough to convince him that to engage Vogel would only result in unnecessary deaths – especially his own.

And suicide was not on his list today.

'I'll give you a choice,' Vogel said to Steinaugen's men, smiling. 'Join me, or leave now. And when I mean leave, I mean leave the district. If I see you here again, or hear you've touched a hair on the head of my people, I'll have you all gutted.'

'And who are your people?' the leader asked.

'I'm glad you asked,' Vogel replied. He turned and addressed the whole inn. 'All the thieves and beggars south of where *Teufelstrasse* meets *Langenstrasse* and the *Rittersbrückestrasse Sud* now belong to me – the Watchman.'

'That's quite a large slice,' Markus growled.

Vogel jerked a thumb at Stefan. 'I got large bodies to feed.'

Stefan smiled and threw Markus a kiss. 'You wanna dance?'

Vogel turned to the templar with a raised eyebrow. *Well, someone's getting into their role.*

Markus ignored Stefan and turned back to Vogel. 'Why should I serve you?'

Vogel pointed at Steinaugen's corpse. 'The king's dead, in case you hadn't noticed.'

Markus turned to his men, a couple of whom nodded before he turned back to Vogel. He paused for a moment before he shook his head and spat. He walked out with seven of his cronies in tow.

Vogel turned to the remainder.

'What about you lot?' he said.

They exchanged glances before one of them turned to Vogel and smiled.

'Long live the king!' he said.

Those with him mumbled his words.

Vogel smiled at them. 'Welcome to the Watch.'

He told them to sit, relax and have a drink. He'd introduce them to their new commanders later. He then gestured to Stefan and the group who commandeered a corner of the inn.

Vogel then motioned to Feelix, Lutz and Mikael, who had been watching the whole affair from another corner, to join him. 'I've kept my end of the agreement,' he said to them as they settled into chairs opposite him. 'Now, what about you?'

'We haven't found the boy yet, Vogel, but we have located Max Dietz,' Lutz whispered.

'It's only a matter of time before we locate the boy, Vogel,' Feelix promised. 'And now that we have more…manpower, I'm sure we'll find him, or find out what's happened to him.'

'Good. Now drink up and then I'll introduce you to your new guards and enforcers.' Vogel said, looking at Steinaugen's thugs and the Watchman's newest recruits.

Lutz, Mikael and Feelix exchanged looks and then turned to Vogel. And grinned.

It was a different group that made its way back to the *Rittersbrücke Sud*.

Stefan walked with a spring in his step as he strode along the *Viertel's* cobbled streets, but he was the only one. The rest of the group marched along with faces as smouldering as the burnt-out and ruined buildings that surrounded them. Whenever Vogel looked at any of the old boys and girls, he was met with menacing snarls on wrinkled old faces.

The spy had gradually fallen back until he fell into step beside Stefan.

The templar placed a sympathetic paw on his shoulder.

'Will you apologise to them for me?'

Stefan smiled as one of the old templars turned and glared at him, muttering all too clearly about being cheated.

They were right, Vogel said to himself with a sigh and shrug. He had promised them action and had failed to deliver.

A disturbing thought suddenly crept into his mind.

'They're not going to do anything to me, you know, because I didn't give 'em the violence I promised?'

'No! I'll make sure they're appeased,' the templar said.

'How?'

'By telling them that you *will* deliver on your promise, soon,' Stefan said.

313

'And how the fuck am I supposed to do that?'

Stefan shrugged before slapping Vogel on the shoulder. 'I'm sure you'll work something out, Herr Schlosser.'

Stefan suggested that they first seek out Brother Arnold Guerk and inform him of their progress when they returned to Marienburg.

Vogel groaned but agreed.

They found the *Komtur* in one of the High Castle's spacious gyms, exercising with the two-handed greatsword, or *zweihander*.

'Stefan!' He greeted his favourite student and protégé warmly with a hug while Vogel received a grunt and a dirty look.

'What news?' Arnold asked Stefan.

'Good, for a change, *Meister*,' Stefan replied, a big grin plastered across his beautifully tanned and square-jawed face. 'Today we killed two birds with one stone. We took down a very powerful racketeer, Toby Steinaugen, who ran the thieves and scumbags in the south west of the *Viertel*.'

'And the other?' Arnold said, smiling approvingly at Stefan's news.

'We have Maximillian Dietz's location,' Stefan said.

'You believe you can learn something useful from this Dietz about Konrad?'

Vogel shrugged. 'We're hoping Dietz can shed some light on Konrad, maybe even help us locate the boy.'

'Well, let's get to it then!' Brother Arnold roared. 'Oh, and Stefan, excellent work. I knew you had it in you.'

'You're welcome,' Vogel murmured, staring at the gym's ornate ribbed vault ceiling.

'When are you going after Dietz?' Arnold asked them.

'As soon as we've informed Grand Master Heinrich and Bishop Vassiliev of our developments in the hunt for Konrad,' Stefan said.

'Good,' Arnold declared. 'Let's go and give them the good news and then I'll grab my armour. I'm coming with you. I've been idle long enough. It's time I lent my sword arm to yours, eh, boys,' the old dog said, slapping Stefan's arm.

Stefan turned and beamed at Vogel. 'Isn't that great?' The templar almost bounced up and down with excitement at the prospect of having his mentor along.

'Yeah,' Vogel said, unenthusiastically, as he trailed after Brother Arnold and Stefan. 'Fantastic.'

***

'Come!' Heinrich said when Arnold knocked on the door of his study. 'Arnie, gentlemen.'

The Grand Master was not alone. He and Bishop Vassiliev faced each other across a chess board.

The bishop looked up. 'I can tell by the look on your faces you have news regarding Konrad and the deaths of our Fathers, yes, gentlemen?'

Before either could reply, Arnold stepped forward. 'We were just going to question a key suspect now, my lord – the racketeer Maximilian Dietz.'

'The one you suspect kidnapped Konrad?'

'Yes, my lord,' Vogel replied. 'We hope we'll learn more about the events concerning Konrad's capture and escape once we speak to Dietz.'

'And maybe we'll be able to determine if Konrad is the Demonheart or not,' Stefan added.

'And we came to inform you and the Grand Master,' Arnold said, looking at Heinrich.

'He's at a brothel, the Blue Mermaid, in the *Viertel*, *Hochmeister*,' Stefan added.

'Good work, both of you,' von Wilnowe said.

'They might need some extra help with this one, Grand Master,' Arnold added, 'so I thought I might go and lend a hand?'

Heinrich pointed a warning finger to his old friend. 'Keep sharp. Cornered rats fight hard.'

Bishop Vassiliev rose. 'May the blessings of Almighty God go with you, gentlemen,' he intoned.

'Thank you, my lord,' the group chorused.

Chapter 24

The carters were out in force in the *Viertel*, clearing houses of corpses before marking the doors with red crosses so the clergy and workmen in the area would know which buildings were empty. As soon as the bodies had been removed, the homeless scrambled to occupy the buildings, which meant rusty knives in filthy alleys and yet more bodies for the carters.

Shelter was just the beginning of their problems as the poor of the South Bank appealed to the Church and Teutonic Order for food. The authorities were doing their best to aid the starving but were overwhelmed by the sheer number of mouths they had to feed.

As they marched through the district yet again, Vogel noted the lack of rats and cats and wagered Stefan that they were either boiling in the residents' pots or sizzling over their fires.

Stefan grimaced when he heard that and stared grimly at the hollow faces of the people they passed. For their part, the residents glared back at the group with unashamed hunger, those that weren't lying on the ground in the grip of fever or throwing up their stomachs into the gutters.

After the double-punch of fire and famine, disease now swept through the district, flooring any survivors.

Vogel shook his head. The inhabitants of the *Viertel* were feral at the best of times, but now they would be desperate enough to kill anyone who didn't travel with a significant amount of protection.

The spy marched warily through the eerie smoke-shrouded streets, alert for ambush by ruthless gangs.

'We're here,' Stefan said to the group. The excitement was evident in his voice and his eyes blazed with desire.

The Blue Mermaid was a typical Rittershafen pub – a two-story brick and timber affair on the corner of *Dunkelmesse* and *Hoffmannstrasse*. Before the fire it would have bubbled with raucous life, but now the doors and windows were barred shut and painted with black crosses to warn people away. Only a few surviving whores were left to cater to a select list of clientele–Rittershafen's master thieves and most prominent scumbags. The kingpins of the city's underworld.

The templars, cloaked and hooded, moved into the shadows of an alley opposite the brothel and waited while Vogel slipped away to reconnoitre the building.

They didn't have to wait long for him to reappear.

'Is he there?' Arnold asked.

'He's on the first floor.'

Arnold and Stefan hefted short war picks from under their cloaks.

'Vogel, you and six of the brethren go round the back. Stefan and I will take the rest and go in the front. Questions?'

There weren't any.

'Let's go then!'

***

If someone had blown the doors off their hinges, the effect would not have been far removed from the chaos Stefan and Arnold caused as they stormed through the front doors. Naked women either bolted or froze in terror as screams echoed through the building at the sight of the templars in their full plate armour with the Order's distinctive surcoat, brandishing evil-looking tools of war.

Thieves and older gangsters with no stomach for a fight also made a dash for the exits. They tugged on their pants and grabbed shirts before they tumbled out of windows in their desperation to escape.

And then, from nowhere, the brothel's muscle suddenly appeared, wielding clubs and short swords.

The templars roared as they leaped to meet them.

Stefan ripped a thug's gut wide open, spilling his stinking innards on the floor. His scream lasted only a moment before the templar mercifully slammed his off hand pick into his enemy's heart and he died with a geyser of blood bursting from his mouth.

Two dull clangs rang out as a short sword and club bounced off the giant templar's armour.

Stefan tore his pick from the man he had just slain and whirled and smashed his helmeted head into another guard, whose face exploded like a pulped melon. He reeled back, clutching and

319

screaming at the bloody ruin that had once been his nose before Stefan swung his pick at the man's head, sending him flying into tables and chairs with one side of his head caved in.

Stefan barged the remaining thug who tried to stand his ground, but he might as well have tried to stand against a thundering warhorse. The effect would have been the same.

Stefan's three-hundred-and-twenty-pound bulk of armour, muscle and momentum slammed his opponent back against the wall with a sickening crunch. As the thug struggled to right himself, Stefan stood back and planted a pick into the crown of his foe's head. Blood exploded, splashing the wall crimson as the thug sank to the floor.

Stefan ripped his pick from the dead man's skull with grind and crunch of bone.

He turned and saw his mentor busy engaging three guards as the other templars fought furiously with the remainder of the brothel's muscle.

Stefan would have helped, but facing him now were five grim-faced men armed with maces.

Plenty for all! Stefan grinned before he hurled himself at them.

***

Vogel's entrance was markedly different to the Teutonic Knights. He waited for his cue to enter and, at the sounds of the templars crashing through the front door and ensuing screams, kicked open the back door and darted inside.

It was only his superb reflexes that stopped him from being trampled by the herd of panicked scumbags and whores.

Vogel flattened himself against the wall. He was about to move when the stragglers stampeded by – a few busty, scantily clad whores pursued by skinny old thieves wobbling on bandy legs.

Vogel raised an eyebrow before moving, nodding to the templars with him as he stole cautiously into the building's interior.

He headed towards the sounds of combat, through a kitchen and hall and into a large drawing room littered with cushions and the torn bodies of the brothel's guards. He was about to breathe a prayer of thanks to the Almighty that the room was empty when its doors exploded open and a dozen armed men burst in.

Vogel raised a knife but before he could hurl it, the templars charged forward, roaring, as they crashed into the thugs.

He paused, ready to provide throwing knife support if needed, but the battle was over in heartbeats as the knights smashed in the faces of their foes with headbutts, warpicks and broad-bladed daggers. When it was over, they turned to Vogel with broad smiles and nods.

He stood with his hands proudly on his hips and took a moment to admire his troops' handiwork before letting out a satisfied sigh. He then sped off to join up with Stefan, Arnold and the rest of the templars.

***

To the casual observer, it would have looked like a chaotic scrum with Stefan bellowing like a behemoth. He flailed wildly and furiously at his foes who ducked and dived as they tried to dodge or parry his picks, with the ring of their clubs and short swords clanging off his armour.

The trained eye would have picked out the speed, accuracy and power of the templar's blows which pounded his five foes into mush in a matter of heartbeats. Only one of them managed to grapple him in an attempt to wrestle him to the floor.

Vogel walked in to see Stefan flip a man over his shoulder and plant his pick in the man's face, which was met with a piercing shriek, violent spasm and fountain of blood before the enforcer lay still.

The templar twisted his pick free and turned, expecting more foes, but the battle was over.

He dragged off his helm and regarded the scene – a wreckage of tossed cushions and scattered bloody bodies of the brothel's henchmen.

The templars' armour was caked with the blood of their foes, their huge chests heaving from the exertion of combat.

Arnold pulled off his helm and turned to Stefan and his brethren who hadn't bothered with helms. They all grinned. There were no losses on their side, just bruises.

Vogel grimaced at the carnage.

Floorboards creaked above their heads.

Movement.

The group looked up, exchanged glances, and dashed upstairs, Arnold in the lead, Stefan hot on his heels and Vogel bringing up the rear.

Vogel barked the location of the room and Arnold crashed through the door.

***

It was a huge room with an equally huge bed. Cowering on one side was a young girl, bed sheet wrapped around her tiny frame. On the bed, semi-naked, sat Maximillian Dietz, the racketeer.

His large once-muscular body had given way to comfortable living and now his bloated belly hung over his britches. His biceps, though still bulging, were generously sheathed in fat.

His bald tattooed head and bearded face twisted into a sneer when he saw the templars and he raised his meaty fists – out of each a d'hazi black powder pistol sprouted.

There was a fizz, a bang and smoke with the strong acrid tang of gunpowder and the sound of two dull pings.

The smoke cleared to reveal a grinning Arnold who tapped his breastplate. '*Heiligesstahl*, Max!' he said and lunged forward with the speed of a striking cobra. His gauntlet closed like a metal vice around Max's throat.

The racketeer tried to struggle but another pair of steel vices grabbed his wrists, pinning his arms as Stefan held him fast.

A group of the templars had gathered outside the room to watch the show as the rest looted the building.

Vogel stepped forward. 'Hello, Dietz. Tell us about the boy you kidnapped, the young novice, Konrad.'

'Konrad?' Dietz struggled to fit a face to the name. 'Nah, don't know the boy. Got loads of 'em, Vogel. Yeah, that's right - I know who you are, mate.'

Vogel raised an eyebrow and snorted. 'Are you serious? Do you think that I'm scared of a cunt like you? If I thought for a moment that you were any kind of threat, I'd have you, and everyone you know, even your fucking dog, scrubbed!'

The racketeer glared at Vogel and then, as suddenly as it had flared up, the fire of defiance in his eyes sputtered and went out.

'I had the boy. I was keeping him safe.'

'It means he kidnapped Konrad,' Vogel clarified to the templars.

'Do we really pay these scum ransom for kidnapped novices?' Stefan asked Vogel and Brother Arnold.

Dietz barked out a laugh. 'Is he for real?' he asked Vogel, nodding at Stefan. 'Course the Church pays for their novices. Boys and girls with the gift of divine magic – worth a fucking fortune.'

'So you kidnapped him – Konrad?' Vogel said.

Dietz glared at Vogel again. 'Course I did.'

'How did you do it, Dietz. Tell us,' Vogel pressed.

Max Dietz frowned in confusion. 'Why d'you wanna know that?'

Arnold stepped forward and cuffed the racketeer across the jaw, drawing a trickle of blood.

Dietz snorted in defiance and spat a glob of bloody phlegm on the wooden floor.

'Answer him,' Arnold growled.

Dietz took a moment to glare at the Teutonic Knight defiantly before turning slowly back to Vogel. 'It wasn't hard to find the boy. He stumbled upon some of my lads - I was actually with 'em when he comes rolling along. Thought he was drunk at first, then realised he was off his head.'

'He was troubled,' Stefan said.

'Probably panicked and not thinking straight,' Vogel mumbled.

'Too right,' Dietz supplied. 'The boy was mumbling and crying like a baby. So I gives him a drink and tries to calm him down, but he insists on leaving. Can't have that now, could I? Not an initiate wearing the robes of the Church and worth a fortune.'

'*If* he had the Gift of magic,' Stefan said.

Dietz shook his head and chuckled. 'Doesn't matter whether he had the Gift or not - the Church always pays for their novices. Gifted ones fetch higher prices is all. Maybe the Fathers really are close to the boys – know wot I mean?' He leered at the templars and gave them a wink.

That earned him two more solid cuffs which split open one of his fat lips and chipped a tooth.

Dietz swore. 'Do that again, you fucker…'

'And you'll what?' Arnold said, moving his face an inch away from Maximillian Dietz's. He grabbed the racketeer by his long black oily beard and jerked his head up.

Vogel placed a gentle hand on Brother Arnold's arm and the templar released his hold on the criminal lord.

'You tried to detain him, and then what?'

Dietz remained silent, breathing hard to control his anger. He was bathed in sweat. 'What do you think?' he snarled at Vogel. 'I stopped the boy, gave 'im a couple of slaps and 'ad my men tie him up.'

Vogel and Stefan exchanged glances.

'And he didn't resist?' Vogel pressed. 'Didn't try and fight back?'

'That weedy little fuck? Don't make me laugh,' Max sneered.

'So what happened after you tied him up?'

'I left him alone with my men. Told them to look after him, properly. Make sure he was well fed, an' all that.'

'At one of your warehouses near the docks in the *Viertel*?' Vogel leaned forward to stare into Dietz's eyes.

Dietz nodded. 'Several nights ago, I sent one of my boys round to check on the lad but he comes back, white as a sheet, nearly pissed himself. Tells me the warehouse was torn up. Some of my boys ripped up like paper dollies. So I goes to have a look and, fuck me, he wasn't stretchin' the truth. The place was a mess – blood and shit everywhere. So I fucked off.'

326

'Do you know who was responsible?' Vogel shot Stefan another look.

'Nah! My boys were torn to shreds. That ain't gang work. I thought it was one of you lot, rescuing your own.' Dietz nodded at the templars.

'One?' Vogel asked curiously. 'What makes you say that?'

''Cos I only saw one set of bloody footprints leading away.'

Vogel was pleased. It confirmed his and Stefan's findings when they had visited the warehouse.

'Thought a templar like him,' Dietz nodded at Stefan, 'had attacked the place, butchered my lads, chucked the boy over his shoulder and strolled back to his monastery, humming a hymn.'

'It wasn't us,' Stefan said.

'Well, I know that now, don't I?' Dietz growled.

Arnold moved forward to strike the racketeer but stopped when Vogel shook his head. He backed off, swearing.

'What else, Dietz?' Vogel pushed. 'There must've been other signs. What about after? Do you know where the boy went? You must have had your people look for him.'

Dietz stared Vogel in the eyes and shook his head emphatically. 'Like I said, I only saw one set of bloody footprints leaving the area. No idea where the boy went after. He disappeared and no way I'm chasing that. Lost enough already.'

'Bollocks!' Vogel spat.

'Liar!' Arnold roared.

'Why would I lie?' Dietz roared back.

'Because you want to pay the boy back personally for the deaths of your men and because you're a cunt!' Vogel snarled in Dietz's face.

'Fuck off!' Dietz growled.

Vogel and the templars exchanged looks.

Stefan asked. 'What do we do with him?'

'Take him in for kidnapping,' Vogel replied. 'Throw him into a dark hole with a couple of desperate men who haven't fucked anything in years, except rats, and let them have their fun with him. Or maybe, give him to the Dominicans and let them "interrogate" him. How does that sound, Max? Not your lucky day today, is it, you greasy cunt!' Vogel growled at the racketeer.

'Oh, I dunno, Vogel,' Dietz replied. 'I'm a sharp bloke. I'll be out eventually and then I'll settle *all* my debts! Understand, Vogel?'

Vogel snorted. 'I'm trembling.'

'Mind you, I probably won't have to. Whoever's tearing up my boys is probably the same fuck that's doing in your priests.' The racketeer laughed. 'Good on 'em, I say. I don't mind losing a few men as long as it means less interfering old, perverted wankers around. Trying to make my men honest and Godly while they diddle the novices. Thank fuck they're gone. Good riddance, I say!' Dietz chuckled, a quiet wheezing laugh, his huge gut wobbling up and down, a large grin painted across his dirty, bearded face. 'I wish I could meet the killer – I'd buy him a round.'

'You've heard of the deaths of our Fathers?' Stefan asked, fury burning in his eyes.

'All the underworld has,' Max jeered.

'What do you know of the deaths?' Vogel whispered to the racketeer.

Max shrugged, grinning. 'Nuffing.'

Vogel turned to Arnold and Stefan and saw Max Dietz's death sentence written in their eyes.

'You're an arrogant arse, Max,' Vogel whispered to the racketeer, shaking his head, as he backed up.

'Max Dietz,' Arnold intoned formally. 'You have been found guilty of kidnapping, racketeering, murder and transgressing against the Church. As a Knight of the Order and *Komtur* of Marienburg, with jurisdiction and law over the city and surrounding lands, I exercise my right as a Holy Servant of God and the law, and as a judge, to pass sentence on you. For your crimes against the people of the City, God and the Order, you are hereby sentenced to death. And may the Lord have mercy on your soul.'

The grin vanished. 'I just told you, templar, I didn't...' Dietz sounded desperate.

Arnold drew his poniard...

...Max started to struggle...

...and placed it against Max's eyeball.

Max began to scream...

...and thrust it through his eye. His body bucked with a single sharp jerk before Stefan released him and Dietz's corpse slumped to the floor.

Vogel turned to Arnold. 'He didn't do it. He didn't kill our Fathers.'

Arnold shrugged his broad shoulders and wiped his poniard clean on Max's trousers.

'And? We did *Rittershafen* a service today by exterminating this vermin.' He gestured at the dead racketeer with his dagger before sheathing it.

Vogel looked at Stefan, but there was no remorse there. The Teutonic Knight had loved Father Pohl and Father Dieter and all the slain clergy. They were his family.

He turned to the old templars outside, who gave him toothless smiles and thumbs up.

Stefan slapped his arm. 'There you go - you're back in favour with them.' He smiled at the retired templars. 'Debt paid,' he said as he accompanied Arnold out.

Vogel cast a last glance back at Dietz's corpse, shook his head and followed the clanking templars downstairs and out of the brothel.

Chapter 25

Arnold Guerk headed back to Marienburg to inform Heinrich of the racketeer's death and gather together Bishop Vassiliev, Brother Martin and Gunther.

Vogel wanted to inform the group of their findings thus far – that they had questioned Maximilian Dietz and discovered that Konrad Stich hadn't slaughtered Dietz's men at the warehouse. He was also innocent of the murder of the clergy, although whoever or whatever had murdered Dietz's men had taken the boy.

In the meantime, Vogel and Stefan headed towards the Church Quarter.

'Well, at least we know one thing for sure,' Stefan said.

Vogel nodded. 'Konrad Stich is not the demonheart – if he was, he'd have ripped Dietz apart when they kidnapped him. It could only be the demonheart that took him - the question is, why? And how did it know where he was?'

'Lord knows how it found Konrad, but it's a safe bet it took him to feed on his magic.' Stefan crossed himself and muttered a prayer.

Poor bastard. 'Lord, I could really use a drink!'

'Don't blaspheme,' Stefan said with a sidelong glance at the spy. 'But, yeah, amen to that.'

They ducked into the Grim Reaper to feed and water while they considered their next course of action. They had only just walked into the inn, savouring the smells of beer and food wafting from the kitchen, when a small figure approached them.

Franz Luber's only greeting was to sneer at them. 'A message came for you from the Franciscan abbey.'

'Afternoon, Franz.' Vogel smiled cheerfully.

Luber snorted and then gave Stefan a wary look.

'What *is* your problem?' Vogel drew closer to the little man. 'Have we offended you in some way?'

Luber looked as though he wanted to say a lot but instead stared at Vogel in silent contempt.

'Do you want the message or not?'

Vogel sighed.

'The child is conscious – I was told you'd understand what that means.'

'Thanks, Franz.'

'Vogel?'

'What?'

'What does that mean – "the child is conscious?"' Luber's sneer was replaced by fascination.

Vogel raised a surprised eyebrow. 'Why would I tell you that?'

'Because we're on the same side. Besides, I may be able to help.' Luber looked between the spy and templar.

Vogel was about to tell the little man to go fuck himself when he stopped, folded his arms and stood staring at Franz Luber thoughtfully.

'What?' Franz looked down in case there was pigeon shit on his clothes.

'I propose an information share – I'll tell you about the child and you tell me something juicy, something you've discovered in your investigations.'

'Done!'

Vogel exchanged a surprised glance with Stefan before Luber indicated the trio should sit.

Stefan nodded to Herr Brolle that they would like beer and food brought as the group huddled around a table beside one of the common room hearths.

'You first,' Vogel and Luber chorused.

Vogel pulled out a coin and tossed it into the air. He caught it and slapped it on the back of his hand. Luber called and when the spy uncovered the coin, the little man grinned.

Vogel cursed.

He exchanged an unhappy look with Stefan before turning back to Luber with a sigh. 'The child is one of my eyes and ears. He was attacked by the murderer of the clergy and left for dead.'

'But he survived,' Stefan added. 'We managed to get him to the Franciscans in time.'

'And he may have information on the murderer,' Luber mused.

Stefan and Vogel nodded.

'Your turn,' Vogel said to the little man.

'Not with him here.' Luber glanced at Stefan before turning back to Vogel. 'This is between agents, between you and me.'

Stefan rose, held up his hands and wordlessly seated himself some distance away from the agents. Any affront he might have taken at Luber's demand swiftly melted when his food arrived – loaves of steaming bread and mutton stew accompanied by platters of smoked sausages, cheese and butter. He decided that Luber and his secrets could go and fuck themselves while he dived into his meal.

Vogel watched him eat with a smile on his face. It didn't take much to please Stefan von Stern – good food, better beer and a proper brawl kept him as happy as a pig in shit. He turned back to Franz Luber. 'Well?'

'After the Church seized Silke von Gruenbaum's sorcerous items, she was asked if there was anything else. She denied it, but I know she was lying – I've done this long enough to know. I don't know *exactly* what she's hidden, but I'd guess it's something very valuable and it's somewhere in her ritual chamber.' Luber's eyes were wide.

'And why haven't you gone after it?'

'You don't think I've tried? I have and couldn't find it. Maybe you'll have better luck.' Luber shrugged.

'Why are you telling me this? Why haven't you shared this with Father Richter?'

'Because he would confiscate anything found, whether it's sorcery or money and gems. I'm hoping, one agent to another, you'll reward the information,' Luber said with a sweet smile.

Vogel understood – the little fucker was after loot.

Luber was certainly an agent after his own heart.

'Fair enough. I'll retrieve whatever Lady Silke has hidden and split the treasure with you evenly.'

'I'll drink to that.' Luber raised his mug with a smile. It was the first time Vogel had seen the little agent smile. It made him look like a feeble old man and Vogel suddenly felt deep sorrow for Franz Luber. He shook his head, dismissing his sentimentality.

Franz Luber is a consummate liar and a devious little bastard, he reminded himself.

'One thing, though. This loot - I'm going to make sure that when I go to retrieve it, if anything happens to me,' Vogel jerked a thumb at Stefan, 'he'll know who it was who steered me into danger.'

The smile vanished to be replaced by a look of anger. The real Franz Luber was back.

Stefan's loud belch signalled that the templar had finished dining. He looked at Vogel and formed his hands into a flying bird. It was time they checked on Julian.

Vogel tossed some coins on the table and gave Franz a glare. He rose and nodded to Stefan and the templar necked his beer. The spy grabbed his cloak and hat and, with Stefan in tow, swept hastily out of the tavern.

Chapter 26

'How do you feel?' Vogel asked.

Julian moaned. He was naked and his torso, down to his upper thighs, was bandaged.

'I feel like shit.'

The monk tending to him shot him a stern look for the bad language.

'Sorry, Brother.' Julian cringed.

'God, he's a miniature version of you,' Stefan whispered.

That earned Stefan a rebuking look from the Franciscan brother too for taking the Lord's name in vain.

The templar mumbled an apology.

'You know you look like a mummy.' Vogel smirked.

Julian laughed and immediately clutched his sides as pain lanced through his body. 'Ow! Don't make me laugh, Vogel – it hurts.'

'Is there anything you want?'

'He needs rest,' the Franciscan brother interjected. 'Not excitement.' The brother gave Vogel and Stefan a stern stare before moving to the other patients.

'I could do with some wine, Vogel. The proper stuff nobles drink, none of that weak piss that everyone else has to do with.'

'Yeah, all right,' Vogel agreed, 'but you'll have to earn it.'

'How?'

'Tell me what you remember about the night you were attacked.'

'I saw him, Vogel, the fucker who did this to me. Well, he wasn't really a bloke. He was young and wearing the robes of a novice.'

'Start from the beginning,' said Vogel softly. 'And don't worry about him.' He gestured at Stefan. 'You can trust him.'

Julian nodded. 'We'd gone out for the evening, the gang, to do some thieving, when we spotted this young novice with a Scholar, pretty girl too.'

'Go on.'

'Well, we touched them for some cash and noticed that the novice had a fat pouch so we followed, intending to rob them when we got the chance. We didn't have to wait long. They broke into a chapel in the Church Quarter and started to shag.' The boy flicked a nervous look at Stefan.

'Keep going,' Vogel reassured him.

'We'd just nicked their pouches when another novice appeared, leaping through the chapel's big window. We saw him knock the girl and Jürgen out, but what he did to the novice after that, Jesus, Vogel...' The boy started to sob as he relived the horror of the evening. He choked as tears tracked down his cheeks.

Vogel placed his hand on Julian's face as Stefan moved forward and prayed for blessings of peace and courage. His hand became wreathed in golden energy and he placed it on the boy's forehead as Vogel stepped back.

The sobbing continued for a few heartbeats before Julian's crying subsided. He calmed down and stared at the templar, wide-eyed.

'Have no fear, boy. You're safe here. Go on, tell us what happened next,' Stefan said softly.

'He, the novice that leaped through the window, he went to the other novice, the one that was shag…making love to the Scholar, and ripped out his guts!' The boy was still tearful but nowhere near as upset as he had been.

'And then?' Vogel pressed, gently.

'We legged it. We ran all the way back to Wulfram and when we got there, we were off our heads, laughing and shouting. We thought we were safe. But then he came for us, the novice. He smashed through our bedroom window and just stood there, leering. I swear, Vogel, I've never looked on a face so evil.'

'And then?'

'And then he started tearing out our throats and guts and started ripping arms and legs off. He did it with his hands, Vogel, his hands! And they looked like…like…' He raised his own, forming them into claws. 'Like a beast's, but it wasn't his hands that was the worst thing - it was his eyes. They were like a snake's – yellow with black slits.' Julian started sobbing again. Even Stefan's divine magic couldn't shield the boy from the nightmare of the event.

Stefan and Vogel exchanged another look. Here it was at last – conclusive proof that the murderer was a demon.

'You're safe, boy,' Stefan repeated. 'Finish it now.'

Julian sniffed and took a few moments to compose himself before he continued. 'I fell when he ripped my guts open. Then Wulfram appeared and started to kick and punch it and his hands were glowing – like yours.' The boy pointed to Stefan.

'He was a Trinitarian.'

'He fought hard, did old Wulfy, but the novice was too strong for him and tore his face off. Wulfram fell on me and the novice leaned close to him and started talking to him. I think he was taunting him.'

'What did Wulfram do?'

'Old Wulfy just smiled and then he exploded. His whole body just became golden light. I passed out when Wulfram did that but not before I saw what happened to the novice.'

Vogel and Stefan craned closer.

'Wulfram's light burned him. I saw it! I saw his face burn – I heard him scream – Jesus – I never heard no one scream like that!'

Vogel and Stefan exchanged another look.

'That's it? That's all you remember?' Vogel raised an eyebrow.

'You did well, lad.' Stefan gently squeezed his arm.

The boy's sobs started anew. 'I never want to feel like that again! I never want to feel that scared! I want to join the templars…'

Stefan prayed again, channelling more divine magic. His hand glowed with a fierce golden light that blossomed to completely engulf Julian's small body. The child's hysteria suddenly vanished, his eyelids fluttered and his sobs lessened.

'Sleep, child,' Stefan whispered.

'I want to become a templar,' Julian slurred. 'I want to join the templars. How do I join the templars?'

'Die and be reborn, if you wish to join us,' Stefan whispered, 'as I was. As we all are.'

But Julian was oblivious to the words. He had sunk back into his pillows and entered the embrace of deep slumber.

Stefan walked out of the ward.

Vogel stared at the departing templar for a moment before hurrying to catch up with him.

Chapter 27

Bishop Vassiliev and *Hochmeister* Heinrich were still awake when Arnold Guerk informed them that Vogel and Stefan had important news for them. By the time Arnold returned with Brother Martin and Gunther Hahne, it was well past Compline, and the old friends decided that the gathering was a fine opportunity to catch up and have a proper piss-up.

They had been reminiscing about the good old days for several hours when they were interrupted by a knock on the Grand Master's study door.

Vogel and Stefan entered, and the raucous laughter died instantly, to be replaced by swaying men with grim looks, flushed faces and the occasional hiccup.

'My lord, *Hochmeister*, Brothers, Herr Hahne,' Stefan and Vogel said to the gathering. They received a mixture of slurred greetings and grunts in response, and a hiccup.

'Brother Arnold told us of your success with the racketeer Maximillian Dietz,' Bishop Vassiliev said, with an approving nod.

'Thank you, my lord,' the spy and templar chorused. They exchanged a look before Stefan spoke.

'We learned some valuable things today, and not just from Max Dietz,' Stefan said. 'We are now certain that the murderer *is* a demonheart and that Konrad Stich is not the creature.'

This raised eyebrows and a round of mumbles and hiccups.

Stefan explained how the marks and wounds on Father Pohl's and Father Dieter's corpses could only have been made by a creature with unnatural strength that sucked the *Vis* and souls from their bodies, as it did to the Scholar and novice Aesa and Aelfwine. A divine Sight blessing had revealed this.

Vogel added Julian's account of seeing the demon, in the form of a young man dressed as a novice with snake-like eyes, rip apart the Robins and Wulfram Brenner with taloned hands. This proved without a doubt that the killer was a demon. The spy also added that Julian had witnessed Brenner's Templar's Retribution spell burn the demon which confirmed that they *were* now on the hunt for a young man with burns to the face and body.

'Well done, Vogel, Brother Stefan. I agree with your assessment,' the bishop said, slurring slightly and swaying.

The other men in the room nodded their agreement while the bishop picked up a wine bottle and upended it, but it was empty. He put it down and folded his hands as he stared at the templar and spy.

'We also know from Max Dietz that Konrad Stich was not a demon since Dietz was able to kidnap him,' Stefan said.

The men in the room murmured again.

'Quite!' Bishop Vassiliev said with a hiccup. 'We've heard what happened at Max Dietz's hideout from Brother Arnold.'

'A demonheart would have ripped Dietz apart,' Heinrich continued. 'It is likely that it was the demonheart that took Konrad from Dietz's men at the warehouse and butchered them in the process.'

'It took him for food,' Brother Martin said. 'Poor Konrad, may his soul rest in peace.'

The monk crossed himself and muttered a prayer, causing all in the room to follow suit, except for Vogel.

'That was our conclusion too,' Vogel said to the gathering. 'We think that finding the demon and its sorcerer will lead us to Konrad Stich, whether he's alive or dead, and so we're making the hunt for them our focus.'

'Good,' Heinrich grunted. 'Pass the wine, Vassily.'

The bishop handed the *Hochmeister* his bottle. When Heinrich found it empty, he scowled.

'My lord, gentlemen,' Vogel said, 'I know it's been tried before with Father Hubertus, but I suggest we try to tempt out the demon again.'

The gathering exchanged looks and hiccups.

Vogel cleared his throat. 'I think it'll work, as the demon is in a lot of pain, thanks to Brother Wulfram's spell, and Brother Stefan tells me that the Templar's Retribution can't be cured by sorcery or divine magic. The only way the demon can cure itself is to consume the *Vis* of *powerful* magic users.'

'You really think it'll fall for the same ruse twice?' Gunther said to Vogel and Stefan. 'It was nearly killed last time, so it'll be far more wary.'

'Fair to say,' Vogel said, 'but I think the demon's in so much pain, and is so desperate, it'll take the bait. If it doesn't, it does give us the opportunity to test out a theory I have.'

The gathering exchanged glances and frowns.

'I think I know what he's planning,' Gunther said, 'but let's hear him out anyway.'

'Yes, let's,' Heinrich growled. 'What are you thinking, Vogel?'

Vogel spent the next few minutes laying out his plan, stopping occasionally to embellish on points the gathering wanted clarified. When he finished, Heinrich, Vassiliev, Gunther and Brother Martin rumbled their agreement with approving looks on their faces.

'I see no harm in trying it,' Gunther declared. 'At the very most, it'll only have wasted a week and given these two,' he looked at Vogel and Stefan, 'a bit of a break, which they probably need.'

'Very well,' Bishop Vassiliev declared. 'Vogel, Martin, Gunther, start spreading the gossip and let's see what we catch.'

Gunther raised his glass. 'Luck to you, boys!'

The other men raised their glasses in salute, hiccupping loudly.

Chapter 28

The Three Swords was located at the end of an alley just off *Strasse Des Kunsthandwerker*, the main street of the Artisans District. It had three floors of richly furnished spacious rooms and an arena-sized taproom capable of seating a small army. The real attraction of the pub, however, lay at the back.

The owner of the inn, Bernhardt Lenger, had served as a soldier in the Order for over three decades. He never expected to survive into old age but his tenacity and spirit allowed him to prevail through the years when all his friends had fallen in the Order's numerous wars on far-flung battlefields. Eventually, however, his body had surrendered to age as a dodgy leg and ropey hip had finally forced his early retirement.

In recognition of his loyal service, the Order had generously rewarded the veteran soldier with a substantial retirement bonus, which Lenger spent on purchasing and outfitting the Three Swords. He also added a few exotic extras, and it was *these* additions which really made the ex-soldier a very rich man indeed.

To one side of the common room were a large pair of sturdy double doors carved out of solid oak and reinforced with riveted bands of steel.

Bernhardt hadn't just splashed out on stout doors but had also spent a considerable sum on the muscle guarding them – the largest and meanest money could buy.

He was taking no chances with his wealth, as beyond the doors lay his treasure – a long hall which Lenger dubbed, the "Hall of a Thousand Delights".

It was poetic bollocks, of course.

The first doors on the left and right of the hall led into sumptuously furnished rooms with thick rugs, satin cushions and oil lamps of Arabic design. Here customers could partake of narcotic herbs while enjoying the ministrations of whores dressed to look like the houris of the mysterious Orient.

The sex and drugs were profitable enough, but the *real* earner was the door at the end of the hall which opened into a cavernous room.

Sunk into the floor were two pits where, twice a week, men and women were invited to fight for coin, blood and the baying of the crowd. For the winner, the rewards were huge – accolades, reputation and coin. For the loser it meant a short cart trip to the docks and either the river or the pie shops.

Vogel entered the Three Swords just before sundown the following evening. He had eaten an early supper with Stefan and when the templar had left to attend to his religious and military duties, Vogel had remained in the Bee, drinking and plotting their next move. He had settled back, prepared for an evening of ale and deep thoughts when young Kristian walked through the door.

The boy raised a hand and greeted Vogel with a sloppy smile before he delivered the good news.

Olaf had been located.

Vogel hadn't wasted a moment. He ruffled Kristian's hair, grabbed his hat and cloak and beat a hasty exit.

***

The spy took a seat in a quiet corner of the Three Swords' tap room and nursed a mug of ale while he waited for Bernhardt Lenger to make an appearance. He could have tried to bribe his way past Lenger's guards into the back rooms but knew they were too professional to let that happen.

Ex-Order soldiers. Vogel sighed to himself. There was no breaking that brothers-in-arms bond easily - not that it mattered, he reminded himself. If he needed entry to the back rooms, or to speak with Lenger, he could do so without resorting to skulduggery, because Vogel and Bernhardt went back a *long* way.

Vogel had his first woman when he was fourteen. Her name was Bettina, a local whore, and they liked each other, but there was never any love.

Vogel fell in love for the first time when he was sixteen, and her name was Kerstin Lenger, Bernhardt Lenger's daughter. At the time, Vogel had only just started working for Gunther and his duties were mainly limited to loitering around various dives, picking up bits of information and feeding them back to Gunther or making as many contacts in the underworld as he could, for, as Gunther put it, future use.

His first spy posting for Gunther was to work the wealthy punters who patronised the Three Swords, a lucrative yet dangerous posting as Bernhardt had a reputation among the city's thieves for dealing harshly with cutpurses on his patch. Rumour had it that those who stole from Bernhardt Lenger wound up maimed, at the very least. Repeat offenders ended up floating in the river.

Vogel decided early on that the best way to thieve from the customers at the pub was to earn himself a job and thus a reason to be there, so he started running small errands for the cook. Before long his diligence paid off and he was swiftly promoted to working in the kitchens and from there the tap room. After that it was easy to charm the locals and run small errands for them, earning their trust. Once he had gained their confidence, it was a simple matter to escort drunken patrons home and to listen to their secrets and gossip flowing from loose tongues. It was also the easiest thing in the world to relieve them of a bit of their cash on the way.

Working the customers in this way, Vogel had never been caught. He was loved by the punters for looking after them and when they woke the next morning with their purses slightly lighter, they would put it down to a night of excess. As far as Vogel was concerned, the situation was sweet as he was onto a good earner, as well as a source of intelligence, and the punters and Bernhardt were blissfully unaware of his spying and larceny.

But nothing good lasts forever.

Vogel had been happily working and thieving at the tavern for about six months when he finally met Bernhardt's daughter, Kerstin Lenger.

She had spent the previous three years living with her grandparents in the village of *Königs*hausen, several days' ride from Rittershafen, following the death of her mother, Wictoria, which both she and Bernhardt had taken very hard. On hearing that her father planned to marry Kristen Stein, a local widow and herbalist, she had returned to meet her stepmother-to-be and resume family life with her father.

Vogel could still clearly remember the day she walked through the door.

She was sixteen, tall and slender, with long hair the colour of the setting sun and eyes so clear and blue Vogel could dive into them and never hit the bottom. She was breathtakingly beautiful with curves and bumps in all the right places, and in a few years, she would blossom into the rare kind of woman who captured the hearts of heroes and nobles. This day, however, she had captured the heart of a rogue.

She turned her head, taking in the tavern and its clientele, and when she spied Vogel, gawping at her with his jaw dragging along the floor, she smiled.

She was an angel. Vogel was sure of it. She radiated light and beauty and was the loveliest thing he had ever seen in the world.

All these thoughts chased through his mind at that fateful smile, and Kerstin knew it. But Vogel's response was to turn away, too embarrassed and unsure as to how to react. She giggled at his awkwardness and found it endearing.

Vogel cursed. He had wanted to act cool and mysterious– instead he had acted like an arse.

But just as Vogel was drooling over the fair Kerstin, a figure loomed up behind him and years of finely honed thieving instincts kicked in as he detected the large presence.

He slowly turned his head to find Bernhardt glaring down at him. He managed a weak smile and mumbled an excuse before fleeing with Kerstin's laughter chasing him.

Kerstin Lenger was obviously happy to see her father, but at the same time, her eyes reflected a profound sadness. She missed her mother and returning to the tavern had unearthed memories of her late and much-loved parent.

Vogel noted that, though she was pleasant and polite to her stepmother, there was no warmth towards the woman, and for Kristen Stein, the feeling was mutual, or so it seemed to Vogel.

Kerstin Lenger could have developed into a brat as Bernhardt denied her nothing, yet she matured into the opposite. She was kind and thoughtful and possessed an ocean of charm, so that in no time at all she had the inn's staff won round and the customers long before them. She was also hard-working and conscientious, for whom no chore was too menial. And one fateful morning, as Vogel was cleaning the tap room floor and bar, Kerstin came in with a bucket to help out.

Initially their conversation was limited to the task at hand, but it didn't take long for Kerstin to break the ice and even less time for the young thief to feel instantly at ease. By the time the tavern's front doors were unbolted to allow the early morning stream of thirsty and hungry punters in, the two were chatting away, smiling and laughing like old friends.

And when Vogel eventually left Kerstin to attend to his other duties, he discovered he had also left behind his heart.

Their friendship grew stronger with every passing day and two weeks later Vogel had found that friendship had evolved into something deeper as, one evening, sitting in the beer garden behind the pub, he found himself and Kerstin locked in an embrace, her warm body pressed against his lean chest, stroking her silky hair and kissing her moist lips.

He told her he loved her.

She smiled and giggled. The feeling was mutual.

They smooched and giggled some more. Vogel didn't want the evening to end but alas it did, rudely shattered by Bernhardt's booming voice echoing around the tavern shouting for his daughter.

Vogel kissed her and rose, vowing he would be waiting for her when she woke the next morning. She had kissed him good night and blown him a kiss and said she wouldn't sleep.

He had caught it and bounced home with thoughts of a married life with Kerstin. He imagined them both living in a small house in the city, at first, and then maybe a small cottage in a village. *Königs*hausen perhaps?

Vogel would eventually stop thieving and spying and, having saved up enough money, would buy a small tavern and grow old and fat with Kerstin, watching their children and their children's children grow tall and strong.

He didn't sleep a wink that night, lost in fantasies of love and romance, and when the sun's rays reminded him it was morning, he sprinted back to work as if his heart were a hot air balloon buoying him aloft as he sailed through the streets, his feet barely touching the ground.

His dreamy smile vanished when he entered the Three Swords.

There were no patrons in the tap room, only the servants and cooks. The serving boys looked grim and the girls' eyes were red from weeping.

The inn was closed. Something terrible had happened.

Vogel didn't have to ask. Deep down he knew what had happened. He walked slowly up the creaky wooden stairs that lead to the inn's upper floors and the rooms of the tavern owner, his wife and his daughter.

The door to Kerstin's room was open. Standing at the back of the room was Kristen, the stepmother, dressed in solemn black, her head bowed in grief and prayer.

Kneeling beside the bed, his body shaking as he sobbed, was Kerstin's father, Bernhardt. Standing opposite him was old fat Father Reimer praying over the body.

Vogel stood at the threshold of the room not daring to enter, as if his presence would soil the

352

girl's holy shrine. All he could do was stare at the woman he had loved, at his shattered heart and future lying lifelessly on the bed.

She looked so serene and peaceful. Her skin so smooth and unblemished. So perfect.

Except for the red bloodstain on the breast of her dress.

Kristen had drawn close to Vogel and whispered a single word in his ear.

Burglar.

Vogel hadn't responded. He continued to stare at Kerstin while the priest chanted and Bernhardt wept. He followed suit. Tears slowly tracked down his cheeks. Later, when grief had turned to fury, he thought about Kristen's explanation for Kerstin's death and as he did so a single word rattled inside his head.

Bollocks!

Kerstin's body was moved to the local church where Bernhardt would spend a day and night in vigil with it before its burial the next morning.

Kristen, the devoted wife and grieving stepmother, would stand the watch with him.

Vogel had stayed with old cook and Alfonse, the most senior servants in Bernhardt's employ. The trio had cleaned the inn and prepared the funeral meal. It hadn't taken long, and by late afternoon Cook and old Alfonse had repaired to the tap room and settled in front of a fire, swapping old memories of Kerstin as a baby and child, and later of Kerstin's late mother. They had gotten drunk and thought fond thoughts while Vogel had schemed and thought dark thoughts. And while the old dears

353

drank and reminisced, he searched Kerstin's room for signs of what really happened.

According to Kristen and the servants, a burglar had broken into Kerstin's room. She had woken, surprised him and in panic he had stabbed her, grabbed some trinkets and fled.

There was a goodly amount of blood on the floor of Kerstin's bed chamber and no doubt in Vogel's mind that she had indeed been stabbed.

And then he examined the window where the burglar had, supposedly, entered.

The catch on the shutters was undamaged which meant if a burglar had opened it, he was a consummate professional - and professionals rarely kill. They only do so if they absolutely have to. But Vogel doubted that. Professionals were rarely caught. A professional burglar would have been in and out so quickly he wouldn't have disturbed the dust on the window sill.

A professional burglar would never have killed a young woman and a professional burglar would never have lifted a few worthless family keepsakes.

No. This was murder and Vogel just had to find out who, so he had gone to see his mentor who listened carefully before asking the fundamental question. 'So how do we find the murderer?'

Gunther's training kicks in.

Who would have cause to see Kerstin dead? Who would profit from her death?

Only one person. The stepmother, Kristen.

But before Vogel could exact his vengeance he would have to go to the church and say goodbye to his love.

It was late when he entered, and the air was thick and musty with the scent of old wood, stone and incense.

Kristen was nowhere to be found. Probably returned to the tavern.

Bernhardt sat as if carved from stone, staring at his daughter's face, wringing his hands. His world had become breadcrumbs –meaningless. First his dear wife and now their daughter. He knew Vogel was there but didn't turn or acknowledge him.

Vogel had walked up to Kerstin and placed a bouquet of flowers under his love's hand and kissed her forehead.

He had turned to Bernhardt who was still staring at her and whispered, 'I'm going to find out who killed her and I can tell you now it was no burglar.'

He had started to walk away when Bernhardt's gravelly voice stopped him, made him turn. 'When you find them, you come and get me, boy. Understand?'

'As long as I'm there when you deal out justice.'

'You'll be there,' Bernhardt promised.

Vogel departed, leaving Bernhardt Lenger to his grief, and spent the rest of the evening mourning in his own way.

Vogel now began to haunt Kristen. Wherever she went he was there, her invisible shadow. Whatever she did, he saw. Whatever she said, he heard, thanks to his hearing gift and it was only a matter of time before she fucked up.

And she fucked up big time.

A week passed before she left Bernhardt to make one of her regular visits to her brother, Cecil, a clerk in the Merchant's Guild who lived above a potter's shop just off the Grosser Marktplatzin the Artisans Quarter.

Vogel had only ever met him once and thought him a feckless arrogant layabout with the spine of a jellyfish.

Kristen had made her way to his rooms, carrying a basket of home cooking, hooded and cloaked like red riding hood, but nowhere near as innocent as the fairy-tale lass.

Vogel had loitered outside Cecil's window and eavesdropped on their conversation. It wasn't long before he heard the tell-tale sounds of lust and his suspicions were confirmed - that either the pair were incestuous cunts or were not really siblings.

'They suspect nothing?' Cecil had asked his "sister" in his nasal voice.

'No,' Kristen replied. 'You did well.'

'Yes,' Cecil had said airily, 'I did. Mind you, the girl didn't fight back or try to flee. She just stood there as I pushed the dagger in. Still, at least the last thing she saw was a friendly face. Oh, and I gave her your regards as I did it.'

Got you, you fuckers! Vogel's palms bled where his fingernails dug into them as he clenched his trembling fists as they chuckled.

Cecil had smiled as he stabbed Kerstin.

The nauseating sound of smooching followed, and the pair had another round of bed athletics before Vogel heard creaking and soft footfalls which indicated Kristen must have risen and was getting dressed. Returning to her husband.

'What did you do with the little bitch's trinkets?'

'They're in the box.' Cecil had replied.

'Get rid of them,' Kristen had said. 'Today!'

'When will I see you again?'

'In a fortnight.'

'And your husband?'

'In a few days, the staff and I will find him dead in his room –poisoned with Basilisk Venom and grief, unable to bear the loss of his precious daughter.'

With that she had thrown on her cloak and left the room.

Vogel hadn't followed her. Instead he had waited for Cecil to leave. The man he had thought was a spineless jellyfish wasn't such a drip after all. Quite the opposite. He was a wolf in a sheep's fleece.

Vogel was surprised at how easily the man had managed to deceive him and wondered if Kristen's brother was a professional killer. At any rate, he would have to tread carefully where Cecil was concerned.

When Cecil finally left, Vogel had followed him, tracking the man through his special hearing. Cecil hadn't wandered far from his rooms. He had threaded his way down a few backstreets before turning into an alley.

Vogel didn't follow him into the alley but concealed himself nearby, and when Cecil had left, he had gone to the spot where he had heard the faint tinkle of metal falling to the cobbles, where Cecil had cast away Kerstin's jewellery. He scooped them up and spent several minutes staring at them and turning them over in his hand, thinking of the woman they used to adorn. He had stuffed them in his pocket and walked slowly back to the Three Swords, head down, leaving a trail of hot tears splashing to the cobbles in his wake.

After that it was a simple matter. He had penned Bernhardt a note a day before Kristen and Cecil's next rendezvous. He had ensured that Kristen was nowhere to be found when the note made its way to Bernhardt. It was a simple letter that said:

'The murderers of your daughter will be in the room above Roland Gidde's Pottery Shop, on Bloomenstrasse, tomorrow afternoon. Don't tell your wife.'

Bernhardt had been a seasoned soldier and his instincts were still sharp, so before he left to confront Kerstin's killers, he dressed for the occasion. A sturdy leather jacket and trousers over which he had worn a chain shirt. He strapped on a pair of daggers and pushed a flanged mace through his belt. He covered himself in a cloak and set off.

'What are you doing here?' Bernhardt said, his eyes narrowing.

Vogel had been waiting for him just outside Cecil's rooms when he arrived. 'Waiting for you.'

'You discovered the murderer.'

'Murderers. And I'm here to watch the fuckers die, as you promised.'

Bernhardt stared at him and then nodded. He moved past Vogel and raced up the stairs. He smashed through the front door and the bedroom door as if they were made of soggy bread and had found Kristen and her "brother" locked in the kind of sinful embrace not permitted between siblings.

Kristen had been wordless. Her eyes and mouth wide, stuttering to explain her blatant infidelity.

Cecil reached down by the side of the bed and started to bring something up, but Vogel was much faster. Cecil shrieked and dropped the crossbow he had tried to reach for as Vogel's throwing knife was embedded in his hand. He reached for the weapon with his other hand, but Bernhardt had crossed the room and kicked the crossbow out of his grasp. He had then grabbed Cecil by the throat and lifted him out of the bed. The man squirmed, but he was caught in an unyielding human vice.

'Hey, Cecil!'

Vogel's voice made the man turn.

'Don't worry, mate, it's not all that bad. At least before you go to Hell, you'll see this.'

Vogel had given him a broad grin just before Bernhardt reached into Cecil's trousers, ripped his balls out and crammed the bloody lot into Cecil's mouth.

Cecil thrashed as he gagged on his bloody privates and managed a mewl before Bernhardt crushed his throat and let the corpse fall to the floor. He then turned his attention to his good wife.

Kristen's mouth still moved, as if she were speaking, but she emitted no sounds. Finally she managed a scream.

Vogel stepped up next to Bernhardt and held out his hand so that both Bernhardt and Kristen could clearly see what was in the palm.

Kerstin's jewellery. Cheap and tacky, yet it had meant the world to her as it was given to her by her late mother, just as she had been worth everything to Bernhardt and Vogel.

Kristen's screams died and she stared at Vogel with wide eyes that said – How did you discover us?

She turned to Bernhardt who walked towards his wife with the fires of hell raging in his eyes.

She shook her head, pleading.

He stopped and turned to Vogel. 'You won't want to see this.'

'Yes, I do,' Vogel replied, 'I really do.' He watched while Bernhardt Lenger exacted revenge for the murder of his daughter and though the screams had been piteous, he had felt no remorse for what had been done to Kristen Lenger nee Stein.

After the deed, Bernhardt walked back to the Three Swords with Vogel by his side. Both were silent. Bernhardt knew that Vogel wouldn't be staying on after this and didn't bother to ask how he had discovered Kerstin's killers. He hadn't even said goodbye. His only parting words were, 'If you ever need a favour boy, you know where I am.'

Understood. Vogel had walked away and hadn't looked back.

When he had related the events concerning the Lenger family to Gunther, the old wolf had simply handed him a pendant. A seal. The official seal of an agent of the Teutonic Order. Gunther had told him that he was going to give Vogel a trial to see if he could earn it but had considered the incident with the Lengers trial enough.

Vogel was now an agent for the Teutonic Order.

It had been good news but Vogel had been in no mood to celebrate.

It was many weeks later before he came across Kristen Stein and to his surprise she had not died.

But she probably wished she had.

She was wearing what was once a fine dress, a wedding dress which was now just tattered rags, not that she could see it, or the dirty dishevelled state that she was in.

Bernhardt had taken her eyes. He had also taken her tongue and hands and left her to the streets where, it seemed, every drunken mongrel had taken her.

Vogel was surprised she had lasted this long. He had walked up to her and smiled. 'Hello, Kristen,' he said, cheerfully.

She looked up and to the side at the sound of a familiar voice.

'It's me, Vogel.'

She broke into a smile and started to sob, her whole body trembling.

Vogel's hand shook with fury as he grabbed her chin. 'Just so that you know, Kristen, it was me that found you out and it was me that told Bernhardt.'

She gasped before crying out.

Vogel had walked away, with tears once again tracking down his cheeks.

'Hello, Bernhardt,' he said to the innkeeper when Bernhardt finally decided to make an appearance.

He stopped and stared at Vogel for an eternity before a look of profound sorrow crossed his face. It didn't stop him from walking up to Vogel and extending his hand.

The spy shook it.

'How long has it been?'

Vogel smiled wryly. 'It's been a long time. You look well, Bernhardt.'

'Nah!' He patted his belly, grinning. 'Fatter maybe. But *you* look well, lad. It's good to see you again.'

Vogel shrugged. Bernhardt also looked well, but the deaths of his loved ones had taken its toll on the man. The wisps of hair that had once resided on his head were long gone, replaced with snow-white stubble. The tavern owner's face was a web of lines. Yet his eyes were bright and, while he still had an air of sorrow about him, he also seemed content. Perhaps he had come to terms with outliving his wife and daughter, although Vogel was sure he had certainly never forgotten them. Maybe he took comfort in the knowledge that with increased age he was one step closer to being reunited with them, which made his life, if not enjoyable, at least bearable.

'Good to see you too, Bernhardt.'

'Can I get you an ale?'

'I won't say no to that. Will you join me? I'd like a chat.'

Bernhardt walked to the bar where he filled two tankards with thick foaming brown beer. He returned to Vogel and placed a mug before him before sinking into a seat opposite the spy. 'What can I do for you, son?'

Vogel took a pull on his beer and wiped his mouth with his sleeve before he replied. 'You've a customer who's been frequenting the back rooms. A nobleman.' Vogel described Olaf to Bernhardt.

'What about him?'

'I need him detained. Not harmed, just,' Vogel chose his words with care, 'ready for delivery.'

'Can I ask what he's wanted for?'

'Theft. Serious theft. Sorry, Bernhardt, that's all I can give at the moment. I can also compensate you for your troubles.' He reached into his tunic for his money pouch, but Bernhardt held up a hand and shook his head.

'Put your money away, Vogel. It's no good here.'

Vogel nodded in understanding.

Bernhardt Lenger had never forgotten the debt he owed the spy and Vogel realised it was something that that the innkeeper felt he would never be able to clear.

'I'm grateful, Bernhardt. And after this you can consider any debts between us cleared.'

Bernhardt smiled sadly. 'If you say so, Vogel,' he lied.

363

Chapter 29

Life had become far more exciting for Olaf von Gruenbaum since his encounter with Father Richter which had forced him into hiding. He had returned to the mansion that same evening, bypassing the Church forces on guard, and sneaked into Silke's ritual chamber. He had located the secret compartment in the floor, which Father Richter had missed, which contained enough coin and jewels to keep a nobleman in a lavish lifestyle for a long while.

Olaf had grinned excitedly as he grabbed the treasure and left, not that he had any intention of remaining on the run for long.

Silke was one of the most powerful sorcerers he had met, and he had known many. One way or another, she would gain her freedom – either she would achieve it by herself or she would call on him for help. Olaf sighed. He hoped that they wouldn't have to flee Rittershafen with its excitement and magic. It was a jewel which pulsed with energy – enough even for his insatiable appetite and it was therefore only a matter of time before he found himself inexorably drawn to the temple of vice that was the backrooms of the Three Swords. And while the gambling tables and sexual allure of the brothels roused potent feelings, nothing created the tsunami of emotion quite like the fighting pits.

He poured himself a glass of wine and raised it in toast to the city before draining the goblet and tossing it away. He left his room and made his way down the stairs through the common room to the fighting pits, acknowledging the inn's enforcers, who nodded back at a familiar face.

Olaf inhaled deeply. *What would I do without it?* The nobleman smiled to himself as he waited in the wings, watching as the first combatants warmed to their match. Judging from their stances and the looks of sick terror on their faces, it would either be protracted and messy, or short and bloody. The first exchanges were tentative swipes, each man measuring the skill and mettle of his opponent.

Olaf had them pegged the moment they had waddled into the sandy arena.

The moronic-looking youth was obviously a farm boy who thought that duelling with sticks with other moronic farm boys constituted training and experience.

Blithering idiot.

Farm Boy's opponent had been a soldier once. His movements bespoke some kind of training in arms and though outwardly he was calm, the nobleman could see he was a single scratch away from shitting his britches. He was pale but managing to keep his cool. Just. Probably a deserter from one of the many mercenary companies that washed across the land deluding himself that it was easier to fight a single opponent for a month's worth of coin than to spend months fighting in the armies of greedy and feckless noblemen.

A sudden roar from the crowd brought his attention back to the pit fighters.

Farm Boy had surprisingly scored a cut on Soldier Boy, who was falling back in fear and shock, flailing his sword wildly in an attempt to fend off his opponent.

Olaf smirked and scoffed. It was so obvious, but not to Farm Boy.

With a bellow like a bull in heat, he threw himself at Soldier Boy, hewing furiously at his opponent, trying to batter him down with brute force. To his credit, he managed to get in three mighty swings before Soldier Boy, harnessing every shred of discipline and courage he possessed, dropped the ruse and darted aside from the last swing to ram his sword deep into Farm Boy's barrel chest.

It stopped him dead. Olaf chuckled at the pun.

Farm Boy stood for a moment, gaping like a fish before his eyes rolled up and he crashed back to the sandy floor of the pit.

Soldier Boy didn't stop there. Elated and flushed and with the scent of blood, he ripped his sword from his opponent's cloven heart and, grasping the hilt firmly in both hands, brought the edge down on Farm Boy's neck.

The crowd roared again as he held up the head by its hair, blood dripping from the ragged ribbons of flesh at the neck, so the loser could look into the faces of the mob as they cheered the winner.

'People! People! Your attention please!' The pit master raised his arms, bringing the roar of the crowd down to a rumble while two of the tavern guards disarmed the now traumatised ex-soldier and led him from the pit.

'For the next match we have a literal battle of the classes,' the pit master announced.

The crowd whistled and jeered, and the pit master let their resentment build before continuing.

'So without further ado, in the corner of Swords, I give you the undefeated master duellist, Ziiiiigmund the blaaaaade!' With a flamboyant sweep of the arm, he gestured to a side of the arena.

The tunnel leading into the pit was barred by a portcullis which lifted as Olaf strutted into the arena, rapier held aloft, dressed in a white linen shirt and black leather trousers and boots, his hair and face impeccably groomed, looking every inch the arrogant noble.

The crowd howled their hatred and hammered on the tables with tankards and fists, booing and yelling obscenities at the nobleman as he smiled smugly at them and strutted arrogantly around the arena.

Perfect! Olaf thought. Keep the emotions flowing!

He adopted a casual stance, resting his rapier on his shoulder as he threw the crowd an arrogant smirk.

As expected, they roared in reply, booing as the nobleman stoked the flames of their ire and blood lust.

Olaf smiled, inhaling deeply as he drank in their energy.

'And in the corner of Spears, I give you everybody's favourite –Looothaaar the Aaaaax!

From the opposite side of the pit a portcullis rattled and in strutted the Axe. Not too tall or

367

handsome, with his bald head and bearded face, but grotesquely muscular. Lothar was clad in a loincloth with a long-hafted war axe casually resting on one of his broad shoulders, which he raised high in salute.

The crowd were hysterical, screaming and punching the air in support of the people's champion.

'All right, boys.' The pit master turned to Olaf and Lothar. 'You know the rules.'

Both men nodded. There weren't any.

'Do not engage until the bell sounds. Good luck!' He scurried from the arena.

The crowd fell silent and the entire room held its breath in anticipation of the bell.

Clang!

The ringing bell heralded a storm of yells as voices shouted support while others cursed as wagers and coin exchanged hands furiously.

Olaf blocked them all out and flowed forward.

Lothar moved to meet him.

He was quick, Olaf would give him that, but he relied on the reach of his axe and his strength to batter opponents and had never actually faced someone who was really skilled.

Until today.

The nobleman could have killed him with a single stroke, but what good would that be? It wasn't what Olaf needed. As his opponent closed, Olaf stopped and waited, standing in a bored pose.

Lothar was oblivious to it. The crowd wasn't, and howled for Olaf's death.

Lothar closed to within range and attempted to oblige the crowd's desires. He swung, a downward cut which, had it landed, would have split Olaf from shoulder to trunk, but the nobleman turned gracefully aside as the huge axe blade whistled past his face. At the same time he casually slid the point of his rapier into Lothar's shoulder.

The axe man cried and fell back, one arm hanging limp. The other still held the axe, but now Lothar was forced to choke up on his grip to balance the weapon for single-handed swings.

Olaf smiled smugly at the crowd and held his arms out wide in a gesture that said, *Am I not the greatest?* His face was a mask of ecstasy as he drank in their fury and taunts.

Lothar was returning for more, cautiously inching forwards now.

Olaf turned to face him and assumed a fencer's stance, side-on to his opponent, knees bent and feet evenly spaced, rapier angled at his foe's throat. This time Lothar was determined to carve up the nobleman like the privileged pig that he was.

He unleashed two large decapitating swings.

They never landed.

Olaf danced nimbly back from the first cut and avoided the second by ducking and sinking down to the floor. As the axe whistled harmlessly over his finely manicured hair, he sprang back up and forward and stabbed Lothar in his right eye, not deep enough to kill him but just deep enough to pop the eyeball.

The axe fell as Lothar shrieked and clapped a hand to his ruined eye.

Olaf only gave him a moment's respite, long enough for the audience to feel Lothar's pain and sorrow, before he darted forward and unleashed a hail of cuts and thrusts which Lothar tried to dodge and swat desperately aside with his hands, but was hopelessly outclassed. He collapsed to the arena floor, blood weeping from numerous gashes and punctures.

Olaf stood back and paced arrogantly around the pit, smiling at the crowd yet again.

They screamed their hatred of him, they cursed at him and swore at him, but they also cried and begged him to let Lothar live.

They pleaded with him for mercy.

The nobleman gave a low, exaggerated bow apparently acceding to their wishes and then walked back to Lothar. He stood before his bleeding and broken opponent and held out a helping hand.

The crowd fell silent. They watched fascinated and horrified at what they knew was about to happen.

Lothar was weak and barely conscious, but he could see the gesture and raised his arm in a feeble attempt to grasp the hand in peace.

Olaf craned forward and reached down to help him to his feet but as his fingers brushed Lothar's, he suddenly pulled back and, raising his rapier high for the entire crowd to see, plunged it deep into the man's throat.

There was a moment of stunned silence where the only sound was Lothar's gurgling and choking which carried on for several heartbeats before the spark that was the people's champion was extinguished.

Olaf drew his slim blade out and wiped the blood off it on Lothar's bald crown before he turned to the crowd, blew them a kiss, and gave them another low and flamboyant bow.

The entire room exploded.

Olaf was quickly ushered out, shielded by a wall of guards from the storm of plates and tankards that slammed into the group as they left the arena.

Olaf smiled and lost himself in rapture as he soaked up the crowd's rage and fed well on the tsunami of anger that welled up from them.

As the riot kicked off and Olaf was escorted from the main fighting pit, a cloaked and hooded figure, sitting at the back of the room, also rose and weaved his way carefully past brawling groups and the tavern guards. He managed to make it safely to the door and slip out into the hallway where he stood in the cool passage and took a few breaths to calm himself.

The Olaf von Gruenbaum who fought in the arena was a far different person to the polite and gentle nobleman he had met several nights ago. The man he had seen in the pit was a cruel creature and, after witnessing his performance, Vogel vowed that Olaf von Gruenbaum would not live to see the morning. What was it Arnold Guerk had said when Vogel asked him why he had killed Maximillian Dietz –*We did Rittershafen a service today by exterminating this vermin.*

That was exactly what Vogel planned to do to Olaf.

The spy made his way quickly back to the common room – time to have another word with Bernhardt and make the necessary preparations.

Chapter 30

'Ah, innkeeper,' Olaf said with a smile when Bernhardt entered the changing rooms next to the arena.

Bernhardt was no stranger to blood and battles, but the sight of the smiling nobleman, his face peppered with spots of dried blood and a big smile on his face, made the hairs on innkeeper's neck rise.

'Well fought, sir,' Bernhardt replied, concealing the disgust he felt. He handed Olaf a pouch which the nobleman gratefully took and hefted a few times. He smiled at the sound of the coins inside.

'Thank you. It was an absolute pleasure!'

'Yes, sir. It was quite a spectacle. Would you like me to draw your usual bath?'

'Thank you, my good man. Oh, for your trouble.' Olaf dug into the pouch and handed him two silver coins. Bernhardt pocketed them, dipped his head in thanks and turned to leave.

'Oh, and innkeeper?' Olaf said, stopping the burly man.

'I know, sir,' Bernhardt replied without turning. 'Absolute privacy. I'll have the bathtub sent up to your room with a bottle of our finest wine.'

Olaf smiled, turned away and started to strip.

Bernhardt left the changing rooms and made his way to the tap room which he crossed without uttering a word to any of his customers. He pushed through the door that led to one of the tavern's two kitchens which was a hive of activity as cooks and servants tended to pots hanging over stoves and large carcasses of meat sizzling on spits, while servants dashed in and out balancing plates on their arms. But Bernhardt wasn't interested in the food. He was interested in the figure sitting at one of the preparation tables, swathed in a dark cloak and nursing a pint of ale.

'Do you want one?' Vogel asked, raising his tankard.

Bernhardt held up a hand and shook his head. 'He's preparing to have a bath. He's had them ever since he's been here and he always locks his room when he does. He says it's for his privacy. My men'll take him then.'

'Good. I need another favour. When I've finished questioning him, I'm going to need help dumping the body.'

'Shouldn't be a problem, Vogel. I'll have a cart prepared. The harbour?'

Vogel shook his head. 'Nah. I don't need all that. Just a couple of men to help me carry his body to an alley not too far away.'

'Consider it done.'

'I'm grateful, Bernhardt. I'm sorry, I know he was a big crowd-puller.'

'Don't be, Vogel,' the innkeeper replied. 'He's a sick fucker and deserves what's coming to him. You're doing this city a favour.'

Vogel smiled and raised his mug to the innkeeper. 'I couldn't agree more.'

***

374

Olaf von Gruenbaum allowed his body to slowly sink into the hot water. He let it adjust to the heat before reaching for the goblet sitting on a small table beside the bathtub. He took a long pull from it and leaned back, closed his eyes and sighed with pleasure as the steam relaxed his muscles. He had been performing the same ritual for the past couple of days now and looked forward to his nightly bath and fine wine as much as the adrenaline-fuelled combat that preceded it.

His eyes flicked open, fully alert at the soft creak in the hall that told him there was someone there trying to move stealthily. He sat up and reached for his rapier hanging on a nearby chair.

Vogel watched the drama unfold in the nobleman's room from behind shutters in a darkened room in the building opposite the Three Swords.

Bernhardt sat beside him, chewing on a piece of smoked sausage. They watched as Bernhardt's muscle entered the room and froze.

Vogel could see that they were staring stupefied at something, and he was pretty sure that it wasn't Olaf's bollocks or the fact that the nobleman had expected them and greeted them with a rapier in his hand.

The spy wanted to call out, in the hope of galvanising them into motion, but it was too late.

Olaf moved so quickly all Vogel saw were blurs and heard a series of muffled cracks before one of Bernie's men collapsed with a shattered jaw and neck. Olaf then reached for his other rapier, hanging on a chair close to the bathtub and tugged it from its scabbard.

The death of one of their own seemed to dispel the enchantment that held the mercenaries enthralled and they leapt to attack the naked nobleman.

Olaf killed the next man with a thrust to the eye. He skewered the third in a heartbeat through the chest and then danced back as the last stabbed and swiped at him with both shortsword and club. He forced Olaf back, as both men did the dance of steel – attacking, and parrying as they jostled for position, but Olaf proved to be the more skilful fighter, lashing out with his rapiers to stab his opponent in the knee and chest. With a shriek, the man collapsed. The nobleman stood over him, grinning in pleasure before raising his leg and bringing his foot down on his assailant's head.

Vogel and Bernhardt exchanged an open-mouthed look – not at the grisly death of the hired muscle, but at what they had seen as Olaf stomped on his foe's skull. It explained the men's initial stupor when they had entered the room.

Olaf von Gruenbaum didn't have a right foot. He had a cloven hoof.

'The fucker's a demon!' Bernhardt hissed. 'Literally!'

Vogel swore softly at the sudden realisation of what Silke von Gruenbaum's "husband" really was. Had she summoned him, and if so, why?

He didn't have time to care as something sailed through Olaf's open window, thudding to the floor. The nobleman unwrapped the note from the stone it had been attached to and read it. A heartbeat later he threw it down, tugged on his clothes and boots and leaped out of his room's window. He landed cat-like on the cobbles below and, without pausing sped off into the darkness. Moments later a small figure detached itself from the shadows and raced after him.

Vogel recognised the diminutive man instantly – it could only be Franz Luber, unless there were two child-sized agents in the Church.

The spy chuckled in admiration at the little man's savvy.

Luber had located and been trailing the nobleman for some time without Olaf having the slightest clue, and was keeping an eye on him in a bid to locate Lady Silke's spell books.

The little man had waited patiently for the opportunity to push Olaf to lead him to Lady Silke's spell books and when Vogel's muscle had attacked the nobleman, the opportune moment had presented itself – and Franz Luber had struck like a viper.

'Bernhardt!' Vogel grabbed the innkeeper by the shoulder, startling him from his trance. 'We have to act fast before those bodies are discovered! Get to his room,' Vogel nodded at Olaf's room, 'and keep that note safe for me and then lie low for a day. I'll send guards to protect your inn.'

Bernhardt was no stranger to violence and reacted with cool professionalism. He nodded, slapped the spy on the arm for good luck and quickly moved to comply with Vogel's request.

Vogel dashed after the nobleman and Father Richter's little agent, triggering his special hearing as he went.

378

Chapter 31

'Oh, it's you!' Sister Adelheid said, her tone laden with disapproval as she glared at Vogel, but she knew better than to argue with him – Church and Order agents were regular visitors to the Dominican abbey, reporting to their witch hunter patrons at all hours of the day and night, and this one was one of Father Richter's charges.

'Thank you, Sister. Sorry to disturb you. I was hoping for a word with Father Richter.'

Sister Adelheid raised her chin, her anger lessening a little. *Well at least this one has manners!* She made another disapproving rumble and muttered something about Father Richter not being present before waving Vogel inside and disappearing to leave the spy to make his own way to the witch hunter's chambers.

It was still dark when Rittershafen's cathedral's bells tolled the office of Lauds and Vogel knocked on Father Richter's door. As there was no answer, and the spy found the door locked, he sat down on a bench in the gallery to wait for the priest to appear. He hoped that Franz Luber would be present when he made his report so that the little man could corroborate Vogel's account of the night's events and the truth behind Olaf von Gruenbaum.

The spy had no doubt that Luber had also seen what Olaf really was.

Vogel's only regret was that he didn't have time to send word to Stefan. He shrugged - he'd tell the templar personally.

The sky rumbled as he sat staring out at the darkness, sweating in the evening heat which swelled to oppressive levels with the threat of rain as insects chirped like an orchestra around him. With a loud crack, the heavens opened and the rain spilled down in heavy torrents.

Vogel moved to the ground floor and stood half in the rain and half in the cloistered gallery as he looked out into the grassy courtyard at the heart of the Dominican abbey. He lit his pipe, taking a deep breath of the fresh rain-cooled air which calmed him and focused his thoughts as he replayed the evening's events in his mind. He blew a plume of smoke and established the story he would relate to Father Richter.

He would start by saying how his spies had located Olaf at the Three Swords and knowing of the nobleman's skill with a blade, Vogel had hired muscle to apprehend him only to witness Olaf slaughter them and in so doing reveal his cloven foot and infernal nature.

A heartbeat later, the nobleman had fled after reading the note that had been flung through his window and Vogel had given chase.

Vogel sighed as he leaned back and his thoughts drifted to what had happened next.

Vogel had tracked Olaf and Franz Luber through his hearing, which he was thankful for as Olaf moved like a cat while Luber was a ghost.

The pair made for the Church Quarter and the nobleman proved to be quite adept at stealth as he managed to sneak past several groups of guards he encountered, although his perception wasn't quite as sharp as his stealth as he failed to notice Luber and Vogel on his trail.

Olaf was a gifted swordsman but not very imaginative when it came to concealing treasures. He had hidden Silke's spell books beneath a statue in one of the Church District's parks and when he dug them up and found them undisturbed, he looked around, his face a mask of anger.

Vogel smirked.

Luber's note must have said that the Church knew where Silke's spell books were.

Olaf, still high from the adrenaline of combat, hadn't thought or acted rationally. Fearing the worst for Silke, he had raced off to check on the spell books he had hidden only to realise he had been duped.

Luber deserved a round of applause for that move.

The look on Olaf's face was pure murder but he pushed aside his feelings and looked around. Unable to detect any pursuers, he took off again, racing around the city like a hare.

Vogel had to give it to the nobleman, it was a good ploy. Olaf had the speed and stamina to outrun anyone, even Vogel, but Franz Luber was a bloodhound with unnatural stamina and when Vogel gave up the pursuit, the spy noted that Luber, still unaware that Vogel was tracking him and Olaf, continued the chase.

He was confident Luber would track Olaf to the ends of the earth, no matter how unnaturally fit the nobleman was. He was also confident that Luber would report back to Father Richter, so leaving the little man to track Olaf for him and locate Lady Silke's spell books, the spy had returned to Bernhardt at the Three Swords.

The tavern owner was still in his inn when Vogel walked in and when the spy read the note Luber had lobbed at Olaf, it confirmed his suspicions. Luber had used a ploy to get Olaf to lead him to Silke's spell books as the note said that the noblewoman's spell books and journal had been located. Following her trial in the morning, she'd burn like fat on a griddle.

As Luber had planned, Olaf had panicked when he read the note and raced to secure Silke's spell books – instead, he had unwittingly led the agents to them.

Vogel had suggested Bernhardt lie low for a few days in case Olaf worked out that Bernhardt was involved with the men who had tried to kill him, and came seeking vengeance.

Bernhardt refused, saying that if the demon wanted him, it could come and get him. He wouldn't run or hide.

Vogel should have realised that Bernhardt didn't really care about dying, not if it meant being reunited with Kerstin and her mum. The spy had understood and squeezed Bernhardt's shoulder in sympathy and gratitude.

Vogel had dashed to the Dominican abbey and Father Richter after that. The spy recalled the priest saying that Silke had confessed her crimes, which included the summoning of demons, but had she told the priest that a demon had been impersonating her husband? Vogel doubted it. It explained why Olaf was going to so much trouble to keep Silke's spell books from Father Richter.

He turned and looked up at the sound of booted feet hurrying along the first-floor cloisters and watched Father Richter throw back the hood of his soaked cloak as he fumbled with keys on his cassock belt. His face was as dark as the storm without.

Vogel shrugged as the priest entered his chambers and the spy decided it would be prudent to give the good Father a few minutes to dry off and calm down while he enjoyed a quiet smoke.

The rain lessened in minutes and when Vogel returned from relieving himself, he knocked on the priest's door and prepared to deliver his report on Lord Olaf. When there was no reply, he called out before trying the handle and found the door locked.

Vogel cursed. Father Richter must have gone back out on some errand.

The spy turned to leave when a sudden impulse came over him and he stopped.

Don't do it! the angel on his right shoulder warned. *If you're caught...*

Fuck that! the devil on his left shoulder countered. *You know you want to have a look in there. Who knows what goodies you'll find!*

Vogel had already made up his mind. With another shrug, and a quick look around to ensure that there were no eyes on him, he whipped out his lockpicks, picked the lock within heartbeats, and entered the room.

Father Richter's study was sparsely furnished with a large writing desk to one side and beside that a covered lectern. Along one wall were bookshelves lined with large leather-bound tomes and weathered scrolls, and along the opposite wall was a dresser with a jug and several cups on it.

Vogel locked the main door before swiping the jug from the dresser and swigging from it as he moved to the large writing desk, which he subjected to a cursory search that yielded nothing. The lectern, on the other hand, held an enormous beautifully illuminated bible worth a fortune and Vogel was tempted for a moment to nick the book but decided against it. Aside from the size of the tome, which would be a pain in the arse to lug around, stealing a bible from a witch hunter was likely to bring down a world of trouble on his head. He left it with a sigh and moved on.

There were two doors in the room. The one through which he had entered the study from the first-floor gallery and the other, he guessed, led into the good Father's bedroom. He padded up to it and out of habit listened for the tell-tale sounds of snoring or heavy breathing. But, as he expected, he heard nothing, and when he tried the handle, the door was locked.

Leave now! the angel on his right shoulder said. *There's nothing of value in there and if there is, it belongs to a witch hunter.*

In you go, the devil on the spy's left shoulder urged.

I'll have a quick look in there and then I'll fuck off, Vogel told his angel. *Besides, I'm only doing my job.*

Yeah, right! the little angel scoffed. *You tell that to the interrogators when they're sticking molten rods up your nosey arsehole.*

Vogel ignored it and resolved to tread carefully as he examined the lock. It looked straightforward enough so, with a shrug, he fished out his picks and set to work.

The lock should have tumbled in seconds but instead Vogel spent several minutes wrestling with it until it did finally give way.

The spy stared at it with a frown. *That shouldn't have been so difficult to pick. Did the clergy have magic that they could place on locks to ward places and containers?* He made a mental note to ask Stefan later as he lit his lantern and slipped into the room, closing and locking the door behind him.

Vogel raised his lantern to reveal Richter's bedroom with a small desk in one corner, a large cupboard in another and a simple cot against the far wall. A quick search of all the furniture and items in the room revealed nothing of value.

He stood with his fists on his hips, shaking his head. *You arse. There's nothing in here.* With a sigh, he was about to unlock the room door and leave when he froze.

Wait one fucking moment! He turned and crossed to the table in the room and opened one of the drawers, where he found a strange-looking key. He opened the bedroom door and entered the study, crossing to the main door and the cloaks hanging on pegs beside it. He bent closer and smelled and felt one of the cloaks.

It was bone dry but stank of rain.

Father Richter, like most clergy, lived a life of humility and so only possessed two cloaks; a heavy winter cloak, and the other, the one Vogel had seen him wearing minutes ago, was his lighter summer cloak. But if he had gone out, what was it doing here?

Vogel looked up with the light of realisation dawning on his face. *He couldn't be – could he? Father Richter?*

One way to find out? the little voice inside his head said.

Vogel returned to the bedroom and closed and locked the door before replacing the key back in the desk's drawer. He then stood in the centre of the room and let his gaze slowly pan around it.

Something felt off. The spy sensed it instantly but couldn't quite put his finger on what it was, except that *now* he knew it was sorcery. It had to be. Fearing that there might be something supernatural in the room, Vogel triggered his hearing.

Nothing.

He took a deep breath and let it out slowly, which helped him to focus. He searched the room

386

again while trying to be thorough and quick, but his search proved fruitless, and he cursed in frustration.

He returned to the centre of the room, scowling, and as he did so, he realised why his instincts had been screaming at him.

The table. There was something on it that was out of place.

You're slipping, he berated himself.

Vogel crossed to it and picked up a small silver lamp. Why was this here when there were lanterns in the room?

He examined it closer. It was a small ornate lamp of Arabic design made of silver and chased in delicate filigree with tiny runes scattered above and below small prancing demonic figures. With a shrug, Vogel held it close to his ear.

And then he heard it. Only just. A conversation, one that was nearing its conclusion.

'Is there nothing you can do for the pain, master?'

The desperate voice belonged to a young man.

'If I don't feed on someone powerful, I'll go mad!' the boy pleaded.

'There's nothing I can do for the pain – no sorcery can cure the Templar's Retribution, except consuming the energy of a powerful magic user,' a voice replied.

Vogel swore softly to himself. They were in the lamp!

The voice of the young man could only be the demonheart, but there was no mistaking the other voice, that of the demonheart's "master".

387

'But all the priests and Church sorcerers are heavily protected,' the boy whined, 'and the energy of the novices just isn't strong enough!'

'Maybe we can find you someone who isn't protected...' the master mused aloud.

'Is there a sorcerer in your dungeon? One I can feed on?' the boy said, hopefully.

'No,' the master said, 'but I overheard one of my brethren, Father Gerhardt, talking about taking a secret visit to a village to help with disease there. The point is, he'll be alone or lightly guarded, as I understand it.'

'If he's guarded, I'll need help,' the boy said.

'Very well,' the master growled. 'I will give you aid. Here, take this.'

'What's this?'

'It's called a Sorcerer's Volcano. A spell designed to create a lot of smoke which will choke and blind a target for a while,' the master said.

'This is wondrous! Where did you get this? What's in it?'

My thoughts exactly, Vogel thought. *I'd love one of those.*

Then the spy heard him scream.

The boy shrieked as if hot pokers were being pressed into his flesh.

'Please, master, stop – I beg you! Forgive my insolence!'

Though he couldn't see what the sorcerer was doing to the demonheart, Vogel had grown up among enough street kids to know abuse when he heard it. He swore as he clenched his fists, forgetting that he was feeling sorry for a demon.

'Where I obtain my sorcery and its secrets are not for you,' the master growled. 'Keep your questions focused to the tasks I have given you.'

'I hear and obey, master,' the boy whined.

'Good,' the master purred.' Know your place. I will call you when I know more of Father Gerhardt's destination and situation.'

'What if I cannot take the priest, master – what if he's *too* well guarded?'

'I have a sorceress in my custody, but you may not feed on her. If Father Gerhardt proves beyond your prowess then you may feast on her, but only with my permission.'

'I hear and obey, master.'

'Go,' the master commanded. 'Come when I call.'

'Your will, master.'

He's leaving the lamp! The spy couldn't believe he was thinking that as he replaced it and quickly slipped inside the large wardrobe.

The boy was the first to leave.

Vogel peered through slats in the wardrobe's door with wide eyes as the boy slowly trickled out of the lamp, like sand being slowly poured from a bag. His booted feet gradually appearing first and then the rest of his body and finally his head, cloaked in the mud-coloured habit of a novice. When the manifestation process was complete, he strode to the window, stuffing a small ball in his robes as he crossed the room.

Vogel thought it looked like a silver thurible, judging from the way it glinted.

That has to be the sorcery his master gave him! The spy reasoned.

The demonheart opened the shutters and crouched on the window ledge where he poised to leap when he suddenly paused, raised his head and sniffed the air. He turned and looked back into the room, his gaze slowly tracking across the darkened chamber.

Vogel's mouth fell open. *Sweet Mother! Can he smell me?* It almost seemed like he was going to start searching the room but changed his mind and without a backwards look, leapt into the hot night.

The spy muttered a prayer of thanks as he slowly exhaled before he frowned, realising that he had got a good look at the boy's face, which showed no signs of burns.

How could that be? Vogel asked himself. Hadn't the boy told his master he was in pain from the burns? Maybe it was his body that was burned and not his face, or maybe sorcery was being used to conceal the burns on his face?

As if on cue, the sorcerer finally appeared, also gradually emerging from the lamp to stand before the spy fully dressed in his priest's cassock.

Vogel still couldn't believe it and shook his head in disbelief as Father Jozef Richter went to stand at the window the demonheart had leaped out of. He folded his hands behind his back as he looked out at the Church Quarter which even at this early hour was still busy with clergy scurrying between abbeys, chaperoned by heavily armed templars or Trinitarians.

'Come!' the priest said, without turning around, to the knock on the door.

'Master,' Franz Luber said. He closed the door and bowed low to the priest.

'What news?'

'Good news, master – I have located the witch's books.'

Vogel frowned. Who was this fawning lickspittle? This was not the cocky Franz Luber he knew.

Father Richter turned and looked at his servant.

Vogel shuddered at the look on his face. Gone was the warmth the spy usually found glowing in the priest's face. Instead, Father Richter's eyes were a pair of large dark pools, the sort of eyes a shark might have – dead and cold.

'I found the witch's husband and followed him, master. He buried the books under a statue and then, suspicious that someone might be following him, tried to give me the run around and lose me. He was fit and fast,' Luber said.

The blow came without warning.

Richter held out a hand wreathed in blue flames. He twisted his fingers and made gestures with the hand and as he did so, Luber writhed on the ground in abject agony, his mouth open to scream but in such pain that he couldn't utter a sound.

Vogel swore as his hand drifted to the hilt of one of his throwing knives.

'If I wanted a fable, I would read a romance or hire a troubadour,' Father Richter growled. 'Get to the point!'

The pain stopped and Luber gasped in relief.

'Forgive me, master.' Still lying on the floor, he turned and looked at the armoire.

Vogel froze. *He knows I'm here. He's going to give me away, the little bastard.* His hand tightened around the hilt of his throwing knife. *What hold does he have on you, Franz?*

The spy shook his head. The Franz Luber grovelling before the priest was a beaten dog and he felt a wave of pity for the little man wash over him.

'Lord Olaf has stashed the witch's spell books in a tomb in Rittershafen's central cemetery,' Luber said. He proceeded to tell the priest exactly where the books were.

'You're sure they're there?'

'Yes, master. Any normal person would never have been able to keep up with him when he moved them from the statue. He was confident he was alone when he concealed the books in the cemetery.'

'You didn't retrieve them?' Father Richter said softly.

The anger and menace in the priest's tone made the hairs on Vogel's neck rise.

Run, Franz! he prayed. *Just fucking flee!*

Terror locked Luber for a moment, but he recovered swiftly.

'I couldn't, master. The witch placed a ward on them.'

'You didn't have the strength to bypass it? Why do I not believe you? The only reason I keep you around is because of your skills and abilities and now you tell me that you're not good enough. What should I do with you?' The priest moved slowly towards his agent.

Luber, still on the floor, cringed backwards and raised his hand in fear. 'Please, master – I couldn't. I really couldn't!'

Father Richter held out his hand with the threat of torturing the little man with nerve-excoriating sorcery.

'Please, master! Please!' Luber begged.

Father Richter held his hand inches from his agent and watched Luber squirm for a few moments before pulling back.

'Try *harder*. Do *better* next time, Franz.'

'I'll go and retrieve the books immediately, master.'

'No!' the priest barked. 'I will go to the cemetery later in the morning, to pray over the tomb of an unfortunate. *We* will seize the books then. What about your other task?'

'I searched Lady Silke's ritual chamber, master, but could find no secreted treasures.'

Father Richter chewed his lip thoughtfully. 'It must be hidden with sorcery that requires her personal touch to reveal. I will arrange for Sister Adelheid to have Lady Silke's hair cut - she will need to look suitably groomed for her repentance ceremony and entry to the Scholars. You will keep an eye on Sister Adelheid when she attends to this and, after, you will take some of Silke's hair and try searching her ritual chamber again.'

'Yes, master,' Luber fawned.

'Don't fail me again, Franz.'

'I won't, master. I swear. When am I to attend to this?'

'Tomorrow, after we have retrieved Lady Silke's spell books and journal.'

'I will keep an eye on the tomb in the meantime, master.' Luber bowed low and after kissing a ring on the priest's hand, fled.

Father Richter sighed before seemingly remembering something.

The witch hunter must have had a lot on his mind as he paused only long enough to pull on his boots and throw a cloak about his shoulders before he left his rooms.

Vogel could hear him talking to his templar bodyguards outside. The spy was just about to walk out of the wardrobe when the door to Father Richter's bedroom opened again and the priest hurried to the table where the enchanted lantern sat. He grabbed it and stuffed it into a small leather satchel before rushing out of the room, closing the doors after him. When Vogel was satisfied he was far enough away, he too left by the main door, checking first to ensure that the gallery was clear.

He quickly and quietly padded down to the stairs, praying that Sister Adelheid wouldn't discover him. He reached Lady Silke's room undiscovered and pressed his ear to her door, praying. The Lord, it seemed, was in the mood for answering the prayers of thieves this night as he could hear deep and even breathing that indicated the lady slept.

Vogel quickly picked the lock to Silke's door and nipped inside. He crouched in the darkness, giving his eyes the opportunity to adjust to the gloom. When they had, he ghosted to the lady's bed.

Silke's long golden hair was spread like an open fan on her pillow, making it the simplest thing in the world for the thief to slice a few long locks off with one of his razor-sharp throwing knives. With his prize secured, he shot the noblewoman a wink before slipping quietly out of the room.

Vogel escaped the abbey unchallenged, after which he took off at a run towards the north bank and Silke von Gruenbaum's mansion.

The eventful night was about to become even more interesting.

Chapter 32

The sun was peeping over the horizon, setting the sky to blushing when Vogel reached the von Gruenbaum mansion.

'Morning, Vogel,' the guards at the mansion gate said, as they stared warily at the cloaked figure with the broad-brimmed hat approaching them.

'Morning, lads,' Vogel replied. 'Relax, I'm here on routine inspection for the Order.'

'Very good,' one of the guardsmen said.

'Anything to report?'

The guardsman looked at his comrades and then back to Vogel and shook his head. 'All quiet.'

'Good. I'm going to the house to see the servants and complete my inspection.'

'As you please.' The guardsman and his companion stood aside so Vogel could pass.

Once he was far enough away from the gate guards, Vogel veered off the path and made a beeline for the family chapel.

The servants had given the place a wide berth after Silke's ritual chamber had been discovered below it, which suited Vogel just fine. The guards stationed outside likewise gave Vogel privacy when he stated he was performing his perfunctory inspection of the chapel and waved him on without fuss.

He slapped them on the shoulder in thanks with promises of food and wine to follow, and entered the building. Once again he ventured down the stairs under the trapdoor in the vestry with his lantern in hand, half expecting to find the chamber guarded and warded. He shrugged when he found it empty. No doubt, the Church would leave it to Lady Silke to dismantle her sorcerous room, supervised by witch hunters, of course.

All such thoughts vanished as Vogel entered the noblewoman's ritual chamber, which had been screened off with a curtain since Father Richter had destroyed Silke's demon door.

The ritual chamber had the same effect on Vogel as it did the first time he entered it – tension drained out of his body and he felt light and carefree.

Choosing one at random, he crossed to a small a circle near the middle of the room and knelt within it. He wound the locks of Silke's golden hair around his forefinger and ran his hands over the sorcerous script etched into the stones, muttering to himself and praying that he would locate the sorceress's safe. He raised an eyebrow when he was rewarded with a faint click and a portion of the stone, with a strange rune etched into it, lifted slightly.

Vogel thanked the Lord as he carefully lifted the stone out, checking the safe for any mundane traps. As he couldn't see any, he reached inside the narrow compartment, where his fingers brushed against three cloth-wrapped bundles.

The first could only be a pouch of coins, judging by the feel. Vogel tucked it secretly up his sleeve. The second was a silver thurible engraved with the flowing script of sorcery which looked a lot like the Sorcerer's Volcano that Father Richter had given to the demonheart.

Something to ask Brother Gerome about, he decided.

The last bundle was wrapped in black silk cloth, possibly three inches wide and about a foot long. Vogel unwrapped it to find a sheathed throwing knife. He drew the blade and held it up, staring in open-mouthed wonder at it.

For the second time in his life, Vogel fell in love.

The blade was leaf shaped and the whole weapon looked to be made from a single piece of polished black jet and was slightly chilly to the touch.

Vogel hefted it, noting that it weighed about the same as a steel weapon of the same length and thickness, but he knew that the knife was not made of any material to be found on the earth. As he stared at it in wide-eyed stupefaction, the fine silvery script of sorcery appeared and disappeared along the length of the blade along with delicate silver dragons, their wings unfurled, as they sailed along the length of it, somersaulting, rising and dipping.

It was the most beautiful thing Vogel had ever seen and he could have stared at it until he died from hunger, but a noise in the chapel, probably the guards wondering what had become of him, brought him sharply back to earth. With a soft sigh, he sheathed the weapon, recalling Stefan's warning words about sorcery in their discussions –*Sorcerous items are never to be taken lightly. They have intelligence and are capable of subverting your will. They can make you do things you may live to regret.*

He heeded that warning as he felt the knife's psychic tendrils boring into his mind the moment he picked it up. Touching it made him feel that he would do anything, *anything*, to possess it.

Vogel started, and quickly sheathed the weapon before swearing. He now understood Stefan's warnings and his reaction at the *Dolphin*.

I'll be careful, Vogel vowed as he strapped the sorcerous throwing knife to his back so that its hilt peeped just over his shoulder. He could feel it writhe against him and fought the urge to unsheathe and admire the weapon again. He pushed the desire to the furthest corners of his mind until it was nothing but an annoying buzz.

Time to leave! he thought. The knife on his back writhed in response – it couldn't have agreed more.

***

It was light when Vogel reached the Church Quarter and he was panting and sweating from running in the humid early morning air. He noted with relief that the cemetery was still closed.

The spy's first port of call was the Franciscan abbey and Brother Gerome. He knew he wouldn't be disturbing the old monk as he and his brethren were always up early for prayers and chores. He found Brother Gerome in his kitchen, tending to bubbling pots and cauldrons and greeted the old monk with a warm hug and received one in return.

Vogel apologised for his haste, saying that he had a time-sensitive errand to run and promised to fill Brother Gerome in on the details later. The old monk understood and asked what the rush was about. The spy's response was to produce the thurible and request two favours. First, what the fuck was it? And, second, Vogel needed a habit along with a bunch of novices to accompany him on an errand. Worry not, he assured the old monk, they would not come to harm, or so he prayed.

Fifteen minutes later a group of seven novices shuffled solemnly towards Rittershafen's central cemetery with their cowled heads bowed and their hands concealed within the folds of their habits.

***

Franz Luber sighed in boredom. He was perched on a rooftop, overlooking Rittershafen's central cemetery in the Church District and watched as groups of young novices and their guards went about their business.

The sun was blazing down fiercely, promising another scorching day, when the office of Prime had concluded. The clergy spilled out of their chapels and monasteries to walk and enjoy the humid and quiet morning before it yielded to the melting heat of the day.

One small group from the Franciscan abbey caught the agent's attention as it made its way to the cemetery, which was now open.

Luber watched the group of seven novices make their way towards the tombs of the rich and split off to pray before individual graves. It was a common enough practice for monks to pray for deceased family members and loved ones, after receiving generous donations from their living relatives who were either too busy or sinful to attend to the deed themselves.

Pious little pricks, Luber sneered. He paid them only the slightest bit of interest and went back to his vigil as they regrouped and started walking out. He was about to lean back and relax when he suddenly sat bolt upright.

Something was wrong.

Six of them left the cemetery but seven had entered. One was still inside.

Maybe he's still praying, or maybe not? Luber said to himself. *And why didn't his brethren wait for him?* Either way, Franz Luber dared not take the risk of the missing novice being there for Silke von Gruenbaum's spell books. If they went missing on his watch, the master would kill him.

Swearing softly, he slithered to the ground and after a quick look around, to ensure that he was not being watched, Franz Luber walked purposefully into the cemetery.

***

Once in the cemetery, Vogel, dressed as a novice, had turned to the novices with him and thanked them for their aid. He told them to pick a grave, say a quick prayer and then to piss off. Whatever they saw and heard, under no circumstances were they to look back or stop for a moment to help him. If they were unsure what to do, they were to run to the nearest group of templars for help.

The disciplined novices had followed Vogel's request to the letter. Once they had left the cemetery the spy made his way to the mausoleum where Luber had informed Father Richter that Olaf had hidden Silke's spell books and journal.

Vogel approached the tomb from what he hoped was a blind side to anyone who may have been watching the building, namely Luber.

He scanned the roof but couldn't see the little agent, only statues.

Vogel pressed himself to the side of the building and looked around again to make sure that there were no eyes on him. Satisfied that he was unobserved, he triggered his special hearing.

He didn't have to wait long for the drama to start.

The knife on Vogel's back twitched, warning him something dangerous was approaching. He looked around for a place to hide or something that could help him from the approaching danger and, as he did so, spotted a sight that made his eyebrows rise.

A funeral was taking place yards away from where Vogel stood with a couple of dozen mourners standing in solemn silence as a priest droned prayers.

Vogel smiled. Whoever the deceased was, he was about to do the spy and the Teutonic Order a large service. *The Lord will reward you in heaven, mate*, he said to himself as he walked towards a trio of young gravediggers who, judging by their sweaty faces and grubby hands, had just finished digging a grave and were proceeding slowly towards the funeral the spy had just spotted.

'Oi!' Vogel called out to them.

They stopped as the spy, still dressed in novice's robes, approached them. He didn't have time to mince words and wasn't in the mood for lengthy explanations. He dug out thirty silver coins from a pouch and pressed ten into each man's hand.

They stared at him in open-mouthed surprise at the small fortune in their palms.

'Now, if you want to double that, I need you to do me a favour,' Vogel said to them.

***

Father Jozef Richter had spent the early hours of the morning attending to his priestly duties, after which he paused only long enough to collect his two templar guards before making his way quickly to the Church Quarter cemetery.

He sweated under the heat which, even at this early hour, was unbearably sticky. It caused his robes to chafe and put him in a foul temper which evaporated when he reached the cemetery and his mood brightened at the prospect of acquiring Silke's spell books and the knowledge and power that he would soon command.

He kept his composure cool and displayed a suitably solemn expression as he entered the cemetery and approached the tomb Luber had indicated Olaf had secreted Silke's books. As he neared the building, however, he found a curious spectacle unfolding before his eyes.

What must have once been a funeral service, complete with priest and mourners, had degenerated into farce as two young men, stark naked, were running around, leering and capering insanely at the mourners, some of whom were chasing after them in a bid to restrain them. If he hadn't been on such serious business, Father Richter might have found the sight of the two nude boys racing around the graveyard ludicrous and amusing.

Father Richter and his guards exchanged bewildered looks before the witch hunter shrugged and continued on to the mausoleum. He approached it just as a figure, dressed in a novice's robes, was leaving with a cloth bundle in his arms. He froze before the witch hunter and his entourage and, given the nature of his predicament, said the only thing appropriate.

'Fuck!'

The multiple scraping of steel on leather rang out as Father Richter's guards drew their swords and moved to surround the figure.

'Drop that!' Father Richter commanded, pointing at the bundle in the figure's hand. 'And surrender peacefully! Now!'

The figure dropped the bundle and raised its hands. 'Please don't kill me…'

And then something thumped to the ground at Father Richter's feet.

The priest looked down to find a silver thurible with delicate arcane writing and images etched on it. His eyes widened and he managed to bark a single word before the world exploded.

'Shit!'

***

Vogel had given one of the gravediggers his novice's robes, as underneath it he still wore his trousers and tunic, and asked the man to wait for a minute before entering the mausoleum. While the grave digger loitered, Vogel scrambled onto the roof of the building, praying that Franz Luber hadn't spotted him, before giving the signal to the disguised gravedigger to enter the building.

Hidden among the statues on the roof of the tomb, it wasn't long before Vogel spotted the cloaked figure of Luber gliding towards the building.

Vogel drew his enchanted knife and waited until Father Richter's agent closed to within striking range. As the little man drew nearer, Vogel felt his blood race but just before Luber came within range of his throwing knife, he suddenly stopped and looked up.

Vogel almost screamed with terror.

Franz knew where he was. At the same time, Vogel's adrenaline surged and his ability with throwing knives flared. He felt the world shrink and slow so that only he and Luber existed. He let fly the knife in a fluid motion and watched as it sailed towards Luber, lazily turning end over end.

Luber was quick but everything always moved at a snail's pace when Vogel's throwing-knife ability triggered, Luber included. Though he tried to dodge the knife, the hilt of the weapon smacked solidly into his temple with a meaty whack.

Franz Luber folded to the ground.

Vogel held out his hand and the knife whipped back to his palm. He kissed it before sheathing it, scrambled down from the mausoleum and raced to Luber's unconscious form. He dragged the little man behind a gravestone before quickly returning to his position atop the tomb and gave a loud whistle to the other gravediggers – the cue to begin their mayhem.

They were in full chaotic swing when Father Richter finally arrived and as he was busy relieving the gravedigger of the bundle he was carrying, Vogel dropped the Sorcerer's Volcano, as the magic thurible was called, according to Brother Gerome, on him and his templars.

The spy couldn't help chuckling at the mischief he had unleashed when he paid the young gravediggers to chase through the funeral service naked, and when Father Richter had thought he had caught a thief making off with Silke's prized spell books. But nothing beat the look of utter shock and horror on the witch hunter's face when the Sorcerer's Volcano landed at his feet.

The thurible exploded in a cloud of hot choking smoke which left the priest and his templars unable to do anything except collapse to the ground writhing and gasping.

Vogel didn't waste a moment. He let his enchanted knife fly again, catching Father Richter's templar guards on the side of the head with the butt of the weapon, knocking them out cold.

Vogel had something different planned for the good Father. Instead of rapping him on the head, he hurled the knife at the witch hunter's groin. Its hilt slammed into Father Richter's balls with a meaty thwack and the priest collapsed to the ground, clutching his bollocks and whining in agony.

Vogel slid to the ground and booted the priest in the guts before putting another good kick into Father Richter's chin which snapped his head back as his eyes rolled up and he sank into darkness.

That's for the torture, you cunt! He reached into Father Richter's satchel and snatched the witch hunter's enchanted lamp which he tucked safely into his own pack. He then entered the tomb and, after a quick search, located Silke's spell books and journal which he carefully placed in his pack.

Olaf hadn't bothered to try and hide them, assuming that people rarely ventured into tombs.

Good thing too! Vogel reflected with a relieved sigh – he feared Olaf may have hidden the books in the sarcophagus or coffin and the thought of rooting around in those sent a shiver down his spine.

Vogel grabbed the gravedigger he had disguised as a novice and hauled him to his feet, ignoring the bundle the gravedigger had dropped - they were only the man's clothes.

After giving Father Richter's unconscious form another kick in the head for good measure, and a final look around at his handiwork, Vogel, supporting his gravedigger, walked quickly away from Rittershafen's central cemetery.

Chapter 33

The sun was a fat orb hanging in a cloudless sky when Vogel walked to Marienburg an hour after leaving the Church Quarter cemetery.

Stefan von Stern was pleased to see the spy and gave him a crushing hug. 'Where've you been?'

'Had a busy night. Come to think of it, had a busy morning as well.'

'Come in and tell me all about it.' He frowned when he saw the glint in Vogel's eyes. 'You've discovered something, haven't you?'

Vogel smiled. 'Oh yeah! But it can wait. First, I really need a bath and something to eat.'

Stefan wrapped a huge arm around Vogel's shoulders and steered him towards the High Castle's stairs. 'Come on, then. Let's get you washed and fed.'

A couple of hours later, feeling refreshed after a good bath and a little drowsy following a meal of bread, bacon and cheese, Vogel sat opposite Stefan in one of the High Castle's refectories. He puffed on his pipe while Stefan stared at him.

'You stare at me any harder and you'll bore holes through me,' Vogel said as he blew out a cloud of smoke.

'You keep me waiting any longer and I will… By God! You've found the demonheart.'

Vogel smiled as he held up Father Richter's enchanted lamp. 'I found our sorcerer, too.'

He flicked his eyebrows up and down before telling Stefan about the previous night's events – how he found Olaf von Gruenbaum and followed him and Franz Luber.

Vogel decided Stefan didn't need to know about Lord Olaf's demonic nature or that the spy now possessed Lady Silke's spell books.

When he lost Olaf and Luber, he returned to Father Richter to report on having located Lord Olaf, but the priest was out.

He was having a smoke when he saw the Father return with a sodden summer cloak, as he had been caught in the rain. It must have annoyed the priest as he had a face like thunder, so Vogel decided to give him some time to calm down before he briefed him about finding Lord Olaf.

'And?' Stefan said, his eyes burning with curiosity.

'I went for a piss and when I came back and knocked on Father Richter's door, there was no reply,' Vogel said.

'He went back out.'

'That's what I thought,' the spy said.

'What happened next?'

'I broke into his rooms.'

Stefan stared at him with his mouth open.

'Anyway, I searched his rooms–'

'Why?'

Vogel shrugged. 'Felt like it.'

The templar shook his head in disbelief and gestured at Vogel to continue.

'I didn't find anything of interest in his rooms, at first, but then I noticed his summer cloak was on its peg by his door.'

'So he didn't take it with him.' Stefan frowned. 'Maybe he's got another summer cloak?'

'That's what I thought. But that's not what set my alarm bells ringing. It was the fact that his summer cloak was bone dry. And I smelled it – it was the *same* cloak he had been wearing when he entered the abbey.'

Stefan could only stare again wide-eyed. 'But that means–'

Vogel smiled slyly. 'Exactly. How could Father Richter walk in with a sodden cloak and have it dry minutes later, unless…'

'He used magic,' Stefan finished. 'And there isn't a divine blessing that can dry clothes in an instant.'

'You know where this is going, don't you?'

Stefan face was grim as he nodded. 'Go on, finish it.'

'I heard the front door being unlocked and thought Richter was returning so I hid. But it was Luber who walked into the bedroom. He stood there, in the middle of the room, waiting for a moment before Richter and the demonheart emerged from this.' The spy gestured at Father Richter's lamp which sat on the table before Stefan.

Stefan stared at it with a raised eyebrow before turning back to the spy. 'How did you get that?'

'I attacked Richter and his templar guards and knocked them all out when they went to get Lady

Silke's magic. You should've seen the kicking I gave him! You'd be proud!' Vogel beamed.

The templar stared at him for a moment before shaking off his horror. 'And where is Lady Silke's spell books and magic?'

Vogel shrugged. 'No idea.'

Stefan gave his friend a sidelong glance. 'Right. And was the demon dressed as a novice?'

Vogel nodded.

'Was his face burned?'

Vogel shook his head.

'How do you know it was the demonheart then?'

'Their conversation,' the spy replied. 'The boy said he was in pain and asked Richter if there were any clergy he could feed on. Richter promised him Father Gerhardt. Then it leapt from the window!'

'All right, that's our demonheart for sure and Richter must be hiding its wounds with sorcery,' Stefan mused. 'Did you recognise the novice?'

'No. You know, you're taking this rather well. I thought you'd be outraged or shocked, but you seem...'

'What?' Stefan asked.

'Satisfied? Relieved?' The spy shrugged.

The templar sighed. 'Richter being our sorcerer explains a lot.'

'Oh?'

'The evening we accompanied him when he discovered Lady Silke's ritual chamber,' Stefan began.

'What about it?'

411

'He was exhausted after destroying both of Silke's guardian demons.'

'I remember.'

'At the time, I thought it a bit odd that Father Richter should be so drained after only casting a couple of blessings, but I put it down to him being low on *Vis* and didn't think any more of it.'

Vogel shrugged. 'Why would you? Nobody would've guessed that a renowned witch hunter would be a sorcerer.'

'That also explains why Richter went after Lady Silke, and his benevolent treatment of her.'

'He wants her sorcery.'

Stefan leaned closer to the spy, his eyes wide. 'It's more than that. Vogel, he's treating her kindly because he may need her guidance with some spells because she has *powerful* magic.'

'Like what?'

'The Gate. Do you know how potent that spell is? It can transport people across hundreds, even thousands, of miles in an instant!' The templar snapped his fingers. 'That's ancient magic. Exiles magic!'

The spy shook his head. He had stopped puffing on his pipe.

'It's not just the spell that's unique, but the casting of such a spell requires power and ability *far* beyond most sorcerers,' Stefan said. 'And who knows what other powerful spells she possesses!'

'Just how powerful is she?'

Stefan looked around the refectory before whispering to the spy, '*Meister* Arnold told me that the Grand Master and the bishop believe that Lady

412

Silke may be the most powerful sorceress in the west. She's definitely the most powerful they have ever met.'

Jesus! Vogel could only stare at the templar. What would Richter have done with such power when he had already unleashed a demonheart on the clergy?

'What's going to happen to Lady Silke?' Vogel asked softly. *As if I don't already know.*

Stefan hung his head, refusing to meet the spy's eyes.

Vogel cursed. Of course they were going to kill her. How could the Order and Church allow such a powerful sorceress to live? How could they allow *any* powerful sorcerers to live, even those that that served the Church through the Scholars?

The spy knew the grim answer to that.

'Did Luber tell Richter where Olaf was?' Stefan said. 'Where Lady Silke's magic was?'

'He didn't say a word about Olaf, only that he knew where Lady Silke's spell books were, but Olaf must have moved them again as I didn't find anything on Richter aside from the lamp.'

Stefan sighed in relief. 'We need to find Olaf and Silke's magic. That can't get into the wrong hands. We'll brief Brother Martin about it; the Trinitarians are already hunting Olaf.'

'There's one other thing,' Vogel said. 'Richter's treatment of Luber.' The spy described how the witch hunter had intimidated and tortured the little agent with sorcery. When he finished, Stefan growled.

'Bastard!' he hissed.

413

Vogel nodded before he and the templar lapsed into silence for a while, lost in their own thoughts.

'How is Richter still able to cast divine magic? Doesn't being a sorcerer mean you can't cast divine spells?' the spy said.

Stefan shook his head. 'In theory there's no reason why a magic user can't cast both divine blessings and sorcery. The problem is, both paths are a way of life – you have to devote yourself to one. There are no half measures. The more you focus on sorcery, the more your devotions to your faith dwindles. And sorcery requires constant practice – more so than any art.'

'But if you start casting evil spells – summoning demons, doesn't that affect divine blessings?'

Stefan shook his head. 'It's not about evil spells – after all, what are evil spells? Members of the Scholars argue that there aren't evil spells. The evil is in the sorcerer, not the spell.'

'So Richter can't be a powerful sorcerer *and* an equally powerful priest – it's like a set of scales. The more you grow in sorcery, the harder it becomes to cast divine blessings.'

'Well put,' Stefan said.

'*That's* why Richter was exhausted after Smiting Lady Silke's guardian demons,' Vogel mused.

Stefan nodded.

Vogel pulled a thoughtful face. 'So, what do we do about Richter? We could go to *Meister* Gunther and Brother Arnold with this. They'd support us.'

Stefan shook his head. 'Father Richter is a witch hunter with the full weight of the Church behind him. I can't see the bishop sanctioning his interrogation.'

Vogel sighed. He was right – it would still be their word against his.

'We need evidence,' the templar said.

'We need his spell books and journal,' Vogel replied.

'They're probably in his lamp.'

'Yep.' Vogel tapped the artefact. 'Probably.'

'And you don't know how he enters and exits the lamp?'

Vogel shook his head. 'No idea, which is why I plan on giving it to Brother Gerome to crack. He should have its secrets for us when we get back.'

Stefan rumbled his agreement. 'And what about Luber – is he in league with Father Richter?'

'From what I saw in his chambers, Luber was being coerced by sorcery to comply.'   'So what, we leave him?'

'For now. We'll attend to him later.'

'What's our next move?'

'We stick to the plan,' Vogel said. 'We draw out the demonheart, then we deal with the sorcerer. We can't let him know that we're onto him.'

Stefan frowned. 'We can't have him releasing or banishing his demon, can we?'

Vogel sucked on his pipe, 'Or have him flee or take his life.'

'Oh no!' Stefan balled his fists. 'He'll not escape that easy.'

'No,' Vogel agreed, 'he won't. I'll set people to keep an eye on him. But first, we need to pay the Dominican abbey a visit.'

'Absolutely. We must get Lady Silke away from Richter.'

'Where can we take her?'

'Edward Poffhenger,' Stefan said, 'Dean of the College of Sorcerous Studies at Rittershafen University. Ed has loads of room at the College and we can rely on him to keep an eye on her and keep her stay a secret between us until we decide to tell the bishop and *Hochmeister* Heinrich about Richter.'

'Great idea.'

'Too bloody right, It's genius.'

Vogel snorted a laugh. 'Is that right?'

'It allows us to kill two birds with one stone.'

'Huh?' Vogel frowned.

Stefan rose. 'I think I might know how Father Richter is concealing the demonheart's burns.'

Vogel rolled his eyes and fell into step beside his friend as they walked out of the refectory. 'So the answer to how Richter is concealing the demonheart's appearance is at Rittershafen University?'

Stefan smiled slyly at Vogel and draped an arm over his shoulders as they walked out of the hall.

'Come on,' he said, 'I'm going to give you another lesson in sorcery.'

Chapter 34

Königshausen lay just outside Rittershafen to the north-west. It was a picturesque village with typical Rittershafen-style timber and brick houses set around a neat town hall and village square which was empty most days except market days.

To the west, the village caressed the fringes of the Nord Forest and to the east a row of cottages, inns and small warehouses were set back from the banks of the Ochs. It was a popular stop for river traffic coming from the south and among travellers who stopped by to enjoy the calm and tranquillity of the place. It was also just off the main road, which meant those using it generally bypassed it in favour of Rittershafen. It still, however, managed to make a comfortable living off the merchant traffic from Rittershafen to the south as well as adventurers who drifted through, preferring quiet retreats to the bustle of a big city like Rittershafen.

It was also where Father Gerhardt Sprecher had chosen to spend a few days in a cottage on the outskirts of the village which he had rented for the duration of his stay.

Every morning the old priest would rise early and take a brisk walk to farmer Senf's farm where, after exchanging the usual pleasantries and small talk, he would collect his breakfast, walk back to his cottage and spend the rest of the day either tending an herb garden or engaging in a little writing or reading of the scriptures.

417

It was a boring routine and he hated it.

It was the first Friday of his sabbatical and the day threatened rain as thick grey clouds massed menacingly on the horizon. Father Gerhardt limped home from one of his morning visits to farmer Senf's farm to find a horse tethered outside the cottage.

The sight of the lone animal triggered something in Father Gerhardt and he felt slightly edgy. He checked to make sure that his throwing knife and daggers were secure and easily accessible before proceeding to the house.

'Hello!' he called.

The door opened and he was greeted by a tonsured young man in the robes of a novice with a shock of straw-coloured hair, and eyes which varied in colour but today were as grey as the clouds above.

'Good morning, Father,' he greeted cheerfully, holding his arms wide open in the threat of a hug.

'Pieter – you young rogue! Come here and give an old man a hug!' The priest limped forward with his arms open wide.

He embraced the boy warmly before he stepped back and held him at arm's length as he looked sternly into the novice's eyes. 'Now, what have you been up to, hmm? What's the news? And have you got a cold – you're sniffing a lot?'

The young man shook his head. 'I'm fine, Father, and there's nothing new. The Church is still trying to hunt the murderer of our brethren and I've been assigned to Father Richter. He thought I

418

should pay you a visit to see how you are, and for a change of scene.'

'Quite right,' Father Gerhardt said. 'A change of air will be good for you. I also suspect Father Richter wants you out of the city for your own safety.'

Pieter nodded. 'It's a risk, but Father Richter doesn't think the murderer will pursue a single novice so far from the city. I'm small fry so I should be safe here with you, if you'll have me.'

Father Gerhardt patted the boy on the shoulder. 'You've been through quite an ordeal recently, Pieter, losing Father Pohl in such a fashion, but you're safe now. Is there any word for me from the lord bishop or Father Richter?'

'Not from the bishop. Father Richter said I was to help out and not be a burden.'

Father Gerhardt chuckled. 'Well, my young friend, your company and help will be most welcomed. To be honest, I was getting a bit bored out here alone in the wilderness.' The old priest winked. 'How about some breakfast?'

'Sounds great, Father, I'm starving!' Pieter beamed.

'Come on then.'

Father Gerhardt set about readying breakfast and bullied Pieter into drawing fresh water from a nearby well and collecting firewood from the shed.

He had his back to the door when Pieter returned. 'Just throw a faggot on the fire and put the rest in the bin, would you, there's a good lad,' he said without looking round.

'Alright, Father.'

It wasn't only the slight squeak of the novice's boots that gave him away.

Father Gerhardt hadn't for a second believed the pile of horseshit the novice had fed him about being sent to aid him in his work.

Father Gerhardt's mission in Königshausen was supposed to be a secret. The old priest was therefore on his guard when the attack came and, as he was expecting it, dived aside with cat-like speed that belied his bulk and age.

It was lucky he did.

The faggot smashed into the table, scattering utensils and food, missing the spot where Father Gerhardt had been standing moments before. He rolled into a crouch, a black-bladed throwing knife in hand, throbbing with sorcerous energy.

'You're not Father Gerhardt!' Pieter snarled.

'Clever boy!' Vogel replied and tore off his Mask.

The form of Father Gerhardt, the fat old priest, shimmered for a moment before melting away to reveal a leaner figure with hazel eyes and mud-coloured hair.

'You!' Pieter spat.

'Gotcha, you little fucker,' Vogel said. 'Stefan!' he bellowed.

They had removed the door to the larder and then walled it off with a wafer-thin plaster facade. Stefan had lived behind it for two days, meditating and gathering his divine powers, waiting for the signal to pounce.

At Vogel's yell, he crashed through the wall in a shower of splinters. His momentum carried him all the way across the room where he careened into the far wall and staggered back, slightly dazed and winded.

Pieter sprang at Vogel with terrifying speed, but not before Vogel flicked his enchanted throwing knife at the novice.

He was rewarded with a dull *thuck* as it buried itself in Pieter's breast where his heart should be. The boy howled, but it didn't stop him, only slowed him for an instant.

Vogel reached out and his knife sucked itself out of Pieter's body and flew straight back to his hand as Pieter's bulk slammed into him. Fast as he was, the spy had been too preoccupied with retrieving his precious knife to avoid Pieter's attack.

The novice was not large but his inhuman strength, combined with momentum, knocked Vogel flying back.

The spy was lifted off his feet and slammed into the wall with a thump that sent cracks spider-webbing across it. As Vogel struggled to rise, Pieter's faggot crashed into the side of his head and he sank into darkness.

Pieter turned to face Stefan and grinned, revealing two rows of pearly white fangs. 'It's just you and me now, templar!' He tossed the faggot over his shoulder.

Stefan glanced at the prone form of his friend and then looked at the demon. He drew his longsword with the audible rasp of metal on leather. 'Good,' the templar growled. 'I was hoping for a one to one.'

Pieter walked slowly towards the templar. As he did so, he held out his hands and stretched his fingers wide.

They began to change.

They cracked and stretched and before the templar's eyes elongated into thick horny talons.

Stefan snorted. 'Is that supposed to *scare* me?'

'Take a good look, templar. I'm going to tear your guts open and feast on your *Vis* as I bathe in your blood.'

'Of course you are.' Stefan raised his sword high and prayed as he slammed the tip into the ground.

Steel rang on stone and light flared. Thick golden syrupy energy poured out of the templar. It flowed along his blade, bleeding into the floors, walls and ceiling of the cottage where it sizzled and writhed like fiery snakes, covering the cottage and completely surrounding the Teutonic templar and his foe. The glow of the divine magic lasted for a few heartbeats before it died, leaving a trail of gold-painted sigils on every surface of the small house.

Pieter snorted. 'That supposed to scare *me*? You think you're the first to try the Sorcerer's Bane on me?'

Stefan shrugged. 'But I will be the last.'

'You pious lummox,' Pieter sneered. 'You really don't know what you are facing, do you?' He too tore something from his face and tossed it to the floor – a mask, just like Vogel's and made of a strange wood with a green tinge, etched with sorcerous script.

Stefan paused as Pieter began to change.

His body swelled and as his form expanded. His charred human skin, unable to contain his form, split and burst apart in a shower of blood and gore as the folds of his fleshly shell flopped to the floor and a creature emerged from it like a grotesque butterfly from a chrysalis.

It resembled a human in that it stood about seven feet tall and had two arms and two legs, but the similarity ended there. It had unnaturally long arms and slender, bony fingers which ended in large talons. As the creature drew itself up to its full height, Stefan could appreciate the horror of what he faced. It was utterly devoid of skin so that its flesh was laid bare for all the world to see and even the templar grimaced at the sight of the bands of muscle criss-crossing its body, and its organs throbbing and pulsating behind the bony cage of its bleach-white ribs.

It stared at the templar with snake's eyes – golden orbs with narrow black slits that burned with hunger.

As the demon closed to within striking, the templar slid into the *Ochs* fighting posture, sword ready, and sang another blessing which encased him in a bubble of glowing amber energy, a protection against weapons and physical damage.

The demon stopped just out of range of Stefan's blade.

'Don't resist, templar,' it crooned, drooling as thick saliva dribbled from between its fangs and dripped on the floor. 'I promise, it'll feel like the softest kiss.'

Stefan wanted to move. He wanted to leap at the demon and sink his sword deep into its body, but he couldn't. He could only stare at the creature, swaying slightly, as though he were drunk and a little tired.

'So potent! So sweet!' The demonheart crooned as it closed on the Teutonic Knight.

And then Stefan screamed.

The templar and demon had been so preoccupied with each other they hadn't noticed the figure lying on the floor come round.

Vogel opened his eyes to find himself in a waking nightmare – a horror drifted towards Stefan, its snake-like eyes wide with desire while drool dribbled from between its pointed fangs.

Fighting down the urge to scream and shit himself at the sight of the demonheart's true form, the spy crawled towards his friend, resisting the allure of the demon's voice, a task made easier as he struggled to keep conscious in a room that wouldn't stop spinning.

Riding out the carousel, Vogel dragged himself to Stefan and grabbed his legs.

The templar was oblivious to the spy, stupefied by the suggestive voice of the demonheart, and Vogel could only think of one way to bring Stefan out of his trance with the little energy he had left.

Stefan looked down.

Vogel stopped worrying the templar's leg and looked up with a bloody mouth.

'Snap the *fuck* out of it!' the spy slurred. His eyelids drooped and blood soaked one side of his face from the wound where Pieter had walloped him with the log.

Stefan swore as he emerged from his stupor. *Nearly!* He thought. He glanced at Vogel, but the spy had sunk back into unconscious oblivion.

The demon hissed at being cheated of its much-needed meal and the knowledge that its voice would no longer affect the templar.

Stefan dropped into a low guard, *Neben*, sword pulled back, left side presented to his foe.

The demon was a blur as it dashed in. It swept a taloned hand down, intending to rip Stefan's face to shreds, but the blow swiped empty air as the templar danced back and delivered a flawless upper cut which severed the demon's arm at the elbow in a spray of thick black blood.

The demon stopped as it shrieked.

Stefan delivered two more lightning cuts – an overhead chop which sheared through the creature's leg and sent it to one knee, black ichor pumping from its stump, followed by a horizontal slice which swept the demon's head from its shoulders. It sailed through the air and thumped against the wall of the cottage before thudding to the floor where it rolled a couple of times. When it came to a stop, it was still leering at the templar.

Blood arced from the demon's neck and splashed Stefan's armour before its body pitched forward, pumping thick blood over the cottage's floor.

Stefan stood, panting. He felt light, a sensation he always experienced whenever he defeated the supernatural.

Even as he watched, the creature's body and blood began to hiss and spit, like a piece of fat on a griddle, and thick black smoke poured off it.

Stefan coughed and gagged at the stench which, as quickly as it had appeared, disappeared, taking with it all traces of the demon's existence.

The templar turned to Vogel, who was slowly coming round again and hoisted the spy to his feet.

Vogel turned a wobbling head to Stefan. 'Still alive, then,' he slurred.

Stefan laughed as he pulled him into a hug and kissed his head before he helped Vogel hobble to his horse.

Together, Teutonic Knight and spy made their way slowly back to civilization.

Chapter 35

Father Jozef Richter woke to find someone was kicking him in the side of the head.

To add insult to injury the room was spinning and his mouth felt dry and furry, like a small mouse had crawled in there and died. All he could do was lie still and hope that the spinning room would eventually stop. It didn't, but it did slow its rotation enough to allow the priest to get his bearings.

He was in a bed in an infirmary and, judging by the nuns and monks quietly drifting from bed to bed, it was his own Order's monastery. He raised his head a little and tried to speak but all he could manage was a croak. It was enough to alert one of the nearby nuns who floated across to him and picked something up from a wooden bowl on the small dresser by his bed. She pressed a cool wet towel to his forehead and the kicks to his head lessened considerably.

He turned and looked at her.

'Rest easy, Father,' she said softly. 'You've taken a nasty bump to the head and groin. You've also experienced some nasty sorcery, but you'll live.'

Father Richter remembered. Someone had tossed a Sorcerer's Volcano at his feet and for a moment he thought it his creature. That was not possible. The creature was under his command and could not hurt him.

The priest groaned as another wave of pain marched through his skull. He raised a hand to the side of his head to feel the bruise there, but the sister gently caught his hand and pressed it back down.

'Best leave it for now, Father,' she said. 'The swelling will reduce in time if left alone.'

The witch hunter was in no state to protest. He let the sister dab his brow with a cool wet cloth before changing his bandages. Finally, she smiled and threatened to return a little later with some food.

She flitted to a couple more beds where she chatted to the patients as she fed them, washed or changed their bandages. Her last stop before leaving the ward was a bed nearest the doors. Its occupant was unconscious and the nun didn't bother to rouse him. Neither did she change any bandages, wash or feed him. Instead she knelt by him, bowed her head and prayed. A few seconds later she rose, crossed herself and left the ward.

'How long do you think he has?'

Father Richter turned and stared through squinting eyes at the figure standing beside his bed. The room was revolving slowly enough for the priest to recognise the slender child-sized man grinning down at him. He pointed weakly to a jug and cup on the dresser beside his bed, and the small man poured him a cup of water and held up his head while he sipped. When he had drunk enough, he slumped back into his pillows.

'Report,' the priest managed to croak.

'I have no idea who attacked you in the graveyard, yet. You should know they didn't just take Lady Silke's spell books. They got your lamp too. My eyes and ears are out, trying to gather intelligence. I'll let you know when I have something solid. Also, no word on Olaf von Gruenbaum, but I'm confident he'll be found soon. Vogel and Stefan have dropped off the face of the earth. Do you still want him apprehended – the nobleman?'

Father Richter nodded.

'If I can't apprehend him, shall I have him eliminated?'

The priest shook his head and winced in pain. He wasn't going to do that again.

'What if I can't take him alive?'

Father Richter glared at his agent. 'Hire more men,' he growled. 'I need him alive. He's no good to me dead. Understood?'

Franz Luber bowed. 'Yes, master.'

'Anything else?' Father Richter whispered.

'Yes, but you're not going to like it.' Luber's smirk returned.

The witch hunter gestured for him to continue.

'You've been out for a couple of days and in that time Lady Silke has disappeared. She was last seen in Vogel and Stefan's company as they escorted her from the Dominican abbey the day we were attacked.'

Richter glared pure murder at his agent. *Two whole days!*

Whoever attacked him would be bleeding and screaming for mercy soon enough, the priest vowed.

429

The little man continued. 'That was the last time anyone saw Lady Silke or Vogel and Stefan.'

Father Richter beckoned for his agent to draw closer and listen. 'Time to end this. Hire the muscle you need and have Silke found and secured somewhere private. Then torture her until she divulges the whereabouts of Olaf and her spell books.'

'Very well, Father.'

'Oh, and Franz?'

'Yes, Father?'

'Remember, she's a powerful sorceress. Take every precaution when you detain her.'

'Your will, Father.' Franz bowed and turned on his heel.

Father Richter watched his little agent stroll away, seething. Not only had he lost Silke's books, but his beloved lamp too.

It had to be another sorcerer – it was the only explanation. They must have somehow found out about Silke's books and his lamp, hence that was stolen too. And what were Stefan and Vogel doing with Lady Silke? Did the Bishop want to question her?

He had to find and deal with this other sorcerer. *Shouldn't be too hard*, the witch hunter reflected, not when one had the power of the Church and Teutonic Order behind them, and his own *Meister* in the arts of sorcery – one of the most potent sorcerers the priest had ever met.

And then I'll strip them of their sorcery and make them beg for death. Father Richter smiled at the thought, which made him relax. With a sigh, he closed his eyes and drifted back into sleep's deep embrace.

Chapter 36

It took Vogel and Stefan a day and a half to return to the city. They reached the gates as the last rays of the sun were fading and were it not for the fact that Vogel was an agent of the Order and Stefan a Teutonic Knight, the guards would have probably thrown them a couple of moth eaten blankets and told them to wait until sun-up.

Vogel was still suffering from the blow to the temple the demonheart had dealt him and was not in good shape. He was pale and in need of food and rest, so Stefan made for the nearest inn, *die Tür zur Hölle*. It wasn't the cleanest tavern in the city, but at least the linens weren't infested with rodent shit and lice, which meant that it was good enough.

They spent the night there and woke late the next morning.

Vogel looked better after a good night's sleep. He hadn't eaten the night before as he was too tired and weak and had crawled into bed and passed out instantly.

It was a different spy sitting up in his cot, Stefan noted.

The sun streaming through the window warmed Vogel's face and brought a healthy flush to his cheeks. His mouth watered at the sight of Stefan carrying a tray laden with porridge, bread and cheese.

The spy's stomach roared at the smell of hot food after a day of fasting, so Stefan set the tray down on the bed and he and Vogel set to breakfast like the starving.

They feasted for an hour before pushing back their plates and sighing contentedly. After their morning meal, Stefan noticed that Vogel's eyelids no longer drooped and he stared at Stefan with alert eyes.

'Glad to have you back,' the templar said.

'Glad to be back,' the spy replied. 'Thanks, by the way, for saving my arse back in Königshausen.'

'You remember what happened?'

'I know you told me about the demonheart's true form, but I wasn't prepared for the real thing. Fuck me – I'm going to have nightmares for the next decade!'

'Probably longer,' Stefan said. 'And in case you forgot, you saved my arse too. Thanks for that.'

Vogel smiled. 'Yeah, I did, didn't I?'

Stefan chuckled as he handed the spy his pipe and tobacco pouch.

Vogel lit his pipe and blew a cloud of smoke before continuing. 'Why didn't the Sorcerer's Bane protect against the demonheart's voice?'

'It only affects certain demonic powers – it prohibits the demon from using most magical abilities like spitting acid, lobbing fire and magical travel.'

'Fair enough. So, the demonheart still had its power of suggestion?'

'A nearly irresistible suggestion. It also retained a lot of its strength and speed. Lord in heaven, that was a *powerful* creature!'

'It was a greater demon and Richter was powerful enough to summon it.'

Stefan nodded, his face grim as he and the spy shared the same thought – how the fuck had Father Richter been able to summon such a powerful creature?

'We'll know more about how he did it when we find his spell books and journals.'

'At least we do know how he was able to hide the demonheart's burns,' Vogel said with a smile.

Stefan reached into his pack and produced two ornate masks, similar to the Harlequin masks favoured by the Venetians. They were made of a strange, polished wood with a greenish tinge which Edward Poffhenger, the Dean of the College of Sorcerous Studies, had informed Vogel was called *Drachenholtz*. When Vogel had asked the obvious question – why was it called *Drachenholtz*? – Edward had responded by handing him a book on the substance.

Vogel had thanked the Scholar and tried his best not to look frustrated.

'A Sorcerer's Mask,' Vogel said as he took one of the masks from Stefan and held it up, turning it this way and that. 'To think, this thing,' he gestured at the mask, 'can change your appearance, size and voice to any person you've seen and heard – fucking awesome!'

'It's potent magic,' Stefan said softly. 'Exiles magic.'

'Well, it's as we thought – Richter used one to disguise the demonheart.'

'Which is why you couldn't see any burns on Pieter when you were in Richter's bedchamber.'

Vogel blew a plume of smoke through the mask's eyes. 'Do you think Richter got his from Ed too?'

Stefan nodded. 'I'm sure if we check Ed's records, it'll show that Father Richter took one for "study".'

'This maybe a daft question, but does the College of Sorcerous Studies and Magical Artefacts have other, er, artefacts?

Stefan's expression grew serious when he saw the hunger in Vogel's eyes.

'You can forget that right now.'

'Forget what?' Vogel's face was pure innocence.

'Getting your grubby paws on any sorcerous artefacts – or one of these, for that matter.' He held up the Sorcerer's Mask.

'I was actually considering playing with both of'em–'

'Have you not heard a word I've said to you about sorcerous items? They're *dangerous* and exact a terrible price on those that use them.' Stefan shook his head. 'Look at what his hunger for sorcery has done to Father Richter – murder, trafficking with dark forces and other unspeakable acts.'

'All right, all right, I hear you.' Vogel held up his hands in surrender.

'Do you?' Stefan growled. 'Is that why you've got that?' He pointed to Vogel's enchanted

435

throwing knife on the table beside his cot. 'And *where* in the nine hells did you get that from?'

'Procured it from Lady Silke,' Vogel said. 'And that's something I *need*.'

Stefan opened his mouth, but Vogel held up a hand, cutting him off.

'If we're going up against the supernatural, I need something to defend myself with. You saw what the demonheart was capable of. And before you say, "You've got my back," bear in mind you might not always be there, and what do I do when that happens?'

Stefan sighed, shaking his head. 'All right.' He threw his hands up. 'Keep it for now, but heed my words and watch yourself.'

'I'll be careful.'

'Too right you will,' Stefan fumed, 'because I'll be keeping an eye on you. And if I think that thing is gaining control, I'm taking it.'

'I can live with that.' *No fucking way is anyone parting me from you*, Vogel thought as he glanced at his enchanted knife.

It hummed as a blue halo sprang up around it.

Stefan snarled.

'Speaking of sorcery.' Vogel threw back his blankets. 'We should get moving.'

'Brother Gerome?'

Vogel grinned. 'Let's see if he's been able to discover anything about Father Richter's lamp.'

Chapter 37

'Well, well, three visits within a fortnight, Stefan, I must be blessed,' Brother Gerome said when the spy and templar turned up at the Franciscan monastery asking for him. He greeted them warmly and led them into one of the monastery's kitchens.

As Brother Gerome pottered about, attending to his herbs and bubbling pots, Vogel wandered over to the hearths where he picked up a spoon and dipped it into one of the cauldrons. The soup had the look and texture of glue.

'Don't eat that!' Brother Gerome cried. 'If it didn't kill you, it'd certainly make you very ill.'

'By God, what is that?' Vogel put down the spoon and backed away.

'It isn't soup. Some of these,' Brother Gerome waved his ladle sternly at Vogel and at one or two of the pots, 'are potions. Others are ointments, designed to be rubbed on the body for various ailments, like boils and other diseases of the anus, skin and flesh.'

Vogel grimaced.

'Actually, some of these potions might be what you need, Vogel. You look unwell,' Brother Gerome said, seizing the spy's head and turning it left and right. He lifted the spy's eyelids and peered into his eyes.

'Er, thank you, Brother, maybe later?'

'Mmm,' the old monk said thoughtfully. 'Well, you look sound enough in body and mind though you could do with plenty of rest and a few hearty meals, and possibly ease back on the ale for a bit.'

'Understood, Brother.' Vogel made a mental note that it would be wine until Brother Gerome gave him the all-clear to return to beer.

Brother Gerome gestured for his visitors to sit at the trestle table dominating the room while he poured three mugs of ale – Vogel begged for a last cup – and laid out platters of bread and cheese before moving to a shelf and fetching Father Richter's lamp. He placed it in the middle of the table.

'Now then, let's talk about this,' he said with a grin, pointing at the lamp and rubbing his hands.

'Well – what is it?' Vogel said, craning forward.

'It's a demon,'

'Of course it is.' Vogel rolled his eyes. He was up to his neck in them these days.

Stefan grunted and picked at his plate of bread, cheese and pickled onion.

'A demon has been bound into this lamp, one with the ability to hold items,' Brother Gerome explained.

'What, like a demonic storeroom?' Vogel said.

'That's a very good way of describing it.' Brother Gerome looked at the item. 'I'll bet that if you entered it, you'd find yourself in rooms or a large chamber.'

'Demons can do that?' Vogel said, looking at his companions.

They nodded, Stefan without looking up from his meal.

'I know you want it kept a secret, boys, but I have to ask – where *did* you get this?'

'I took it from the witch hunter, Father Jozef Richter, after I saw him appear out of it,' Vogel replied.

Brother Gerome stared at him for a few moments before turning to Stefan.

'He's pulling my leg, isn't he?'

Stefan shook his head slowly and shrugged.

'You're mad, Vogel. When the witch hunters find out you stole a magic item from one of their fathers…' The old monk stopped and frowned in confusion. 'Hang on – you did steal it, didn't you?'

'I stole it.' Vogel smiled proudly.

Brother Gerome shook his head before turning to Stefan. 'He's telling the truth, isn't he?'

Stefan nodded, staring at the floor.

'Do I want to know why?'

'You'll find out soon enough, Brother. For now, though, we still need you to keep this matter,' Vogel nodded at the lamp, 'between us.'

'We *can* tell you that the clergy in Rittershafen have nothing to fear from the demonheart anymore,' Stefan said.

He looked at Vogel, who nodded his permission to continue.

'You killed it,' Brother Gerome said softly with an approving look. 'How?'

Stefan told him how they had laid a trap with Vogel using a Sorcerer's Mask to disguise himself as Father Gerhardt Sprecher before renting a cottage

439

on the outskirts of Königshausen where they had lain in wait.

The powerful priest was too fat a prize for the demonheart to resist as it was hurt by Wulfram Brenner's Templar's Retribution blessing. The priest's plentiful supply of *Vis* would sate the demon's hunger as well as heal most of its wound and so it had walked knowingly into the trap, gambling on its strength and power to be able to escape from it.

It had gambled badly.

Stefan had faced it and sent it howling back into the void.

Brother Gerome slapped the templar on the shoulder.

Vogel lit his pipe.

'Poor Pieter!' Brother Gerome said as he hung his head, tears in his eyes.

Stefan placed a hand on his shoulder and they both muttered a prayer before crossing themselves.

'Anyway.' The old monk looked up and smiled at them. 'Good on you both for getting rid of the monster, but I can see it wasn't easy.' He gestured at Vogel's tender condition.

'You both know who's responsible for summoning the demon, don't you?' Brother Gerome said, his eyes glittering with excitement.

The templar and spy looked smug.

'By God – it's Father Richter, Isn't it?'

The spy and templar exchanged another look and smiled.

'But you need to keep that between us for now,' Stefan said.

'Until we have evidence of the Father's guilt,' Vogel added.

'Mum's the word!' Brother Gerome vowed.

'Is it possible that Father Richter's ritual chamber is in there?' Vogel nodded at the lamp.

'Possible,' Brother Gerome replied with a shrug. 'But I have no idea what's inside. The little beast wouldn't tell me.'

'Let me guess, it'll only let Father Richter have access.'

Brother Gerome nodded.

'Can't you force it open?' Vogel asked.

'No!' The old monk and templar chorused.

The spy held up his hands in surrender. 'Just a suggestion.'

'If we try and force it open, Vogel,' Brother Gerome explained, 'we may destroy the demon and if we do that...'

'We destroy its treasures,' Vogel finished.

'Actually,' Brother Gerome added with a sly smile, leaning forward, 'it does also permit another person to enter.'

Stefan and Vogel exchanged a look.

It didn't tell me exactly who the other person is,' Brother Gerome said, tapping his chin as he squinted at the lamp, 'but I did see images of someone dressed in black.'

'Well, that doesn't help,' Vogel mumbled.

Stefan silenced him with an elbow to the ribs.

'The person was small,' Brother Gerome continued, 'a child maybe? But how can that be? What would a child have to do with Father Richter?'

441

Vogel and Stefan exchanged another look, this time grinning like idiots.

'You know who it is?' Brother Gerome rolled his eyes. 'Of course you do.'

Stefan nodded.

'Oh yeah!' Vogel puffed on his pipe, looking happier than a cat with cream. 'We know exactly who it is.'

'Right.' Stefan stood. 'We have an agent to find.' He looked at Vogel who shook his head.

'Not we. Me. This is going to require stealth.' The spy held out his hand and Brother Gerome handed him the demonic lamp.

'What if you need me?' Stefan said.

Vogel patted his hip and Silke's enchanted throwing knife concealed there. 'I'll be all right.'

'Then I should report in to Marienburg,' Stefan said.

'Tell them the demonheart's dead but ask them not to announce it yet. I'll have something for them soon.'

Stefan gripped his shoulder. 'Good luck!'

Vogel winked at his friends. 'It's got nothing to do with luck,' he said as he slapped on his hat and grabbed his cloak. 'It's skill!'

Chapter 38

Franz Luber was not a hard man to find if you knew where to look, and Vogel knew *exactly* where to look, thanks to Kristian and the army of urchins he had set on Father Richter and his agent before he and Stefan had left for Königshausen.

The spy caught up with Luber on the *Rittersbrücke Sud* as he was heading north to the Central Isle.

'Franz!' Vogel roared, holding his hands up in a halting gesture, but Luber only saw the desperation and alarm in Vogel's face.

Fearing the worst, Franz Luber bolted.

Vogel groaned and took off after him.

The small man ran up to the guards at the southern end of the *Rittersbrücke Sud*, to the gatehouse that led into the *Viertel,* and spoke to them in a rush, looking and pointing at Vogel occasionally.

Vogel slowed to a walk and casually strolled up to them. As he drew closer, he could hear Luber frantically trying to persuade the guards to detain him. He raised a hand and smiled.

One of the guards glared at the two men doubtfully and ordered them to stay put. He disappeared for several minutes before returning with a tall lean Teutonic Knight.

'Right, you.' He pointed to Luber, tossing away the apple he had been munching. 'My man here,' he jerked a thumb at the guard who had summoned

443

him, 'tells me that you're an agent for the Witch Hunters and that you say you're in danger from this man here,' he pointed at Vogel, 'a Teutonic Order agent.'

Luber held up his seal of office. 'Don't believe a word he says, Brother. He's probably got a false agent's seal on him that he'll try to deceive you with.'

'Is that right?' the knight asked, looking at his guards and then at Vogel. 'And why would he do that? Why exactly is he after you?'

'Because I've been spying on him,' Luber replied. 'I overheard him plotting against the Order and the Church. He plans to murder a priest, Father Jozef Richter.'

'Really? Murder a priest?' the knight said casually, pulling a thoughtful face as he turned again to his men and Vogel.

'And why would he do that?'

'I haven't been able to determine that, yet, Brother,' Luber said, giving Vogel a sidelong glance. 'He maybe in league with some people, sorcerers even, but I haven't exactly established his motive.'

'Well, then,' the knight leaned closer to Luber, 'why don't we ask him?'

Vogel sighed.

'Why are you trying to kill Father Richter, Vogel?'

Vogel looked up and to the side, his brows furrowed in thought, before he turned back to the knight and shook his head. 'Nah, sorry, Uli. I want to come back with a witty retort, but I've got nothing.'

'Wait – you know him?' Luber asked the knight.

Uli Venke nodded. 'For some years now.'

Vogel and Uli grinned at each other.

Franz Luber groaned, his eyes darting between Uli and Vogel, but the gate guards had already surrounded him. There was no legging it now.

Vogel walked forward and placed a hand on the small man's shoulder.

'Come on, Franz,' he said gently. 'Let's have a quiet chat, shall we?'

Chapter 39

'Are you fucking serious!' Vogel roared.

He crouched on the roof of a Church in the *Rittersbrücke Sud* with Franz Luber standing opposite him, shifting his weight and balancing with the same ease as Vogel.

He had taken Luber into a room in the guardhouse where Vogel had revealed that he knew all about Father Jozef Richter – the sorcery, his desire for Lady Silke's magic and finally his abuse of his agent.

Luber had listened patiently before standing up and motioning with his head for Vogel to follow him.

Vogel had readily agreed, assuming Franz Luber would lead him to Father Richter's secrets. Instead the little man had led him onto the roof of the tallest building in the area.

'If you want to know what I know about Father Richter, you'll have to meet my demands.'

'And I have to do that here?' Vogel shook his head in disbelief. 'Look, if Richter's forcing you to do this through sorcery, I can help.'

'And how are you going to do that then?' Luber sneered.

'Tell me how to break the spell.'

The sneer vanished to be replaced by furrowed brows. 'Why are you helping me?'

'Because Richter's a cunt and needs to be stopped.'

'Yeah, but you're a cunt too.'

Vogel pulled a thoughtful expression. 'True – but he's a rabid one, and needs to be put down. So, how do I break his hold on you?'

Franz Luber shook his head. 'I can't. Not until you meet my challenge.'

'What challenge?' Vogel gave him an uneasy look.

Luber drew a throwing knife. 'I believe you're versed in the art?'

'You want a duel? Here and now?'

'You defeat me and I'll tell you everything I know about Father Richter. I defeat you and you fuck off and forget about all of it – me, Father Richter, Lady Silke, the lot.'

It must be the abuse, Vogel reasoned. *All the shit he's had to endure at Richter's sick sorcerous hands has driven the little bastard mad.*

Vogel rolled his eyes and threw his arms in the air. 'Fine! I'll meet your challenge.'

Luber grinned and Vogel suddenly noticed how similar his eyes were to the man he served, large dark pools filled with cold indifference. He could have been the witch hunter's own progeny.

'There's one other thing, Vogel.'

'I'm listening.'

'If I win, I want your secrets, starting with your story.'

Yeah, definitely fucked up by Richter. 'Fair enough.'

'You ready?'

Vogel grinned. 'Let's dance, short arse!'

The agents edged to the centre of the roof where they stood ten paces apart, eyeing each other before Vogel tossed his cloak over one shoulder to reveal a sheathed throwing knife at his hip.

Luber mirrored him. 'On the count of three. Ready?'

'Wait!'

'What?'

'Are you going to count up to three, or just say "three"?'

Luber glared at him for a few heartbeats. 'I'll count up to three. Ready?'

'Ready.'

'One...'

Okay, Vogel said to his knife, *don't kill the little bastard – whatever you do, you can't kill him. Just give his blade a gentle nudge.*

'Two...'

Vogel's hand hovered over his throwing knife.

Luber did the same. 'Three!'

Both men's arms were a blur.

There was a ping and an audible *thuck* of metal burying itself in flesh, followed by a grunt and a groan. There was also the sound of metal skittering on tiles.

Luber folded silently with Vogel's throwing knife growing from his shoulder.

The spy moved closer to the little man who lay on his back. For a moment, Vogel thought that he was crying before he realised with a start that Franz Luber was laughing softly.

The little agent looked up at the stars and breathed in deeply before letting out a long sigh of relief.

Vogel looked down at him with a raised eyebrow. 'Still alive then?'

Luber snorted and chuckled softly. He held out a hand which Vogel took and pulled him to his feet.

'You knew I was going to win, didn't you?'

'Not for sure,' the little man replied. 'But I was fairly certain. Not that I didn't try my best.'

'Why did you do it – make the deal if you weren't sure you were going to win?'

'It's the only way to break the hold Richter had on me. I couldn't just tell you about it because that's part of the enchantment – it doesn't allow me to tell you how to break it.'

'So that's how it works – you issue a challenge and if your opponent wins, the enchantment's broken.'

Luber winked at him as if to say *Spot on, mate!*

'We still have an accord, don't we?' Luber said, grasping Vogel's hand.

'We do.' Vogel shook it, feeling as though a manacle had been securely clamped onto his soul with the other end attached to Franz Luber. For good or ill, they were tied to each other now.

'Vogel, Richter will know his hold on me is gone. He may come after whoever broke that. He'll *definitely* be coming after Lady Silke.'

'Don't worry about Richter - I'll deal with him,' Vogel said.

'What happens now?'

'First off, you now work for me. You're my agent.'

'Fair enough, but still I want to be paid in information – it's, er, my thing,' Luber said, scratching his ear awkwardly.

Vogel rolled his eyes. 'Done.'

'What about the Church? I'm privy to what Richter did. They'll want my head.'

'You leave them to me. Now, to business – Richter's secrets?'

'You'll need his lamp.'

Vogel fished around in his pack and withdrew the witch hunter's lamp.

Luber's eyes widened in surprise. 'When did you…you fucker! It was you that knocked Richter out.'

Vogel puffed out his chest proudly.

'And me – you knocked me out too, didn't you?'

Vogel had the good grace to look apologetic. 'Sorry, mate, didn't have a choice – you're a deadly little bastard, as I've just witnessed.' He nodded at Luber's throwing knife.

Luber grumbled before he frowned at the spy. 'How were you able to knock me, Father Richter *and* his guards out? And how did you know where I was?'

'That's a secret for another time.'

'You know that Richter will come for that with all his power.' Luber nodded at the lamp.

Fuck! Vogel had a sudden disturbing thought. 'He can't enter the lamp from wherever he is now and appear here, can he?'

Luber shook his head. 'He needs to be within a few yards of it. Any further than that and he can't.'

Vogel breathed a sigh of relief before turning back to the little man. 'You saw me in there, in Richter's room, in the closet?'

Luber gave an enigmatic smile.

'How?'

'That,' Luber said, extending his hand for the lamp, which Vogel gave him, 'is a secret I may reveal to you in time.' He pointed to the lamp. 'Shall we?'

Vogel held up a hand. 'I need a witness to whatever's in there. A credible witness.'

'I'm not taking the templar,' Luber said, shaking his head vigorously. 'He may snap and lash out when he sees what's in there. I'd rather not be near him if that happens.'

'Don't worry,' Vogel said. 'I know just the person – a kind and gentle old feller.'

Luber shrugged. 'Fair enough.'

***

The room was made of stone the colour of flint – black, with fudge-coloured veins swirled through it. Carved into the walls, floor and ceiling were the flowing lines of sorcerous script and a number of circles, artfully etched and inlaid in silver with a precision no human hand could hope to match.

Oil lamps of Arabic design hung from the high ceiling and walls, bathing the room in light which winked off the silver sorcerous script and arcane circles.

In one corner of the room stood a small ornate cupboard made of lacquered wood with elaborate gold fittings, while dominating the heart of the room was a large circle with the language of sorcery traced inside and outside it.

Brother Gerome cried out and moved to the circle and the two bodies dressed in novices' habits lying at its centre. He turned them over and gasped, covering his mouth with his hand as tears tracked down his cheeks.

Vogel and Luber exchanged looks.

'Welcome to Father Richter's ritual chamber,' Luber whispered.

In some ways it was similar to Silke's ritual chamber and in others, so very different.

Father Richter's ritual chamber had all the expected circles and sorcerous calligraphy, but where Silke's ritual chamber lightened the soul, Richter's was dark and cold.

The room made Vogel uneasy, and he desperately wanted to leave, but he suppressed the urge and crossed to Brother Gerome, who prayed as he wept.

The old monk crossed himself before he rose.

'Let me guess,' Vogel said. 'Konrad Stich and Markus Ganz.'

Brother Gerome nodded as he wiped his eyes and nose with a sleeve.

'I'm sorry, Brother,' Vogel said, placing a hand on the old monk's shoulder.

Brother Gerome patted his hand.

Vogel left him and crossed to the small cabinet. Inside it were a few chubby pouches which he knew contained gold or gems. He stuffed them inside his tunic. Next to them was the real prize – four large fat books.

Father Jozef Richter's beloved spell books and journal.

Vogel flicked through them but quickly slammed them shut as the words writhed and crawled before his eyes when he tried to read them.

He leafed through Father Richter's journal for a few seconds before hugging it to his chest.

'It's all here!' He grinned at Luber. 'Everything Father Richter has done and plans to do. I've only read a bit of it, but it's detailed and more than enough to damn the man.'

'You're going to turn him over to the Church?'

Vogel turned at the sound of Brother Gerome shuffling over.

'Are we going to Bishop Vassiliev and *Hochmeister* Heinrich now?' the old monk asked.

'Yes. What do you think they'll do to Father Richter?'

Brother Gerome looked at Vogel with fury raging in his watery blue eyes. 'Whatever they do to him, it won't be enough!'

'Too right,' Luber said.

Vogel placed a hand on Luber's shoulder. 'Don't worry, you've done your bit, mate. I'll take it from here.'

He looked around the chamber before they left. Luber was right not to bring Stefan, Vogel reflected. He'd have killed the little agent.

And he still might, the spy thought, *when I tell him what we found.*

Chapter 40

Father Jozef Richter could not be still. He sat. He stood. He sat at his desk, drummed his fingers on it, and cursed. He rearranged it and then rearranged it again. He did the same with his shelves of books and scrolls all the while cursing and wishing he could magically move time to Vespers.

A week after Father Richter woke from the hospital, Bishop Vassiliev's novice, Wolfgang, delivered the invitation to dine at Marienburg with the Bishop and *Hochmeister* Heinrich. It was accompanied by a short and cryptic message saying they had news for Father Jozef as well as a surprise – a magical object for him to study.

The witch hunter launched a barrage of questions at Wolfgang, who could only shake his head and shrug.

The priest would discover everything at the dinner.

For Father Richter, it couldn't come quickly enough.

He knew the news would give details about the destruction of his beloved demonheart. He had felt its loss and heard the news about its destruction from one of his witch hunter brethren who had visited him recently.

Father Richter shrugged. So he lost his demonheart? He would summon another one, and next time he would use a stronger vessel to house the demon, a Teutonic templar maybe, or even a Dragon Disciple or a Sword Brethren.

Imagine a demonheart in one of them! It would be unstoppable. Besides, he could live without the demonheart but dealing with the loss of his steward –*that* was something else entirely. That stung. Hard. As hard as losing his beloved lamp.

Franz was his mentor and guide in the beginning. Yes, the good Father had been stern with Franz, even harsh at times, but unruly children required a firm hand.

Luber had to be found and repossessed. Unlike the items in his lamp, for which he had duplicates or could be recreated, Luber was irreplaceable and had been Father Richter's sole preoccupation since he felt his bond with the agent suddenly severed the previous day.

It had come as quite a shock and for the rest of that day, the priest had to take to his bed to recover his wits and gather his thoughts. By Compline he had pulled himself together and realised that the best way to find Franz Luber would be to use the considerable power of the Church.

And by God would he use it! He would task the Trinitarians, the best bloodhounds in the west, to hunt Luber down. Perhaps his brothers in the Order would help, lending him their agents? Some witch hunters had armies of them.

He was about to request a meeting with them, and Brother Martin, this morning when the dinner invitation arrived.

Father Richter smiled at its heaven-sent arrival, as he knew Brother Martin would be present at the meal. So would the Bishop. By the end of it, he'd have the Trinitarians and his lordship's agents hunting Luber and tracking his precious lamp down. It was only a matter of time before he repossessed them and in the meantime, he'd have a new toy to play with.

It had to be sorcerous, else why present the item to him?

Father Richter had earned a reputation as one of the foremost researchers into magical artifacts, a reputation which had drawn scholars from all over the world to consult with him.

The priest took a deep breath which he released slowly. *I need this*, he told himself. *I need a distraction to stop from obsessing on all I have lost.*

The witch hunter had spent the day at the libraries of the College of Sorcerous Studies and Magical Artifacts before returning to the Dominican abbey to bathe and change into a fresh cassock.

When the bishop's carriage came to collect him, he was waiting for it outside and shot inside without waiting for the footman to open the door.

Father Richter's heart pounded as the carriage rumbled into Marienburg's Lower Castle bailey and he sprang out before the carriage came to a stop.

A horse was waiting for him when he jumped from his carriage with a novice in attendance to take him to the High Castle. It took all of the witch hunter's willpower to stop from vaulting from the saddle and sprinting into the building.

He dismounted, keeping a cool composure, and after a wave of dismissal to the novice, casually strolled through an arched doorway into the High

Castle and up the north wing staircase towards his sorcerous prize.

'Ah, Jozef, welcome!' The bishop was standing outside the High Castle's main refectory. As he and Father Richter embraced, the priest could hear the sounds of people talking and making merry coming from inside.

'My thanks, my lord, for the invite, though I'm not sure why I'm being so favoured,' Father Richter said.

'Well then, Jozef, come with me and I'll show you.' Bishop Vassiliev smiled as he guided the witch hunter into the hall. 'For your efforts, you deserve what's coming to you.'

The refectory was a grand affair with tall arched windows and slender stone columns that opened into fan vaulting at the ceiling.

The room's polished wooden floor was swept clean and all the trestles and benches removed except a single long table and pair of long benches that dominated the centre of the chamber.

Surrounding the diners on the four walls of the refectory were paintings and murals of angels and demons, along with scenes of the Teutonic Orders' battles against their supernatural and mundane foes.

As Father Richter entered the hall, the men seated on benches dipped their heads in greeting to him except for two who rose.

'Ah! There you are!' the priest said to Vogel and Stefan as he held his arms open.

'Hello, Father,' Vogel said as he embraced the priest with a copy of the smile Father Richter wore.

Stefan likewise hugged the priest, but it was a hasty embrace, after which the templar seated himself. There was no smile on his face and his jaw was tightly clenched.

Father Richter turned to Vogel with a questioning eyebrow.

The spy shook his head slightly, indicating he would fill the priest in later.

Father Richter seated himself at the table.

'I'm sorry we didn't come to see you when you were injured, Father,' Vogel said. 'But time was of the essence if we were to successfully trap the demonheart, and we decided we'd give you the good news when you were up. We prayed for you – didn't we?' He turned to Stefan.

'*Ja*,' Stefan growled, his face red.

'Are you alright, my son?' Father Richter frowned at Stefan.

'It was a difficult battle, Father – to take down the demonheart. It took a lot out of us.' Vogel dug his elbow into Stefan's rib.

'Yes,' the templar repeated. 'Difficult. We nearly died, Father.'

'But you didn't.' Richter beamed. 'Not only did you prevail but sent the creature back to the abyss. I was overjoyed when I heard the news.' He turned to the Bishop. 'As were all the brethren.'

'Quite, Jozef. Well, now,' Bishop Vassiliev declared loudly, 'you're probably curious as to why we're having this celebration and with such a large company.' The bishop flashed a smile at the gathering. 'But let us save that for later. For now, let us celebrate and feast.'

This was met with a loud rumble of agreement by the diners, and his attendant novice, Wolfgang, disappeared and reappeared moments later with kitchen servants carrying trays laden with bread and fruit. This was followed by platters of roasted vegetables and fowl, a spit-roasted hog, cauldrons of stew and more platters of cheese.

Barrels of beer stood in a corner of the hall, neglected for the time being as Wolfgang filled the diners' goblets with a wine the colour of a fresh bruise that smelled of honey and spices.

Father Richter chatted easily with Gunther, who sat to his left, and Sister Beate, a Trinitarian nun, who sat on his right. She had red dragon tattoos on her arms.

Vogel and Brother Martin likewise seemed at ease and enjoying themselves, engaged in some absorbing discussion which made them frequently smile.

Everybody seemed happy, Father Richter noted, except for the Teutonic templars who drank and chatted with grim expressions plastered on their faces.

He turned to Edward Poffhenger, the curly haired and bespectacled Dean of the College of Sorcerous Studies at Rittershafen University, sitting at the opposite end of the table from him.

The Herr Professor raised his goblet to the priest.

Father Richter smiled at him and returned the gesture. The fact that Edward was among the gathering boded well and reinforced the witch hunter's belief that he was going to receive a magical item from the college's stores. Why else was the Dean here if not to shed light on the item?

Edward turned away from him as Arnold Guerk wrapped a large arm around the Scholar's skinny shoulders and started regaling him with an anecdote which Edward found far from interesting, though he pretended to look eager as he smiled and pushed back his spectacles.

A wine jug entering Father Richter's field of vision pulled him from his reverie. Gunther filled his cup and began another tall story from his younger days when he, Heinrich, Arnold Guerk and Bishop Vassiliev were adventurers travelling the world, fighting evil. He allowed the spymaster's tale to carry him away until the Bishop stood, rapping his spoon against his goblet which drew the gathering's attention.

'Now then,' the Bishop said. 'I know we're still dining and it goes against the Rule to do these things during mealtimes, but I think we can be forgiven this little sin, since we're celebrating. So, now we come to the items.'

Items? Father Richter smiled. *More than one?*

Though outwardly Father Richter remained calm, Vogel could see the priest's eyes shining with desire as he sat up.

Vassiliev smiled before nodding to Heinrich, who left the hall and returned moments later carrying a large and long bundle wrapped in silk cloth. He placed it on the table, untied the bindings on the object and unwrapped it for all to see.

'A *zweihander*,' Father Richter said, trying to keep the disappointment from his voice.

The greatsword was sheathed in a plain leather scabbard with a hilt fashioned in the image of an angel clasping a downward pointing greatsword and whose outspread wings formed the quillons. The angel's feet rested on an orb which served as the pommel and like all the blade's fittings had a slight glow and showed not a speck of blemish.

'The hilt and guard are *Heiligesstahl*,' Heinrich said as he slid the blade from its scabbard with the sweet ring of metal on metal.

The gathering stood and gasped softly, as did Vogel.

The sword was over six feet long with a mirror-like blade that shimmered and rippled slightly. Every now and again, Vogel noted that divine sigils appeared on the blade, before vanishing again, in the same way that the sorcerous script had appeared on the greatsword Vogel had seen on the *Dolphin*.

The blade was passed around until it reached Stefan. When the templar held it up, the metal rippled and shimmered like waves in a storm and the sigils on the blade writhed and blaze into life with golden fire.

'Isn't the whole thing *Heiligesstahl*?' Vogel asked the templar.

Stefan shook his head, his eyes still locked on the blazing sword. 'This is an angelic blade.'

'That's when an angel joins to *Heiligesstahl*, making the metal a living sentient artefact, right?'

Stefan nodded, 'Well remembered, Herr Schlosser. The fittings are still *Heiligesstahl* but,

461

yes, the weapon is no longer metal but living divine steel.'

'And not just a sentient angelic weapon,' Bishop Vassiliev added, hearing the exchange between the templar and spy, 'but the most powerful type of magic artefact on earth.'

Try as he might, the Bishop couldn't keep the note of pride out of his voice.

And priceless! Vogel fantasised.

'You summoned this, my lord?' Father Richter said, his eyes wide with awe.

The bishop gave a slow, satisfied smile.

'I'm honoured, my lord, brothers, that you chose to share this with me,' Father Richter said. 'It is truly wondrous.'

'The angelic weapon is something I wanted to share with all of you, but it is not the object I was referring to in my letter, Jozef,' Vassiliev said. 'Now we come to that.'

'But first a display of this fine item, I think,' Heinrich said.

The Bishop placed his hands on his hips in mock outrage and looked around at the gathering with a broad smile. 'What do you say gentlemen? Sister Beate?

The group rumbled their approval.

Father Richter had no choice but to play along. 'Of course, *Hochmeister*. A display of the weapon's power would be a treat.'

Heinrich handed the weapon to Stefan, who paused a moment in surprise before the Grand Master's nod persuaded him to accept the sword. He raised it and muttered a short prayer which caused

462

the sword to flare with golden brilliance, forcing everyone to turn away from the fierce glare. When the light of divine magic finally faded, the walls and floor of the room glowed with honey-hued sigils.

Vogel smirked knowingly.

'Truly, this is a wondrous item, as you said, Father,' Stefan said to Father Richter. 'Not only was I able to cast the Sorcerer's Bane on this room – but the entire building. Without the blade, I would only have the strength to cast the blessing on this and the adjoining rooms. And that's just a taste of its might. Praise the Almighty!'

'Amen,' the gathering chorused.

'Now then, everybody,' Bishop Vassiliev said, 'let us be seated for dessert. I think we've kept Father Richter waiting long enough. Brother Martin, will you, please?'

The diners returned to their seats except for Father Richter.

'Thank you, my lord,' the priest said. 'I must say, this has been a most wonderful evening. Not only have I been treated to a lovely feast and privileged to be shown a holy divine weapon, but I am now to be presented with a magical artefact. I thank your lordship for favouring me thus. Thank you all.' The witch hunter dipped his head to the assembly.

The Trinitarian nodded and left the refectory as Stefan handed the angelic *zweihander* back to Heinrich. When Brother Martin returned, he carried a covered silver platter which he placed directly before Father Richter before taking his seat next to the priest.

'The sorcerous artefact I mentioned before, Jozef.' The Bishop gestured at the platter.

Father Richter kept his cool as Brother Martin lifted the lid to reveal a single item sitting in the middle of the platter.

A lamp.

His own sorcerous lamp.

'This is yours, is it not, Jozef?' Vassiliev said. 'An item you were studying?'

'It seems to be, my lord,' Father Richter said with a forced smile. 'It was taken prior to my assault just over a week ago. I was going to report it in the morning but now I have no need to. God be praised.'

'I can confirm that is definitely the lamp I signed out to Father Richter over a year ago,' Edward Poffhenger added.

'May I?' the witch hunter asked the bishop.

Vassiliev indicated to him to proceed.

Father Richter picked up the lamp and examined it, gently running a finger along the sorcerous script on its body.

'This is definitely the lamp I was studying, my lord,' he said to the Bishop. 'Where – how – did you find it?'

'We'll come to that in a moment, but first, did you manage to plumb its secrets, Jozef? Do you know what the lamp is?'

Father Richter shook his head. 'Not entirely, my lord. I understand a container demon is bound to the lamp and holds something, but what exactly is inside the lamp is still a mystery.'

'You've yet to enter the lamp, Jozef?'

'Not yet, my lord.'

'I see. Well, that brings us on to our next item.'

'Next item, my lord? There's more?' Father Richter raised an eyebrow.

The bishop nodded to Brother Martin, who reached into the leather satchel that he had stashed under his seat. He brought out a square bundle wrapped in cloth which he placed on the table before the gathering and stood back.

Vassiliev untied the knot and opened the cloth to reveal a stack of two large leather-bound books and a third smaller book.

Father Richter's spell books and journals.

'Yours also, I believe,' the bishop said.

Father Richter could only stare at the books. After an eternity he looked up at Vassiliev and then at the gathering around the table.

There were no smiles on their faces now. Just stares of pure ice.

Well, that explained the little demonstration of the Sorcerer's Bane, Father Richter smiled to himself. There would be no escape with magic at all.

Bishop Vassiliev picked up the smaller of the books and opened it, flicking through the first few pages before he closed it and held it up, his face a mask of disgust.

'The writing is unmistakable and certainly yours Jozef. It details how a witch hunter in the Dominican Order went from a man of God to a heretic obsessed with sorcery and willing to commit every unspeakable sin in his pursuit of power in the art. Are you going to deny this journal is yours,'

Vassiliev pointed at the books on the table, 'and that these are your spell books?'

Father Richter opened his mouth slightly and, for a moment, Vogel thought he was going to deny the evidence against him, but he snapped shut his mouth and shook his head.

'In case you were wondering, Jozef,' Vassiliev said, 'the books were discovered in your lamp along with the bodies of Konrad Stich and Markus Ganz, which you fed to your pet demon, according to *this* piece of filth!' Vassiliev flung Father Richter's journal onto the table. 'The spell books detail the summoning of your foul demonheart, and one of your last journal entries states that you sent it to pay Father Gerhardt a visit because it was starving.'

The silence that followed was heavy enough to cut and Vogel was grateful when Father Richter broke it after a few moments. 'So what happens now, my lord? Torture and then the fire?'

The bishop gestured to Brother Martin who produced a pair of bracelets made of a black metal shot through with veins of silver. He clasped the *Sonderbarer Stahl* cuffs on Father Richter's wrists before standing back.

'Jozef Richter!' the bishop intoned. 'I hereby find you guilty of heresy, blasphemy and trafficking with dark forces. I also find you guilty of murder and crimes against the Teutonic State and the Church and hereby excommunicate you.'

Vassiliev muttered a prayer and Father Richter's body became encased in a halo of golden energy which flared brightly for a moment before dying.

Father Richter gasped.

The men and woman in the room nodded and rumbled their approval.

No more would Father Richter use divine magic. The bishop had placed an impenetrable barrier between the priest and his ability to channel it.

'Now, Jozef,' Bishop Vassiliev said. 'I want to hear it all from you, from your own mouth – how and why you became a sorcerer. Confess everything you've done. There will be no torture and death as long as you tell me *everything*– and tell me the truth!'

The ex-witch hunter looked him in the eyes for some moments before speaking, 'Very well, my lord.'

Vogel half expected him to take a deep breath before he launched into his story, but he told it as nonchalantly as someone relates what they had for dinner the previous evening.

Father Richter told them everything.

How over time he went from hunting sorcerers to admiring them and the power they wielded, to finally craving that power. So he threw himself into mastering it by befriending the sorcerers he captured, offering them pardons in exchange for tutelage in the art.

He tortured those who refused into compliance before disposing of them. In this way he progressed, scuttling up the chain of powerful sorcerers until he finally met his *Meister* in the sorcerous arts, the man who called himself *Der Drachen,* the Dragon.

It was the only name he ever used with the priest and it was he who guided Father Richter into the deeper secrets of the art and taught him the summoning and binding of demons and necromancy. But it was the summoning and binding of demons that was the priest's passion.

And who exactly was the Dragon? Heinrich demanded. What did he look like and where did Father Richter meet him?

The witch hunter gave a description of his master but the men in the room knew that sorcerers could disguise themselves. At least it was a place to start the hunt for the *Meister*.

Father Richter had met his master in Freiburg where they trained. Later, when Father Richter returned to Rittershafen, he constructed his first ritual chamber beneath a small house he purchased in the Merchants Quarter. Later, he destroyed that ritual chamber for the one he constructed in the lamp, well over a year ago.

The *Meister* was the only sorcerer he had contact with. Those he had learned from in the past had either disappeared or were dead.

Under the *Meister's* tutelage, Father Richter grew in power to the point where he felt confident to try and summon a powerful demon. A greater demon.

That was when the *Meister* taught him to summon an emissary of Beraak, demon lord of disease and decay, who he promised the souls of the clergy and innocent to in return for the names of a sorcerer whose spells and magic he could steal.

Father Richter was rewarded with Silke von Gruenbaum's name and the summoning spell of a greater demon, the demonheart.

Ah, the demonheart! What a gift!

He used Pieter Gesell, Father Pohl Heinz's novice, as the vessel for the demon. After it killed Fathers Dieter and Pohl, it waited for an opportunity to kill more priests, but the Church reacted surprisingly swiftly, putting guardians on all their priests and monks, so that it had to feed on novices.

Markus was first. When he ran away, he confided in Pieter where he was going to hide, so the demonheart had a food source on hand just waiting for it.

Konrad Stich was different.

The demonheart stumbled across him by accident when the creature was wandering the streets of the *Viertel* and some of Max Dietz's thugs tried to kidnap him – the fools! When it was done with them, they were begging for their lives and one of them let slip that some of their mates were holding another novice in a warehouse and that, if the demon let them live, they'd give him the location.

The demon had scoffed, obtained the location of Konrad and butchered Dietz's men anyway, just as it butchered the men in the warehouse holding Konrad. It had then taken the terrified and traumatised novice back to Father Richter's lamp and feasted on him.

The demonheart had done everyone a favour, Father Richter casually pointed out, because by the time the demon had found him, Konrad Stich was quite insane.

Where Aelwine and Aesa and the urchin in the chapel were concerned, the demonheart had attacked them for their *Vis* and had then tracked the children back to their hideout where it was burnt with the Templar's Retribution by the children's guardian. In its pain and desperation, the demon had tried for Father Hubertus but he and Brother Martin had proved too strong.

While the demonheart was left to wreak chaos and slaughter among the clergy in the city, Father Richter focused on obtaining Lady Silke's powerful magic. How he desired the Gate spell and her other magic! But, alas, Lord Olaf thwarted him at every turn and finally disappeared with it all.

The rest was history.

Father Richter fell silent.

The gathering exchanged glances.

'And your master.' Bishop Vassiliev broke the silence. 'Was he of the Order of the Magi?'

Richter shrugged. 'If he was, he never mentioned it.'

The bishop glanced at Brother Martin who indicated that he thought the ex-priest wasn't lying.

'And what happens now, my lord?' Richter said.

'As I said, Jozef, there'll be no torture and execution for you. You were once a witch hunter and a bloody good one. That's earned you the right to clemency. But you have still committed heinous crimes which you must answer for,' Vassiliev said. 'I'm going to destroy your lamp, Jozef, and in a few days, you'll be taken to a Trinitarian convent far away where you'll spend the rest of your life in prayer.'

'His Holiness will be informed of your crimes and our verdict and sentence,' Heinrich growled.

'Is there anything else you want to tell us, Jozef?' Bishop Vassiliev said.

Father Richter shook his head before raising his hand as if suddenly remembering something.

'There is one question I would like to ask, if I may. Who discovered my spell books and how?'

Vogel and Stefan stood.

'It was your summer cloak,' Vogel smirked, 'that gave you away.'

Father Richter frowned.

'The evening that Franz Luber told you he had found Lord Olaf, it rained heavily, and I was in the garden at the heart of the Dominican abbey. I saw you storm into your rooms with a soaked cloak, but when I entered your rooms minutes later, it was dry. Now how could that happen?'

Vogel could see from the look on Father Jozef's face the priest could have kicked himself for the simple oversight.

'We all know priests lead a life of humility and only have two cloaks, one for summer and one for winter. So I checked, and when my suspicions were confirmed that the cloak you entered with was your summer cloak, I knew you had dried it using sorcery.'

He gave Richter a wink.

'You're addicted to the art,' Stefan growled. 'That's why you'd do anything to get your hands on

Lady Silke's books – it's why you were so desperate to get your hands on Lord Olaf and why you were so lenient with Lady Silke.'

'I hid in your room that evening, when you last saw Franz, and watched a novice emerge from your lamp before leaping from your window. I then saw you emerge from the lamp. I also saw what you did to Franz Luber – torturing him with sorcery,' Vogel said.

'And then we killed your demonheart.' Stefan couldn't help looking satisfied.

'Yes, but how did you enter the lamp? Who let y–' Father Richter began.

'Enough!' Bishop Vassiliev barked. 'You merit no exposition, Jozef. You can contemplate it in the time you'll have to consider your crimes – and you'll have *plenty* of time to do that. Get him out of our sight, Martin!'

The monk hoisted Father Richter to his feet and walked him out with Stefan and Vogel in attendance.

Father Richter was silent throughout the short walk to his cell on the highest floor of the High Castle.

Brother Martin gently ushered him into the room and as he closed the door, Vogel couldn't resist a last parting shot at the former witch hunter.

'It was Franz Luber, Jozef,' he said with a smile and wink. 'He let me into the lamp.'

Father Richter's eyes widened and he cried out something, but it was muffled as Brother Martin slammed shut the room's heavy door and locked it.

472

'Come on!' the Trinitarian said to the spy and templar with a grin. 'Now we can really celebrate!'

Chapter 41

'What do you want?' Hengist rasped when he opened the door.

'I need to see the *Herr Doktor*. The Church know Richter's responsible for the demonheart,' Franz Luber said.

Hengist grabbed the little man by his tunic and dragged him into the building.

'So let me see if I understand you correctly, Franz,' Horstmann said.

They were gathered in the doctor's study.

'The Church know Father Richter is the sorcerer responsible for summoning the demonheart that murdered the clergy in the city.'

'That's right, *Herr Doktor*.'

'How did they discover it was Jozef, Franz?'

'He was discovered by a Teutonic Order agent.'

'And what has the good Father told them?'

The little agent shrugged. 'Beyond knowing that he has been detained and his spell books and journal found, I don't know anything else. I'm not his seneschal anymore, *Herr Doktor*.'

The doctor and Hengist exchanged a look.

'I see,' Horstmann said. 'Franz, I suggest you stay here tonight. Don't worry about Jozef - I'll deal with him.'

'Thank you, *Herr Doktor*.'

'Hengist, why don't you show Franz here to a guest room?'

Hengist beckoned Luber to follow him as he walked out. When he returned to the doctor's study, Horstmann whispered in his ear, after which the big man collected his cloak and left the building.

Well, that's Father Richter dealt with! Horstmann sighed to himself, smiling. Jozef Richter had turned out exactly as he had predicted – a deranged power-hungry sadist who was too arrogant to heed wisdom.

Horstmann stared up at the floor above him. *And what part did you play in your master's downfall, eh, Franz?*

For his part, as soon as Hengist had left him, Franz Luber opened his window and crawled down the wall into an alley beside the doctor's practice. He ghosted to the front of the alley from where he could keep an eye on the doctor's front door while concealed within the shadows. As he expected, moments later a stocky cloaked figure emerged, moving quickly through the warren of alleys of the Merchants Quarter, constantly looking over its shoulder.

Luber trailed Hengist until the doctor's manservant entered the Church District, whereupon the little man raced to confront him.

Hengist whirled to face him.

'You weren't trying to hide.' The big man was intrigued.

'No. I know what you intend to do, and I want in.'

Hengist grunted in surprise. 'Why?'

Luber moved close to the big man. 'I owe him. I owe him for the things he used to do to me.'

Hengist knew only too well of Father Richter's penchant for cruelty, thanks to the doctor's own penchant for gossip at breakfast.

The look of anger and pain on the little man's face told the minder that whatever the doctor had told him about Richter didn't come close to describing the priest's sheer brutality.

'I want to be there when you *end* him!'

Luber fully expected Hengist to tell him to fuck off, end him even, but instead the large man stared at him for several heartbeats.

'Fair enough,' Hengist growled softly.

Luber raised an eyebrow. Did the big man also know what it was to suffer abuse?

'If you get in my way, or try anything...' Hengist began.

'I know. I know,' Luber said. He made a squashing sound. 'I'm dead.'

Hengist gave him a glare before motioning with his head for Luber to follow. Together, the pair continued to Marienburg.

***

Father Jozef Richter sat in his cell, trembling uncontrollably.

For the first time since he could remember, he was utterly defenceless, thanks to the bishop's excommunication preventing him casting divine blessings. Not that he had much divine magic left since his descent into sorcery.

Once, it had thundered through him like the mighty torrents of a huge waterfall. Now it trickled through him like a pathetic puddle.

Then there was his "mighty" sorcery.

He looked down at the black and silver *Sonderbarer Stahl* bracelets and chuckled without humour.

Such little things, yet capable of so much – thanks to them he couldn't summon or contact his demons or any of his bound entities, denying him their abilities. Even the simplest spells were impossible to cast.

Father Richter cursed.

'Hengist!' He looked up wide-eyed as a figure suddenly emerged at his window and squeezed itself into his small cell. 'You have no idea how happy I am to see y–'

The figure that followed after the large man cut Father Richter short. He looked between the little and big man, his mind trying to understand why they were here and then, in a flash, he understood.

Father Richter held up his hands haltingly. 'I can still be of service. I haven't told them anything worthwhile – look!'

He pointed to the blank parchment on the table.

'The bishop asked me to write down my confession, naming all the sorcerers I have had contact with. I haven't complied – and I don't intend to,' Father Richter said.

Luber barked a laugh. 'You've told them enough. You've done enough.'

Father Richter's sneer was impossible to suppress as he turned to his former servant. 'You're here to gloat.'

'You bet your stinking rotten balls I am, you cunt!' Luber spat. 'I wouldn't have missed this for the world!'

Father Richter acted first.

He tried to throw up a sorcerous shield. And screamed.

In his panic he forgot about his *Sonderbarer Stahl* cuffs, and his bark of sorcery produced nothing, not even the tiniest spark of power.

Hengist focused his will and his eyes flared with emerald fire as his inner *Vis* surged through his body and into his hands, causing them to shiver with power.

He slammed the palm of his left hand against Father Richter's chest, sending the former witch hunter reeling back to crash against the wall of his cell.

Father Richter stared at him in surprise as if to say, *Is that it?*

And then pain suddenly flared in his body.

He doubled over in agony and collapsed to the floor, thrashing like a fish out of water before, with a final choking gasp, Father Jozef Richter coughed up a spume of blood and lay still, staring up at the big man with dead eyes.

Franz Luber spat on Father Richter's corpse before climbing out of the room's solitary window and slithering down to the ground.

Hengist gave the ex-priest a final glance, shook his head, and followed after the little man.

478

Chapter 42

The council had gathered in the chapter house on the uppermost floor of the High Castle where the room's tall arch windows allowed the daylight to pour through in thick shafts.

Seated around a large oval table, in high backed wooden chairs, were representatives of all the Holy and Military Orders in the city including the Trinitarians, Witch Hunters, burgomeisters and representatives from the city's guilds.

Seated at the head of the table, chairing the meeting, was Heinrich von Wilnowe II, *Hochmeister* of the Teutonic Knights, rulers of the city of Rittershafen. He tried not to look bored as he listened to the proceedings while novices flitted between those present with jugs of wine and ale and platters of bread, cheese and fruit.

Vogel and Stefan stood at the back of the hall, also trying not to look bored as Brother Wilfred von Buxtehove, head of the Grey Knights, the administrative arm of the Teutonic Order, stood and addressed the council.

He opened with an account of the treasury and finances, droning on for nearly an hour about other financial issues, including various trade talks.

Heinrich yawned.

Stefan sighed softly while Vogel fidgeted.

He then talked about the state of the city's services and utilities – all good – and recruitment for the watch and soldiers for the Teutonic Order.

With a loud clearing of his throat, Brother Wilfred's report then turned to the recent fire and the resultant damage, homelessness and poverty it had caused. With that also came crime and disease.

'And that concludes my report for this quarter,' Brother Wilfred said with a nod, before sitting.

'Amen,' the gathered men and women chanted.

Thank fuck. Vogel thought as he turned to Stefan. The look of joy on the templar's face told him that the large man shared his sentiment.

Heinrich glared at Brother Wilfred for a moment before standing and thanking the old cleric for his report. He then announced decrees to tackle the issues Brother Wilfred had outlined.

The *Hochmeister's* declarations were met with nods and rumbles of approval by Bishop Vassiliev and the assembly.

'This brings our meeting to an end,' Heinrich said. 'I would ask our clerical brethren to remain as the next report is on ecclesiastical matters.'

He sat as novices escorted the burgomeister and guilds' representatives from the chamber. When they had left, Bishop Vassiliev stood and addressed the congregation.

'We now come to the murders of our brethren in the city,' the bishop began, 'which I am pleased to report has been solved. Let me start from the beginning and, I promise, I'll be brief.'

He took a deep breath before launching into his account which began with the deaths of two priests and witch hunters, Father Pohl Heinz and Father Dieter Schenk. This coincided with the disappearance of the bishop's own novice, Konrad Stich, and Father Dieter's novice, Markus Ganz.

The novices' disappearances made them suspects in the murders as Konrad had displayed violent and mentally unstable behaviour prior to his disappearance. The Fathers' deaths also suggested that the supernatural was involved as their innards were torn open and they were strangled, with deep blue markings on the lips. All this suggested a rare and powerful breed of *Nachahmen* demon, a demonheart, could be involved since the creature fed on the *Vis* of powerful magic users, leaving such marks when it did so.

The assembled clergy rumbled and exchanged grim looks.

But then, it could also be the work of criminals disguising the crime as supernatural, the bishop pointed out, which is why the Teutonic Order paired together an Order agent and a Teutonic Knight, under the watchful eye of an experienced witch hunter, Father Jozef Richter, to investigate the Fathers' deaths and the disappearance of the novices.

This was met by approving nods.

A day or two after the spy and templar had started their investigation, the murderer struck again, killing a junior Scholar and novice in the Church District in exactly the same fashion as Fathers Pohl and Dieter. Then Father Hubertus and his lone Trinitarian bodyguard, Brother Martin, were attacked by somebody or something dressed as a novice and protected by sorcery.

This was a strategy employed by the Church and Teutonic Order to draw out the killer.

Novices went about in large groups, and Teutonic Knights, Sword Brethren and Trinitarians were used to guard senior clerics and monasteries around the clock with the exception of Father Hubertus and Brother Martin.

Not only did the trap work, but it confirmed that the supernatural and a sorcerer was definitely involved in the clergy killings although, alas, the attacker escaped alive but not unscathed.

The Church and Teutonic Order decided to employ the same trap that it had used previously with Father Hubertus and Brother Martin to lure out the demon again, only this time the Order's spy and templar would be the bait.

As the Teutonic Order and Church had rightly predicted, the demon was starving and took the bait, and the spy and templar were attacked in the village of *Königshausen* where the templar slew the demon. It was indeed a demonheart disguised as a Church novice, one Pieter Gesell.

This was met by prayers for the novice sacrificed to the demon and claps and roars of approval at the creature's demise.

Stefan and Vogel exchanged grins and winks.

The hunt for the demonheart's sorcerer became the sole focus of the Order spy and templar on the case.

Days after their return to Rittershafen, the pair discovered by chance the identity of the sorcerer in question and accompanied their mentor, Father

Jozef Richter, and a large force of templars to arrest him.

Alas, the group had underestimated the sheer viciousness and power of the sorcerer in question who, though hopelessly outnumbered, chose to stand and fight. He fell, of course, but not before unleashing a devastating sorcerous attack which killed Father Jozef Richter.

This was met by cries and wails.

Stefan and Vogel exchanged another look utterly devoid of smiles.

The sorcerer's lair contained his spell books and the bodies of Konrad Stich and Markus Ganz which he must have fed to his demon.

Moans and tears followed.

Bishop Vassiliev bowed his head and led the congregation through another prayer for the fallen before he fell silent and sat. His account was over.

Grand Master Heinrich stood again and asked the assembly if there were any further questions.

There were a few, mainly from the Witch Hunters Order.

Did the Church and Order discover the identity of the sorcerer responsible for the demonheart? Who exactly was he? Where was he from? How exactly was he found and did he have accomplices?

Bishop Vassiliev rose and explained that the identity of the sorcerer was still a mystery, but he and his lair were discovered beneath the *Viertel*.

As for how he was discovered, that was down to the Order spy on the case. One of his contacts had seen suspicious occurrences in the *Viertel*, strange figures coming and going in the night. On

483

further investigation, the agent had stumbled across the sorcerer's lair.

The rest was history.

As for the sorcerer's accomplices, that would remain a mystery as his journal was never discovered.

Bishop Vassiliev waited to see if any further questions would come. When they didn't, he sat.

Heinrich stood.

'Are there any further questions?'

He received blank faces and shaking heads in reply.

'Then, if there's nothing further, I hereby bring this council to a close. May you all go with God,' Heinrich intoned.

'Amen,' the assembled men chorused before they rose and filed out, chatting softly as they exited the chamber.

Vogel turned as Gunther approached. He motioned with his head to leave the chamber, but Gunther shook his and placed a hand on Vogel's shoulder, stopping him.

The room quickly emptied, leaving Heinrich, Bishop Vassiliev, Brother Martin, Gunther, Arnold Guerk, Edward Poffhenger, and Vogel and Stefan behind. When the doors finally boomed shut, Heinrich beckoned the spy and templar closer.

They stood before the gathering with Vogel looking around the room uncomfortably while the bishop and Grand Master stared long and thoughtfully at him, especially Bishop Vassiliev, who did so through steepled fingers.

Outside the rain gently pattered against the window. The mood of the gathered men matched the weather outside – sombre.

Heinrich broke the silence.

'You two did bloody well. I'm impressed,' the Grand Master said to the spy and templar.

Arnold Guerk, sitting beside him, nodded. 'Yeah, me too.'

Stefan grinned.

Vogel almost swooned.

Bishop Vassiliev coughed, drawing everyone's attention.

'Brother Stefan, Herr Schlosser, thank you for keeping our council regarding Father Richter. If the assembly knew that a priest and witch hunter was the sorcerer responsible for the deaths in the city, it would have had catastrophic consequences for the Church and Order both here and elsewhere – Father Richter had powerful friends in the Church.'

'We also have no idea how deep this goes,' Brother Martin said. 'How many more clergy are involved in the practice of dark sorcery.'

'So what happens now?' Vogel asked.

'We will conduct a thorough investigation into our brethren to root out the heretics within our ranks,' Bishop Vassiliev said.

'And you two have earned a reward,' Gunther said. 'Isn't that right, *Hochmeister*?'

Heinrich scowled.

'If there's any requests you two have, now's the time to ask,' Heinrich said. 'Stefan?'

The big templar shook his head.

'I'm happy to do God's work,' the big man said.

Vogel rolled his eyes. *Arselicker*.

'What about you, Vogel?' Heinrich growled.

The spy cleared his throat before stepping forward. 'I'd like to make a small request, *Hochmeister*. Er, for a loan. There's an inn in the Artisans Quarter I'd like to make an offer on.'

'Sensible choice.' Gunther nodded. 'Investing in your future and retirement. Very prudent. Don't you think so, Heinrich?'

The *Hochmeister* grunted. He glared at Vogel for a few uncomfortable heartbeats before snatching a quill and scratching on a piece of parchment. When he finished, he sprinkled sand on the paper before dribbling hot red wax on it and pressing his ring into it. He shook the sand off before tossing the parchment to the spy.

'That gives you permission to take a loan from our treasury,' he said. 'Anything else, Vogel?'

The spy shook his head. 'Thank you, Grand Master.' He bowed before stepping back and couldn't resist exchanging a grin with Stefan.

'The two of you have our deepest gratitude for what you've accomplished,' Bishop Vassiliev said with a smile.

There were mumbles of agreement from the gathering and Heinrich grunted in approval.

'Well, if there's nothing else?' Heinrich turned to the men around him who shook their heads. 'Right, you two.' The Grand Master turned back to Vogel and Stefan. 'You've earned yourselves a well-deserved rest. Von Stern! Take a day off!

Vogel, since you're not a templar, take two! Oh, and here.' He tossed them a silver shilling. 'Have a beer on me. Dismissed!'

The duo bowed, turned on their heels and strode out.

***

Arnold cornered Stefan outside the chamber and Vogel watched the old warhorse hug and congratulate his protégé. He turned as Gunther approached.

The old spymaster placed a hand on Vogel's shoulder and pulled him into a hug and ruffled his hair before pushing him back. 'Questions?'

'How did Richter really die?'

'Mysticism, we think. A technique was used against him.'

'What kind of technique?'

Gunther shrugged. 'I'll let you know when I know more.'

'Fair enough. What about Lord Olaf and Lady Silke – what's going to happen to them?'

'The Trinitarians are still hunting Olaf. As for Lady Silke, we're keeping her in the Scholars where we can keep an eye on her. As long as she doesn't misbehave, she has nothing to worry about.'

Yeah, right, Vogel scoffed. *Keep an eye on her, my arse. They'll wait until everyone's forgotten about her and then they'll have her quietly bumped off.* 'And Richter – are they really going to give him a proper burial?'

Gunther shook his head. 'That's just for show. They're burying his robes and jewellery. The bishop had his body cremated.'

'So that's it?' Vogel said. 'Another cleric's crimes just get swept under the rug?'

Gunther stopped smiling. 'Like the bishop said, Richter had too many powerful friends among the clergy. If this all came out, the scandal would create serious splits in the Church and rock people's confidence in us.'

'You think this is best dealt with quietly?'

Gunther nodded. 'Absolutely. Richter's associates are not getting away. Not when sorcery's involved.'

'So what's going to hap–' Vogel stopped, his mouth hanging open as the light of realisation dawned. 'No!' he whispered.

'Inquisitor's been summoned.'

Vogel could only gape as the old rogue winked and walked away, patting Stefan on the shoulder as they passed each other.

'A whole day!' Stefan said. 'Where are you going?'

'Where do you think?' the young spy replied sourly. 'To drown my sorrows on a measly shilling!'

The templar's face fell.

'What?' Vogel frowned.

'I thought he was a good man, a really good man. How was he able to deceive us?'

Vogel shrugged. 'By being like the demon he summoned – Richter was a wolf in a sheep's fleece. He fooled us all.'

Vogel turned.

Stefan watched him walk away.

The spy took a few paces before he stopped and looked back. 'You coming then?'

The big templar's grin returned as he wrapped a large, mailed arm around the spy's shoulders and together, they walked out into the rain.

Epilogue

Stefan's dreams never varied. Every night when he shut his eyes and sleep claimed him, he relived the event again in all its intensity.

They had stopped to make camp, not far from the main road, near the fringes of the Schwarz Forest, three days east of Bergdorf. After the evening meal, Father Wolfgang was leading the men through prayer when the figures suddenly appeared, black cloaked, swooping out of the darkness.

Men's screams mingled with the smell of blood and death.

Chaos swirled around the young templar and then he turned and beheld a figure.

A young man, perhaps in his late teens, roughly the same age as Stefan, but where Stefan's hair was the colour of wheat and his eyes bluer than a clear sky, this young man had hair and eyes the colour of deepest night and skin paler than the moon at its zenith.

He smiled, revealing ivory fangs longer than any wolf's, before he shot forward, too quickly for the young templar's eyes to follow.

Something slammed into Stefan's abdomen, hurling him onto his back, knocking the air from his lungs. All he could do was gasp. When he tried to stand, a paralysing pain shot through his gut and he looked down to see a huge rent in his stomach and his life blood pumping down his legs.

He looked up. The figure was gone. All around him his brothers were being torn apart by the vampires, so he lay back and prepared for death, trying to block out their screams. Then he heard a bang and smelled smoke, and he could hear soft chanting.

Suddenly he was looking down at himself, all pain gone.

I'm dead, he thought.

'Not quite,' said a husky voice beside him.

He turned and found himself staring at the most beautiful woman he had ever seen.

Her skin had the lustre and shine of the sands of the Arab desert, and her long chestnut-coloured hair flowed from beneath a circlet of the purest gold. Her sword and breastplate were likewise made of a gold and glowed with a faint golden hue.

A pair of sparkling emerald eyes regarded the young templar. Her entire being shimmered with a faint radiance.

Stefan could only gape and gawk.

'But you are dying,' the figure continued. 'I was sent by the Almighty, drawn to your bright soul. I come to you with an offer from Him.'

'Wha...' Stefan gasped.

'Life! In return for swearing eternal service to the Lord, I will restore you and give you a gift from the Almighty to one of his chosen.'

Stefan didn't hesitate.

'I accept!' he blurted.

She smiled then, and to Stefan it felt like the early morning sun shining on his face, and his spirit soared.

491

'Kneel, templar!' she said in a voice as loud as thunder.

Stefan dropped to one knee, still gazing in rapture at her shining face.

With the clear ring of steel, the herald drew her sword and placed the flat of the blade on Stefan's head.

'Swear, that when your apprenticeship is over, you will not leave but will remain and serve the Order to your dying day, waging war on the enemies of the divine. Swear!'

'So I do swear!'

'Stefan von Stern, the Lord hears your vow. Let it never be forgotten. He also gives you this, the Gift of the Templar. Let your sword arm reflect the strength of your faith. It is your hammer. With it, may you smite all foes, mundane and supernatural. Let your body be strong and steadfast, like your faith in the Almighty, that even though you be pierced by sword and arrow, your faith shall heal and sustain you, and you will serve the Lord until He deems it nigh for you to appear before him.'

As the words passed her lips, Stefan felt a warmth creep through his body and then suddenly a heat flushed his entire being and he found himself on the ground again. His stomach wound had stopped bleeding and was closing. The pain had vanished. As he lay there, he realised that all the pain he had ever suffered had also been washed away.

All the bitterness had vanished.

He looked around. Father Wolfgang had passed out from the strain of divine magic use and the rent bodies of his templar brethren lay strewn around the campsite.

The vampires had fled, driven away by the presence of a divine herald.

He heard it then, a faint ringing sound which grew in intensity, finally swelling into thunderous pealing which plucked him from the world of dreams back into the harsh reality of the waking world.

Stefan von Stern awoke to the sound of the High Castle's bells tolling the early morning summons to prayer.

Panting, smiling and bathed in sweat, he rose from his pallet, shivering, his breath steaming in the chill morning air as he shuffled off to join his templar brethren for morning mass.

THE END

'Demonheart' Characters

Our Heroes

Vogel Schlosser
A spy and agent for the Teutonic Order

Brother Stefan von Stern
A Teutonic Knight with the gift of divine magic

The Church, Teutonic Knights Order and Sword Brethren Order

Martin of the Trinitarians
A master in the Trinitarian Order

Cordula Broche
A nun in the Trinitarian Order

Beate Grote
A nun in the Dragon Disciples Order of the Trinitarians

Brother Gerome the Franciscan
An ex-witch hunter, priest and sorcerer. Now a monk in the Franciscan Order devoted to the healing arts and study of medicine

Reinhardt Schiller
Teutonic Order's master-at-arms

Heinrich von Wilnowe II
Hochmeister (Grand Master) of the Teutonic Knights in the city of Rittershafen

Hermann von Balk
Grand Master of the *Schwertbrüderorden*, Sword Brethren Order. Responsible for training the monks of the Order in the 'inner' arts, i.e., the martial mysticism of the Order

Arnold Guerk
Supreme/Grand Commander (*Grosskomtur*) of Marienburg fortress in Rittershafen. Heinrich's best mate and 2nd in command

Vassiliev Ignovovitch
Bishop of Rittershafen. Head of the Witch Hunters Order

Gunther Hahne
A spymaster of the Teutonic Order and friend of Heinrich's. Vogel's teacher and mentor

Jozef Richter
A priest and witch hunter

Pohl Heinz
A priest and witch hunter. Murdered.

Dieter Schenk
A priest and witch hunter. Murdered.

Konrad Stich
A novice witch hunter and Bishop Vassiliev's personal assistant

Hubertus Schweinebraten
Priest and witch hunter

Franz Luber
Jozef Richter's agent

Wolfgang
Novice in the Witch Hunter's Order and personal assistant to Bishop Vassiliev

Brother Georg
Weapons master for the Sword Brethren Order. Teaches the 'outer' or technical weapon skills

Sister Adelheid
Dominican nun and user of divine magic

Wolfgang Schmidhuber
Priest and witch hunter

Gerhardt Sprecher
Priest in the Witch Hunters Order

Marianne Breitmayer
A Trinitarian posing as the madam of the Lewd Elf brothel

Wulfram Brenner
A retired Trinitarian living beside the Naked Elf brothel who acts as guardian for a gang of Vogel's urchins, the Robins

Thomas Backstedt
A priest and witch hunter

Pieter Gesell
Father Pohl's novice and a trainee of the Witch Hunters Order

Markus Ganz
Father Dieter's novice and a member of the Franciscan Order. Missing

Professor Edward Poffhenger
A member of the Order of Scholars and Dean of the School of Sorcerous Artefacts, College of Magic, Rittershafen University

Achim
A novice in the Witch Hunters Order and another of Bishop Vassiliev's personal assistants

Other Characters

Herr Doktor Gerhardt Earnst Horstmann
Sorcerer, necromancer, mortician and physician living in the Merchants Quarter of the city

Hengist
Doctor Horstmann's bodyguard

Weasel
Thief and one of Vogel's contacts

Four Fingered Rolf
Master thief and head of a gang/guild of pick pockets and burglars

Ingvald
Violent racketeer who operates in the Artisans District and the Church Quarter of the city

Siegfried
A sorcerer. Ingvald's brother

Kristian
A teenager. One of Vogel's agents and his right-hand man

Herr Helmut Wulf
Proprietor of the Honey Bee tavern, on the *Rathaus Marktplatz*

Maximillian Dietz
A crime lord

Rutger
An assassin in the employ of the racketeer, Maximillian Dietz

'Old' Knut

Ex-prize fighter and proprietor of the Scabby
Lobster tavern, Artisans District docks

Lady Silke von Gruenbaum
Noblewoman married to Lord Olaf von Gruenbaum.

Lord Olaf von Gruenbaum
Nobleman married to Lady Silke von Gruenbaum

Toby Steinaugen
Racketeer operating in the South Bank

Feelix, Lutz and Mikael
Master thieves. Vogel's first teachers and mentors

Herr Johann Brolle
Innkeeper and proprietor of the Grim Reaper tavern,
Church District

Herr Bernhardt Lenger
Innkeeper and proprietor of the Three Swords
tavern, Artisans District

Frauline Kerstin Lenger
Bernhardt's daughter. Deceased

Frau Kristen Lenger nee Stein
Bernhardt's second wife. Kerstin's stepmother

Frau WictoriaLenger
Kerstin's mother. Deceased

Ludwig Schlosser

Vogel's older brother

Sonja Schlosser
Vogel's older twin sister

www.ingramcontent.com/pod-product-compliance
Lightning Source LLC
Chambersburg PA
CBHW011400010726
47495CB00009B/2709